PRAISE FOR KILL CREEK

"A menacing and cinematic story that starts off merely creepy but evolves into a bloody, action-driven terrorfest [and] a thought-provoking and enjoyable look at the genre itself, as the characters discuss horror, its history, and its tropes at length. A match for readers who enjoyed Shirley Jackson's *The Haunting of Hill House*." —*Booklist* **(starred review)**

"Intensely realized and beautifully orchestrated Gothic horror." —**Joyce Carol Oates**

"Not since I read *The Shining* in eighth grade has a book scared the crap out of me as much as *Kill Creek*. The combo of a great premise and an exquisite ability to conjure dread and terror make Scott Thomas's debut the perfect Halloween treat." —**Andy Lewis,** *Hollywood Reporter*

"*Kill Creek* is the horror debut of 2017 . . . An intimate, twisted gothic testament to horror as a genre . . . *Kill Creek* is a book from a horror fan to horror fans—creepy, atmospheric, and messed up in all the best ways . . . a must-read for anyone who likes it when their fiction goes to dark places." —**Barnes & Noble Sci-Fi & Fantasy Blog**

"Scott Thomas splendidly creates a fascinating co-dependency between the spooky edifice and the folk that perpetuate (and amplify) its morbid history. Thomas does a fine job with his characters, and the atmosphere is chock-full of delightfully unsettling images. Horror aficionados will welcome it with open arms." —*Scream* **magazine**

"Suspenseful, foreboding, and macabre, *Kill Creek* is high-grade horror, successfully bringing together old-world classics like *The Haunting of Hill House* by Shirley Jackson, elements of the highly stylized Japanese scare movies like *The Ring*, and a bit of *The Amityville Horror* to give readers original twists and deathly scares." —**Fantasy-Faction**

"There'll be no admonitions to read this one with the lights on or alone at night. That's a given. Alone or with friends, lights blazing, or a single reading lamp casting shadows over the page, it won't matter. The result will be the same: shivers for many nights afterward. *Kill Creek* is the perfect novel to read on Halloween." —**New York Journal of Books**

"*Kill Creek* is a slow-burn, skin-crawling haunted house novel with a terrifying premise and a shockingly brutal gut-punch of a conclusion. This debut establishes Scott Thomas as a force to be reckoned with on the horror scene. His remarkable ability to build tension and suspense had me on the edge of my seat until the last page." —**Shane D. Keene,** *HorrorTalk*

"*Kill Creek* delivers the cinematic scares of *The Conjuring* without losing a literary feel. This is the kind of book that reminds you binge-reading came way before binge-watching." —**Kailey Marsh, BloodList**

"Gives us just the right kinds of Halloween-spirit thrills while throwing in some new twists, and great characters." —*Horrible Imaginings* **podcast**

"I thought there were no more good haunted house stories to tell until I read *Kill Creek*. Scott Thomas uses a foundation of the expected tropes to build a story with not just a classic horror ambiance but also a unique architecture of tension." —**J-F. Dubeau, author of** *A God in the Shed*

KILL CREEK

SCOTT THOMAS

A NOVEL

Published by Inkshares, Inc., San Francisco, California
www.inkshares.com

Edited by: Philip Sciranka, Matt Harry & Adam Gomolin
Cover design by: M. S. Corley
Interior Design by: Kevin G. Summers

ISBN: 9781942645825
e-ISBN: 9781942645832
LCCN: 2017955309

First edition

Printed in the United States of America

For Kim, Aubrey, and Cleo.
For my parents.
And for Old Parker,
because the tallest tales
cast the longest shadows.

Gossip is mischievous, light and easy to raise, but grievous to bear and hard to get rid of. No gossip ever dies away entirely, if many people voice it; it too is a kind of divinity.

—Hesiod

Only the silent, sleepy, staring houses in the backwoods can tell all that has lain hidden since the early days. . . . Sometimes one feels that it would be merciful to tear down these houses, for they must often dream.

— H. P. Lovecraft

PROLOGUE

NO HOUSE IS born bad. Most are thought of fondly, even lovingly. In the beginning, the house on Kill Creek was no exception.

The house was made from nothing more fantastic than wood and nails, mortar and stone. It was not built on unholy ground. It was not home to a witch or a warlock. In 1859, a solitary man constructed it with his own two hands and the occasional help from friends in the nearby settlement of Lawrence, Kansas. For a few good years, the many rooms within the grand house were filled with a passionate love, albeit one shared in secret, a whisper between two hearts.

But as with most places rumored to be haunted, a tragedy befell the house on Kill Creek. The man who built it was murdered, mere feet from the woman he loved. His outstretched hands attempted to span that mockingly short distance between them, to touch her dark skin, to caress her hair; his mind insisting that if he could just hold her, they would both be saved, that if he could just wish hard enough, they could still be together.

They were not saved. His love's body was taken from beside his own and hung from the only tree in the front yard, a gnarled beech. She was already dead, and yet they strung her up in one final insult. The bodies became as cool as the steamy August night would allow, the silence of the house and grounds lying over them like a death shroud. They would remain undisturbed for several weeks, forgotten as the town of Lawrence endured its own tragedy. As dusk fell, the horizon to the southwest flickered with the orange glow of flame. Lawrence was burning.

A house stained by spilled blood cannot escape the harsh sentence passed by rumor. The townspeople, traveling the quiet dirt path to Kansas City, began to speak of the house as if it were alive. How badly they felt for the poor, sad place, orphaned as so many children had been during the bloody border battles preceding the Civil War. It was impossible to say what happened within that empty house on long, dark winter nights, when the wind cut through the barren forest to rattle its windowpanes. There was just something about the place that inspired travelers to quicken their pace as they passed Kill Creek Road.

Because of its size and grand architecture, the house did not remain empty forever. A few tried to call it home. Yet no one felt completely welcome in the house, and most moved out within a year. They could not explain why they were compelled to abandon it. It was as if the walls refused to absorb their warmth. Even in the middle of summer, the temperature dropped a good ten degrees as one passed over the threshold.

It had become a bad place. A thing to be feared.

In the late 1920s, Kansas Highway 10 was built, linking Kansas City and Lawrence. By the 1970s, the modest paved road had been expanded to a four-lane highway. To someone speeding by at fifty-five miles per hour, the exit to Kill Creek Road was easy to miss, as was the sign that marked the creek itself. As life raced forward and simple times grew ever more hectic, the house on Kill Creek became just another empty farmhouse, left for the prairie to reclaim. Even the creek that had once fed so greedily from the Kansas River began to dry up, the sun baking its bed until it cracked like old flesh.

The closest neighbors still shared stories about the strange things they'd witnessed over time—lights passing in the windows, pounding on the doors, whispers in the darkness—but the house and its bloody history had been reduced to nothing more than a tall tale that parents told their children as they tucked them into bed. Most did not believe the stories; they were told simply to keep the children safe, to warn them of the dangers of exploring the dilapidated structure. The house must have been lonely then, the passion that had built it lost, pulled down into the earth like morning fog.

In 1975, the Finch sisters, Rachel and Rebecca, bought the estate from the county, which had owned it since the last occupant abandoned it in the spring of 1961. The Finch sisters were not concerned about the house's dark history. They were sixty-eight-year-old identical twins, and they had seen and endured much worse than a few bumps in the night, especially Rebecca, who was confined to a wheelchair, the victim of a tragic accident of which neither woman spoke.

When the Finches hired local hands to help them refurbish the once-grand mansion, many welcomed their arrival, thinking the sisters would finally give the house the care and attention its original owner had intended. The *Lawrence Journal-World* and the *Kansas City Star* both ran articles about the Finch sisters' arrival. KILL CREEK MANSION FINALLY A HOME announced one paper. TWIN SISTERS RESURRECT "HAUNTED HOUSE" proclaimed the other.

The Finch sisters did not live up to those expectations. They were, as people in the region were wont to call them, "odd birds." The Finches rarely spoke to the carpenters working on the house, and, once moved in, they almost never stepped foot outside. If one of them could be regarded as friendly, it was Rachel, with her long, flowing black hair, who always paid the workers promptly and fairly. Rebecca, hair pulled painfully tight in a bun, was almost never seen, choosing to stay behind the closed door of the third floor's only bedroom. An elevator was one of the first additions, allowing wheelchair-bound Rebecca to roam freely throughout the spacious house. Yet she was never about for long, always returning to that one room, a single two-foot-wide window providing her only view of the outside world.

Once, a plumber inspecting the pipes asked Rachel why her sister did not come downstairs more often. "It must get awfully lonely up there," he said. Without missing a beat, Rachel turned to the man, gave the closest approximation of a smile she could muster, and replied, "She has all the company she needs."

Two years later, Rebecca Finch was dead. According to the coroner, her heart had simply given out. Rachel continued to live in the house on Kill Creek, refusing visitors, even those who came to express their condolences for her sister's passing. No one except Rachel Finch walked the halls of that house for nearly five years. No living being, that is.

So it came as a surprise when, in 1982, Rachel granted an interview to world-renowned parapsychologist and author Dr. Malcolm Adudel. Although most of the scientific community regarded him as a fraud, Dr. Adudel's books based on his adventures into the paranormal were devoured by a public desperate to believe.

Only Rachel Finch and Dr. Adudel witnessed the occurrences during his weekend visit to that house. The resulting book, *Phantoms of the Prairie: A True Story of Supernatural Terror*, brought the house on Kill Creek to national attention. While critics and skeptics discounted the book as pure fiction, eager readers kept *Phantoms of the Prairie* on the bestseller list for an astounding thirty-six weeks. The story Dr. Adudel wove was short on details and long on atmosphere, but for those seeking proof of the existence of ghosts, the book was all they needed. The house on Kill Creek was officially crowned a doorway to the other side. It was a house of nightmares. More importantly, it was once again known by name.

Rachel Finch died in 1998. She was ninety-one years old. Just like the man who'd built her beloved mansion, Rachel's body was not discovered until several weeks after her death. Teenagers from suburban Kansas City had, on a dare, crossed the weathered bridge spanning the dry, dusty ravine that once was Kill Creek. They made it one hundred feet from the front porch before coming to a sudden stop. There, swinging slowly in the beech tree, from the very branch that had once supported the dead, slack weight of the original owner's forbidden love, was Rachel Finch. An amateurish knot dug into the stretched, rotting flesh below her chin. Her thin black hair fluttered softly in the breeze and then settled upon her shoulders. As the onlookers tried to make sense of this sight, the rope creaked, and Rachel's body spun around to face them. A beetle crawled happily in one of the empty sockets that had housed her gray eyes.

Many speculated as to what drove the old woman to hang herself. Some assumed it was sheer loneliness; the loss of her sister had become too much to bear. Others suggested that it was the house—the house had driven her to do it—although no one could say exactly why. And then there were the few, those who took morbid glee in tales of tragedy, who whispered in slow, deliberate voices that Rachel had not killed herself at all. She was dragged out of the house and hung from that branch against her will. Someone—or *something*—had done that to her. It was a reminder that the house was best left alone.

After Rachel's death, all of the Finch sisters' belongings were left in the house, as stipulated in Rachel's will, including, one would presume, the furniture in the third-floor bedroom. No one knew for sure what that room held. Its entrance had been scaled shut, the staircase now ending in a wall of brick as if no third floor had ever existed.

Word spread once more that something was very, very wrong with the house on Kill Creek. Rachel Finch's death was just another chapter in its dark legacy. Eventually the house and lot became the property of Douglas County. And, despite being on the market once more, no one dared move into the infamous structure. It still attracted its fair share of curiosity seekers, a constant source of busywork for the sheriff's department, who routinely patrolled the area. In 2008, a chain-link fence was erected around the grounds to keep out trespassers. The owners of the local business that donated the time and equipment for the job simply said they slept easier knowing that they had helped discourage others from approaching that house. They even threw in a coil of razor wire at the top of the fence for good measure.

So the house fell silent once more, the yard overgrown with knee-high tallgrass and clinging ivy.

The house on Kill Creek still stands. Empty. Quiet. But not forgotten. Not entirely. Rumors are its life, stories its breath.

PART ONE

INVITATION

Last October

I took another step into the abyss. "What's down here?" I called to her. I could sense her presence at the top of the stairs.

"Don't worry," Rachel replied. "It's more scared of you than you are of it."

I heard her chuckle, a laugh that stuck in her throat, never quite reaching her lips.

As usual, I would have to see for myself.

—Dr. Malcolm Adudel
Phantoms of the Prairie

ONE

THE AIR WAS on fire.

Set into the stone wall was a towering Gothic window, the beveled panes of its enormous, narrow body glowing in the afternoon sun. Dust motes swirled in the shaft of light blasting through the glass.

Just beyond the light, in the shadows, things shifted restlessly.

Faces.

Staring. Silent. Hungry.

Their eyes were focused on a man in his late thirties, his brown hair buzzed to the scalp. He was handsome, just over six feet tall, dressed in old black Levi's and a henley that showed off a thin, slightly muscular build. The shirt's long sleeves were pushed up to his elbows, revealing a collision of tattoos covering his left forearm. There was a strange, pitted texture to the skin into which the ink had been set, his entire left arm and the back of his hand wrapped in scar tissue. Dark lines snaked seemingly random courses across the flesh, but within the abstract arrangement, images emerged. Trees. A wildflower. The hollow eye of a skull. And flames, so many flames, devouring all.

The man looked out at the three hundred students stacked upon each other in the stadium seating of Budig Hall's Hoch Auditorium. No matter where he turned, he met someone's rapt gaze. Technically they were here to attend a freshman-level class called Introduction to

Horror in Popular Culture. But he knew why every seat in the lecture hall was currently filled. He was not only a Lawrence resident and a KU alumnus, but a best-selling author, an "expert" on the subject of horror.

Sam felt the bristles of hair rub against his palm as he ran a hand over his shorn head.

Don't blow it—you're supposed to be a master of the macabre.

He walked the length of the floor of the lecture hall, feeling every set of eyes tracking him like prey.

"What don't we know?" he asked rhetorically, his voice echoing from the highest, darkest corners of the cavernous room. "What is hidden—*purposely* hidden—from us? The Gothic tradition is about secrets, dark secrets, *awful* secrets, hidden just behind the façade of normality. Modern horror is still heavily influenced by this tradition. But it's not creepy old castles that hold these secrets anymore. The Gothic has invaded our everyday lives. The old farmhouse in *The Texas Chain Saw Massacre*. The suburban Japanese home in *The Grudge*. Even a videotape in *The Ring*. The infectious evil that used to be confined to crumbling ruins in eighteenth- and nineteenth-century literature, like Lewis's *The Monk*, Radcliffe's *The Mysteries of Udolpho*, and Maturin's *Melmoth the Wanderer* has spread to our cities, our small towns, our homes. And that makes it even scarier, doesn't it?"

There was a murmur of agreement, a few heads nodding within the many-eyed mass before him.

Sam began to pace more quickly, his own excitement on the subject growing. "So what makes some stories innately Gothic? *A Nightmare on Elm Street* hinges on the secret that the Elm Street parents are keeping from their children, that they took the law into their own hands and killed Freddy Krueger. *Saw* keeps us guessing about Jigsaw's true identity and motive. So why don't these feel as entrenched in the Gothic tradition as other horror movies?"

The students glanced uneasily at each other, no one wanting to be the first to give a wrong answer.

"Okay," Sam said finally. "I believe there are several key reasons."

The chemical smell of a dry-erase marker drifted into the air as Sam uncapped it. He turned to a massive whiteboard mounted on the back wall and quickly jotted down the first entry on his list.

"One: Emanation from a Single Location," he said aloud as he wrote.

He turned to lean over a heavy wooden lectern as he spoke directly to the class. "Yes, we're told in the very title that the nightmare is happening on Elm Street, but in the movie itself, we never get a sense that the evil truly emanates from this place. It does very little to give us a sense of the geography of Elm Street, the close proximity of the targeted kids, or even if Freddy's horrible acts, both past and present, are confined strictly to this part of Springwood. In the end, the antiseptic safety of 'Elm Street' just juxtaposes nicely with the all-consuming threat of 'Nightmare.'

"*The Texas Chainsaw Massacre*, on the other hand, is confined mostly to an old house in the Texas countryside. If those fatally curious kids never wandered over to Leatherface's house, they would have remained in one piece. The evil is behind that door. Don't open the door, and you got nothing to worry about."

The dry-erase marker squeaked its chipmunk voice as it sped once again over the board.

"Two: a Sense of Forbidden History. The location must have some dark history associated with it, whether it's the illicit affair of Quint and the former governess in *The Turn of the Screw* or the suburban wet dream of the brand-new housing development in *Poltergeist*, a neighborhood that just happens to have been built on top of the bodies of a relocated cemetery. Even in these examples, which are firmly rooted in the supernatural, the secret history is purposely kept from our protagonists.

"Three: an Atmosphere of Decay and Ruin. This could be the physical decay of classic Gothic literature—the aforementioned crumbling castles and shadowy manors that continue to show up in films like *The Others* and *The Woman in Black* and *Crimson Peak*. But it could also be mental decay, like the main character in Roman Polanski's *The Tenant*, who moves into a seemingly innocuous apartment and proceeds to lose his mind. More often than not, it's a combination of the two—the ruin and decay of the physical structure leads to the ruin and decay of the mind of the protagonist. We see it again and again in books like *The Haunting of Hill House* and movies such as *Session 9*, in which the cleaning of an abandoned mental institution coincides with the mental degradation of the homicidal leader of the cleanup crew. And finally—"

Sam wrote the last item on the board.

"Four: Corruption of the Innocent. That's you guys."

This drew a laugh.

He replaced the cap on the marker, set it on the ledge that ran along the bottom of the board, and returned to the lectern.

"This is perhaps the most important element of any good Gothic horror story. Without it, what do you have? A shitty old dump with a dark history no one remembers or cares about. You need that one person who ensures that the evil lives on."

From a shelf inside the lectern, Sam picked up a well-worn paperback. He held the book high so the entire class could see the elegant hand-drawn cover art and the classic font of the title and author's name.

"*Last One Out Kills the Lights* by Sebastian Cole. You all should have a copy of this now."

The majority of the students nodded, some displaying their own copies as evidence that they had done as Sam had asked.

"You're probably wondering why I made you buy the entire book if we're just going to discuss one of the short stories inside. Well, it's because Sebastian Cole is one of the greatest horror authors *ever*. And I want to know that all of you own at least one of his books. Who here has read Sebastian Cole before?"

Several hands shot into the air, though sadly not as many as Sam had expected. From the center row, a pimply faced kid called out: "*A Thinly Cast Shadow.*"

Sam nodded enthusiastically. "Arguably Cole's best book, although picking a favorite from his vast body of work is, at least for me, incredibly difficult. Now, the story I asked you to read for today is—"

A hand shot into the air. It belonged to a young man of Middle Eastern descent. Even sitting down, he was clearly an exceptionally large person, his long legs bent awkwardly, knees pressing into the seat before him. His hand seemed to be reaching to touch the ceiling above.

"Yes?" Sam asked.

"What about your own books?" the young man asked. "How does all of this apply to them?"

Another voice, a female, from somewhere on the right side of the hall, followed this by calling out: "Tell us about *Under the Rug!*"

Several overzealous students whistled and whooped.

Careful, Sam warned himself. *They want to peel you like an onion.*

He gave the rough, reptilian flesh of his scarred arm a squeeze.

The applause died away.

"Okay. Fair enough. How is the Gothic tradition represented in my work? Well, in *Under the Rug*, I tried to take advantage of these four elements to create a modern Gothic horror novel. A blue-collar worker, a single dad, moves his young son to an old, dusty Oklahoma farm. There's number one on our list: Emanation from a Single Location. He hopes that his blood and sweat will breathe new life into the rocky soil, that he can coax the earth into once again growing something, but he doesn't realize that this forgotten patch of land is barren because of what had happened there a century before. If you've read the novel, you know what I'm talking about. If you haven't, I won't spoil it for you, but it involves a child murderer and a stolen baby and an act of violent revenge. That's number two: Forbidden History. Number three—Decay and Ruin—comes in the form of the farm itself. But it's also in what happens to the relationship between the father and his son. First, when the father's efforts to grow a crop result in nothing more than weeds, and later as the son begins to show signs of a strange, frightening psychic power. And there's number four: Corruption of the Innocent. See, the power this boy begins to exhibit isn't a gift from God, but the side effect of a greater evil attempting to be reborn. Stir in some thematic parallels regarding fertility and the fragility of masculinity, give it a good shake with some hopefully unexpected deaths and startling violence, top it with a trapdoor literally 'under the rug,' and you've got yourself a smooth, tasty sip of modern Gothic horror with just enough bite to remind you it ain't a kids' drink."

There was a soft ripple of good-natured laughter. A pale, red-haired girl raised her hand. Before Sam could even address her, she asked, "So what's your secret?"

Sam tasted smoke. His breath caught in his throat, nearly choking him. The air suddenly had a harsh gray taste to it, like cinder and ash.

"I'm sorry," he said when he had managed to swallow the breath. "What do you mean?"

"You said these types of books and movies, they're all about secrets, right?" Her thin lips barely moved as she spoke, her voice so faint that Sam realized she was forcing him to lean toward her. The involuntary action filled him with a sudden, inexplicable anxiety.

"Yes—" he began.

She didn't let him continue. "You've said that writing is personal, that an author always puts a piece of themselves in their stories. So, you know, what's your secret?"

Sam fell silent.

From the last row of the stadium seats, a voice called down: "She wants to know why you write horror."

He peered up at that last row. The narrow shaft of sunlight had begun to arc across the seats of the lecture hall, but it had only reached the middle rows. The upper rows were in almost complete darkness. It was impossible to tell from which of the featureless shadows the statement had come.

That thin wisp of smoke slithered down his throat and between his lungs, constricting, pushing breath through his teeth. The smoke serpent twisted beneath Sam's ribs and squeezed tighter, its gray head slipping around the ribbed stalk of his trachea. It pressed its upturned snout against the upper lobe of his lungs, probing for a way in.

"Why do you write horror?" the deep voice boomed again.

Sam McGarver was no longer in a grand lecture hall on the campus of the University of Kansas.

He was ten years old, clothes spattered with blood that wasn't his own, the angry light of an unstoppable fire illuminating his face. He was just a boy, a tiny silhouette against the inferno.

Sam, now a grown man, stood silently before his students until the bell rang, saving him from a question he did not want to answer.

Eli Bloch sat in a crumpled suit on the porch of the Free State Brewery, a pint in one hand and his phone in the other. He'd barely touched the beer. He was only concerned with two things: writing a *fuck you* email to his assistant using as few characters as possible, and meeting with his number-one client, Sam McGarver.

"Jesus, you look miserable," someone said.

Eli looked up. Sam. Finally.

"Yeah, well, I am. I hate this place. I want you to move to New York immediately."

Sam gave a weary smile. "Not gonna happen."

Eli made what room he could on the crowded bench. "Sit."

"I'll be back. I need a beer."

"Drink mine." Eli passed his glass to Sam without waiting for a reply.

Sam sat down on the bench's limited real estate. He tipped the glass and drank half the beer down in two large gulps. Tiny, lighted pumpkins dangled overhead in zigzagging strings. One pumpkin was flickering on and off, on and off, threatening to give up the ghost at any moment. Sam leaned back against the wooden rail and took a deep breath, watching the pumpkin flicker. On and off. On and off.

"That bad?" Eli asked.

Sam swallowed another mouthful of beer. The glass was now almost completely empty. "What do you want, Eli?"

"Just checking in. Wanna know how you're doing."

"And you fly in for that? You can't just call and ask?"

It was Eli's turn to fall silent as he searched for the right words. There were none. May as well rip the Band-Aid off.

"Erin called me. She's worried about you."

"She shouldn't have done that."

"I'm worried about you too."

The last of the beer slipped through Sam's lips. He held the empty glass up to a nearby waitress, mouthing the words "pale ale." She nodded and disappeared inside.

"You're not writing," Eli said bluntly.

"You don't know what you're talking about, Eli."

"Yeah? So you have something to show me? You have pages to share?"

"When it's done."

"And when's that?" All of the pleasantry was gone from Eli's voice. "*Bad Blood* slipped off the paperback bestseller list over a year ago. People are asking when your next book is coming out, and I don't know what to tell them. I'm starting to doubt it ever will."

"It's close," Sam said defensively.

"Bullshit. I haven't seen page one of it. Neither has your editor."

"You both will when it's done."

"And when will that be?" Eli asked, a bit of desperation bleeding through. "You've been working on it for two years. Or you say you have."

There was no discernable movement in the crowd, but the wait-ress was somehow miraculously there again. She handed the fresh beer to Sam, who tilted his head toward Eli. "Put it on his tab."

She looked to Eli. He gave a sharp nod, and the waitress disap-peared once again.

Eli rubbed his sweaty hands on his pant legs as if trying to smooth out the wrinkles. "What are you doing, man? You're not writing. You're hiding out in a damn classroom, teaching—talking about other people's books." He paused, not quite sure if he should bring this up. "And you're about to go through a divorce."

"We're separated," Sam corrected Eli.

"Mm-hm. Fine. And how many *separated* couples do you know who worked things out?"

Sam said nothing.

"Why are you trying to throw your career away?"

"I'm not."

"Well, you're not fighting to keep it."

The crowd shifted suddenly as someone made their way toward the front door. The entire mass rippled like a segmented insect inching its way up a leaf. The movement caused a bearded guy in front of Sam to take a step back, bumping Sam's shoulder. The beer in Sam's hand sloshed over the rim of the glass, a cold line coursing down his wrist and into the haphazard grooves of his scars.

"Everything I write feels thin, fake," Sam admitted abruptly. He frowned, as if surprised by his own words. "Everything I write, I hear Erin saying there's a better story in me."

"Is there?" Eli asked. It was not an insinuation of doubt. It was an honest question.

"I'm sorry you flew all the way here," Sam said. He downed half of the new beer. "I love ya, Eli, but you could have just called."

"I know," Eli said.

Sam stood, patted Eli on the shoulder, and started to push his way through the crowd. He was almost off the porch and onto the sidewalk when Eli called after him.

"Why do you write horror?"

Sam stopped cold.

There it was. The voice that had called down from the shadows high in the corner of Budig Hall.

Slowly, Sam turned back to face him.

"That was you?"

Eli did not look away. He was ready for a fight, if that was what it would take. "I had to see what was keeping my most talented writer from actually writing. Whatever's stopping you from finishing your book, you need to face it and move on. You can't hide out in a class-room forever."

"Fuck you, Eli."

"If you think Erin is right, Sam, if you think there is a better story in you, then tell it. Write something you actually give a shit about. If there *is* something you give a shit about these days."

Sam didn't bother with a response. He slipped through an opening in the crowd and was gone.

The bottle of Bulleit was still on the counter.

There was the clink of glass as Sam took a tumbler from a cabinet and poured himself two fingers of whiskey. He sipped, the burn loosening the constrictor in his chest. The suffocating cloud of ash and smoke was replaced by the soothing heat of alcohol. He closed his eyes and felt the warmth spread from his chest to his extremities.

Sam drifted into the living room and stood in the perfect stillness of the empty house. There was a separate dining room beyond this, and above, two bathrooms and three bedrooms, one of which he used as his home office. All were exactly as they'd been when he and Erin had first moved in five years ago. Only they were *his* rooms now, *his* house.

Sam raised the glass to his lips but did not drink. He stood there, an insect frozen in amber as time marched on without him. He wished he could exist only in this spot. He did not want to go to bed alone. And he did not want to sit in front of a blank page on his computer and be judged. He wanted to be here, right here, never moving, safe from the dangers of his own momentum.

From the room at the end of the second-floor hallway came a faint *ding!*

His office computer announcing the arrival of an email.

A second later, his phone buzzed in his pocket.

Sam fished out his phone and the screen illuminated.

There she was, Erin, more beautiful in her midthirties than she'd ever been, green eyes bright and filled with joy, arms wrapped around Sam's waist, her cheek pressed against his.

Time to change the ol' wallpaper, Sammy.

He pressed the Home button, grateful as the photo was covered by a sea of apps.

A 1 in a red circle hovered over the corner of his Mail app.

Sam tapped it. His inbox appeared. The new email stood out in bold, black letters.

His brow furrowed as he read the subject line:

An Invitation

And above this, the address of the sender:

Wainwright@WrightWire.com

He opened the email and scanned the body of the message.

Around him, the empty house waited patiently for Sam to break the silence.

TWO

THE BLADE SLICED downward, easily exposing the wet red flesh beneath. The man's thick tongue licked his lips anxiously as he slipped the bit of meat between his crooked teeth. Clear juices ran down to the edge of his chin.

"You know how excited we are to work with you," he said around the mouthful. "We mean it. We're still very, very excited to work with you."

T.C. Moore watched the doughy, balding man in the baggy black suit devour his steak and thought to herself, *So this is what it is. Not a chance to repair the fissure. This meeting is a complete fingerfuck. And not even a good one.*

She had gone to the dinner hoping it would defy her expectations. They had greeted her with smiles and hugs, with kisses on the cheek. One of them had actually pulled out her chair for her, as if the four-legged piece of furniture were too complicated a contraption for her to operate. They had ordered stiff cocktails, each trying to impress with their intimate knowledge of whiskey and scotch. They had nibbled on small plates of house-cured meats and local cheeses, on grilled octopus and hamachi, beef tartare and lamb belly. They were all easy smiles, even as she sat in the dim light of the West Hollywood steak house with her sunglasses on, arms folded across her chest. They assured her that they were here to discuss the project on equal terms. They wanted to move forward with a clean slate.

But they were all full of shit. She could tell by the hollow compliments, the tentative praise. There was another shoe to drop.

Goddammit, she should have known this was going to happen.

The man in the baggy black suit wiped his mouth on a linen napkin and began to eagerly cut off another slice of filet mignon.

"So," he said, tongue lapping at the juice on his chin. "We just wanted to hear how *you* see this project. You know, what *you* think it's really about."

He shoved an even larger hunk of steak into his mouth and chewed noisily.

Moore looked from this man to the men sitting on either side of him. The man in the center was Gary Bryson, the head of the studio. To his left was his vice president of development, Tanner Sterling, a rail-thin weasel in baby-blue glasses and a checkered button-down shirt. Tanner always had half a smirk on his stupid face, as if everyone he met was a flat-out idiot and therefore deserving of endless contempt. To Gary's right was Phillip Chance, the producer on the project and a genuinely okay guy. But a nice disposition rarely came paired with a backbone. Phillip shifted uncomfortably in his seat, his underseasoned and overpriced meal barely touched. He was in his midsixties, thin skin hanging loosely from his skull. Above deep canyons of shadow were kind brown eyes. He clearly did not enjoy being caught in the middle.

"What *I* think it's about?" Moore asked. Each word was a sliver of ice.

"If you don't mind," Gary said, lips smacking loudly.

Tanner leaned in closer while Phillip shrank back in his seat.

Moore ran a hand over the jet-black length of hair draped over her shoulder as if it were a beloved pet. The sides of her head were shaved to the scalp. The darkly tinted lenses of her sunglasses caught the reflection of a nearby candle, the flame dancing as if her eyes were on fire.

"What do I think the screenplay based on my own novel is about? Are you fucking serious?"

Gary's mouth hung open as he froze mid-chew.

"We just . . ." He swallowed hard and cleared his throat. "We want to know what your vision is."

My vision. You mean my book?

Moore leaned back in her chair and looked at the people seated at the tables around them: a shallow collection of wealthy industry types in skinny suits; bearded hipsters with poofy, greased-back coifs; and skeletal blondes with lips as thick as blood-filled leeches. Unidentifiable electronic music thumped from round white speakers mounted in the ceiling.

For an uncomfortably long time, Moore said nothing.

Tanner rubbed his sweaty palms together. When he spoke, Moore thought of an annoying little cartoon mouse in thick, round glasses. The kind of character you hope gets ripped to shreds by a hungry cat.

"We're just trying to get on the same page here."

Moore snapped her head around so quickly, her mane of black hair rose up from her shoulder like a striking snake.

"Have you read my book?"

"Of course I've read it."

"Describe it to me."

Tanner shifted uncomfortably in his seat. "I don't think I have to—"

"Describe it to me," Moore repeated.

Tanner was in the hot seat. He gave a sharp, incredulous snort. "Are you serious?"

"You seem to be the expert."

Tanner looked to Gary. He did not want to speak out of school.

This was not lost on Moore.

"Fuck you, Tanner." She tilted her head to stare at the boss man in the baggy black suit. His steak was momentarily forgotten, its juices beginning to congeal on the plate. "What is this really about, Gary?" Moore asked. "Why did you ask me to dinner?"

Gary set his fork down. "Look, sweetheart, it has nothing to do with your novel."

Sweetheart. Call me that again.

"We love it. That's why we bought the rights to it."

"Love it," Tanner repeated.

"It's just a little . . . extreme."

"Just a little," Tanner parroted again.

"We want to tone it down a bit. Try to reach a wider audience."

"You mean you want to turn it into a PG-13 teen romance," Moore seethed.

"No," Gary insisted. "No, we're simply focusing more on the dark love story at the heart of it. Make the subject matter a bit more palatable."

Reaching down into the sleek leather purse hanging from the back of her chair, Moore pulled out a paperback book and tossed it onto the table. It landed dead center, the weight of its four hundred and thirty-two pages causing silverware to clank against plates and ice to bob in cocktail glasses.

"Tell me what you see." It was not so much a demand as a dare.

All three men looked to the book's cover.

The image was simple and explicit, like the cover images of all of Moore's novels: a teenage girl's hand held a bloody razor blade over her bare thigh. Carved into the thigh in crude, jagged letters was the title of the book: *Cutter*. The shadow of a second hand, this one clearly male in its size and menace, fell over the girl's wrist, as if it had guided her in the self-mutilation of her supple flesh. The spine of the book was creased with countless lines. The upper right corner bulged with dog-eared pages.

Gary was the only one to take the dare. "Well, it's a very complex book. It's sexy, it's dark. That's why we want to tell this story, why we want to capture the *essence* of your novel—"

"Okay," Moore cut him off. "So obviously no one's bothered to take your dick out of their mouth long enough to give you the back cover synopsis. So allow me."

She picked the paperback up off the table and turned it over to read the paragraph printed on the back. "'Set in a seemingly idyllic suburban town grappling with a rash of teen suicides, *Cutter* is the pitch-black tale of a clique of high school burnouts growing bored of homemade drugs and casual sex. Desperate for a new thrill to shake up their painfully dull lives, they decide to break into and vandalize a classmate's home. They find the girl dead by her own hand, her body covered in thousands of slices from a bare razor blade.'"

Tanner gave an irritated sigh. "Please, Ms. Moore, we know what the book is about."

"This is where it gets good," she said, ignoring him. "'Open on the floor is an ancient, unholy tome: a self-hurt guide to astral projection through self-mutilation. Soon the teenagers are engaging in increasingly violent rituals as they leave their bleeding bodies to surf the outer edges of reality on orgasmic joyrides.'"

"Is this really necessary?" Tanner asked.

"Yes. Yes, it is," she said clearly and plainly. And then she continued reading. "'But something wants to keep them from returning. Something far more perverse, far more powerful than anything they've dreamed in their wildest fantasies or darkest nightmares.'"

"What is your point, Ms. Moore?"

Without warning, Moore ripped off her sunglasses. Her eyes were gray and cold. Flecks of green in her irises offered the hint of life, like moss creeping over ancient stone. But there was something distinctly different about her right eye. The pupil. It was ruptured like the smeared black yolk of a bad egg. Its oblong body bled into the iris, threatening to devour what little color existed there.

"What about that sounds like a goddamn love story?"

"No one wants to turn *Cutter* into a love story," Gary assured her.

Slowly, Moore turned to face him. Her ruptured pupil seemed to expand, sucking in what little light hovered around their table. "I know you've brought a new writer on board. I've read the latest draft of the script."

Gary's eyes flashed to Tanner, who immediately shrugged and passed the buck by turning his own accusatory glare on Phillip.

"She had every right to see it," Phillip said.

Gary rubbed a hand over his slick, pasty forehead. "Oh Christ, Phillip. What the hell is wrong with you?"

"All we're doing is trying to appeal to a larger audience," Tanner insisted. He was trying to regain control. "So we've taken the most sympathetic characters in the book and elevated them."

"*Elevated* them," Moore sneered.

"That's right."

"What you did was invent a love story that doesn't exist in my novel in order to turn the whole movie into some sort of pathetic, mystical *Twilight* bullshit."

"And honestly, what the fuck is wrong with that?" Gary spat.

"It's not my book!"

"You're right. It's not your book." Gary leaned back in his chair. "It's *our* movie."

There it is. The truth. Finally.

The time for pleasantries had long passed. Gary had Moore right where he wanted her, and everyone at the table knew it. "We own the rights. You had your pass at the screenplay. Our deal with you is done. And now we're going to make *Cutter* the way *we* see it. Hell, we'll probably end up changing the fucking title too. You know, to something less grotesque. You want to scream and stomp your stilettos at somebody, try the lawyer who made your deal in the first place. Now, if you don't mind, I'm going to finish my steak. I might even order dessert. You can stay or you can go. It's up to you."

Picking up his knife and fork, Gary hacked off a chunk of cold steak and popped it happily into his smirking mouth. He stared straight at her as he relished both the meat and the moment.

Slowly, Moore replaced her sunglasses. And then, to everyone's surprise, she began to nod.

"You're right," she said.

For the second time that night, Gary stopped mid-chew.

Moore ran her hands over the shaved sides of her head as if throwing back a hood that had temporarily blinded her. "You're right. I guess I wasn't thinking about it that way."

Gary's eyes darted to Tanner and narrowed as if to say, *What the hell is this bitch up to?*

Tanner shrugged.

Reaching across the table, Moore touched Gary's hand. The edges of her silver fingernails lightly grazed his sun-damaged flesh. A shiver ran from the base of his skull down to the tip of his cock.

"I'm sorry, Gary," she said. "I really didn't come here to fight."

Gary turned his attention from his meal, letting his gaze pause briefly on the exposed curve of Moore's breasts before settling on the dark lenses of her glasses. The flickering flames where back. Captured there. Dancing.

"It's just . . . horror is very important to me."

She took his stubby fingers in hers and drew his hand closer.

"Well, I mean, I get that," Gary babbled. "I don't blame you for speaking your mind."

Moore laughed, relieved. "Thank goodness. I'm sorry, I hope I didn't offend you."

With his free hand, Gary waved the apology away like a foul odor. "Not at all. It's fine, really."

Tanner and Phillip were watching the exchange with growing disbelief. Neither man had ever heard T.C. Moore apologize for anything.

"I just need you to truly understand something." She was staring at Gary's hand with something close to adoration. With one of her silver nails, she traced an ambiguous pattern up over his hairy knuckles and across the back of his hand, to his wrist.

Gary straightened up in his seat.

Moore let her caress drift back down to the tip of the man's index finger. His nails displayed the perfection of a top-dollar manicure, the only part of him that appeared meticulously kept.

"You see, to me, horror is something that must be experienced."

"I understand."

"It's not light and fluffy."

"Yes."

She gave his index finger a light tug, like a farmer testing a teat.

An almost imperceptible gasp escaped Gary's plump lips.

Tanner looked to Phillip in disbelief. They were both realizing they no longer existed at the table. They were unnecessary. This moment belonged to Moore and Gary and no one else.

"Horror is a lot like sex," Moore continued. "It's raw and it's primal and when it's good—when it's *really* good—it even hurts a little. But the good kind of pain, you know?"

The doughy man nodded and made a sound that he meant to be a word but in reality was nothing more than a breath.

Moore stroked his finger. Up and down. Up and down.

"Because that's what horror is. Pain. Unbearable, all-consuming pain. So real and brutal that we almost crave it in a sick way. It prickles our flesh and gets our pussies wet and our cocks hard. We need it to feel real. It reassures us that we exist. And what's truly frightening is when we realize that our pursuit of that sensation—of that reassurance of our own validity—has led us to a dark, terrible place from which there is no escape. That's *true* horror. When the seducer turns on us, and we are no longer in charge. We've lost control. And now we have to pay an awful, unspeakable price."

Moore gripped Gary's finger so tightly, the tip went white. With her other hand, she snatched the steak knife from his plate.

"Like how a second ago, you actually thought I was coming on to you."

Moore pressed the point of the knife against his finger, resting it just under the beautifully manicured nail.

"And now I'm about to jam a fucking steak knife under your goddamn fingernail."

Moore pushed the knife forward ever so slightly, its tip sinking into the soft flesh. A tiny spot of blood blossomed under his nail.

A horrible sound, like the terrified yelp of a kicked puppy, escaped Gary's open mouth. He jerked his hand back, and Moore let him, releasing her grip on his finger.

Tanner lunged across the table, but Moore had already set the knife down and was on her feet.

"You bitch!" Gary hissed. "You crazy fucking bitch!"

The entire restaurant came to a standstill, all eyes on Moore and the three men at her table.

"Thanks for dinner, Gar. It's been a real pleasure." She slung the steel chain-link strap of her purse over her shoulder, her black hair curling around the links like the tendrils of a sentient plant.

She pointed a silver nail at the paperback on the table.

"Keep the book," she said. "You might even want to try reading it."

"You're done, you hear me?" Gary's body heaved with anger.

But Moore was already pushing through the front door and into the still warm air of a California autumn night.

Headlights streaked across the face of the hilltop home, illuminating the midcentury modern's unforgiving façade of concrete and glass.

The chrome Maserati GranTurismo whipped into the driveway. Tires chirped as it came to an abrupt stop.

The engine had barely died when Moore burst out of the driver's side. She was shaking, her entire body racked with uncontrollable spasms. She had been fine when she left the restaurant, her hands steady on the steering wheel. But the higher she drove into the Hollywood Hills, the closer she got to home, the more she began to tremble. Had her house been one block farther up the twisting, narrow road, she feared her quivering hands would have sent her sailing over the edge and into the canyon below.

But she was home now. She was safe.

Then why am I still shaking like a fucking Chihuahua?

The sensation filled her with rage, and an explosion of adrenaline shot through her veins. She felt her heart pound furiously in her chest.

Take a breath, she commanded herself. And she did, drawing the cooling night air deep into her lungs.

She began to steady. Her hands stopped shaking, and the rest of her limbs followed suit.

For a solid minute, Moore stood at the edge of her driveway and just breathed.

In and out. In and out.

Okay, she thought.

Okay.

She was in control again. The panic, for the moment, was defeated.

"Bitch, you need to get a grip," she said to herself, chuckling at the sound of her own voice.

She was halfway up the front walk when she saw the small, pale rectangle hovering, apparently in midair, before her front door.

As she got closer, she realized it wasn't actually floating; it was taped to the heavy oak door, the glow of a nearby street light bouncing off the surface of the cream-colored envelope to create the optical illusion.

Written across the front of the envelope, in an elegant script, were two words:

An Invitation.

Moore was reaching to rip the envelope from the door when she paused, suddenly frozen in place.

There was no stamp. No return address. It had been hand-delivered.

Don't open it, her mind warned her.

It was an irrational thought. There was no reason to fear the contents of the envelope. Yet her mind turned over every stone, every possibility: a love letter from a stalker; hate mail from an angry parent who blamed her for their child's self-harm; pleasantries from a neighbor she did not care to know.

And then there was the most troubling prospect of all, that it was none of these things, that it was something entirely unexpected.

The words came again, louder this time.

Don't open it.

T.C. Moore stood at her front door, the October breeze running invisible fingers through her wild mane of black hair.

THREE

IT WAS THE house.

Something was reaching inside. Surrounding him. Suffocating him. Silence.

A silence that made it hard to breathe.

Outside the large picture window in the second-floor office, the dark, jagged shapes of bare treetops swayed against a night sky illuminated by an unseen streetlight. Branches jutted out of the blackness like piles of misshapen bones, clinging desperately to brittle autumn leaves. The wind whipped up, angry and invisible, and swirled past the double-pane window. It whistled softly as it went, a strange minor tune. And then it was gone. The house was silent once more.

Sam sat at the heavy wooden desk with its flaking white paint and ghosts of coffee cup stains. He stared at his monitor, the cursor on the blank page taunting him. *Blink, blink, blink*, the cursor went, a beat to which his fingers had once danced. No longer. Now they were folded reluctantly in his lap. He willed them to life, to leap to the keys and put on their best Fred Astaire. They did not.

He had started this new novel at least a hundred times. He had exhausted more first sentences than he could remember. They were single lines on one-page documents, saved on his hard drive in a folder named, appropriately, "Crap."

Little Keller Reed woke up in the middle of the night, his breath like a frozen cloud in the dark, and he knew the man had come out of his closet again.

It took four of them to lift the sun-bleached headstone in the field behind Keller Reed's house.

Sarah Ann stared at her reflection in the mirror and waited for it to make the first move.

At a quarter past three in the morning, on her sixteenth birthday, Sarah Ann Baker came stumbling home and saw the pale face staring out from her bedroom window.

It was a tradition for fishermen to hammer the head of their biggest catch to a telephone pole along River Road, but the head Sheriff Beaumont was staring at did not belong to a bottom-feeding catfish—it belonged to Sarah Ann Baker.

The doll was not where she had left it the night before.

And perhaps Sam's most inspired first sentence:

Sam, you suck as a writer and will never write anything that anyone cares about because you are a fraud and your books are shit.

Yet here he was, another night facing a blank page.

High on a built-in bookshelf, the second hand of a metal alarm clock pulled the minute hand closer to two a.m.

Sleep. He needed sleep. He had to teach at ten o'clock in the morning, and the five beers he'd consumed were going to make it even harder to shake off the haze of exhaustion.

Blink, blink, blink.

Sam rested his fingers on the keyboard, lightly and deliberately as if he were resting them on the planchette of an Ouija board.

Blink, blink, blink.

He had other stories in reserve, fragments written on yellow pages of legal pads, scribbled on napkins, stored away in the recesses of his mind. Many of them stalked similar ground as his four published novels—*Under the Rug, Crimson Moon, A Mounting Scream,* and *Bad Blood*—the books that held a place of honor on the shelf just below that damn clock that refused to stop ticking toward dawn. He could switch gears, take another idea for a test drive, see if he could lay down some pages. They didn't have to be great. They didn't even have to be good. They just needed what his readers had come to expect from a Sam McGarver book: men who worked hard and drank harder, the women who loved them, and the unspeakable thing that lurked just below the surface of their picture-perfect Midwestern town.

Pivot, he thought. *Change direction. Just write something. Anything. Write a goddamn paragraph. A sentence. A word!*

Blink, blink, blink.

"There's a better story in you."

Sam gasped and twisted around in his chair.

He had heard it. A voice. Echoing from down the hall.

The doorway was an empty black monolith.

There was no voice. There was no one there.

He was alone.

For another thirty minutes, Sam sat obediently before the blank Microsoft Word document. Then, with no more than a sigh, he shut down the computer. The hard drive whirred to a stop. The monitor blinked its weary eye.

It shouldn't be this hard. This was his job. This was the only thing he knew how to do. Just tell the damn story.

There's a better story in you.

He touched a finger to the computer's power button, but he did not press it. He listened as the house gave the occasional pop and creak. Night sounds.

The sound of settling.

He closed his eyes.

He tasted smoke again.

A boy stood before a burning house, a shadow dwarfed by the inferno.

Sam let his finger drop away from the power button. The computer would stay off for the night.

In the master bathroom, he prepared for bed, brushing his teeth, washing his face, and slipping out of his worn blue jeans. From the medicine cabinet, he took an orange prescription bottle and shook out a single green pill, thirty milligrams of Paroxetine. *For anxiety,* he told himself. But it was for depression. It was to take the edge off the sadness. A pill was supposed to defeat the thing he had fled since he was a child.

He got into bed wearing only his boxers, even as the chill of mid-October penetrated the walls. He did not bother pulling the covers up over his body. He lay there in the darkness, still restricting himself to "his" side of the bed, eyes fixed on the blackness where he knew the ceiling must be.

There's a better story in you.

Something caught in his throat. Something gray and harsh and of the earth. He couldn't breathe. He didn't want to breathe. He wanted it to take him. He deserved to be pulled into the darkness. The thing in his throat twisted tighter, smoldering, threatening to catch fire. He wished it would consume him. He should feel his body peel into charred strips. He should know the agony again, smell the sickening stench of his own meat cooking.

He gripped his left forearm, and the scarred flesh beneath his tattoos twisted awake like a reptile in the warm sun.

The orange light flickered at the base of his skull. Shadows danced on the cave wall.

It wasn't enough. He'd gotten off easy. He should have killed himself long ago. God knows he had thought about it countless times. Firing a bullet into his brain. Slicing his arm from wrist to elbow with a box cutter. Hanging himself from a beam in the garage, feet kicking stupidly in the open air.

Eventually, Sam rolled over on his side. He lay there in the silence, and the deep gray fist in his throat exhaled in a long, resigned breath. He stretched a hand out over the right side of the mattress. Felt the coldness of the sheets that had once been warmed by Erin's body. Before he fell asleep, in that moment as he tumbled into unconsciousness, Sam swore his fingers sensed her touch. The smoothness of her skin. The invitation of her body.

Five hours later, Sam woke to sunlight on his face, the bright morning rays streaming in through the bedroom window. It was a new day.

He closed his eyes as tightly as he could, fighting the light.

A skinny young sophomore, his unabashed love of the genre worn like a badge of honor in the form of a too-tight *Fangoria* T-shirt, called down from the second-to-last row. "What about Stull? That place is for sure haunted."

The bitter kiss of lukewarm coffee slipped into Sam's mouth as he took a sip from his travel mug. Having completed the Gothic part of the syllabus, he'd moved on to shallow cuts in supernatural literature, starting with Sheridan Le Fanu and M. R. James and ending with . . . well . . . did it really matter? Once the students had started asking questions, the conversation had quickly gone sideways.

"Stull." Sam closed his eyes and rubbed his temple. "Gateway to hell. We've all heard the stories. When the Pope flew to Denver in 1993, he'd ordered the pilot to avoid passing over this 'unholy ground.' You can read all about it if you can find the 1993 *Time* interview with Pope John Paul II, which you can't, because it doesn't exist. Legend says if you throw a glass bottle against the church's stone walls, the bottle will not break—which it will, as evidenced by the hundreds of broken bottles littering the churchyard. Stull, I hate to say it, is nothing but an urban legend, albeit a uniquely regional one, which is something to be proud of in itself."

Sam left the safety of the lectern and approached the class.

Careful, he thought. *They want to dig. They want to discover your secrets.*

There was a faint crack in the dark abyss at the base of his skull. A shift as uneven levels collapsed upon each other. A pale orange flicker as the pain was consumed. As something fed from it. And then it was gone. Smothered by shadow.

He pressed a thumb hard into the opposite palm. Gotta get back on track. "Stull . . . it's . . . Look, we all want to believe, right? Even the way the church was mysteriously torn down, we try to tell ourselves there is a supernatural explanation. Because if we can prove that there are ghosts, that the supernatural does exist, it in turn proves the existence of the afterlife and, finally"—he thrust his index finger into the open air for effect—"of God. And without the weekly obligation of church. It eases our minds because, with that proof, we will be certain that death is not the end."

"The Finch House, then," a girl spoke up. Sam turned to face her and was taken by the fact that she, although completely tangible, seemed to not be there, her dark features fading into the shadows behind her. "I know that place is haunted. I've been in it."

"Except you haven't!" an anonymous male shouted down from the top row.

The girl straightened up in her chair, ready for a fight. "I have. Last summer. Found a hole in the fence and got up to the house.

Opened the front door. Walked right in. And I was standing there—I'm serious—I was standing right there and . . . and I heard, like, a moan. Like . . . like, a woman in pain. Coulda been an animal. But something told me . . . it wasn't."

"What'd you do then?" This from a different girl.

"I got the fuck outta there. What do you think I did?"

The class erupted in laughter, nearly drowning out the sound of Sam's phone chiming. He slipped a hand into his pocket and silenced the alarm.

"And that's time," he announced. "See you all on Friday."

The lecture hall echoed with the uneven rhythm of six hundred feet shuffling toward the exit. It took a few minutes for all of the students to clear out. And then Sam was alone again.

Returning to the lectern, Sam snatched up the silver travel mug and swallowed down the last, awful sip of old coffee.

"Mr. McGarver?"

The voice was deep, with an Irish accent.

Sam turned. There at the edge of the first row of seats was a young man in his late twenties, dressed in skinny black pin-striped slacks, a white V-neck shirt, and a dark leather jacket that matched the odd brownish-purple hue of his penetrating eyes. He was handsome with a full head of wavy brown hair, but there was something strange about his face. It was as if the flesh matched too perfectly to the bone structure beneath. It reminded Sam of the smooth clay a forensic scientist spreads over a skull when creating a facial reconstruction. It gave the man's face the uncanny appearance of being close to his likeness but somehow not exact.

"Sam McGarver?"

Sam cocked his head, confused. "Yes?"

The man grinned and leaned back casually on one foot, his hands in his pockets.

"Care to tell me why you ignored my email, mate?"

The door clicked softly as it swung shut. Sam turned to the young man now seated in his tiny office on the second floor of Wescoe Hall, which housed the University of Kansas's English department.

He had introduced himself as Wainwright. Just Wainwright. No first name.

Not that one was needed. Sam knew exactly who he was.

"It's good to meet you, but you're wasting your time coming here."

"So you got it then?" Wainwright asked. The heavy bass of his voice did not match his youthful appearance. It was the voice of a much older man, like a second person speaking from deep within his chest.

Sam sat down in the scuffed leather chair behind his cluttered desk. "Yeah," he said. "I got it."

"And?"

"And it made no sense."

"How's that now?"

"Well, I assumed it was a joke."

"And why would I joke about something like that?"

Sam gave his head a small shake but said nothing. He had no answer for him.

"It's no joke," Wainwright assured him. "I want to feature you on WrightWire."

"You want to interview me."

"For the site, yeah."

"And that's worth a hundred grand?"

The young man stared blankly at Sam as if he truly did not understand the confusion. The unforgiving glare of the fluorescent lights only increased the oddness of Wainwright's face. The dimensions just seemed . . . off. The eyes a bit too far apart. The eyebrows too straight. The lips too thin. And those eyes, such a strange color, as if the irises had been wrapped in the flesh of a long-extinct beast, its skin stripped and tanned and pounded soft. He was at once captivatingly attractive and utterly generic, like a police sketch of a movie star.

"One hundred thousand dollars for two full, uninterrupted days."

"That's insane."

Wainwright did not even blink.

"Why would an interview take two days?"

"You know my site?"

Sam nodded. *I'm a writer. I spend half my day procrastinating on the internet.*

"Then you know I have—I guess you could say, an *unconventional* way of promoting the genre that I love."

Wainwright pinched his thumbs and index fingers together and moved them apart as if stretching an invisible string. "Horror is more popular than ever, right? But until now, no one has figured out a way to reach an online audience beyond hardcore fans." He chopped the air with his hands to represent a space beyond the invisible string. "What I saw was an opportunity to capture the casual fan, even win over those who have never considered themselves interested in the genre. And I did it by making WrightWire a destination for horror *events*. It's why the site gets over one hundred million unique visitors a month. It's why we're not only the twenty-first century's hottest horror destination—we're the hottest *pop culture* destination. Period."

"Yeah, I've seen your work."

"Have you now? Did you check out the latest? The *Underground* premiere?" Wainwright didn't wait for a response. He leaned in closer, as if he were about to share a juicy piece of gossip rather than the description of a video viewed well over fifty million times.

"We sold it to the public as a simple live stream, the entire cast and above-the-liners—the director, the producers, the studio execs—all taking the movie's namesake, London's Underground, to the premiere in Leicester Square. Then we stopped the train right there in the middle of the Tube. Dead stop. No explanation. Soon it was all over the news: '*Underground* stars stranded in Underground.' And still the live stream continued, our only link to our helpless heroes. . ."

Wainwright ran a single finger through the air in a straight line to suggest the live stream's tenuous connection.

He's loving this, Sam thought. *The thrill of the show.*

"After half an hour, our live viewers grew from ten thousand to over a hundred thousand. And that's before the creatures began to emerge from the darkness."

He smiled, yet only the corners of his mouth reacted; the rest of his rubbery face remained still. Even his eyes seemed to resist the hint of joy.

"Everyone was in on this, of course. The folks from the movie, the London Underground Limited, even the police. In reality, the train was on a discontinued line. There was never any threat of another train coming through. It was our own private movie set for the evening. The media gobbled it up, and a thousand calls flooded in. For a full day, *#underground* was trending at number one. It was our own little *War of the Worlds*. Eventually we got the gang to their movie premiere, everyone alive with limbs intact, and the ruse was up. By the next morning, the video had over a million views. Ten million by week's end."

The internet mogul was out of his seat now, hands gripping the edge of the desk.

"We transformed what could have been an ordinary movie premiere for a fairly forgettable horror movie into a once-in-a-lifetime experience that blurred the lines between fact and fiction. It was a bigger bloody event than the movie itself."

"So you want to, what?" Sam asked dryly. "Put me on the subway and let people watch me type?"

Wainwright tipped carefully back into his seat. There was a long moment of silence as the young man collected his thoughts.

"I created WrightWire to not only promote the world of horror and fantasy in general, but to champion the things I believe people should be losing their minds about. Movies. TV. Music. Websites. *Books.* I want to take the stigma out of this genre and cement it firmly in the mainstream, to show the world that it's okay to embrace your dark side, to celebrate the unknown. And so, with Halloween coming up, I figured now was the perfect time to remind people that they should be going absolutely mental about Sam McGarver. Remind them about the stories that have scared the piss out of millions of readers. Give them some insight into what makes McGarver tick. Maybe tease them with a taste of your new novel."

In a room in a house across town, on a desk below a picture window, a cursor on a computer screen went *blink, blink, blink.*

Sam winced as he felt his chest tightening. "Look, Wainwright, I really appreciate it. I do. It's a generous offer."

"You're right about that, mate. So do it."

"Right now I just need to focus on the new book. Maybe when it's done. Maybe then you can bury me alive or whatever and stream it to your followers."

Wainwright's thin lips pulled tight. He nodded slowly, not in agreement but in acknowledgment of a stalemate.

Sam suddenly felt compelled to fill the silence. "It's just not a good time. Things are a little crazy right now."

"You're busy."

"Yes."

"Writing."

"That's right."

"And teaching."

"Yes," Sam said. The word sounded painfully inadequate. Even he didn't believe it.

Wainwright rose from his seat, glancing around at the bare, dingy walls of the eight-by-eight office.

"Well then." He extended a hand.

Sam stood and shook it. "I really do appreciate it."

"Mm-hm."

Sam tried to pull his hand back, but Wainwright tightened his grip. With the slightest twist, he turned Sam's hand—and with it, his wrist, exposing the scarred forearm covered in ink.

The streaks of violet in Wainwright's brown eyes seemed to glow as he grinned.

"You should do this. It's only two days of your life, but for your fans, it's an all-access pass, a chance to see their favorite master of horror in a *unique* setting."

"What setting? What do you have planned?" Sam asked, but Wainwright was already opening the door to the hall.

"You have my email," he called back over his shoulder. "When you change your mind—and you will—just respond to that. We'll take care of the rest."

"I really don't . . . ," Sam began.

He was speaking to an empty doorway.

Wainwright was gone.

FOUR

THURSDAY, OCTOBER 20

MOORE GRUNTED FURIOUSLY as she thrust the bar away from her chest. The veins in her biceps bulged under the weight. Sweat coursed down the sides of her shaved scalp and into the twisted knot of her ponytail. Her arms were on fire, her back wet against the smooth, rubbery surface of the workout bench.

She lowered the bar in a slow, controlled descent. Felt the cold iron kiss the bare skin just above her sports bra. She let out another animalistic growl as she forced the bar up again.

Her right arm quivered, threatening to buckle.

"Fuck you," she hissed through clenched teeth. She gripped the bar hard enough to squeeze all color from her fingers.

The bar clanked down on its cradle. Moore sat up straight. Snatched up a towel from the floor. Wiped the sweat from her face. Felt her heart pound, pound, pound in her chest. It felt good, the pain. It was both the threat of death and the reassurance of life. It was nothing to fear. Pleasure and pain, Moore knew, came from the same area of the brain. The extreme of one became indistinguishable from the other. The pleasure of pain. The pain of pleasure.

She ripped off her sweat-soaked sports bra, pulled her hair free of her ponytail, and marched through an open archway into the bathroom of the walk-out basement. She twisted the shower handle protruding from the wall of white subway tile and, slipping out of her exercise shorts, immediately stepped into the cascading water. Her flesh prickled in the freezing deluge. Gradually, the water grew hotter, until great clouds of steam billowed up around her.

Barefoot, she was barely five-six, but the power she radiated added half a foot. She was thirty-eight years old and cut like marble. Defined, but not obscenely muscular. Sexy, but not grotesque. Every line, every curve, was deliberate and necessary.

She cranked the handle hard to the right and the water shut off. Warm droplets fell from the chrome showerhead and onto the nape of her neck as she toweled herself dry.

She did not bother getting dressed.

Padding naked up the spiral staircase to the first floor, Moore crossed the sleek, cool living room of her Hollywood Hills home to where a hinged metal stand rose from the floor like the rib of a robotic god. She opened the laptop that rested on a shelf of corrugated steel. For the next two hours, she wrote, her naked body kissed by the early-morning sunlight. This was her pagan ritual, writing nude as the last of the stars were forced from the brightening blue sky. She barely slept, three or four hours at most. Each waking moment was devoted to a necessity: eating, drinking, fucking, exercising, writing. Her mind was like a series of intricately connected traps; as soon as one was sprung, the next one was set.

Every day, she tried to adhere to the same strict work routine. Three hours of writing, no interruptions, no exceptions. An hour for lunch. At least four more hours of writing in the afternoon. Most writers were lucky if they produced ten pages a day. When her routine went undisturbed, Moore never failed to add twenty pages to her latest novel. If she was working on a screenplay, the total was never less than thirty. Moore never suffered from writer's block. That was for the weak, she thought, the undisciplined. She likened writing prose to fucking. It was raw. It was rough. And, as long as she was satisfied, nothing else mattered. The readers would feed from her strength, or else they would be cast aside. If they couldn't handle her stories, she didn't need them. Let them curl up in their easy chairs with that crusty old Sebastian Cole bullshit.

The ceaseless tap of Moore's fingertips on the keyboard was the sound of a heavy downpour, as if a black cloud had broken open right in the living room.

Today was a special day. Today was the start of a new novel.

Screw *Cutter*. Screw Gary. Screw Tanner and Phillip. Screw the studio and her lawyer and every other pathetic little man who wanted her on her knees.

She would leave them all behind. They were already little more than blurry mile markers in her rearview mirror.

Words raced across her computer screen as particles of a story collided in her brain.

It came to her as most stories did, with a single image smashing into existence. It was the image of a painting in a museum. As with her other tales, Moore began to ask questions.

What is so special about this painting?

The painting is being restored by a woman.

Who is she?

Her name is Sid. She has recently broken up with her boyfriend and is burying herself in work. Because of her young age, as well as her many piercings and tattoos, she is not taken seriously by her colleagues. One night Sid discovers something unexpected about the painting.

But what? What does she discover?

That there is another painting beneath it. The seemingly straightforward restoration has taken a turn. She is no longer restoring; she is revealing. Against the wishes of the museum's curator, Sid begins to strip the top layer away.

What does she find?

An eye. The eye of a god. Cold and cruel. And within it, the markings of an ancient language, long thought lost.

And what does it say?

It says that through the suffering of others, she can finally rid herself of her own pain.

Moore had let herself free-fall so deeply into this new tale that the sound of her cell phone ringing actually made her flinch as if she had been electrocuted. Her fingers left the keyboard, the connection broken as she took a step backward.

"Dammit!" she yelled.

Her heart was racing, her pulse thumping noticeably in the bare flesh above her left breast. She snatched up her phone from the glass coffee table behind her. She glanced at the name on the screen: Anaya Patel.

She let out a slow breath. If it were anyone interrupting, she was glad it was Anaya.

She answered the call.

"So?"

The flat, unemotional voice of her agent spoke from the cellular abyss. "So I still think you're making a mistake." Despite being born in Los Angeles, Anaya had more than a hint of her parents' Indian accent.

"That's not what I meant, Anaya."

A distorted sigh crackled in Moore's ear. "So they wouldn't tell me any more than you already know," Anaya said.

"Why are they being so damn secretive?"

"Because it's Wainwright. He likes to play games."

Moore felt a momentary sense of unease. She quickly swatted it away like an annoying insect. "And it's one interview. In and out."

Silence. Only the soft crackle as the call ricocheted between towers.

"That they did tell me. It's not quite in and out," Anaya said finally. "They've requested two days, two nights."

"For an interview?" Moore cocked her head to one side, closing her eyes. Her black mane draped down over her breasts. "I get the feeling I'm being messed with here, Anaya. You know I don't like being messed with."

"Then pass." It was what Anaya wanted. She had called every day since Moore had told her about the unnecessarily dramatic note stuck to the front door. The fact that it happened on the same night as Moore's ambushing at the West Hollywood steak house only served to make the agent more skeptical. It wasn't a good idea. Not right now. Now was the time to retreat and plan their next attack in the form of a new T.C. Moore bestseller.

When Moore did not reply, Anaya relented. "Or take the offer. But Wainwright has the upper hand on this one. He likes stunts. It's probably not as clear-cut as it seems."

Moore twisted her long hair around her wrist like a boxer wrapping her hands for a fight.

"I want to do it," she said.

"Okay, fine, but listen, Moore, you can't use this as an opportunity to slam Gary and the studio."

"It's my interview. I can say anything I damn well want."

"And they can damn well sue you. Please, if Wainwright tries to go there, don't take the bait. Talk about your work. Talk about *Cutter* the book. Just don't talk about *Cutter* the movie, unless it's to put asses in seats when it hits theaters."

Moore clenched her fist and gave her ponytail a hard tug. "I have work to do."

"Moore—"

A silver nail tapped the "End" button, and Anaya was gone.

Moore tossed the phone onto the white midcentury sofa and turned back to the computer. Once again, her house was filled with the sound of typing.

FIVE

THE VINES DID not want to give up their hold.

Green tentacle-like arms snaked through every empty space of the chain-link gate, securing it in place. Cappie Kovac slipped his gloved fingers through several of the diamond-shaped holes and gave the gate a hard shake.

"Deke!" he shouted over his shoulder to his son. "A little goddamn help here!"

A pair of thirty-six-inch bolt cutters bit into the lower corner of the gate and snapped it free. Deke quickly worked his way up the side of the gate, row by row, veins starting to bulge across the crest of his biceps. He was in his late twenties and already beginning to show the hint of a beer belly, but he was a strong kid. Ready to work. All commitment. No sass.

"Almost done," Deke announced in a high-pitched voice. It was the last sound one would expect to hear from his broad-shouldered, thick-necked frame. He forced the handles of the bolt cutters together, their sharp teeth cutting through the final row of fence.

Cappie wrapped his stumpy gloved fingers around the center of the gate and gave it another tug. It was free from the rest of the fence that bordered the land around the house. Yet it still would not budge.

"Help me get this bastard down!" Cappie ordered his son.

Deke stepped up next to his father and took hold of a section of gate. Together, they pulled backward with all of their might. The vines actually seemed to tighten. Tendrils twisted tighter.

"Pull!" Cappie shouted.

Without warning, the entire gate came free. It was as if every twist of vine released at the same moment. Cappie and Deke had no time to shift the direction of their power. They both fell flat on their backs, the eight-by-six-foot-gate landing on top them.

"Holy mother of Christ," Cappie exhaled.

"Sorry," was all Deke could offer.

Carefully, they slid the gate away and got to their feet.

"Jesus," Deke whispered.

Before them was a mound of vines that, only moments before, had been secured to the gate, keeping any visitors from entering the house on Kill Creek. Beyond the fence was a field of tallgrass, the blades swaying in the soft breeze like rows of soldiers standing in Cappie's way.

"Want me to get the brush cutter?" Deke asked.

Cappie barely heard him. There was something about this expanse of overgrown countryside that gave him pause. The wind was blowing to the east, but the tallgrass seemed to be swaying in the opposite direction. There was a pattern to the movement, like the jitter of a snake's rattle.

Cappie rubbed the bald spot on the back of his head and gave a snort. It had been a good hour since his last drink. He could almost hear the sound of the flask in his jacket pocket calling him, begging him to suck it dry.

"Yeah," he finally said.

From this distance, he could see only the second and third stories of the house rising above the field of tallgrass.

He took a step through the opening in the fence.

Something seemed to slither away from his foot. Cappie hopped back, expecting a rat snake or, maybe, if he were truly unlucky, a copperhead.

There was nothing there. Only a cluster of tallgrass stalks.

The wind picked up, and the entire overgrown yard suddenly collapsed. What had appeared as an impenetrable pass to the front porch was now a relatively clear path.

It was as if the house wanted Cappie to enter.

The sound of Deke firing up the brush cutter made Cappie leap a good foot into the air. He yelled, "Christ Almighty!" but Deke was already hard at work, the roar of the gas-powered brush cutter drowning out all sound. He must have gone back to the truck to retrieve it.

Deke gave a thumbs-up and continued plowing through the overgrowth, creating a clearing through the field of tallgrass. Clumps of stalks went flying into the air. It would take a while, but Deke would clear most of what could be called the "front yard."

The job was simple. Make an abandoned house habitable for a few nights. Clear the yard. Clean the main rooms. Install a generator.

Cappie watched as Deke reached the front steps. Deke killed the brush cutter's engine. He turned back and waved to his father.

Cappie waved back. Time to get to work.

Cappie stared at the last of the sunlight glinting off the third-story window. He unscrewed the top of his stainless-steel flask, his mouth already watering at the thought of a much-needed swig. The window looked like a cyclopean eye, staring out at the horizon, unblinking.

"Don't stare at the sun there, bub, you'll go blind," Cappie said to himself, then added, "Plentya ways to go blind. Fun ways too." He gave a raspy chuckle that quickly became a cough that rattled the phlegm deep inside his chest.

Behind him, parked on the now-cleared gravel driveway, was his beat-up old pickup truck. Fresh paint on the doors stood in contrast to the rust that was quickly devouring the automobile from hood ornament to trailer hitch. Kovac & Son, the paint proclaimed. There was little fanfare beyond this. Just stenciled letters. Clean and simple.

The faintest hint of a "Dammit!" blew in from around the house, and Cappie grinned. That was Deke. Cappie pictured him grunting and cursing as he put his weight into a stubborn nail in a window plank that refused to budge. For the son of a professional handyman, Cappie was shocked at how often Deke complained about the jobs they landed. Maybe he should have been harder on the kid. Maybe he should have whipped him a few times when he was younger. Really taken the belt to him. Toughened him up. Like Cappie's old man had. That was the way they brought you up on the farm. You complain, you give the old man any lip, and *whap!*, your skin would be on fire from a lash of the strap.

Ah, who was he kidding. The kid meant no harm. He worked hard. He tried his best. Cappie couldn't ask for much more. He gave his flask a shake. "Except maybe for a bit more hooch," he said, the comment sending him into another fit of hacking laughter.

Cappie screwed the top back onto the empty flask and slid it into the inside pocket of his flannel jacket. He shivered. It was cold out, strangely cold. The chill seemed to snake under his clothes and across his flesh. He took a few steps away from the house, tilting his head back to take it all in. The structure loomed over him, the peak of the triangular roof like a fang sinking itself into the purple clouds of the darkening sky. White paint flaked like dead skin from the house's weathered wood. At its base, thick weeds sprouted, burrowing into the brick foundation wherever they could. Yet for all the time it had been abandoned, neglected, the windows were not so much as cracked. The glass panes remained intact, the light of each passing day reflected upon their surfaces.

The house made Cappie nervous. He couldn't say exactly why. Cappie was not a superstitious man. He did not believe in God. But he had heard stories about this place. And now, being here, it seemed . . . what was the word? *Sinister.* That was it. If he were drunker, he would have sworn this place was waiting for something, biding its time in the last of the open prairie.

Cappie shuffled uncomfortably. He checked his watch. It was a quarter to six. "Come on, Deke!" he called out. "Finish 'er up and let's hightail it back home! Your mama's gonna have dinner on soon!"

There was no reply. Not the angry screech of nails being pried from wood. Not even a random curse word for good measure.

"Deke?" Cappie called again. Nothing.

A flock of black birds suddenly sprang from a cluster of oaks nearby. They circled the edge of the forest once and flapped off into the darkness. He hesitantly took a few steps closer to the house.

From just inside the front door of the house, someone giggled. It couldn't have been Deke, though. The giggle sounded immature, like a child's, but it had the weight of an adult's.

Cappie had made it to just a few feet from the porch. He tilted his ear toward the closed door, but there was no other sound. Cautiously, he moved up the uneven front steps to the wraparound porch. The warped stairs groaned under his weight. His work boots knocked dully as he slowly approached the front door, his footsteps echoing under the porch.

Thick, thorny vines had curled their way up the door and around the doorknob. They should have removed these hours ago, but neither Cappie nor Deke had been in a hurry to step up to the front door. Now Cappie tore them away. He reached for the tarnished brass knob, and he paused. Behind the door, something shuffled. He heard it draw a quivering breath. Whatever was there, it was excited. Anxious for him to enter.

"Hello?" Cappie heard the fear in his own voice.

His fingers touched the knob, and he paused again.

An image confronted him, from countless nights of passing out in front of the TV: Bette Davis in *What Ever Happened to Baby Jane?* Her old hag face smeared white with thick makeup in a hideous attempt to look like a baby doll. Black lips that grinned below wide staring eyes.

Cappie didn't want to open the door. Sure, Deke could have gone in one of the back entrances to pull one over on his old man. But something deep down inside him—deeper than the love he felt for his wife and son, deeper even than the fear that his rattling lungs may be the first signs of cancer—something at the very core of his being told him not to open that door.

But open the door Cappie did. He gave a soft push, and it slowly swung inward on its ancient hinges.

Footsteps scampered away, farther into the house.

Even in the dusk, Cappie could see that the front entrance was empty.

Cappie allowed himself a sigh of relief. He gripped the knob, preparing to pull the door shut and look for Deke around the side of the house when, without warning, a gust of wind whipped past him, whistling wildly into the foyer. Cappie looked over his shoulder and saw that the outside world remained undisturbed by the strong breeze. In the doorway, though, the wind picked up speed, the whistle growing to a howl. Cappie could feel its weight on his back, an invisible hand pushing him forward, ushering him into the house. He risked a half step, planting his foot to steady himself against the phantom gale.

And then, as quickly as it had begun, the last of the wind slipped by, spun itself wildly up the staircase, and was gone. In an instant, all was still.

"Dad?"

A tiny yelp escaped Cappie's mouth. He spun around.

It was Deke, a hammer in one hand, the keys to the truck dangling from the other.

"We leaving?"

Cappie pushed past him, taking the porch steps two at a time. "I been ready to leave for near twenty minutes now," he snapped, hoping Deke wouldn't ask why the hell he was suddenly so jumpy.

"But what about the rest of it? What about the generator?"

"We'll deal with the rest tomorrow," Cappie barked, knowing damn well he would be sending Deke out with someone else from the shop, maybe Ricky or Clayton. Cappie would not be returning to the house.

The pickup's engine turned over on the second try, and Deke was soon piloting it down the winding gravel road back to K-10. It was true that Deke's mama probably had food on the table by now, but Cappie had no intention of devoting his evening to a sit-down family dinner. He wanted nothing more than to belly up to the bar at the Innkeeper on Sixth Street and drink himself numb.

He couldn't tell the boys at the bar what he'd experienced. He couldn't even tell Deke. They would think he was crazy. It *was* crazy. But back there, on the porch, Cappie could have sworn the house had taken a breath.

SIX

A SKYLIGHT HIGH above cast a single stream of sunshine down into the darkened room. At its center was a wooden bench.

Moore listened to the soft click of her footsteps echo off the concrete walls and distant corridors. There were others here, moving slowly in silent contemplation, but she ignored them. She came to this place not to be inspired like so many other visitors but to turn everything off, to flick the switch in her mind, and just . . . be.

Now she needed it more than ever.

Shut off the thoughts. Just exist. Float. Be nothing.

The Getty Center was a fairly new addition to Los Angeles, opening to the public in 1997. Perhaps that was what Moore liked most about it compared to other art museums—its lack of true history. It was pretending to be as ancient and important as the works of art it sheltered. It was an old soul in a new shell. The building thought it was doing the art a favor, protecting it, displaying it. The shell had invited the soul in. One day the shell would collapse, and the soul would move to a new place.

The soul was a parasite.

Moore watched as darkened figures slid along the walls, appreciating genius in thirty-second increments. They were shadow people. They were nothing to her.

She took her usual seat on the bench beneath the skylight and looked over at her favorite painting in the entire museum. *Judith Slaying Holofernes*, completed by Artemisia Gentileschi in the early seventeenth century. A servant held the villain Holofernes down while Judith forced the blade of a sword through his throat. He struggled, his hands pushing desperately against the chin of the servant woman, yet she refused to let go. The panic he must have felt, to wake up and find his head being severed from his body. The weakness. The impotence.

Moore narrowed her eyes and stared into the absolute darkness between the servant and Holofernes. It was not the murderous women's cold, calculated expressions that excited her. It was the abyss between these two struggling bodies. That space meant the strength of a woman above, the helplessness of a man below. Moore felt the collision of forces there—him pushing her away, her holding him down.

The crossroads of pleasure and pain.

The darkness seemed to expand before her, like a wormhole opening in deep space, pulling her further inside until it was all she could see. It wanted her. To know her. To devour her.

Someone was approaching, a man in his fifties, thin hair ridiculously combed over his bald head.

"T.C. Moore?" the man asked. He did not bother to hide the annoyance in his voice.

"Yes?"

"Patty asked me to bring you to the Conservation Center." He followed this with a sharp breath.

Moore let the corners of her mouth cut high into her cheeks. It was like seeing a snake smile.

"Lead the way," she said.

The man identified himself as Chad. No last name. No title. Moore assumed he was a lackey sent to babysit the author during her research, and his increasingly dismissive attitude seemed to confirm this.

The area into which Moore was led was not the dismal subbasement she had anticipated, but a brightly lit research space with long steel tables lined with computer monitors. She passed several men and women in lab coats who eyed her curiously, several smiling warmly. Moore kept her gaze straight ahead.

"We have two impressionist paintings being restored, if you would be more interested in seeing that," Chad offered.

"Do I look like a fucking sixth grader on a field trip to see water lilies, Chad?" Moore asked.

Chad glanced back at her and his eyes narrowed. "No, you don't," he said.

At the far end of the room, a wooden table was set perpendicular to the others. A bright LED light rose up from the table on a long metal arm. Below this, illuminated in a soft halo of white light, was a clay tablet on a length of plastic sheeting. Etched into the tablet were crude images: a roaring lion, a one-horned goat, a buzzing insect with a human head.

Standing nearby, his back to the wall, was a security guard in black pressed pants and a white shirt. He watched Moore out of the corner of his eye as she stepped up to the tablet.

Chad thrust a hand out, stopping Moore from going any closer.

"You can look from here," he said.

"Calm down," Moore snapped. "I'm not going to lick the damn thing."

She scanned the various images. In the far right corner was a woman in a long cloak lined with an intricate pattern. She wore what looked like a square crown covered in flowers. A single braid curled down the back of her neck. The single eye in view was wide and knowing.

Chad nodded toward the image. "That's Kubaba. She was a Sumerian queen—"

"I'm in a bit of a hurry here, Chad," Moore interrupted. "You can spare me the history lesson."

"I just thought you might like to know—"

"About the only queen on the Sumerian King List? Ruled in the Third Dynasty of the Kish? Started her career as a tavern keeper before becoming one of the most powerful women in the world and later a Mesopotamian goddess, worshipped by multiple cults well into the second century? How am I doing?"

Chad frowned. Clearly some of this information was new to him, and he was fighting the urge to challenge Moore on its accuracy. In the end, he simply chose to ask, "What exactly are we helping you with here, Ms. Moore?"

"Research," Moore explained. "For a book. Don't worry, I can't stay long. I'm on my way out of town."

"And why is viewing this tablet so important to your . . . *book?*" He said the word as if he found it hard to believe that the woman before him could be responsible for such a thing.

"I wanted to see her eye," Moore said.

"Her eye?"

Moore ignored the man at her side and leaned in closer to the tablet. She stared into the eye of Kubaba.

How many kings did she see in her day? Moore wondered. *How many men questioned her authority? How many Hittites looked into that eye, just as I am now, and attempted to channel her strength through sacred rituals of their own invention? How many succeeded?*

Chad cleared his throat.

"You can go, Chad. There's a guard right over there. He'll Tase me if I try to run off with your tablet."

Chad did not bother to weigh his options. With an annoyed snort, he turned and walked away.

Moore hovered over the tablet and soaked up every detail of the carving of the Sumerian queen. As she did, she began to imagine a kind of dark magic, one that could turn the inspirational strength of this woman into something destructive. Something intoxicating. Something addictive.

For another twenty minutes, Moore did not move. Then, without warning, she turned on one heel and marched away, out of the Conservation Center and into the bright light of late morning.

She had a plane to catch.

SEVEN

HE HAD ONCE heard that driving was a form of hypnosis.

The hum of tires on the highway. The comfort of knowing that muscle memory is in complete control. Your mind begins to wander, and twenty minutes later, you don't remember what you passed or if you signaled before changing lanes.

The fire.

The smell of burning flesh.

His brother by his side as young Sam clutched his scorched arm to his chest and sobbed into his sleeve. Stop. Stop, stop, stop.

Sam shook his head, clearing away the thoughts.

He needed to be here. In this moment.

Stay right here.

There was a sudden thunk as his right front tire hit a pothole, and adrenaline shot through Sam's bloodstream. Good. He was awake again. His mind cleared.

In the backseat of the Audi was a duffel bag, stuffed haphazardly with random clothes for two full days. Someone named Kate from WrightWire had informed Eli that the interview could turn into a full-day walk-and-talk, something Kate had referred to (with what Eli presumed was a straight face) as *celebrity vérité.*

It was beginning to make more sense to Sam. The absurd paycheck, the lack of details. It was how Wainwright operated. Keep the subject guessing. Change the rules often. Elicit an honest response.

Fine. If a former club kid from Dublin wanted to spend an extra day with a Midwestern horror writer, Sam was willing to play ball.

What else did he have to do? Sit alone in his house *not* writing his next novel?

Sam exited onto Fourteenth Street and curved around to Broadway, past the Kansas City Convention Center, taking a hard right onto Tenth Street. Some of the buildings along this narrow street had been renovated, but many were still the same low redbrick structures that had lined the streets of downtown for decades.

On his right, office and apartment buildings gave way to the towering spines of classic books: *Catch-22*, *Fahrenheit 451*, *The Lord of the Rings*, *To Kill a Mockingbird*. This was the exterior of the Central Library, its main façade designed to resemble one long line of three-story-tall vintage novels.

This was where Wainwright had suggested they meet; the interview would begin with Sam McGarver walking into a giant bookshelf.

It did not matter if Sam remembered every detail of the drive from Lawrence to downtown Kansas City. He was there now.

No turning back.

The library was empty. Silent.

Sam's footsteps echoed off the marble floor as he made his way across the main lobby. Despite the fact that it was just barely evening, the interior of the library was surprisingly dim.

"Hello?" he called out, and listened as the cavernous building devoured his voice.

He glanced around. There was no one there to meet him. Not even another patron or a security guard.

He was alone.

Directly ahead of him, track lighting illuminated a set of wooden double doors. Sam pushed them open. The click of their latches was like a gunshot in a cave.

He was now in some sort of grand hall. Large white pillars extended into the darkness above. And in the open space between these pillars were books. Stacks and stacks of books. It was a primitive skyline of literature stretching across the room, a miniature cityscape of bound pages.

Thick, burgundy curtains had been drawn over the floor-to-ceiling windows on either side of the hall, plunging the immense room into darkness. Strategically chosen track lights cast glowing white beams down onto each stack, a mixture of hardcover and paperbacks. They dotted the dim room like markers in a prehistoric burial ground.

Sam slowly came to a stop.

"What the hell . . ."

At the center of the hall was a long wooden table covered with even more books. They were piled so high, they were spilling over. Several lights were angled directly at the piles of books, giving the table the unearthly appearance of a glowing toppled monolith.

Sam realized for the first time that soft music was playing through unseen speakers, a strange industrial ambience with a vaguely hip-hop beat.

He moved farther into the room, reaching the first of the book towers.

Paperbacks. Suspiciously thin. Barely room for the titles and author's name on the spines. The cover art was juvenile. Cartoonish. Reminiscent of the EC horror comics of the 1950s but without the subversive charm. Words were printed in an over-the-top, ghoulish font better suited for Halloween decorations. The titles, a collection of groan-inducing puns, suggested stand-alone stories in a series set at a haunted high school: *Six Feet Underclassman*, *Homecoming Scream Queen*, *Killer Ride*, *The Ghoul Next Door*, all under the series banner, *Fear Resurrected*. The intended audience was clearly teenagers looking for a gratuitous scare wrapped in heavy-handed morality. Even the author's name sounded like a bad joke: Daniel Slaughter.

Sam picked up the book on the top of the heap and gave its sides a light squeeze. The slender paperback easily buckled between his fingers. These were not multilayered narratives to be savored. They were candy.

And just like candy, consuming too many of these in one sitting could make you sick.

Confused, Sam set the book down and drifted out of the first shaft of light, into the darkness. He was beginning to see the room for what it was—a temporary museum, each tower its own exhibit. But why? What was the point?

His shoes padded softly across the marble floor as he slowly made his way over to the next stack of books.

Again, he picked up the book at the top of the stack. Much like Slaughter's novels, the top cover of this book said it all, but that was where the similarities ended. In a photograph aged and blurred at the edges by a hazy vignette was the lower half of a naked woman, a man's head pressed forcefully between her legs. Upon closer inspection, Sam noticed the ragged edge of the man's severed neck and the glimpse of a straight razor handle held in the woman's hand.

The name of the author was scrawled into the cover as if by the blade of a Buck knife held in a quivering hand, but Sam didn't have to read it to know who had written this aggressively sexual slice of horror fiction.

T.C. Moore.

Sam glanced around, now recognizing the telltale signs of Slaughter's and Moore's works on the sides of other nearby stacks. The books curved at odd angles, like the deformed vertebrae of twisted spines.

What is this? he wondered. *A museum of modern horror? Is this the setting for his interview? And if so, why are there stacks of books by other authors and none by—*

He froze.

There on the table was a mound of his books. Hardcover. Paperback. English. French. Spanish. His four novels multiplied by format and language; his output made to look more prolific than it actually was.

And yet it was a tribute, the same as the sloping towers for Daniel Slaughter and T.C. Moore.

"Hello?" he called once more into the darkness. "Anyone here?"

There was no reply.

Sam sighed, annoyed. He did not like playing games.

From behind him came the sharp click of the double doors opening.

There in the doorway was a woman dressed in black skinny jeans, a body-hugging T-shirt randomly slashed to show glimpses of skin, and dark sunglasses in a chunky black frame. Onyx hair poured over one shaved side of her head and down her shoulder like spilled ink.

Suddenly it came to him, the realization of who this person was, slamming into his brain like the key of a typewriter. Although they had never met, he knew who she was the moment he saw her. After all, he had just held one of her books in his hand.

T.C. Moore cocked her head, equally confused by the sight of Sam.

"Are you . . . Sam McGarver?"

The gears in Sam's mind locked.

Moore marched into the room, heels striking with each controlled, deliberate step. She vanished into the shadows for a moment, then reemerged into the soft illumination of the first spotlight. She was strikingly beautiful, with knife-sharp features. Her entire body was tight, like a single contracted muscle.

Despite the room being exceptionally dim, she still wore her sunglasses.

"What the hell is going on?" she asked, her irritation loud and clear. "Where's Wainwright?"

Sam shrugged. "I don't know." He nodded toward a stack of books to Moore's left. "But I think those are meant for you."

She turned, regarded the stack with complete disinterest at first, then her face slackened as she stared at the spines, lost and confused. For the first time since arriving, she removed her sunglasses, letting them dangle, forgotten, in one hand. With the other, she picked up the paperback on the top of the pile and ran a silver-nailed thumb over her name.

"What . . . what is this?" she asked, more to the room than to him.

"I was hoping you knew."

She gripped her book tightly as she took in the rest of the stacks, recognizing Sam's works. She spun to face him, and even in the low light, Sam could see her trademark pupil cutting a black swath across her iris.

"You're here for Wainwright too? *You?*"

"Is it so unbelievable that he would be interested in me?"

"Him, I believe. But his followers . . ." She shrugged. "Or maybe WrightWire is more middle-of-the-road than I thought."

Sam stiffened at the slight. "I prefer *mainstream*," he said.

"I'm sure you do," Moore replied.

The squeak of tennis shoes made both authors jump. Moore huffed like an irritated bull. She did not like being startled.

A massive form filled the entire doorway, a perfectly round torso set atop short, stubby legs. The man's chest rose and fell as he tried to hide the desperation of his breaths. He had obviously hurried to get to this section of the library, and he was not a man built for hurrying.

"Is this where I come for the interview?" he asked in a breathless yet chipper voice.

"And the hits keep on coming," Moore growled.

Sam recognized Daniel Slaughter immediately. He had seen Daniel at a couple of horror conventions early in his career, but the two had never spoken.

Nothing like officially meeting in the most awkward way possible, Sam thought.

Daniel was in his midthirties, a bright-eyed, rosy-cheeked man who was quick with a warm smile. He was conservatively dressed in khakis, a light blue polo shirt, and a navy blazer. Around his thick neck hung a delicate cross on a thin gold chain, and squeezing the ring finger of his left hand like a string tied tightly around a sausage was a simple gold wedding band.

Slaughter's jolly grin slowly retracted as he saw the faces of Sam and Moore.

"Am I in the wrong place?" Slaughter asked innocently. "I was supposed to meet someone named Wainwright."

"Oh, hell no," Moore spat. She thrust a hand into a small leather purse hanging on her shoulder by a strap of black ribbon and pulled out her cell phone. "This is not . . ." She didn't bother finishing her thought. She was already storming across the room, her face illuminated by the pale glow of the phone's screen as she searched for a number.

Slaughter turned back to Sam. "I don't understand."

"I think I'm starting to," Sam replied.

And so Sam explained what he had just moments ago realized: it was a setup. They had all assumed they were the only ones being interviewed, and the fine folks at WrightWire hadn't told them otherwise. Both Sam and Slaughter admitted they hadn't bothered to ask; it didn't even occur to them that there would be others involved. From the way she was furiously shouting a string of profanities into her phone, it obviously hadn't occurred to Moore either.

"So it's a group interview?" Slaughter asked, tugging the bottom of his polo down over his bulging belly.

Sam nodded. "Yeah, it seems that way."

"Just the three of us?"

Sam frowned. He hadn't considered that there might be more.

His gaze drifted from the large, ruddy-cheeked man before him to the towers of books rising from the hall floor like paper stalagmites. There were at least twenty stacks positioned in an arc around the room table, and several piles heaped on the table itself. After finding his own novels there, Sam hadn't bothered looking at the other piles.

He crossed to the nearest pile: T.C. Moore. The next pile: Daniel Slaughter. The pile after that: T.C. Moore. The next stack was immediately familiar to him; the books were his own.

"What are you doing?" Slaughter called after him. Sam didn't bother responding. He was picking up speed, moving farther around the arc. There were towers of their books in various languages. Slaughter in Spanish. Moore in Japanese. McGarver in French. Slaughter in German. He was halfway around the arc, and still it was only the three of them. Maybe there were no others. Maybe everyone Wainwright had invited was already there.

Across the room, Moore's face floated, disembodied, in the glow of her cell phone as she tapped the screen to end the call. She looked over at Sam, now working his way around the other side of the arc.

"I'm leaving," she announced.

Despite having barely met her, Slaughter made a face as if he truly regretted Moore's decision. Sam, on the other hand, didn't react.

"You two can blow Wainwright all night long for all I care," Moore continued, "but I didn't fly all this way to be—"

Sam wasn't listening. He was staring at a monstrous pile of books on the far corner of the table. Books by another writer.

Someone's missing.

The heap of books spilled to the very edge of the table on three sides, a massive collection of paperbacks and hardcovers, every cover different, every book unique. It was a body of work by an unfathomably prolific writer.

"There's a fourth author here."

"Even more reason to leave," Moore replied. "Have fun, fellas." She turned sharply on a heel and marched toward the double doors that led into the main lobby.

"Whose books are those?" Slaughter asked Sam with good-natured curiosity.

Sam noticed a single word of one title before he even picked up a book.

Shadow.

There was no way Wainwright had gotten him to come. It made no sense. It had to be a trick, another one of Wainwright's mind games.

Sam's hand trembled with a troubling mixture of excitement and anxiety as he picked up the book he had recognized so quickly.

A Thinly Cast Shadow.

Moore was a few feet from the double doors when one of them swung slowly open.

Before her stood a wisp of a man impeccably dressed in a slim gray suit, a white shirt, and a maroon tie. His face was cleanly shaven, flesh hardened from years in the sun, his high forehead speckled with liver spots. His white hair was parted neatly to one side. When he saw Moore, he smiled, and wrinkles shattered the skin at the edges of his clear, gray eyes.

"Pardon me," he said in a voice as crisp as spring linen drying on a line. Moore did not need an introduction, even as the old man shuffled into the room, even as he held out a thin hand to her.

She knew who he was. Every writer knew who he was.

"Sebastian Cole," the man said. "A pleasure to make your acquaintance."

When Sam was eleven years old, his father took him to the small pawnshop located on the second block of Walnut Street in what their microscopic town of Blantonville ambitiously called "downtown." The plastic sign above the door displayed the name of the store: RED ROBBIE'S PAWN AND LOAN. A single light bulb buzzed angrily within the sign, every now and then flickering as a warning that soon it would be joining its dead brother in broken filament heaven.

Robbie was a barely functioning alcoholic, which explained the trademark red nose with its burst blood vessels and bulbous tip, and the early closing time of four p.m., which just happened to coincide with the start of happy hour at the Brick House. As far as Sam knew, no one had ever taken Robbie up on his loan services, which gave unintentional irony to a sign's promise of "low interest rates." But many in town had brought in items to be pawned. The rows of crooked metal shelves and smudged glass cases were overflowing with a collection of unsorted, used wonders displayed with neither rhyme nor reason.

Sam's dad, a slight, timid man with a voice like a thin whistle, had stopped at the counter to ask Red Robbie himself where he might find a toaster for under ten bucks. It had been two years since the fire. They were still living in the "temporary" accommodations of West Hook Apartments—Sam and Jack and their dad in a cheap two-bedroom, although Jack was almost never around. Jack spent almost every night sleeping over at his girlfriend Crystal's, whose mother was warm and loving and supportive, all the things Sam and Jack had never known.

While his father haggled over toaster prices with Robbie, Sam was left to wander the aisles and gaze in astonishment at the treasures most would call "junk." His left arm was still wrapped in gauze like the arm of a mummy, although it no longer needed to be. The skin grafts on his arm had healed over in a rough, mottled sheath of scar tissue, but he wasn't ready for anyone else to see it. Sam had not said a word when they entered the store, and his dad had offered Robbie a sad little smile of apology. Most people in town knew not to expect much conversation from the boy. Not now. Not after what had happened.

On his last visit to the pawnshop, Sam had stumbled upon a ninja throwing star that his dad had let him buy after agreeing to use his own money and promising not to throw it at stray cats. Sam was hoping to find another weapon, maybe a throwing dagger or a butterfly knife. Despite the tragedy that swirled constantly over him like a funnel cloud, he was still a boy, and there was nothing quite as satisfying as flinging a sharp object at a tree trunk and watching it stick. But on this day, this summer afternoon in mid-July, Sam instead found a book.

It was the third from the top in a stack of random paperbacks, just below *A Guide to Edible Mushrooms* and a tawdry romance novel featuring a man on the cover whose shirt appeared to only have one working button (the bottom button, of course). The title of the third book intrigued him instantly, although he couldn't exactly say why. It was the simple yet inexplicably disturbing image it conjured up in his mind, that of a dark humanoid shape stretched long and thin, the fingertips of one extended hand ending mere inches from Sam's own shoe.

The book was called *A Thinly Cast Shadow*.

The author was Sebastian Cole.

And the moment Sam read the first paragraph, sitting in the cab of his father's Dodge pickup truck, his pocket fifty cents lighter, he knew this book was worth a thousand throwing stars. Every word was a thing to be chased, and chase them he did, away from the memory of the fire, away from the unspeakable solutions to his pain that no child should consider, and eventually away from the tiny town of Blantonville, in search of better things. He chased Sebastian Cole's words for the next three decades as he first mimicked, then rejected, and finally honored the author with his own stories.

Sebastian Cole was the single greatest influence on Sam's artistic life. He was the savior of his actual life. And now the man was walking toward him, pulling Sam back to the present with each elegant step.

"It appears Mr. Wainwright has decided to throw a party."

Cole's words reverberated through the darkness, the sound of a rosined bow being drawn over the strings of a perfectly tuned instrument.

This is the voice you hear right before you're born, Sam thought. *The voice that says, "Fight the good fight," before you are thrust into the unforgiving world.*

"I'm—"

"We know who you are," Sam said, immediately hating himself for being so dramatically reverent.

You sound like a goddamn fanboy, his mind scolded.

Daniel Slaughter apparently did not share Sam's fear. He eagerly thrust out a chubby paw that seemed to devour Cole's frail hand.

"Mr. Cole, what an honor. I am such a fan of your work. Everything you've written is a classic."

Sam may have imagined it, but he thought he glimpsed the hint of a grimace tugging at the corners of the old man's lips.

"Yes, well, thank you," Sebastian said.

A shadow was slipping up behind him, slow and catlike. The shadow passed into the edge of a spotlight, and Sam found himself staring into the ruptured pupil of T.C. Moore.

"I thought you were leaving," he said.

"I was." She nodded to the old man. "But then things got interesting."

As if on cue, a flash of light exploded above them, a brilliant white beam cutting through the darkness. It collided with a large white screen, up to this point lost in the shadows, and the four authors watched in shocked silence as the blurred image of a man's face appeared.

Slowly, and in absolute silence, the face came into focus. Thick, swooping hair. Brownish-purple eyes. Flesh like clay.

"Welcome," the image of Wainwright said, the sound of his impossibly deep voice booming from speakers hidden somewhere in the dark. "By now you all know the truth: you are not alone."

Slaughter glanced excitedly at the others. They did not return his enthusiasm.

Wainwright continued, "I hope you'll forgive my deception, but I felt it was the only way to make this dream come true: four of the most influential horror writers of the last fifty years, together for the first time in one room. You've each had a profound impact on my life, from having the piss scared out of me in middle school by Daniel Slaughter . . . to discovering in college the elegant, refined terror of Sebastian Cole . . . to peeling back the dark curtain of small-town America as I devoured the novels of Sam McGarver . . . and finally somehow loving every second of having my soul ripped out through my goddamn ass by T.C. Moore."

Sebastian gave an amused snort. Moore scowled, assuming Wainwright meant some form of disrespect, but when Sebastian smiled warmly at her, even the famously prickly Moore softened.

A screech jolted the entire group. On the screen, a series of flash frames shot past so quickly, it was nearly impossible to glean any necessary information.

They saw a house. Trees. The swaying tops of overgrown grass.

And then Wainwright's face was back, peering out at them from the shadows.

"I *love* horror. There's something about letting another person lead you into darkness that is both unbearably terrifying and exquisitely thrilling. And I have trusted each of you to lead me into that darkness . . ."

Another shriek, like a nail being pried from its decades-long grave in a plank of stubborn wood. The images flashed by even faster this time:

A house. Vines creeping over a closed door. The branches of a tree. White clouds in a blue sky. A window under a gabled roof.

When Wainwright returned, he was farther from the camera, standing in a field of tallgrass. The bushy tips swayed in the breeze.

". . . and now I hope you will trust me to lead you."

There was the angry pop of electricity, and the screen went black.

One by one, each spotlight followed suit, snapping off and leaving the stacks of books—books written by Sam, by Moore, by Slaughter, by Cole—to be devoured by shadows.

The four writers stood in confused silence, there in the dark.

"Seriously," Moore finally whispered, "what the shit is this all about?"

"It's a show," Sam said. "His show. It's what he does."

Without warning, the spotlights popped back on, then off, then on again individually, flashing in a seemingly random sequence, faster and faster as if an angry spirit had taken control of the power to the building. The strobing effect gave the whole thing the appearance of a light show at a rock concert.

There was a beat accompanying the lights, a steady thump that grew louder, drums swirling around them in an invisible aural cyclone until—

The shock and awe was complete.

The entire room was illuminated from above. There at the far end of the conference table was Wainwright, in the flesh, standing casually with his hands in his pockets.

He looked even younger in the company of his heroes, his excitement barely contained. Dressed in a jet-black suit over a white linen shirt unbuttoned to the base of his sternum, hair teased into a wild nest of unwashed curls, his face shaved smooth, he didn't appear a day over twenty-five.

"You're all still here," he said. Even without the aid of a PA system, his deep voice filled the large room. "Then let me tell you about our next step into darkness."

Moore ran her tongue over the bottom of her front teeth, stopping on the slightest hint of a chip. "Cut the crap. What are we really doing here?"

Wainwright smiled. He had been waiting for someone to ask that very question.

"Who wants to spend the night in a haunted house?"

EIGHT

MOORE HAD JOINED the others in taking a seat in one of several chairs around the table when she heard the sound of footsteps.

A young African American woman had entered the room. She was in her late twenties, tall and thin in a white tank top, black bra, and camouflage cargo pants. Her hair was a beautiful, lush bed of natural curls, her cheeks glowing at the ends of a warm smile. Dangling at her side by a long shoulder strap was a high-end digital SLR camera. In each hand, she carried two copies of a paperback book.

She introduced herself as Kate—just Kate—in an undeniably Southern accent, the full-mouthed twang of a Georgia upbringing. She set a copy of the book down in front of each of the writers.

Moore turned her copy so that it was perfectly perpendicular to her.

I remember this book. From when I was a kid, she thought.

The cover was tattered at the edges, the pages dry and slightly yellow. On the cover was the faded image of a field, not unlike the one Wainwright had stood in during his grotesquely theatrical introduction. Across the field, just off-center, was the dark shape of a house. A single window glowed brightly from the third story.

Written in an embossed, self-consciously creepy font popular among similar horror paperbacks from the 1980s was the title: *Phantoms of the Prairie: A True Story of Supernatural Terror.* And at the bottom of the cover, the author's name: Dr. Malcolm Adudel.

Kate took a seat next to Wainwright, the edge of her elbow brushing his.

Moore watched them all as they turned the books over in their hands.

"What is this?" Slaughter asked with genuine interest.

Wainwright smiled. "Our tour guide. Have any of you read it?"

"When it was published," Sebastian said in his elegant, measured way. "It was just as I suspected: a hastily written money grab, a trashy piece of hokum."

"Yeah, that's what most educated people think." Wainwright held up his own copy of the book, a well-used paperback, and flipped through its brittle pages. "But back in the day, there were plenty of people who believed it, enough to put it on the nonfiction bestseller list. In this part of the country, the house on Kill Creek is still a local legend, as Sam can attest."

Moore looked to Sam, who nodded. "It's just a campfire story told by teenagers."

"Wait, I remember this place," Daniel said, turning the book over in his hands as if he'd just been handed an ancient artifact of great value. "This was huge—"

"For, like, a minute," Kate added.

Moore rolled her eyes. *A minute. We get it. You're a kid. You won't be forever.*

Daniel nodded. "Yeah. Yeah, this was the house where those two creepy women lived—"

"The Finch sisters," Wainwright said.

"That's it. No one's been able to live in that place since it was built. When people move in, the house just, like, comes alive!" He tapped the cover of *Phantoms of the Prairie*. "It's all in the book. I remember it now. Didn't they make a movie out of this?"

"They were going to," Wainwright informed them. "Never happened."

Moore crossed her arms and leaned back in her chair, eyes narrowing as she studied the young internet tycoon at the head of the table. "So what does the Kill Creek house have to do with us?"

Wainwright met her gaze. He did not shrink under her scrutiny. "Every October, WrightWire does something huge for Halloween. But this year, nothing we came up with felt right. Our ideas were either too obvious, things anyone would think to do, or they were too cheap, lacking the . . . well, the *indie cred* that WrightWire has become known for. WrightWire is a genre site, right? But it's also a pop culture site; that's how we think of it. What separates us from similar sites and magazines is that we focus as much on the *culture* as we do on the *pop*. If something's already mainstream, I want to come at it from another, completely unexpected angle. If something has been forgotten or overlooked, I want it to be a household name.

"So our big stunts sort of need to exist in two spaces: they need a big, loud, trashy component that is strangely complemented by an air of respectability, usually in the form of an artist or artists who are so inarguably great that they elevate the trashy hook, creating something . . . profound."

Wainwright was flushed with life. When Moore had first seen him, she thought the young man appeared as if he were made of rubber, as if the person standing before them were wearing a Wainwright mask, his true identity hidden. But the more Wainwright spoke about his passions, the more that rubbery flesh came alive.

"And then one day an image appeared in my mind, of an old, dark house on Halloween night. A haunted house. Everyone loves a haunted house. It's timeless. That's the *pop*. Then I needed the *culture*. That's the four of you."

"While I respect your ingenuity, this is not what I signed up for," Sebastian said.

Wainwright glanced over at Kate, who gave him a supportive smile.

The brief exchange did not escape Moore. *They're together,* she thought, filing the detail away for future use.

From a leather satchel on the floor by his chair, Wainwright took out a thick stack of papers and set them on the table.

"This here is the document you or your representatives signed. By doing so, you all agreed to a two-day interview for WrightWire. I promised your travel, meals, and accommodations would be covered. But I didn't say where that interview would take place, or if there would be others involved. You all assumed you were the only ones taking part in it and that the interview would be in a more, uh, normal venue."

"You tricked us," Sam said. There was no anger in his voice. It was a statement of fact, plain and simple.

Wainwright sighed. "Well . . . yes. I guess you could say that. But if you had known the plan from the beginning, would you have come? Would I have been able to get you all together in the same room?"

"Well, you did it," Sam said. "Congrats. You got us in the same room. But I'm not interested."

Sam pushed his chair away from the table. He was going to leave.

"What's the matter, Sam? Give any one of your *students* a six-pack and they'd be knocking down the front door of the Finch House. Don't tell me the modern master of horror is afraid of a . . . what did you call it . . . a campfire tale?"

Moore expected the Midwestern mainstreamer to take the bait, but he did not. Sam remained seated and silent.

Wainwright turned to the others. "We could do the interview here in this library, we could do it in a conference room somewhere, or we could do it in a place that is guaranteed to light up the goddamn internet."

Wainwright paused, long enough for any one of them to stand and walk out. They did not move.

"I can't force you to do this. You're free to leave now. Or you can stay the night—we have rooms booked for each of you at a hotel on the Plaza—and you can leave in the morning." He leaned over the table, the spotlight overhead casting long streaks of shadow down his face. "Or you can come with me to Kill Creek and, by the first of November, you won't just be the four most famous horror authors on the planet; you'll be the four most famous *authors* on the planet."

"We're already famous," Sebastian countered, his posture stiffening.

Wainwright slowly nodded. "Yes, sir, you are. To a certain generation. But what happens when they forget you?"

He looked to Daniel Slaughter. "Or they outgrow you."

To Moore. "Or they misunderstand you?"

To Sam. "Or they give up on you?"

A heavy silence fell over them. No one wanted to confirm that Wainwright's shots had hit dead center.

Screw this guy, Moore thought. "This is bullshit."

"Is it?" asked Wainwright. "Or is it exactly what each of you needs at this moment?"

"Baby, you don't know what I need," Moore told him. "And even if you did, you couldn't give it to me."

Wainwright gave a sharp laugh. It was not meant to be mocking; it was genuine amusement. "Look, I promise, it'll be a good time. We'll have all the comforts of home. The house really isn't that old. Rachel Finch lived in it until 1998. A few days ago, we had the water turned back on. There's a generator for power. A cleaning crew went out this afternoon to give the place a bit of sprucing up."

Daniel Slaughter sat up in his seat. "So people have gone in the house?"

"Just the cleaners. A handyman. A few other workers, maybe."

"And did anything . . . happen?"

"Whaddya mean, mate? Like supernatural?"

Daniel nodded. "It's sort of what you would expect in the Finch House."

Wainwright shook his head. "Nah. But they were only inside for a few hours, in broad daylight."

Sebastian rapped his knuckles lightly on the table. "In broad daylight," he repeated. "So what you're implying is, at night, all bets are off."

Wainwright gave a sharp, gravelly laugh. "Look, if you're asking me if I believe the house is really haunted, the answer's *no*. If you're asking if I have something planned to make the house *seem* haunted, well, same answer. I really mean it—this is an interview, a chance to dig deep into your genius brains in a, you know, appropriate setting. I've purposely kept the party cozy. Just us. A few cameras. A simple sound package. Nothing slick. No place for bells and whistles. I want my subscribers to feel like they're there with us, not watching a cable show. Which is why I've purposely kept my team small. Kate and I will be the only ones joining you in the house."

Wainwright touched Kate lightly on the hand.

Moore shook her head. *Way to give the girl permission to speak.*

Kate lifted the Nikon into the air with one hand. She looked each of them straight in the eye as she explained: "I'll document our time in the house through several mounted wireless cameras and a handheld.

We'll be live-streaming from the moment the interview starts to when it ends. Giving the viewers access to every minute we're in the house would only dilute things, spreading our viewership over hours instead of minutes. We want to create an event that will bring a big audience for the live stream and still be short enough to go viral. This is about reaching as many people as possible, as quickly as possible. Any other footage we gather from the night will be recorded wirelessly to hard drives and edited later. This isn't *Ghost Hunters*. We're not rigging the whole place with night vision. This is about your time together. This is about your conversation with Wainwright. The focus should and will be the four of you."

"Thanks, Kate." The legs of Wainwright's chair squeaked as he stood. "So? Who's in?"

"I'm in," Daniel announced with nervous excitement.

Moore rolled her eyes. "Of course you are."

"What?" he said. "It sounds like fun."

Sebastian breathed in through his nose and exhaled slowly. "I'm in as well," he said, though with much less enthusiasm than Daniel. "I'm not dead yet, and I suppose this old man could use a bit of excitement."

"Are you both serious?" Moore asked. She looked to Sam. He was rubbing a hand lightly over the intricate tattoos that covered his left arm. "You're not doing this, are you?"

Sam glanced from Moore to Sebastian Cole, who appeared content with his decision, his gaze steady, posture ruler-straight. The chance to spend more time with literary royalty was clearly swaying Sam.

"Screw it. I'm in," he said.

Moore gave a disgusted snort.

But Wainwright turned to her as if he had noticed nothing.

"The men are on board. What about you, Ms. Moore?"

Much later, after the reality of their situation had come horrifyingly into focus, Moore would look back at this moment and curse herself for not walking out of that room. She had wanted to leave. She was free to do so. But just like the others, something made her stay, made her take a seat at the table, made her listen quietly as Wainwright explained his master plan. Moore could not speak for the others, but when she truly pressed herself for a reason for her participation in Wainwright's grand charade, the answer was so pathetically simple that it sickened her:

She stayed because the men did. She stayed because of pride. She had fought too hard against these condescending pigs to walk out now.

Room 819. Sam inserted the key card and heard a sharp click. He pushed the door open.

Stale, recycled air rushed at him. He let the door swing shut behind him. He tossed the key card onto the dresser, dropped his duffel bag to the floor, and fell back onto the bed.

For ten minutes he lay there, staring up at the ceiling. A single water stain blemished the whiteness.

He closed his eyes.

This is ridiculous.

The hum of the air conditioner filled the room.

His fingers began to slowly trace the burned flesh of his left arm.

The air-conditioning unit below the window blew a cool, steady breath across the room.

Sam could taste the ash at the back of his throat. He could smell the sickeningly sweet aroma of charred skin. He recognized his own. But there was another, in the fire, being consumed by the flames. . . .

He sat up.

His cell phone came to life as he picked it up. No messages. Who the hell did he expect to call? Eli, perhaps, checking in on his client. Erin. Not likely. Although Halloween *had* always been one of their favorite holidays. They would rent a stack of horror movies, fill a large tub with candy for trick-or-treaters, and turn off all the lights so that only the flicker of the television illuminated the room.

It was October 30, and not a word from her.

Maybe tomorrow, he thought. *While we're at the house.*

He knew she wouldn't call. She was done with him.

Sam got up from the bed and paced the small room. *What am I doing here? I should be at home, writing. Or at least trying to write. I should have brought my laptop. No,* he reconsidered, *what kind of writing could I get done locked in a house with three other authors? Maybe none. But maybe the visit will inspire me. Maybe a first sentence will come to me, there in that old ghost-filled house. A phrase might suddenly appear in my mind, perfectly formed, like a healthy child.*

On a table near the window was a complimentary pad of Fairmont stationery and a single ballpoint pen. Sam snatched them up, unzipped his bag, and tossed them in. He let out a breath. There. He felt better. One problem solved. A million to go.

He dug into his bag and pulled out the small dopp kit. He unzipped it. Inside was a travel pill case, and inside this were three green pills. He popped one in his mouth and swallowed it dry.

At quarter to seven, the lounge at the Fairmont was like every other hotel lounge—appropriately dim, artificially constructed, and packed wall to wall with businesspeople. Light jazz tinkled through the air.

Sam entered and scanned the room, almost immediately spotting Sebastian Cole perched at the bar, a glass of what looked to be single-malt scotch dangling loosely in his hand. He was staring at the window behind the bar, through which darkness was beginning to engulf the city. The infinitely blue sky was riddled with stars, the once-white clouds glowing a warm pink as if they had been slapped. The lights of the Plaza shops blinked on one by one, each window a warm invitation to the shivering shoppers outside. A horse-drawn carriage rolled leisurely down the street as cars trailed patiently behind it.

Sebastian's eyes were widened slightly, unfocused.

"Hope I'm not disturbing you." Sam's voice startled Sebastian. He turned sharply.

"I'm sorry," Sam continued. "If you want to be alone—"

"You're not disturbing me at all." Sebastian offered a warm smile. "Please. Have a drink with me."

Sam pulled himself up on the next barstool and ordered a beer. The bartender delivered a perfect pour. "So," Sam said after a much-needed sip, "here we are."

"Of all places."

Sam took a cocktail napkin from a nearby stack and began to twist it into a tight roll. *Just get it over with,* Sam thought. *There's no casual way to say it, so just say it.*

"Mr. Cole, I—"

"Please. Sebastian."

Sam nodded. "Sebastian. I'm sure you get this on a daily basis, but your writing really does mean a lot to me. It's safe to say your books are the reason I became a writer." He fumbled nervously with the mangled cocktail napkin.

"Not to sound like an arrogant old man, Sam— May I call you Sam?"

"Of course."

"Good. Yes, I do get fans telling me how much they've loved my books, particularly *A Thinly Cast Shadow*."

"A classic," Sam blurted out, instantly ashamed. He remembered the way Sebastian had flinched when Daniel used the same word earlier that day.

"A classic," Sebastian agreed with a melancholy smile, "much like myself." He took a hard swallow of scotch. "But coming from a writer like you, Sam, a talented writer, an honest writer, the accolades have weight. Because I believe you know a good story from a bad one. And if my stories are some of the good ones, well, then I've done my job."

Sam nodded. He raised his glass to his lips, but he stopped short of drinking. There was something else that needed to be said.

"I read *A Thinly Cast Shadow* when I was twelve. Two years before that, my mother died. I wasn't . . . Well, let's just say I was having a tough time. Your book, your writing, it didn't just inspire me. It . . . It saved me."

Sebastian nodded slowly, but he said nothing. For a moment, the two men drank in silence.

"I've read your books, too, Sam," Sebastian said finally.

Sam could not help feeling a flutter of excitement in his chest.

"I liked them very much," Sebastian continued. "You have an honest way of writing, especially your first book. It's genuine. That may not seem like the most thrilling compliment, but a voice like yours—a real voice—is rare these days."

Now it was Sam's turn to repay praise with silence. Sebastian's kind words meant the world to him, and yet one phrase chipped away at Sam's confidence like an ice pick: *especially your first book.*

Sam took a long gulp from his glass, hoping the beer would mix with the slowly dissolving pill in his stomach and numb his nerves.

"As for our other brethren . . ." Sebastian did a quick visual sweep of the room, making sure they were nowhere in the vicinity. "Mr. Slaughter writes for teenagers, a group I never have understood, nor ever will. And Ms. Moore, besides being insanely successful, panders to a—I'm just going to say *unique* crowd that thinks sexual liberation means letting a demon fuck you in the asshole."

Sam almost choked on the beer but managed to swallow it down around a laugh.

"If I may be frank," Sebastian added dryly.

Night had finally fallen on the outside world, the last streaks of dusk quickly pulled below the horizon. The bar seemed to welcome the darkness, the music taking on a slightly more electronic sound, the dim lamps that had been easily overlooked in the daylight now casting narrow orange streaks upon the bloodred walls. The place felt smaller, the patrons crowding closer and closer to the bar. When had it gotten so busy? It was loud, voices over voices, a steady bombardment of muddled, drunken banter.

Through the window, Sam could see things moving in the darkness. He assumed they were people, but they scurried through the streets like beetles, seeming to stick to the shadows, just out of sight.

"Is there a story there?"

Sebastian was looking down at Sam's arm. He knew the old man wasn't referring to his tattoos.

"Yes."

"Have you told it?"

Sam swirled the last of his beer around in the glass. "Part of it. To my wife. *Ex*-wife."

"Why only part?"

"Sometimes . . ." Sam paused. The acrid gray cloud of smoke was rising in the back of his throat again. "Sometimes stories have too much power. They change who people think you are."

The old man nodded. "They do indeed."

At a nearby booth, a group of businessmen in ill-fitting off-the-rack suits erupted in a startlingly loud roar of laughter.

Sebastian sat up straight on his barstool, the intimacy of their conversation lessened a bit. "Well, I would hate to think we're only going to get four books out of you."

"No, I'm working on something new. It's going well."

You're lying, he scolded himself. *You just lied to your idol.*

Sebastian seemed to sense the dishonesty, for the smile he gave faltered a bit at the edges.

"Sam, agents talk. Nothing stays a secret for long in this business. Sometimes a writer just needs a break, to regroup."

Sam gave a sharp laugh that he hoped sounded incredulous. "I don't know what you've heard, but I promise, they're only rumors."

"Funny thing about rumors," Sebastian said softly. "It doesn't matter if they're true or false, only that people believe them."

NINE

DANIEL SLAUGHTER HAD always been an early bird.

Even when he was at home in his own bed with his wife, Sabrina, by his side, his eyes would click open as soon as the first rays of dawn broke the horizon. He would roll out of bed as quietly as possible, wincing as the bed frame squeaked, as if it were relieved to be temporarily rid of his bulk. Sabrina rarely woke. She was a heavy sleeper. Her petite body, unchanged since they had met in their early twenties, would remain curled in a tight ball under the sheets.

So it came as a shock to Daniel that in a strange hotel room in a city he had visited only a handful of times in his life, he had slept in.

When his eyes blinked sleepily open, sunlight was already cutting like a knife across the foot of his bed. He checked the digital clock on the nightstand: 10:14 a.m. His hand swept out from under the covers to grasp the clock. He had to touch the clock, actually feel it in his thick fingers, to believe that the numbers it was displaying were correct.

"Gosh darn it," he whispered.

They'd planned to meet in the lobby at eleven thirty. After showering and getting dressed, he would barely have time to wolf down a late breakfast.

He rocked forward in the bed, but the pillow-top mattress seemed to only sink beneath his immense weight.

A sudden thought, totally irrational, surfaced in his mind:

Holy heck, I'm not gonna be able to get up.

He swept his hand from the nightstand to grip the bed frame for added leverage. As he did, his hand hit a paperback book beside the clock and sent it tumbling to the carpeted floor.

Daniel looked down.

It was the book Kate had given him the previous evening.

Phantoms of the Prairie.

Daniel groaned, irritated with himself.

That book was why he had slept in.

He knew he should have gone straight to bed after returning from the hotel restaurant shortly after nine. But the book had intrigued him from the moment Kate had handed it to him. It was something about the cover, which was deceptively simple compared to the outrageous artwork that adorned his own novels. There was the farmhouse adrift in a sea of tallgrass, a single light on in the uppermost window, glowing with supernatural menace. He'd held the cover close to his eyes. Were there faces peering out from the trees beyond the house? He couldn't be sure, but the shadows between the slim tree trunks seemed to twist into vaguely human forms.

He had settled himself down into a chair at the small table by the window and opened the book.

A True Story of Supernatural Terror, the subtitle proclaimed.

He began to read.

The writing was journalistic in style, verging on the academic, but there were enough lurid flourishes that Daniel found himself, somewhat guiltily, pulled away from his hotel room in Kansas City and out to the dark countryside of Kill Creek.

He was there with the author, Dr. Malcolm Adudel, as Rachel Finch greeted him. Her face was moonlight made flesh, a stark contrast to her hair, which was as black as a starless night. He was at Adudel's side as the parapsychologist explored the house, room by room, listening as a phantom breeze swept through hallways and corridors like air into lungs. When Daniel closed his eyes, he could see the ghoulish face of Rebecca Finch, dead by the time Adudel visited the house but no less a presence than her sister, Rachel. Several times Daniel jumped in his chair as a maid's cart wheeled by in the hall outside his door.

He was sure, *absolutely sure*, that it was the squeaking wheels of Rebecca Finch's wheelchair.

He was two-thirds of the way through the book before he realized he had been reading for four hours. It was after one o'clock in the
morning.

He quickly jumped up, brushed his teeth, and pulled on his
striped pajamas. Daniel slipped into bed, fully intending to leave the
book where it lay and go to sleep.

But there were faces in the woods on the cover. He was now positive it wasn't just his imagination.

It was almost four in the morning when he turned the last page.

He had set the paperback on his nightstand, right next to the
digital clock. He was reaching for the switch on the lamp when a voice
in his mind screamed:

Don't!

It was not his own voice. It was lighter. Sweeter. Yet there was
unbelievable power in it.

It was the voice of his daughter, Claire.

His Claire. Barely sixteen years old, every bit a teenager, and still
she was his rock. His hope. His life.

Daniel's hand had hovered inches away from the light switch as
he felt the residual vibrations of that voice fading into the darkness.

He was a grown man. He was not going to sleep with the light on.
But he could also make sure that doggone creepy cover wasn't staring
at him all night.

Opening the nightstand drawer, Daniel had dropped the paperback inside, right next to the obligatory copy of the King James Bible.

Strange bedfellows, he thought.

Hopefully old King James would keep those shadow faces at bay
until dawn.

And there he was, at a quarter past ten in the morning, staring
down at the floor and the book he knew—he *knew*—he had put in the
nightstand drawer.

Come on, buddy, you're remembering it wrong, he told himself. *It
was late. You were tired.*

"Sure," Daniel said aloud. "Maybe."

He hoisted himself up out of bed, making sure to take a wide step
over the book as he crossed to the bathroom.

He left it on the floor until he was ready to go.

Moore stood at the curb, the handle of her bag clutched tightly in one hand as she stared out through black cat-eye sunglasses at the monstrosity parked a few yards away. Behind her, the automatic front doors of the hotel opened with a whoosh, and Daniel hurried out, pulling a large suitcase. His face was flushed and sweaty even in the crisp October air.

He, too, came to an abrupt stop when he saw it.

"Is that our ride?" he asked.

Moore ran her tongue over her top front teeth. "Unfortunately, I believe it is."

Son of a bitch, she thought. *We've officially joined the circus.*

The side door of the vintage Volkswagen Microbus stood wide open, revealing a center row and a third in the far back. Kate leaned against the pale yellow body of the bus. She was dressed in fitted cargo pants and a long-sleeved thermal shirt. Unlike the night before, she was free of makeup, revealing small clusters of acne scars on each cheek. Her dark brown hair was pulled back into a simple ponytail. Her camera hung on a strap from her shoulder. She was talking quietly to Wainwright, who was decked out in dark blue jeans and a black leather jacket over a plain white V-neck. His thick hair fluttered in the soft breeze, strands falling down around the tinted frames of classic aviator sunglasses.

Kate's brown eyes flashed over to the authors at the curb. She smiled warmly as she instinctively brought the camera up. Her thumb hit a button on its body to begin recording. "Mornin'," she said, quickly focusing the wide-angle lens.

"Good morning," Daniel replied.

Wainwright turned, his face smooth and strangely artificial in the late-morning light. He slapped the metal side of the bus with an open palm.

"What do you think? She's a beauty, right?"

Moore groaned softly. "Let's get this over with," she said as she crossed to the open door and climbed inside.

The old bus bounced down the road.

Sam looked out the window, his face long, his eyes tired. He had not slept well the night before. His nerves were like millions of tuning forks humming in different keys.

Here I go, on my way to camp, he thought. *I feel like a kid. I hate feeling like a kid.*

"She's a 1975 VW," Wainwright said, his voice booming from the driver's seat.

When no one else responded, Sam leaned forward from his seat in the third row. "What was that?"

"The bus. She's from 1975, the same year the Finch sisters moved into the house on Kill Creek. The same year, I believe, Mr. Cole published two novels: *At the End of the Tunnel* and *The Dark Before Dawn.*"

"That's correct," Sebastian said, obviously a bit embarrassed by Wainwright's comment.

Moore gave a sarcastic whistle. "We get it: Sebastian has written a lot of books in his hundred years."

Sebastian gave a good-natured chuckle. "Don't worry, Ms. Moore, *The Dark Before Dawn* was complete shit."

"And *Tunnel?*" Moore asked.

"Well, it was genius, of course," he said with a wink.

Sam leaned back, listening to the drone of the highway under the wheels. Daniel Slaughter sat beside him on the leather bench, his hands folded obediently in his lap. He was clad in an unremarkable green polo shirt. This was tucked into tan Dockers and cinched with a brown leather belt, a little too tightly, Sam observed, based on the considerable bulge hanging over. Daniel's chubby arms were pale against the short sleeves of the shirt, his flesh the pinkish gray of a dead fish's belly.

The ride from the hotel in Kansas City had been a relatively quiet one, although Wainwright was determined to change that. Every few minutes, he made a new attempt at mundane chitchat, but so far, every attempt had failed. For this, Sam was thankful. The internet tycoon's over-the-top introduction the night before had been exhausting, and Sam felt as though he had a hangover despite only having three beers at the hotel bar.

For a few more miles, they rode in silence. Sam wished he had snagged the seat next to Sebastian, but Moore had claimed it first, leaving the backseat for Sam and Daniel. Now Sam stared at the backs of their heads, Sebastian and Moore in the middle row, Wainwright and Kate up front, each off in their own little world. Coming to terms with their decisions to join Wainwright on his bizarre little field trip, Sam assumed.

"Okay, time for a pop quiz," Wainwright announced, trying a new approach.

"Oh Christ, here we go," Sam grumbled under his breath.

From the passenger side, Kate swung her camera around the edge of the seat and pointed it at the authors in the two back rows. The sunlight glinted off the wide-angle lens, giving it the illusion of having a slender, reptilian pupil.

Sam shifted uncomfortably in the camera's gaze.

Wainwright tapped his copy of *Phantoms of the Prairie* resting on the dashboard. Sam could see its cover reflected in the glass of the windshield. "You were all given copies of the Adudel book, so this shouldn't be too hard." Wainwright kept his eyes on the road as he called back over his shoulder. "How many owners has the house had?"

They responded with silence.

Sam slid down in his seat. *Enough with the game. No one wants to play.*

The lack of enthusiasm did not please Wainwright. "Anyone care to venture a guess?"

Daniel glanced awkwardly at the others, realizing no one was going to participate. "Uh . . . six, I think."

"Wrong," Wainwright said flatly. "There were five." He sighed. "Anyone know their names?"

Again, there was no quick response.

"Sam." Wainwright adjusted the rearview mirror so that he could see Sam in the third row. "How about you?"

Sam glanced up and found himself staring straight into Kate's lens. He shrugged and shook his head. "I wouldn't know. Sorry."

Wainwright's already deep voice dropped even lower. Any pretense of pleasantry was gone. "But you have the book. I gave it to you specifically for our trip."

Kate seemed to sense something coming, her body tensing, but she held the camera steady.

He's pushing you, Sam told himself. *He wants you to react.* Sam met Wainwright's gaze in the mirror. "It was late. I was tired."

The leather steering wheel creaked as Wainwright tightened his grip. "What's the point of going to this house if you all know nothing about it?" There was anger in his voice now. Sam could see the back of the young man's jaw moving ever so slightly. He was clenching and unclenching his teeth.

"Did no one bother to look at the book?" Wainwright snapped.

Kate lowered the camera, pretending to busy herself with adjusting the settings.

"I gave it a go," Sebastian announced. "But I couldn't quite stomach Mr. Adudel's assault on the English language. His use of exclamation marks was more terrifying than the description of the paranormal events they followed."

Moore swiveled on the bench to face the old man. "You'd prefer he wrote in the self-consciously elegant style of the great Sebastian Cole?"

"Honestly, I would have prefered anything to Adudel's prose, even the self-consciously perverse style of T.C. Moore."

The comment caught Sam by surprise and he snorted unexpectedly.

Moore shot him what, even through her dark sunglasses, Sam could tell was meant to be an irritated look.

Perhaps not entirely irritated. There was the tiniest hint of playfulness there. Despite her best attempts, she was beginning to warm to her companions.

"I read it. I read the whole thing."

They all turned to look at Daniel, surprised by the sound of his voice.

Sebastian cocked an eyebrow. "It's not your fault, Mr. Slaughter. Insomnia has been known to make people do irrational things."

"It wasn't that. I wanted to read it. I wanted to know what you're getting us into."

"And?" Wainwright asked, his voice deep and probing. He was nothing but a pair of eyes in the rearview mirror. "What am I getting you into?"

Sam watched as Wainwright glanced over at Kate. The subtle hint of a smirk played at the corners of his lips.

He likes that we're in the dark, Sam thought.

Daniel shifted nervously. "Well, I mean, I didn't really believe a word of it. Seemed like a bunch of hooey to me."

"I don't know what's scarier," Moore said, "the fact that you read that entire awful book or that you just said *hooey* with a straight face."

"Not everything has to be laced with profanity."

"I guess we just have two different styles, don't we, Mr. Slaughter? I say what people think and you tell people what to think. Don't worry, you're not the first Holy Roller to think he knows better than everyone else."

Daniel's cheeks flushed red. "I don't think I know better. I see writing as a way to teach a lesson through entertainment. You see it as an opportunity to glorify deviant behavior."

"Okay now," Sebastian said.

Moore ignored the old man. She had turned around in her seat to stare Daniel down with those dark cat-eye lenses. "I simply encourage my readers to free themselves of the fabricated morality that is shoved down their throats every day by hypocritical priests and politicians."

"How? By telling teenage girls to cut themselves?"

"That's enough," Sebastian said louder.

Once again, Wainwright looked to Kate, and Sam could see that he was grinning. He gave a sharp nod, and Kate obeyed the order, whipping the camera up and instantly recording.

He's enjoying this, hearing us tear each other apart.

Moore continued: "The only reason teenage girls would even think to harm themselves is because high-and-mighty pricks like you tell them that their own biology is sinful. They only need my release because of your repression. Maybe that's why my first book—a self-published book—sold more copies than an entire series of the church pamphlets you call novels."

"Enough!" Sebastian's tone was that of a father pushed to the limit by his arguing kids.

"Stop fighting over who is the better writer or I'll turn this car around," Wainwright called back in a faux stern voice. He gave a low chuckle, amused by his own comment.

Sam frowned. *There's something off about him. One second he's ready to tear into us; the next he's joking like we're old friends.*

"What's on your mind, McGarver?" It was Moore, looking back at him.

"What?" Sam asked, caught off guard.

"You look like you got something to say."

Sam watched Wainwright's eyes flash up to the rearview mirror. He waited for Sam's response.

"I like your sunglasses," Sam told Moore.

She gave a surprisingly honest laugh, then nodded to Sam's left arm. "I like your ink, but I'm more curious about what it's hiding."

Instinctively, Sam slid his right hand over his scars, doing his best to cover them.

Sebastian sighed. "There, see? We can all get along."

In the rearview mirror, Wainwright's eyes were still on Sam.

What's your game? Sam wondered.

Without warning, the bus swerved. Everyone gripped their seats as Wainwright swung the vehicle past the sign for "Kill Creek Road" and around the sharp curve of the exit ramp.

"Sorry about that," Wainwright said in that flat, deep voice. Soon the paved road gave way to gravel.

Sam pressed his forehead to the cool glass of the window. The trees along the side of the road had already shed their leaves for the winter. Long, bare branches stretched over the road like a canopy of skeletal hands. Blackbirds, grackles perhaps, dotted the trees, their beady black eyes watching as the car rolled past. Every now and then, one would give a shrill squawk at the intruders.

You are not wanted here. You should turn back.

Something flashed by on the side of the road, a chain-link gate covered in twisted green vines. A fence cut through the trees, running perpendicular to the road for about fifty feet before being swallowed into the shadows that stretched between ancient brown tree trunks.

Wood planks rattled under the tires as the bus crossed a small, weather-beaten bridge. The dry bed of a stream snaked beneath them.

"That's the creek," Wainwright said. "Let's try this again: Anybody know why they call it Kill Creek?"

Moore gave an irritated sigh. Sam barely made out the words she whispered: "Please be quiet."

"In his book," Daniel said, "Adudel speculated that this land was the site of a massacre, possibly during the Civil War border battles between Kansas and Missouri."

"I sincerely doubt the creek is named after a massacre," Sebastian interjected. "'Kill' or 'kille' is Middle Dutch for 'creek.' Early settlers probably used the word to describe this pitiful little stream. As more and more folks moved to the area, they must have thought *kill* was the name of the creek, hence *Kill Creek*. Its name is nothing but a redundancy. Like saying 'the Rio Grande River' or 'the Sahara Desert.'"

"Or Christian extremists," added Moore.

Sam glanced over at Slaughter, expecting the tension in the bus to ratchet back up, but Slaughter chose to ignore Moore's jab.

Leaning forward, Sam got a better look through the windshield. They were making their way up a long driveway of gray pebbles. On either side, tallgrass waved in the breeze. It appeared as if it hadn't been cut in years. Through a break in the trees, he could see the dingy white wood of the house. Its crumbling brick chimney peeked over the top branches of the highest oak like a solitary horn. Except for the badly neglected Kill Creek Road, this house was completely cut off from the rest of the world.

Exactly how Wainwright wants us. All to himself.

He shook his head. *Stop. You're trying to make a mildly annoying situation into something worse. But that's your MO, isn't it, Sammy boy?* He closed his eyes and tried to silence his mind.

Two minutes later, Wainwright brought the VW bus to a stop. "We're here," he announced.

Sam was the last one out. He slid the side door shut and turned to follow. But the rest of the group had not moved. They stood in a perfect stillness, staring up at the old house as if half expecting it to jump up and dance. It did not. It sat as a house should, motionless and silent, planted firmly on the secrets of its past.

Had it not been for the size of the structure, Sam would have thought it was nothing special, a Folk Victorian farmhouse, mostly square in shape with an angular porch wrapping around from the front door to the middle of the south wall. Several slender windows dotted the façade, the wood splintered on the sides where, Sam assumed, protective boards had been removed to make the place more inviting. It wasn't an ugly house; on the contrary, the simple architecture and rural surroundings should have made it a quaint little cottage. Except that it wasn't little. It was huge, so big in fact that the word *monstrosity* came to mind. At a mere three stories, the house must have been at least six thousand square feet, maybe more. A good quarter of an acre had been cleared of trees to make room for the foundation and sprawling yard. One tree remained, an ancient, gnarled forty-foot beech, growing just to the right of the front steps. The grooves of its twisted trunk resembled an arm stripped of flesh, the muscles exposed, its long-dead branches reaching upward like an arthritic claw.

"Who in God's name built this . . . *thing?*" Sebastian asked, breaking the silence.

Wainwright had his dog-eared copy of Adudel's book clutched in his hands like a Bible. "A settler named Joshua Goodman built it in the 1850s. With his bare hands. Drove every nail, raised every wall."

"How is that possible?" Sam asked. It seemed that no man, no matter how determined, could construct such an edifice all by himself. That was what it was, not a house but an *edifice*. Its very existence seemed impossible without the help of the supernatural.

"I doubt anyone had the chance to ask him. Goodman was murdered in 1863, the same night Quantrill and his men torched Lawrence."

Daniel took a few heavy steps forward, his eyes never leaving the house. "It wasn't just Goodman who died," Daniel explained. His voice was not distant. It was steady, authoritative, much like Sam's own voice during one of his lectures. "A freed slave named Alma Reed was also killed that night." Daniel motioned to that hideous tree in the front yard. "They strung her body up from one of those branches."

Sebastian and Moore stood side by side and stared up at the twisted beech tree. The two couldn't have looked more different: a bulky wool coat draped over Sebastian's tall, frail body; tight black jeans and an even tighter long-sleeve tee with a lace-up front clung to Moore, barely containing her breasts. Together they were the reluctant intersection of Elegance and Rebellion.

Nearby, at the edge of the high tallgrass, Kate was capturing the moment, the camera gripped in her hands as she monitored the shot on a flip-out LCD screen.

Sam looked straight into the camera lens for no good reason, simply because it was there. He was not aware of making any particular expression, but Kate lowered the camera and stared at him peculiarly, her face suddenly grave. Sam watched as she leaned over to Wainwright and whispered something in his ear. Wainwright placed a hand lightly on Kate's waist and spoke to her in a low voice. Whatever Wainwright said, it had the desired effect. Kate's stark expression softened, and she nodded obediently, agreeing to some unknown pact.

They're up to something, Sam thought. *Both of them.*

From his right pocket, Wainwright produced a single key on a metal ring. He dangled it between two fingers. To the rest of the group, he said, "Well then . . . shall we?"

The others followed Wainwright toward the front steps. But Sam did not move.

"After you," Kate said, motioning for him to go before her. He studied her face for a moment, but she offered nothing more than a pleasant smile.

"Please," she said.

Sam fell in line. He noticed the Adudel book now tucked into Wainwright's back pocket. Every few seconds, Wainwright reached back and touched it, just to make sure it was still there.

They mounted the stairs to the porch. Thick, furry vines curled around the edges of the steps, twisting up the rickety balustrades of the porch's railing.

Crossing to the front door, Wainwright tore away a tentacle-like length of vine that had wound its way up the doorframe and around the tarnished knob. He slid the key into the lock, paused briefly for dramatic effect, then gave it a hard turn.

The bolt withdrew with a reverberating thunk.

What happened next was too brief for any of them to mention.

The house seemed to ripple from foundation to roof.

For a split second, the tallgrass surrounding the structure appeared to bow, and then it rose back up, tall and straight, like hundreds of thousands of obedient soldiers.

A shudder ran through Sam, through Sebastian, through every single one of them.

Wainwright put his hand on the doorknob. He paused again, turning back to the group. One by one, he met their gazes, the light catching in those slivers of purple in his irises.

"So. Over the threshold we go," he said.

He turned the knob.

The door swung slowly open, and Sam watched as Wainwright backed into the house, shadows enveloping him, that knowing smile stretching across his masklike face.

He wanted them to follow.

PART TWO

A WHISPER THROUGH THE WALL

October 3I to November I

Upon first entering the house, I found there was one thing for which I was profoundly unprepared—an overwhelming silence. Nary a sound filled my ears. No clocks ticked. No boards creaked. Only the faint whisper of my own breath and that of Rachel at my side.

"Is it always this quiet?" I asked her.

Rachel smirked. "No," was all she said. And so began my tour of the house on Kill Creek.

—Dr. Malcolm Adudel
Phantoms of the Prairie

TEN

12:54 p.m.

THE FOUR AUTHORS, Wainwright, and Kate all stood one step inside the front foyer, listening to the house and the air drifting invisibly through it.

There was nothing particularly odd about entering the house, no drop in temperature, no feelings of being watched, no sudden sense of dread. There was only the slightest sensation of a change in barometric pressure, a fullness in their ears. It was so subtle, none of them mentioned it. And in less than a minute, it passed.

For Daniel Slaughter, the most surprising thing about the house on Kill Creek was the warmth it exuded. The floor, planed and varnished by hand over a century ago, was an inconsistent pattern of maple and black walnut planks, some lighter, some darker, a collision of grains, of knots and rings, of varying lengths and widths. Yet the imperfections only added to the homey charm of the structure. And by the time the boards met the beautifully carved molding along each wall, everything was flush, everything was right.

A wide federal staircase was set against the west wall, leading up to the second floor. With its square newel post and rounded balusters, the staircase was deceptively simple. But upon closer inspection, each newel featured meticulously carved notches, each baluster adorned with a tightly etched spiral.

Some boards were cracked, some paint had peeled, and a fine layer of dust had settled over every surface. Still, the craftsmanship on display eclipsed any flaws. Joshua Goodman had made sure that every inch was a simple yet elegant labor of love.

The sunlight drifting in through archways to the right and left was not so much reflected as it was absorbed by the wood and then projected out again in a brilliant golden glow. Daniel followed the sunlight across the room to a far wall on which a crucifix hung crookedly. It was simple, made from the same wood as the floor, no doubt carved by Goodman.

Daniel crossed the foyer and adjusted the crucifix twenty or so degrees clockwise.

There we go.

He heard Moore chortle, and he closed his eyes.

"'From the hill there came a loud rumble. They turned to see the devil above them. The ancient one peered into their souls and learned their secrets. It would be back for them. Their lust would be their downfall.'"

"Lemme guess. The Gospel of Paul?" she asked.

"Actually that's from the Book of Daniel," he corrected with a wink as he moved past her. Daniel noticed smiles on the faces of Sam and the frail Sebastian. He smiled himself. "It's okay, Moore, I have enough faith for the both of us."

Daniel glanced over and saw that Kate's camera was up. She had captured the exchange.

Great, just what they want for their big show, Daniel thought.

Wainwright swiveled on worn black work boots to face the group. "Welcome to the house on Kill Creek. What do you say we have a look around?"

Daniel Slaughter took in the house once more. He did not think it was a bad house. In fact, in that moment, he was sure that it welcomed him.

They moved through the front foyer, passing beneath the arched doorway at their left.

Ah, Sebastian thought. *Now this is a room after my own heart.*

They were in a study. Large, dirty windows lined the west wall. Their smudged panes let in enough light, however, to make the room feel cheerful and inviting, despite the gloom of the overcast day. Two mahogany chairs sat at an angle, an ornate table between them. Built-in bookshelves, packed with books, lined the wall directly ahead.

"All of the furniture belonged to the Finch sisters," Wainwright explained. He carried his well-used copy of *Phantoms of the Prairie* in his right hand. "In their will, they stated that, even in the possession of the county, everything in the house was to remain as they left it. Untouched."

Sebastian ran a finger over the spines of the books on the shelf. It did not matter to him what the titles were. They were books. They were filled with thoughts. Their relevance was debatable; he was sure some were exceptional while others were the works of lesser minds. He was not above calling a book *unreadable*. But their literary merit wasn't important at this moment. They were words strung together to represent the firing of neurons and the transferring of information through synapses. They were human minds set into paper, and Sebastian loved every single one of them, even the ones he found disposable.

Like that blasted Adudel book, he thought.

Yes, even the Adudel book deserved to exist, because the man himself had sat down and pounded keys until all of the clutter in his brain was carefully organized and displayed for others to experience.

This is why we do it, Sebastian told himself as he looked down the row of leather-bound tomes.

To live on. To exist when we stop existing.

To be remembered.

"It's a beautiful room."

Sebastian turned away from the bookshelf.

Daniel Slaughter was standing by one of the chairs, his hands in his pockets. He took in the space like a tourist with ten free minutes to speed-walk through Notre Dame.

"The Finch sisters loved this house," Wainwright said.

His voice. I'll never get used to that. Booming. As if it is coming from a speaker pointed directly at my ear.

The others were talking. They were discussing the years in which Rebecca and Rachel Finch were alive, the time when both sisters roamed the rooms of this house. But Sebastian wasn't listening to them. They were a wall of noise. He thought of millions of words he had committed to paper. He thought of the countless ideas that had flitted through his mind like hummingbirds hovering over the buds of newly opened flowers. And he blinked the fog away.

Sam walked through the swinging door that brought them to the kitchen.

This is nicer than my damn house, he told himself.

It was a spacious layout, a standard L-shaped room with dark walnut cabinets lining two of the walls. An enclosed porch could be seen through the French doors to their left, a wicker couch and chair surrounded by the shriveled brown corpses of long-neglected plants. At the center of the kitchen, the modern addition of an island floated in isolation directly in front of a deep farmhouse sink. The grout between the chipped white tiles had seen better days, but otherwise the room was in fine condition. As with the furniture, the appliances were from decades past: a four-burner stainless-steel gas stove and a mismatched white 1950s-style refrigerator with a large metal handle.

Like the foyer and library, the kitchen was bathed in warm afternoon sunlight.

Moore stepped up next to Sam. She was still wearing her sunglasses. "It's a little odd, right?" she asked.

Sam shook his head, confused. "What?"

"How nice the house is. Isn't this place like a hundred and fifty years old?"

She was right. With the exception of the dust and the chipped tiles and the musty hint of air trapped for too long, the house was immaculate.

The pressure Sam had felt when they'd first entered returned, pressing into his eardrums. He pictured himself sinking deeper and deeper into an increasingly dark ocean. Above was the light. Below was the impenetrable depths of a bottomless trench.

He glanced around the kitchen.

He could hear his brother yelling. He could hear his mother screaming.

The kitchen is the heart of the house, Sam thought. *It is a place of gathering, of conversation, of love.*

It should be, he corrected himself.

But this house was not a place of love. It was a place of death. Goodman's hopes, his dreams, his *love* had been brutally taken from him.

Wainwright opened the fridge door and a breath of frigid air wafted out. "Even though we'll only be here for one night, we made sure the refrigerator was stocked," he told the group. "Water, soda, wine, beer. Cold cuts. Vegetables. Fruit."

The cry of tired hinges made Moore jump. Daniel had opened the back door and was staring out at a line of stones dotting the yard.

"What the hell, Slaughter?" Moore snapped.

The large man motioned to the pathway that led from where he stood to a break in the trees. "Where's that go?"

"The well," Wainwright said matter-of-factly, as if the path could lead only one place. "It's pretty overgrown, so watch yourself if you go back there. They told me the well was covered years ago, but please, don't go out for a stroll and end up at the bottom of it."

Sam noticed Wainwright smirk, as if the thought of one of them falling in the well amused him.

"And this?" They all turned to find Sebastian with his hand resting lightly on a closed door several paces down from the stove. "A pantry, I presume?"

Wainwright shook his head. "Basement. No reason to go down there. Nothing but rats and our trusty generator. Besides, the basement only runs a third of the house. The rest is crawl space."

"That's odd," Daniel said. "Why not have a full basement?"

"Perhaps Mr. Goodman started to dig but broke through to somewhere else." There was a sparkle in Sebastian's eyes. "Perhaps he realized he had opened a doorway to a dark, empty place, and so he sealed it and hoped he had caught it quickly enough. That he had stopped it before the darkness could escape."

Daniel nodded quickly, anxious to get in on the game. "Yeah. Yeah, like he broke through to hell, and the sins of his past were coming to drag him down."

"Sure, if you want to be painfully literal about it," Sebastian said dryly.

Moore smirked. "Or maybe—and I'm just riffing here—maybe he got sick of digging a fucking hole."

Sebastian smiled. "It's a bit farfetched, but I suppose it could have happened that way."

"Probably a foundation thing," Sam managed. "Being this close to the creek, they probably get quite a bit of runoff. Back when the house was built, there were no sump pumps, so unless they wanted an in-ground swimming pool beneath the house, Goodman opted to cut the basement short. I bet the house still has a problem with water getting in during a heavy rain."

"You read that in the Adudel book?" Daniel asked. "I thought you said you didn't—"

Sam shook his head. "I grew up about two hours south of here. A lot of storms in Kansas. A lot of basements. And a lot of shitty contractors who don't build them right."

Light glinted off glass. Sam turned to find Kate aiming her lens right at him.

A wave of nausea suddenly hit Sam, and he closed his eyes.

I don't want to be here. I don't want to be in this kitchen.

He felt like he was losing his balance. He was going to fall.

He quickly reached out and grabbed the edge of the counter to steady himself. The counter felt rounded and oddly cold. It was metal.

Sam opened his eyes. He was not gripping the counter, but instead the stainless-steel stove. It looked so familiar, so much like the one in his mother's kitchen.

Where she kept the cast-iron skillet on the back left burner.

Sam flinched as if he had been burned.

"Are you all right, Sam?"

It was Sebastian. His voice was low so as not to involve the others.

For a moment, Sam had no idea how to answer the old man's simple question. Then he nodded and said quietly, "Yeah, I'm fine."

"What's the matter, McGarver? House getting to ya?" Wainwright asked with a smirk.

Sam clenched his teeth. "Just want to keep moving."

Wainwright motioned through the next doorway. "Come on, then. There's more house to explore."

They all shuffled forward, following.

Sam was the first one out.

A narrow hallway ran along the south side of the Finch House. Moore followed the group as they moved in single file past a long row of windows on their left. There were no doors off this hall, only the entrance from which they had come, an archway that opened to the back of the foyer, and a doorway at the far end.

"Head toward that," Wainwright told them.

Moore thought, *His voice. Everything he says sounds like a command. Not one of my favorite things.*

The doorway brought them past a quick succession of joined rooms—a bathroom, a sewing room, a den—to a surprisingly large space at the house's west end. A colorful peacock print decorated an elegantly upholstered sofa, contrasted by the traditional plaid of two sitting chairs, all arranged around a chipped yet attractive brick fireplace. A sturdy oak table was placed near the windows at the front, providing a clear view of the porch and that hideously grotesque beech tree beyond.

Where those bastards hung Alma Reed. She imagined she could hear the creak of the rope and the rippling of fabric as the breeze blew Alma's dress. She could almost see the faint outline of her lifeless body, swinging gently outside the window.

"So, here we are," Wainwright said, clapping his hands loudly. "This is the main living room and our HQ, if you will, the place where we'll spend the majority of our time at the Finch House. There's a nice stack of wood out back, left by the previous occupants, thank you very much, which will provide us with a fire this evening. The house, well, it tends to be rather cold."

"Of course it does," Moore said. "That's some classic haunted house bullshit right there, Wainwright."

"Yes, surely you can do better than cold spots," Sebastian added, his voice as crisp as the autumn air.

"Just supplying the facts." Wainwright's tone was even and assured.

Moore touched the back of a chair.

The living room.

A thought drifted quickly through the dark expanse of her mind, and she snatched it up.

The living *room.*

A place that is alive.

Moore had always hated the term *living room* for exactly that reason. It conjured up images of a family gathered to spend quality time with each other in some ridiculous Norman Rockwell wet dream. She knew some people were convinced this existed in their lives, but Moore refused to believe it. There were always secrets. Daddy is having an affair. Mommy is popping pills. Junior spends a little too much time torturing bugs in the driveway. And Baby . . .

Well, Baby makes mistakes, doesn't she? Baby runs off because she thinks she's in love.

"It's a shame Goodman only got to enjoy this place for such a short time," Daniel said.

Moore gripped the back of the chair, digging her silver nails into the fabric. "Come on. What did he really think was going to happen?"

They all turned to her.

"What do you mean?" Wainwright asked.

"I mean, Goodman was a white dude shacking up with a black girl in the years before the Civil War. What did he think? That the murderous cocksuckers from the slave state next door were just going to let that happen?"

"He loved her." It was Kate, staring at Moore over the barrel of her camera lens. The camera clicked as she snapped a still photograph.

"And it got them killed. What good is that?" Moore asked.

"They couldn't help how they felt." Kate held her finger on the button and rattled off a burst of photos, all of Moore staring back at her. "Maybe they knew that death was a possibility. Maybe it made their love . . . stronger."

Kate turned her head slightly to steal a glance at Wainwright. He was watching her with a strange sense of wonder.

Baby thinks she's in love, Moore thought again. She clenched her fists. "That's some bullshit. Death doesn't make love stronger. Death only makes things dead."

The camera went *rat-a-tat-tat* as Kate fired off another burst.

"I think you have enough pictures of me," Moore said coldly.

Kate lowered the camera. "You're right. I got what I need." She switched the setting back to "Movie Mode." The camera beeped softly, once again recording video.

"What's next?" Daniel asked.

Wainwright motioned through the archway, toward the foyer. "Well, now's as good a time as any to bring in your bags. Then I'll show you to your rooms."

ELEVEN

1:28 p.m.

SAM COULD FEEL his every move being watched.

It's Kate.

She stood several yards away, hip-deep in the tallgrass. She cradled her camera like a child, eyes on the LCD screen as she captured every moment in high-def.

"They're fucking," Sam heard Moore say as she lifted her bag from the back of the van.

"Who?" Daniel asked, blanching at her vulgarity.

"Wainwright and the camera girl," Moore explained. "She's that rich twat's woman. So quit eyeballing her tits."

"I'm married," Daniel said.

"And that's stopped one hundred percent of no one," Moore replied, shouldering her bag.

On the porch of the house, tucked back into the shadows created by the overhang, Wainwright waited for them to retrieve their luggage. As always, the Adudel book was clasped in his hands.

"What do you think he's really up to?" Sam quietly asked the others.

Sebastian followed Sam's eyeline. "Who? Mr. Wainwright? He's harmless. Or as harmless as an arrogant billionaire's son can be."

"They're both weird as shit," Moore said.

Because they're hiding something, Sam thought. And then, almost immediately, he scolded himself: *You don't know that. Stop looking for problems where there aren't any. You'll drive yourself crazy.*

Sam said aloud, "You all saw how he reacted in the bus, when he realized I hadn't read the book."

"Maybe he just wants us to be as excited about this place as he is," Daniel suggested.

Moore leaned into the back of the bus for her bag. "Or maybe he secretly brought us all here to kill us. He and his little Manson girl are going to torture us, murder us, and then upload the whole goddamn thing to the internet. He'll be the most famous name in horror by noon tomorrow."

Sam glanced over at Kate, noticing for the first time the shotgun microphone mounted atop the camera and the earbud wire snaking up from the camera's headphone jack.

Did she hear that? Sam wondered.

Kate lowered her camera and gave a knowing smile.

Sam followed the others across the foyer to the door of the elevator. Behind them, Kate stopped at the foot of the staircase.

"I'll meetcha up there," she said, her charming Southern twang competing with the clatter of the elevator's accordion door. And then she was gone, bounding up the stairs to the second floor.

The rest of them crammed shoulder to shoulder into the tight confines of the elevator, their bags by their sides.

Sam suddenly found it difficult to breathe. *Why are we taking the elevator? We barely have any luggage. Why does Wainwright want us in here?*

"Is this really necessary?" he asked aloud. "We're going up one story."

"Rachel would have wheeled her sister into this elevator," Wainwright said, as if this explained it. "It was Rebecca's only way to get around the house."

Sam pressed his back against the wall of the elevator.

Wainwright reached for the control panel. In addition to the requisite Door Open and Door Close buttons, there were three more, one for each floor. Wainwright pressed the button marked "2." The elevator jolted violently as, somewhere in the shaft above, a cable was drawn over a pulley.

Sam knew the thought was ridiculous, but he couldn't help thinking it: *He wants to kill us. He wants this to drop with all of us on board.*

Daniel shifted in place, suddenly worried. "You had this thing looked at, right? To make sure it's still safe?"

Moore tried to reposition herself around Daniel's bulk. "I don't think the elevator is the problem here, big guy. Maybe you should take the stairs."

"It's safe," Wainwright told them. It offered very little reassurance.

The chain clicked above them as they began their surprisingly long journey to the second floor.

"The elevator was the fastest way for Rebecca to get around the house. Not that she used it much. In the two years she lived here, her final years, Rebecca almost never left her bedroom on the third floor."

The elevator came to a shuddering stop. Wainwright pulled the accordion door open, revealing Kate, already there, focusing the wide-angle lens of her camera. Without looking up from her monitor, she stepped to the side, clearing the way for the group.

There were five bedrooms on the second floor, all indistinguishable from the outside, each marked by a heavy wooden door. Wainwright walked backward as he led the group. Kate trailed behind.

"Slaughter, this is you," Wainwright said, pointing to the first door on the right. "You'll find everything you need for a comfortable night. A nice big bed. Dresser for your clothes."

Daniel gave a little smile of appreciation and disappeared into his room.

Wainwright turned back to the others.

His face, Sam thought. *Why does it look like flesh draped over flesh?*

With his hands tucked into the pockets of his jacket, Wainwright sauntered down to the next door, the first on the left.

"Sebastian Cole." Wainwright tapped the door lightly as if christening it. This time, he did not wait for the named to enter the room. Instead he gave a sigh, apparently bored with his own game. "Ms. Moore—"

"You can all stop with the *Ms.* bullshit. I don't hear you saying *Mister* when addressing everyone else."

"Right," Wainwright said. "Moore, the next door across the hall, that's you. And, Sam, you're next-door neighbors with *Mr.* Cole."

"What about Kate?" Moore asked. "Where will the lovely lady be resting her head?"

"Kate and I are sharing the room at the end of the hall," Wainwright explained.

Moore gave a sharp laugh, like the thrust of a knife. "Can't pass up the chance to squeeze the peach, eh?"

"I'm not biting, Moore."

Moore blinked, feigning innocence. "What's that supposed to mean?"

Sam watched the two of them. They were strange animals that had never been introduced, and he had no idea which was the more dangerous one.

Wainwright turned to face her. "I know you're looking for a fight. Let's just try to be polite, yeah? We're all civilized people."

Moore's eyes narrowed. "Speak for yourself. And I didn't come here to be lectured."

"No, you came here to plug your new project, the one you hope will make everyone forget you've been shut out of the *Cutter* movie."

"How did you—"

Wainwright continued, "You all came here for similar reasons. You came because you know what I can do for you. You know how popular WrightWire is. But just because you're all here for selfish reasons doesn't mean we can't have a bloody good time."

"And what about you? What are you here for?" Sam asked.

Wainwright smiled as warmly as his rubbery flesh would allow. "I'm here to geek the hell out with some of my heroes, mate."

The fuck you are, Sam thought.

Moore gave an incredulous snort, seeming to sense Sam's suspicion.

"I'm quite serious," Wainwright said. "It's an absolute thrill to have you here. Four legends. One amazing night."

"Five legends, if you count the house," said Kate from behind the camera. They all turned to her. The budding filmmaker was unable to resist this perfect staging of faces. Her finger flipped the setting from video to still.

"Say *boo*," she said as the shutter clicked.

Sebastian closed the bedroom door behind him, the latch snapping obediently into place. With a weary sigh, he set his suitcase on the floor and took the bedroom in. It was a fairly Spartan arrangement. A red-and-black patchwork quilt covered a four-poster bed. A streak of gold snaked its way through the quilt's pattern like arms of ivy along a fence. Flanking the bed were two dark oak nightstands. On the left nightstand was a single brass lamp, its shine long tarnished, its shade brittle with age. On the nightstand to the right there was nothing but a fine layer of dust.

That's where Richard's reading glasses would have been, Sebastian thought. He could still picture them, rectangular lenses in simple wire frames.

The only adjoining room was a bathroom. The door was half-open. From where he stood, Sebastian could see only a fraction of the space. Tiny white tiles covered the floor. They were clean and perfectly spaced, glowing in the early afternoon light.

Sebastian placed his suitcase on the bed, running his fingers over the worn, well-traveled leather before popping open the latches. He took out the meticulously folded clothes—a pair of slacks, a white button-down shirt with thin blue stripes, a clean pair of black socks—tomorrow's outfit. Tomorrow, when this self-indulgent stunt would be over.

He placed the clothes in the empty top drawer of a nearby dresser. In the second drawer he placed his pajamas, a cotton plaid top, and drawstring pants. Old man pajamas. Just like his father had worn.

His father. Not even seventy years old, dressed in those same striped pajamas, his face slack, a rivulet of drool winding down his gray-stubbled chin. Sebastian remembered the moment so clearly, reading his father the poems of W. S. Merwin. Sebastian could remember every single verse, every nod of his father's head, every drop of saliva from his lips. A man in his sixties shouldn't have been so sick, but there he was, detached from the world. The worst part had been his father's eyes, vacantly staring out into the great Nothing, blind to his own son sitting before him.

That is horror, he thought. *That's the true awfulness I hope to capture in my books.*

Sebastian took a deep breath and centered himself.

The only things left in the suitcase were his notebook (containing several pages of nearly undecipherable notes he had jotted down during the plane ride), his pens (down to three, the fourth left in his room at the hotel in Kansas City), his copy of *The House on the Borderland,* by William Hope Hodgson, and a dopp kit containing his toiletries. The toiletries—a toothbrush, travel-size Crest toothpaste tube, bar of soap, metal comb, and small vial of aspirin—would go in the bathroom.

He was reaching for the dopp kit like he had done a hundred times before when, just like that, the fog returned.

Sebastian sat gently down on the bed, his eyes moving quickly about but looking at nothing specific. Instead he looked *inward,* searching his mind for any train of thought. It lasted only a moment, and then the dominos fell, each more specific than the last. He was in a house. Not his own. His residence was in New York, just outside of Ithaca. This was a house by a creek. What was its name?

Kill! his mind shouted suddenly. The startling word brought a cover of cold sweat to his skin.

Kill, it repeated, over and over. *Kill. Kill. Kill.*

"Kill Creek." He said the name again, "Kill Creek. You're in the house on Kill Creek."

His hands were shaking. He closed his eyes and heard his heartbeat, deep down in the hollow of his chest, an angry fist pounding ribs.

"It's only a moment," he whispered to himself. "You're fine."

He opened his eyes. His hands had stopped shaking.

He locked in the moment: *You're at the house on Kill Creek. You're here for a publicity stunt. Your name is Sebastian Cole. You're a writer.*

The bedroom was impossibly silent. Not a single sound from the hall or the nearby rooms. Nothing from outside, despite the thin barrier of the single-pane window.

The house is listening, he thought, and immediately wondered where such a ridiculous notion had come from.

Snatching up the dopp kit, Sebastian pushed open the bathroom door the rest of the way and moved inside. He unzipped the dopp kit and removed the assorted toiletries, placing them in the medicine cabinet above the pedestal sink. His toothbrush slid off the shelf. Sebastian saw it fall and bounce off the edge of the sink, but he could not catch it before it hit the floor.

He bent down and picked the toothbrush up off the crooked, filthy tiles. The thought of using it now made Sebastian's throat tighten a bit.

He froze, the toothbrush gripped tightly in his hand. The tiles had been clean when he first saw them. He was sure of it. They were white and—

White and straight. He stared down at the floor. It was exactly as it had been. Not a smudge, not a fleck of dirt, each white tile meticulously placed.

Sebastian shoved the toothbrush into the medicine cabinet and slammed the door closed. On the outside was a mirror, a large smudge streaked across its surface. His reflection was an ambiguous blob floating in the air.

He scolded himself for letting his imagination run wild. Of course the tiles were the same. There was nothing otherworldly about this house. But he was a writer; it was how his mind worked, always looking for a story.

He knew there was another reason why he had wanted to jump to the supernatural. If the rumors were to be believed, he was standing in one of the most haunted houses in the country. Yet except for the Adudel book, which Wainwright and Daniel treated so reverently, there were no documented occurrences, no unexplained phenomena recorded by giddy parapsychologists.

Except Adudel. He's a parapsychologist.

"He's a quack," Sebastian said aloud, suddenly embarrassed by the sound of his own voice.

Get a grip, old man. You're talking to yourself.

Sebastian rested his hands on either side of the sink and stared into the smudged mirror. The amorphous blob of his reflection hovered before him.

He glanced down and frowned. The faucet was dripping. Droplets of discolored water slowly formed on its lip and fell straight into the open drain at the bottom of the basin.

Sebastian tried tightening the handles, first the hot, then the cold. The drip only worsened, the droplets forming more quickly.

Something was strange. What was it?

Think, old man!

The droplets.

They made no sound as they fell. The trap, hidden within the pedestal, couldn't have been more than two feet below the drain. The water hitting the pipe should have made some kind of sound, no matter how faint. But there was nothing. Only silence.

Sebastian leaned down, the vague impression of his reflection disappearing from the medicine cabinet mirror, replaced by the blurred image of the empty bathroom behind him.

With his hands on the sides of the basin for support, he lowered his head into the sink, careful not to put his face in the path of the falling droplets. His left ear hovered inches away from the black hole of the drain.

Without warning, the faucet gave an angry cough and spat out a thick brown substance that splattered the white bowl below. Sebastian cried out and flinched away, but not quickly enough. The brown liquid spattered his face.

It's shit, he thought in disgust. *Actual shit. You'll smell like this soon, old man. Sitting in a nursing home and filling your diaper for some poor nurse to change.*

He swiped at his face, smearing the liquid across his cheek. He held his fingers to his nose and sniffed. The brown liquid was not what he feared it was, although its scent was unpleasant, conjuring up images of things decomposing in darkness. He watched as the water from the faucet dripped brown for a few seconds, then became clear.

The rhythm of the dripping water sped up, and now he heard what had been missing only moments before: the faint *plink* of the droplets hitting the trap.

Sebastian snapped a towel from a small silver hook mounted on the wall and angrily wiped the liquid from his face. He looked into the mirror.

A shape floated before him. A wrinkled face, obscured by the smudged glass.

He ran the towel across the mirror to wipe the smudge away.

There he was, his image clear. His eyes were tired, heavy bags hanging below them. Deep lines cut through his weathered skin. His hair looked thinner than he remembered. It had started to reveal empty patches of liver-spotted scalp.

"When did I get so damn old?" It was a rhetorical question.

The drip from the faucet turned to a stream as Sebastian gave the knob another twist. Water swirled around the bowl, washing away the thick brown spatters, gurgling as it was swallowed by the drain. The odd amplification remained but was now accompanied by a more subtle sound, just under the splash. Sebastian listened. It was a familiar sound.

In that moment, if he had allowed his imagination to run wild, he would have said it was the sound of voices whispering.

TWELVE

3:45 p.m.

DANIEL SLIPPED OUT the back door, making sure it did not slam behind him. The overcast day had burned off to reveal a blue sky just beneath, the way a skinned knee will reveal the redness of fresh flesh. Every few minutes, the wind would pick up and blow from the north, pushing its way like a bully through the woods to the clearing, rocking the bushy bodies of trees gently to and fro.

With one hand, Daniel powered up his cell phone, checking to make sure he had ample reception. Two bars. Good enough. The display read "Home" as the number automatically dialed.

After two rings, a young girl answered.

"Hello?"

"Claire?"

"Who else would it be?" his daughter replied with her perfect blend of childish playfulness and teenage smartass. "Mom told me about your 'interview.' I can't believe you're doing that. It's, like, a little crazy, you know?"

"Yeah, I'm kinda surprised I'm here myself."

"So? See anything scary yet?"

Daniel smiled to himself. He always smiled when he talked to Claire. "Not yet, sweetheart. But the day is young." He followed the trail of chipped pale stones away from the house, closer to where the trees parted like a mouth yawning.

Or screaming.

"You go to church yesterday?"

"Yeah, with Mom."

"How was it?"

"Intense. Heavy on the fire and brimstone. You know, cause of Halloween."

Daniel knew. His church didn't actively discourage the holiday, but the lesson was always the same. Horror is the result of sin. Sin gives way to temptation. Temptation is the number-one weapon of the Devil.

The formula was so simple. When you played it in reverse, you had a guaranteed best-selling book.

"Speaking of, you have any big Halloween plans?"

Claire gave a soft chuckle, obviously meant to go over her father's head. It didn't. Daniel knew what it meant. She assumed he still thought she was interested in trick-or-treating. He may be a lame, middle-aged, churchgoing dad, but he wasn't stupid. Claire had plans with her friends, plans that would undoubtedly expose her to the temptations of underage drinking and premarital sex. But Daniel had a secret, a lame, middle-aged, churchgoing dad secret: he trusted his daughter.

"Jessica's sorta having a little get-together tonight," Claire said off-handedly. The understatement was a bit too obvious.

"A party?"

She was quick to protest. "Not a party. Just, you know, a few friends."

A few friends. Age-old code for *party*.

"Nothing big. Probably just watch horror movies, that kinda thing."

"What's his name?"

A pause. The question had caught her off guard.

"Clint."

Daniel gave a dramatic sigh. "Clint. No, no, no, Claire, not a boy named Clint."

"What's wrong with Clint?"

"Everything."

And Claire laughed. It was the same laugh she'd had as a child, five years old in a frilly pink dress her grandmother had given her, spinning circles until her giggling forced her down. It was the laugh that melted Daniel's heart. The laugh that, if it ever went away, would tear him to pieces.

"I'll put Mom on," she said.

"You do that," Daniel told her. "Have fun tonight." He groaned. "With Clint."

Another laugh, then silence as Claire left her room and wandered down the hallway. Suddenly there was a burst of static, a shrill squelch in Daniel's ear. He jerked the phone from his ear just as a voice broke through it:

"Hello?"

"Hello? Sabrina?"

"Daniel?" There was worry in his wife's voice. "How's it going?"

He felt a warmth in his chest, the hidden flame that meant home.

Daniel reached the last of the stones and stepped through the trees, into the dense forest. He hadn't noticed it before, but the drone of cicadas now enveloped him, as if that one simple step had transported him to another world.

"Daniel?" Her voice quavered, breaking the fluidity of her normally steady tone.

"I'm here," he assured her.

"I don't like this."

The barren branches high overhead seemed to reach for one another, straining to clasp fingers bare of leafy flesh, pointed fingertips desperate to span the distance as the light wind knocked them gently about.

"Like what?"

"This. You. There. You should have just come home."

"I'm here for the same reasons the others are here, baby. It's publicity. I've got the new book series coming out soon. This could help make sure it sells."

"Your books will sell. They always do."

"The Christian bookstores are saying they won't carry this one. It's the beginning of a backlash, Sabrina. They're saying . . . they say my books glorify evil."

"That's ridiculous."

Daniel closed his eyes and took a deep breath. "I know that. You know that. This is the chance to explain myself. And if the church is going to abandon me, then I'll need the mainstream readers more than ever."

"No one's going to abandon you," she assured him.

For a long moment, neither of them spoke.

"I've heard about that house," Sabrina said finally. "I know the stories people tell."

"And that's just what they are. Stories."

A sigh, not so much for her as for him. "I just . . . I don't like the idea of you flirting with the occult."

Daniel gave a sharp laugh. He knew he shouldn't go out of his way to show his irritation, but after seventeen years of marriage, she should know him better. "Sabrina, I'm here at a very ordinary, very *un-haunted* house to promote my books. Tomorrow, I'll be on a plane and back in Chicago by dinnertime."

"Do you promise? I mean, that the house is . . . only a house?"

Something creaked under Daniel's feet. He looked down to find that his shoes were completely obscured by fallen leaves.

He scratched at the ground with his fraying leather shoe.

"Daniel? Is . . . thing okay?" The reception was cutting out.

"It's the signal, sweetie. I'm going to lose you."

His foot did not scrape dirt but a harder substance. Cement, perhaps. But cement did not creak. He shoved the toe of his shoe down harder and there came a sharp crack.

Wood. It was wood.

Daniel was fat. He knew he was fat. But in that moment he found himself to be amazingly agile, hopping into the air just as the wood plank snapped clean through beneath him. As he did, the phone slipped from his sweaty fingers.

He landed a couple feet away, on the safety of solid ground, just in time to watch the phone drop straight down toward the split plank. One moment the cell phone was there, and the next it was swallowed by the jagged black slit in the cracked board.

He heard the tinny, faraway voice of his wife call out, "Daniel?" And then the phone was gone.

"Shoot!" He lunged toward the crack in the board but stopped short, remembering that it was his weight that had snapped the plank in the first place.

"Goddamn it!" he cried out. Immediately he looked around, his cheeks flushed with shame at taking the Lord's name in vain. Luckily, there was no one there to hear him.

Over the tops of the trees, the Finch House silently watched.

The wood that had snapped under his feet covered a well, the same well about which Wainwright had gone out of his way to warn them. Using his foot, Daniel brushed away the cover of brittle leaves and vines to reveal warped, weathered boards placed haphazardly over the well's stone mouth. Years of erosion from rain, snow, and ravenous termites had taken its toll on the boards. Great splintering cracks gouged deeply into the wooden flesh, the sides crumbling at the touch. The planks probably wouldn't have supported the lithe Kate, let alone the largest person in the group. The handyman Wainwright sent out to prepare the house must have missed this, or surely he would have replaced the boards. At the very least, he would have ringed the area in barrier tape.

Daniel reached under the middle plank, and his bare fingers sunk slightly into the deteriorated wood. Thoughts of spiders filled his mind—thin, needlelike legs scuttling in the dark; fangs dripping with teardrops of golden venom; sleek black bodies born of shadows; webs in the nooks and crevices where only they could climb, like a trail of silken nightmares. Daniel could smell the dank odor of the well's mossy walls, of the stagnant water somewhere far below, of the absolute darkness. Glancing around, he located a stone, jagged like the tooth of some long-extinct beast, and, holding it directly above the slit of blackness, he dropped it down into the well. Its fall seemed impossibly long, the splash as it hit bottom far too faint.

It can't be that deep, he thought. It was impossible. No well should go down that far unless the digging of it exposed an immense chasm, a black pit long buried beneath the shifting earth.

The ancient odor emanating from the well hit Daniel, as many lost scents do, with a misplaced memory from mental oblivion. When Daniel was just a boy, he and his family—his parents; his brother, Peter; and his sister, Mary Kay—lived in a ramshackle three-bedroom house forty miles south of Chapel Hill, North Carolina. It wasn't their first house, nor was it their favorite. His father had lost his job as a maintenance man for the city and, with an alarming shortage of jobs in the area, had no choice but to uproot his family and retreat to the only place that didn't demand a mortgage payment: his own father's hunting lodge.

Daniel hated what Peter referred to as "Grandpa's Whack Shack," a nickname Daniel knew was hilarious without entirely understanding its perverse meaning. The Whack Shack was small, drafty, and home to just about every type of insect in the Tar Heel State. Crickets, grasshoppers, cicadas, mosquitoes, hover flies, deer flies, horseflies, silverfish, cockroaches, fire ants, carpenter ants, yellow jackets, honey bees, centipedes, millipedes, ticks. You name it, they had it. Crawling up the bathtub drain. Burrowed under stacks of bath towels in the closet. Nesting in the spaces where the sagging floors and warped ceilings had begun to separate from the dingy walls. The Whack Shack was never intended to house a family; it was Grandpa's escape from the city, where he and his hunting buddies would go for some peace and quiet, miles away from their nagging wives.

Yet what Daniel despised most of all were the eight-legged monstrosities, the arachnids, the spiders. Daniel's father assured him there were only two kinds of spiders that could do any real damage: the brown recluse and the black widow. But to young Daniel—a sensitive teenager with every one of his childhood fears intact—spiders were the most horrifying creatures on the planet.

"I read that at least once in their life, ever'body will have a spider crawl into their mouth while they're sleepin'," Peter said to Daniel one day, knowing good and well what kind of damage this tidbit of information could do to his younger brother. The very thought of it—a spider with its prickly legs and deadly fangs, creeping between his lips, welcomed in by the slow draw of his slumbering breath—it was enough to keep Daniel awake for nights on end.

And then, one steamy summer afternoon, Daniel came face-to-face with the very thing he feared. It was Peter's friend, Kenny, who made him go in. A skinny, red-haired creep who lived next door (next door being a mile and a half as the crow flies), Kenny Milburn must have had a million freckles, and where there weren't freckles, there were pimples, so many that his face looked like a rotting apple, discolored and lumpy.

That afternoon, after much begging and pleading, their mother ordered Peter to let Daniel tag along. It really wasn't much of a demand; Peter and Kenny had plans to go no farther than the front yard for a game of catch, but it annoyed Daniel's older brother and his no-good friend all the same. So when Kenny overthrew Daniel's prized Official Mickey Mantle baseball (complete with faux signature), sending it racing into the crawl space under the house, it was Kenny who insisted Daniel go after it.

Daniel looked from the darkened crawl space entrance to his older brother, not wanting to whine like a baby, hoping that Peter might see the fear in his eyes and offer to go himself.

Instead, Peter stood silently as Kenny's taunts grew louder and louder. Before Daniel knew what was happening, he found himself down on all fours, inching his way across the line of shadow that marked an end to sunlight's safety and the beginning of the underworld, the *realm of the crawl space.*

It was damp underneath. The ground outside had been baked dry by the sun, but in the crawl space, the earth retained the wetness of recent rains. Daniel could feel it soaking through the knees of his blue jeans. He knew his mom would not be happy to find the soiled pants in the laundry hamper. The dank odor left by standing water filled his nose, the thick scent of mildew and mold. Daniel held his breath until little black spots would creep from the corners of his vision; only then would he take in another quick, desperate gasp. His back scraped the underside of the house and Daniel winced, sure that it would leave a blood-speckled spot in the middle of his shirt. He thought of his mom again, how she would totally flip out when she saw what he had done to his clothes.

And then, there it was, a white orb glowing like a pearl in the damp belly of an oyster. Only a few more yards and the baseball would be in his hands.

The black spots were not going away. Daniel took a deeper breath, tasting the years of sediment, the dirt and dust and decomposed leaves, but the black spots continued to close in. He was sure he would pass out. But strangely he didn't feel the least bit light-headed.

One of the black spots spun down on a line of silk no thicker than a human hair, its body twisting to reveal the bright red hourglass on its belly, like the dab of blood Daniel was sure he had on his back. The black spots were not warnings of impending unconsciousness. They were alive. And they were everywhere.

Terror swept through his round body in a million icy pinpricks. Daniel was sure for an awful moment that every deadly spider had decided to bite him at once. Without thinking, he reached out and snatched up the baseball, giving a helpless whimper as he tried to turn around. The crawl space was too tight. No matter how he twisted his body, he could not maneuver around to face the opening, that painfully distant square of light that meant the end to his hell.

He began to panic. His eyes darted from the ground before him to the rough wood above to the cement pillars supporting the house, stopping on a wisp of white just to the right of his shoulder. It was a peculiar substance, like cotton candy, but white instead of pink. From its center, a black body scampered out, tested the air with its two front legs, and reared back like a startled horse. It seemed to sense that Daniel was close, so close, reaching out as if it longed to touch the young boy's skin, to skitter across his rolls of flesh and under his clothes where he wouldn't be able to brush it off, where it could do what it lived to do, to bite, to kill.

With a quick glance down to make sure the area was free of spiders, Daniel smacked his palms to the ground, the baseball still clutched in his right hand, and pushed off with all his strength, simultaneously lifting his knees and propelling himself straight backward. He knew he didn't have a chance of getting out without being bitten. He had never really thought he would see a black widow in the real world. Here was not one but tens, perhaps hundreds of the monsters. His father's warning echoed in his mind: it would only take one bite.

He felt a tickle on his bare skin. One of the spiders had fallen onto his arm and was skittering quickly higher. In another second, it would disappear into his sleeve.

Daniel heard a horrible whimper escape his lips, and then he drew in a deep breath and puffed it out toward the spider. The spider was slipping its long black legs beneath his sleeve, and then the sharp breath whisked it away. But another black widow was on him in seconds. And another. And another.

He was going to die in the crawl space.

So young Daniel Slatterson did the only thing he knew to do in situations like that one—he prayed. He prayed hard, eyes closed tightly, the words spilling from his quivering lips so quickly, they became one solitary thing. *"GodifyougetmeoutofthisIpromisetolivemylifeforyou."*

The faster Daniel recited his prayer, the faster he pushed himself backward. His knee came down on the pointy edge of a stone and Daniel winced, feeling the warm wetness of blood begin to saturate his muddy jeans, but still he did not stop praying.

"GodifyougetmeoutofthisIpromisetolivemylifeforyou."

In his mind he could picture his body swarming with the terrible arachnids. He could imagine their fiery bites, the poison hot as it coursed through his veins. His left palm and the baseball in his right hand dug ravines in the dirt, leaving odd mismatched waves of earth in his wake.

And then an amazing thing happened, the very last thing Daniel ever expected. Daylight warmed him. With one final thrust, he launched himself out of the crawl space and into the open air. A gust of wind blew the spiders free. He rolled across the grass, hoping to crush whatever deadly creatures remained beneath his thin cotton shirt.

"What the hell's the matter with him?" Kenny asked dumbly.

Daniel opened his eyes, squinting in the summer sun. Peter and Kenny were standing over him—black, featureless shapes against the cloud-speckled sky.

Black shapes.

Springing up, Daniel tore off his shirt, his hands running quickly over his loose, pasty skin.

"Are there any on me?" The hysteria made his voice quaver.

"Any what?" Peter asked, confused.

Kenny was bowled over laughing at the sight of Daniel's flab jiggling, barely finding enough air to power his horselike guffaws.

"Are there any on me?" Daniel asked again, shouting this time.

Peter did a quick sweep of his brother's back, not sure what he was looking for, but thinking he would know it if he saw it. Finally, he shook his head. "Nope. Nothin'."

"Nothin'? Are you positive?"

"Nothin'," Peter repeated.

"Hey," Kenny said to Daniel, his horse laugh calming to mild giggles. He cupped his hands as if he meant to catch something. "The ball, dummy."

Daniel looked down to his right hand, to where he still clutched Peter's prized baseball. Even in his blind panic, he hadn't dropped it.

Peter was staring at his kid brother, his brow furrowed, his head cocked. "What was under there, Danny?"

Daniel didn't tell him right then. He waited until he had given himself a thorough inspection, standing with his back to the cracked bathroom mirror, peering over his shoulder for any indication of bite marks.

There were none. Not a single mark.

That evening, Daniel, Peter, Mary Kay, and their mother watched from across the yard as their father tossed a bug bomb into the crawl space, pulling the pin and chucking it like a grenade into a foxhole. As the noxious white fumes rolled out from under the house, giving it the appearance of a rickety square rocket readying for takeoff, Daniel became aware of two unimpeachable truths:

Kenny Milburn was a grade-A asshole.

And God was love.

On the other side of the well, the path became more overgrown, but still there was an apparent route through the foliage. Daniel followed this, mindful of the thorny vines that tried to snag him as he went.

Even in autumn, it was dark under the canopy of trees. The fat, brittle leaves of the oaks and elms above refused to let loose of their branches, reducing what sunlight there was to mere slivers.

Ducking under a fallen branch, Daniel found himself at the edge of a slope. With his arms outstretched, grasping exposed roots for balance, he awkwardly maneuvered the steep terrain and was soon standing at the center of what appeared to be a dry creek bed. In one direction, the creek abruptly curved, cutting a path to the side of the house. Daniel assumed this led to the bridge they had crossed when they arrived earlier that afternoon. In the other direction, the ravine plowed straight through the countryside, a dusty trail that was once a stream.

So this was Kill Creek. Or what was left of it. With the exception of a few shallow puddles here and there, it appeared water had not flowed through this particular channel in years. Clumps of dead leaves formed curiously human-shaped mounds, giving the creek bed the appearance of an ancient burial ground. The only thing that seemed to thrive in the creek were vines—fat, knotted arms snaking through the forest floor, down the muddy slope, zigzagging over the creek bed in a patchwork of woven veins. Yet even the vines looked in desperate need of a drink. Although they were unusually large, about the size of a man's arm, their color was a sickly brown, their exterior covered in coarse, hairlike bristles.

Daniel went to take a step and nearly stumbled, the toe of his shoe wedged beneath one of the thicker vines.

That's odd.

He didn't remember stepping over it to get to this particular spot, although he surely must have. Gone unnoticed, a vine this big would have tripped him. He tried to pull his shoe out from underneath it and discovered that a second vine, slightly smaller than the first, now ran directly behind his heel.

How on earth did I manage to get my foot into this spot without knowing it? he wondered.

He gave his leg a good yank and his foot slid free, but his shoe remained in the tangle of vines. The unexpected smoothness of the sudden action caused Daniel to fall on his ass with a thud. As he did, he could have sworn he saw the vines constrict, tightening over his shoe like a snake attempting to keep hold of its prey.

He sat there for a stunned moment, his eyes never leaving that shoe. The vines, of course, did not move, and after a full minute, he carefully reached between them and pulled the leather loafer out of their grasp.

With a nervous chuckle, Daniel slipped the shoe on and turned back toward the slope, grasping a handful of yellowing weeds and preparing his poor arms for the climb. It was a good struggle, but he finally reached the top and was soon trudging down the trail. When he reached the well, he knelt down and secured the deteriorating planks back in place as best he could.

"I thought I told you to stay away from there."

The unexpected voice made Daniel cry out. He spun around.

It was Wainwright, standing on the path leading back to the house.

"Oh y-yeah, right," Daniel stammered, his heart pounding. "I was just . . ."

Wainwright didn't let him finish the thought. "Let's get back to the house. No reason to be out here."

Without another word, Wainwright turned and disappeared up the trail.

Daniel followed. He pushed through the low branches of saplings and was once again behind the house. The sky had brightened since he left, and a large blanket of warm sunlight now lay over the house. Its brick glowed red. Its windows sparkled.

The Finch House beckoned Daniel Slaughter to come home.

THIRTEEN

4:14 p.m.

KATE HELD HER breath.

She walked slowly down the second-floor hallway, the camera perfectly level and centered. Wainwright always told her to invest in some form of Steadicam, but Kate prided herself on her camerawork. She didn't need a cumbersome piece of equipment when she had two hands and the skill to pull off the shot.

She was almost to the end of the hall, where a stained-glass window was set into the wall of a small alcove, when the toe of her shoe scuffed the wooden floor. The camera in her hands bobbed slightly.

See? He's right. You should have brought a Steadicam, she scolded herself.

She stopped recording and pressed a button on the back of the camera's body to review the footage. Most of it was usable for b-roll. A nice tracking shot down the hall would come in handy for atmosphere when she cut together the longer version of their Kill Creek video.

Moving into the alcove, she realized her right foot was butting up against the edge of a step. It was a staircase leading to the third floor. But at the top, instead of a door, there was a redbrick wall.

Rebecca Finch's bedroom.

She had read about Rebecca's room in the Adudel book. The few times Wainwright spoke of the brick wall, it was with an odd reverence, his voice low as if someone might hear him. He had purposely left it off his tour of the house. He wanted the authors to discover it for themselves. He wanted the house to draw them to it.

The colored light from the stained-glass window spilled across the surface of the first step, but it went no farther. Shadows engulfed the rest.

Kate quickly adjusted the f-stop and shutter speed. She twisted the LCD screen so that she had a good view of the shot. She angled the lens at the multicolored light at the floor in front of the first step and pressed the button to start recording.

She took a breath and held it.

On the screen, the image was exposed perfectly. The richness of the sunlight gave way to the black depth of shadow as she smoothly tilted the camera up. One by one, the stairs led higher. Carefully, Kate began to zoom out to reveal the brick wall at the top.

The wall was gone.

"Holy shit!" she said, blowing out the breath she had been holding.

She stumbled backward. The shot was ruined, but she didn't care. She had seen . . .

What the hell did *I see?*

She looked up to the top of the stairs, everything in her being telling her not to.

Leave. Run. You don't want to see it again!

The brick wall was there, as it had been, as it should be.

Her thumb, now slick with sweat, found the button to review the footage, and pressed it.

On the LCD screen, she watched as the shot made its way gracefully up the steps, up to the brick wall covering the bedroom door. The wall hadn't disappeared. So why did she think she saw—

A woman, Kate realized, the image forming once again in her mind. *The wall wasn't there, but there was a woman with black hair and she was . . . she was . . .*

Kate closed her eyes tight, trying to force her mind to make sense of the memory.

"She was scratching the air," Kate said aloud.

Of that, she was sure.

The woman had been scratching the open air, her fingers curled into claws, fingernails digging into the space before her as if the wall were still there.

Kate shuddered.

She was trapped. And she wanted out.

Like the rest of the house, the living room had the feeling of a museum whose restrictive red ropes had been removed to allow Sam to wander freely.

It's the silence, he thought.

That was partly it. The quiet within the house did encourage a sense of reverence. But it was also the amazing craftsmanship on display in each room. To think that one man was responsible for not only the structure but also its countless intricate details was mind-boggling. The stonework around the fireplace. The images of leaves and vines carved into the crown molding. Even the grain on the wood floors seemed to run and swirl in deliberate patterns.

Sam moved farther into the room and found himself staring out of the large window that looked onto the front yard. Outside, a light breeze softly tossed the tallgrass to and fro. The gravel drive cut through the yard and over the wooden bridge to disappear into a wall of trees. Above the trees, a bit of the gray had burned off to reveal patches of blue sky beneath.

A woman stood just outside the window.

Sam gasped.

The woman had appeared out of nowhere and was now at the porch railing, looking out into the yard. Black clothes clung tightly to her lithe body, and a single rope of hair snaked down her back.

Moore, he realized, immediately feeling foolish.

Sam passed beneath a grand archway and into the foyer. There was the elevator, on his left. Its accordion gate was closed. Thick shadows hung low in the corners of the cab. Beyond the elevator were stairs that led to the second floor. He reached the front door and opened it, stepping out onto the porch.

There was no one there.

Sam pulled the door shut behind him. He looked around, listening.

Only the faint whistling of the breeze and the rustling of tallgrass. He called out, "Moore?"

No response.

Careful, he warned himself. *It could be Wainwright messing with you. He's setting you up for a scare, to make a fool of you for the camera. Or worse. Maybe he has something darker planned for us.*

Sam shook off the thought. The weathered boards creaked under his feet as he crossed to the exact spot where he had seen her standing. He put his hands on the rail, just as she had. He stared out into the yard.

Before him was the twisted claw of the beech tree. The breeze appeared to have no effect on it. Its branches were motionless, its few leaves frozen in place.

"They hung her from one of those branches," a voice called out from nearby.

Moore was leaning against the side of the house around the next section of the wraparound porch. Her head was cocked back at a sharp angle so that Sam had no choice but to stare into her ruptured pupil.

"Goodman's lady. They dragged her dead body out here and strung it up. And for what?"

"They were Confederate raiders," Sam said.

"They were pieces of shit."

"Now you're just being redundant."

Moore stared at him for a silent beat, then pushed off from the wall and crept slowly across the porch to stand by his side. She looked out at the tree. The breeze picked up, and still its branches did not move.

"I hope, when they died, that they saw her bloated face staring down at them from that tree and knew she was waiting for them on the other side." She paused, relishing the thought. Then the mean little smile playing at her lips slowly vanished.

She doesn't believe that could happen, he realized. *She knows there was no justice here.*

Sam listened to the wind whispering between them. Moore seemed lost in heavy thoughts.

"I've read your books," Sam said in an attempt to lighten the mood.

"Oh yeah?"

"They're messed up in the best possible way."

Moore laughed, an honest, out-before-she-could-catch-it laugh. She relaxed, just a little bit.

"I've read you too," she said.

Oh man, here it comes.

"And?"

"And you hold back." She turned to face him. She studied him with her mismatched eyes. "Like you're being cautious. Like you're hiding something."

A wisp of smoke slipped up into Sam's throat and twisted, trying to take hold.

"And you," he managed to say, "you write like you're going to battle. So what is it, Moore? What are you fighting?"

She leaned back against the railing and considered the question. "The same thing you're running from, I suppose. Life is fight or flight. I choose to fight."

Her gaze drifted down to Sam's scarred left arm. She said nothing.

Without the usual cover of her sunglasses, Sam had a perfect view of Moore's ruptured pupil. He knew that in most cases, a ruptured pupil was the result of physical trauma. When he had first seen her eye, he'd found it revolting. He wasn't proud of that fact, but it was true. Now he had a different reaction. That eye was a constant reminder of some past pain.

We both have our secrets, he thought.

Her eyes flicked up and narrowed as she smiled. She knew he was watching her, and she liked it.

"So? What do you think of Wainwright?" she asked.

Careful. Don't sound crazy.

But you are crazy, his mind insisted.

"I don't trust him," was all Sam offered.

"And the house?"

Sam considered this for a moment. "Nothing yet has made me believe that any of the stories are true."

"How would you write it? If you decided to write its story?"

Now it was Sam's turn to smile.

"Oh, I don't know . . ."

"I do," she said confidently. She pushed off from the railing and began to slowly circle Sam as she talked, forcing him to turn to follow her. "You would start with a character from some seemingly perfect small town, someone not unlike yourself. You know, a little bland."

Sam gave a snort. "Sounds good so far."

"And the house wouldn't be in the country; it would be right in the middle of town so you could overpopulate the book with too many characters and Midwestern details. No offense."

She stopped, her back now to the house. She folded her arms across her chest and cocked her head in an overexaggeration of serious thought.

"There would be a boy—some painfully sweet little kid—who is obsessed with the house. Maybe he saw something there when he was riding by on his paper route—by the way, kids still have paper routes in your book—something he can't explain, but no one will believe him. And then the house would begin to infect the people of the town with its evil. Their unhealthy urges and dark fantasies, which up until this point have only existed in their heads, drive them to commit unspeakable acts. The evil in the house pulls every loose thread in that small town until the entire community unravels. And, in the end, that little boy is the only one who can stop it." She squinted and glanced up, sorting out one last detail. "And . . . the kid would probably have some sort of half-assed psychic power or some shit."

Moore looked to Sam. She grinned seductively.

"So? How'd I do?"

She nailed you, he told himself.

Sam pretended to feel the pockets of his jeans for some misplaced object. "I wish I'd brought a pen or something. Would you mind emailing all that to me? It's fucking fantastic."

Moore laughed, her armor down for the moment.

"What about me?"

Sam cocked his head. "I'm sorry?"

"How would I write about this house?"

"Let's see . . ." He ran a hand over the back of his stubbly head. "First of all, the house would be in a city."

"Okay."

"Some rundown, disgusting part of town where people do combinations of drugs that make almost no sense and engage in sexual activity that in no way sounds enjoyable."

"Mm-hm." Moore's jaw had clenched slightly.

The shoe's on the other foot. Guess that's not easy for her.

"There would be a handful of thoroughly unlikable characters, just filthy, filthy people. Except for one. A young woman from somewhere else. An affluent family, perhaps. Or a woman who married young and now feels trapped in her painfully domestic life."

"Who is she?" Moore asked. She took a step closer.

"She's a police officer. No, wait. She works for a security company. She's the only woman on the payroll, which means she's surrounded by blowhard, overweight men with fake badges and Tasers on their belts. The company has been contracted by a real estate firm to keep crackheads and tweakers from squatting in empty houses. And that's where she falls in with the other characters, when she tries to run them out of a house that looks suspiciously similar to this one."

He pointed up at the porch overhang and the unseen stories above it.

"Together, they discover that a power in the house offers them the escape they've always desired. But, of course, it comes at a price."

"Of course," Moore said quietly. She had taken another step toward him without Sam noticing. She was no more than four feet away from him now. Her eyes never left his as he spun his yarn.

Her eyes are actually very beautiful. Not despite the flawed pupil. Because of it.

He continued: "Some entity, older than time, lacking in anything resembling human emotion, is using our heroes as a means to gain access to our world. And it's working. They're becoming addicted to the power, which gives them a high that can't be matched by drugs or sex."

Moore furrowed her brow and stared at Sam. That misshapen pupil seemed to dilate even as the pupil of her other eye stayed the same. "So far I'm not getting what's so bad about their bargain. Sounds like a good time to me."

"Well, that depends on your definition of a *good time*. See, the entity requires sacrifice. First, it's sexual sacrifice. You'll be happy to know there's a lot of spilled seed and an unnatural amount of fluids."

"Perfect."

She's so close. When did she get so close?

"But then the sacrifice becomes emotional as they pull their lives apart, destroying the happiness of anyone close to them. And finally

there is physical sacrifice, each member of the group offering themselves up to be brutally murdered until the only two left are our girl and
the dirtbag she's screwing, whose name is probably something bizarrely
antisocial like *Thrash* or *Bobby Filth*."

"That's pretty bad."

Sam put his hands in the air. "Hey, you're the one who wrote it."

Moore leaned in.

"I guess we really have each other pegged, don't we?"

The breeze picked up, sweeping across the porch and twisting
around them, but Moore's hair did not move; the braid draping down
her back remained still. There was a dangerous smile playing at the
corners of her mouth. Her right pupil was a bottomless pit inviting
Sam to fall in.

You can't trust her, he told himself. But Sam wasn't sure this was
true. He wanted to trust her. He wanted to trust *someone*. And there
was something about her that just felt . . . real.

The sound of the front door opening broke the spell.

Behind Moore, Daniel lumbered out. The porch boards groaned
under his weight.

"There you two are," he said.

Moore pulled her lips tightly against her teeth. "Daniel Slaughter.
Exactly who I wanted to see."

"Seriously?"

Without another word, Moore marched past him and disappeared into the house.

"Oh, I get it," Daniel said to Sam, "she was just being awful, as
usual."

"She's testing you."

"And I feel like I keep failing." Daniel suddenly snapped his fingers, remembering something. "Oh, if you go out back, be careful. The
cover on the well is not at all sturdy. I almost fell into it. Lost my phone
in the darn thing."

The rustling of leaves got Sam's attention.

The branches of the beech tree were swaying, the leaves rippling
from end to end.

Yet this time, there was no breeze.

Moore slipped through the shadows.

She heard faint voices that were growing louder the closer she crept.

She loved being in the darkness, feeling its cold embrace as she moved up the stairs, unseen. She stopped at the top and peered around the corner.

Kate and Wainwright stood in a cramped alcove just off the main hall of the second floor. To their left was a stained-glass window through which the day's last bit of daylight streamed in, the gloom transformed by the window's multicolored panes. Against the light, they were silhouettes.

They were still too far away and their voices too low to make out exactly what they were saying, but Moore could tell by the way Wainwright was holding Kate by the shoulders that there was something wrong with the girl. He bent down to look her in the eyes, but she glanced away. "What was it?" his silhouette was asking excitedly. "What did you see?"

She shook her head, unable to put it into words. Wainwright pulled her closer, encouraging her to slip her hands around his waist. He whispered something to her.

Moore strained to hear what they were saying.

"Try to remember," Moore overheard him tell her.

"It was right there." She motioned to someplace behind Wainwright, farther into the alcove. "I think. Hell, I don't know, maybe it was just a trick of the light."

Moore rolled her eyes. Kate sounded like a goddamn bumpkin with that Southern twang. How could Wainwright take anything she said seriously?

Wainwright looked to where Kate was pointing. "What did it look like?"

"It . . ." Her voice trailed off as she tried to conjure up an image in her head. "Forget it. I'm sorry."

"But you saw something, right?" It was less a question than a statement of fact.

"Maybe."

He pondered this, his foot tapping the wood floor. Then he nodded. "Okay. Okay. Let's keep this between us. Don't tell the others."

Moore frowned. She heard Sam's voice telling her, *I don't trust him.*

Kate gave a small, earnest laugh. "My dad would lose it if he knew his sweet little preacher's daughter was spending the night in a place like this."

"Yeah, well, your dad would be even more upset if he knew you were sleeping with your boss."

"Not because you're my boss," Kate said teasingly. "Because you're white."

"Right. Not much I can do about that then, is there?"

Kate smiled. Wainwright ran a hand up her cheek to the nape of her neck and kissed her. Kate dug her fingers into his thick hair and kissed him harder.

Something about this intimate moment troubled Moore. *That girl would let him talk her into anything,* she thought.

She watched as the two silhouettes merged into one big, oddly shaped shadow.

They finally parted and stepped away from the window; Moore could make out their features once again. Wainwright took Kate's hand in his, and together they disappeared into their bedroom.

Time to find out what's so interesting.

Moore left her hiding place and moved silently down to the alcove where Wainwright and Kate had been standing. She looked to where Kate had pointed.

"What the hell?" she whispered.

Why would someone build a brick wall at the top of a staircase?

FOURTEEN

6:25 p.m.

THERE'S ANOTHER HALLWAY. How the hell did we miss that? Sam wondered.

In the kitchen, when facing the sunroom and back doors, there was a narrow hall to the right that led to the foyer and, ultimately, to the living room. Had one of them bothered to look to the left, however, they would have noticed a second hall, not quite as narrow as the first but much darker, for it lacked any windows. This hall had not been on their initial tour, either forgotten or purposely avoided.

Now Wainwright motioned to the dark hallway, telling the group, "We'll eat in the dining room."

On the kitchen island, Wainwright and Kate had arranged a modest spread of food. Beside the numerous takeout containers was a stack of plastic plates and an assortment of plastic utensils.

The mood was surprisingly light as the group filled their plates, piling on heaps of Midwestern picnic fare: chicken, turkey, roast beef, sides of green beans, baked beans, corn, pasta salad, and potato salad. Sebastian hovered over a plate of cheeses and fruit; Moore went for the rarest of roast beef; Sam made a simple turkey and Swiss sandwich; and Daniel sampled more than a bit of everything. Their drinks were equally appropriate: Sebastian had a glass of Bordeaux; Sam, a bottle of beer from the fridge; Moore poured herself whiskey, neat; and Daniel opted for the more conservative choice of iced tea. Wainwright and Kate prepared their plates and poured their drinks last, allowing the four writers to wander down the hallway as a group.

As he left the kitchen, Sam noticed the dog-eared paperback of *Phantoms of the Prairie* sitting on the counter near the island.

Wainwright's copy, he realized. It hadn't been out of the young man's hands since they'd arrived. And now there it was, forgotten on the counter. Sam made a mental note of this and followed the others.

It was astonishing that the dining room could have existed in the house without them knowing. It was a massive space, easily the biggest in the house. Large windows lined one wall, allowing both the fading evening light into the cavernous room and a beautiful view of the back woods. At the center of the room was a long wooden table covered in a red tablecloth. Red leather was stretched over the backs and seats of each chair and secured with rustic nail heads. There were ten chairs, four on each side and a single chair at each head of the table. A two-tiered chandelier was suspended over the table. Three candelabras were lit and evenly spaced. Opposite the windows, more candles flickered in a small fireplace.

As was customary when writers gathered, they began by complaining about their publishers.

"They want me to join Twitter," Sebastian announced from the head of the table, laughing. "I told them that I still had a rotary telephone and wrote on a typewriter."

"Christ, you're old," Moore said.

Sebastian sighed. "There was something wonderfully simple yet elegant about the old way. The first chapter of your book published in *The New Yorker* or *Playboy*. Full-page ads in the country's largest newspapers. A few well-publicized in-store events at the Strand or City Lights. Your books sold on the strength of your writing, not your number of online followers."

Moore washed the roast beef down with a sip of whiskey. "Hate to say it, fellas, but you're all spoiled. You've had publishers and agents and managers and publicists for way too long. Seven years ago, I was editing my first book, *Biter*, begging any friend I could to read it, paying for cover design out of my own pocket, and then putting the damn thing out myself. There were no 'well-publicized in-store events' or first chapters in jerk mags for T.C. Moore. It was all word of mouth, and I had to have the biggest mouth of all."

"Somehow I doubt that was a problem for you," Sebastian said with an ornery smile.

"Screw you, old man," Moore replied with a grin.

Sam glanced around the room. They were shy two people. *Where are Wainwright and Kate?* he wondered. *Why would Wainwright miss the opportunity to get this all on camera?*

"I made *Biter* a massive hit all by myself, and I pulled in seventy percent of the net profits," Moore continued. "Publishers got down on their hands and knees, begging to take *Biter* off self-publishing so they could put it in every bookstore in the world. So I made a deal, and what was the first thing I got? A new watered-down cover that would appeal to the one-piece bathing suit crowd. What's the next thing I got? My profits cut to a pathetic twenty percent."

Daniel's chair groaned as he leaned back. "But you don't have to hustle anymore. You're a household name. Your books are bestsellers. You've sold the movie rights."

"I sold out. That's what I did."

"To reach a larger audience. To make sure your work lives on as long as possible."

"Amen to that," Sebastian said, lifting his wineglass.

Sam crossed his arms. Wainwright's absence was making him nervous. He glanced around at the others. *They don't even notice. They don't seem to care.*

So why do you? he asked himself.

Because I don't know why he brought us here.

He brought us here because he admires us.

His right hand slid down to feel the haphazard ridges of his scars. *How can anyone admire me?*

Moore took another bite of roast beef, still considering Daniel's last comment. "My work is popular because it pushes boundaries. That's what my readers expect. But the marketing of my books is shit. My books are loud, but the marketing isn't, because my books have gone corporate. So yes, I have a team behind me now that allows me to write from a killer house in the Hollywood Hills while they take care of the rest. But what's the point? I'm willing to go to the darkest, nastiest places in my psyche in order to top my last book, and my publisher is, what? Praying to white Jesus for a starred review in *Publishers Weekly*?"

"You want your marketing to be as extreme as your books?" Daniel asked. He looked completely befuddled by Moore's point of view.

"Yes!" Moore cried out. "Fuck yes! Nero burned down Rome just so he could rebuild it the way he wanted it. Yes, if I'm going to sweat blood to write a book, I want my publisher to bleed in marketing the damn thing."

"I *wish* marketing were my biggest worry." Daniel was holding a rolled-up piece of prosciutto between two fingers. "At least you all still have people who want to publish you."

"What the hell are you crying about, Slaughter? You have, like, a billion books on the shelf," Moore said.

Daniel sighed like he suddenly regretted speaking up. But it was too late now. The other writers were staring at him, waiting.

"I think my publisher's going to dump me soon," he said.

The comment pulled Sam out of his own thoughts. He shot a confused look to the large man sitting beside him. "That doesn't make sense," he said. "They must have made an incredible amount of money off of you."

Daniel shrugged. "My Christian audience isn't as, well, *receptive* to my books as they once were. Maybe I'm just paranoid, I don't know. It's just . . . The print orders keep getting smaller and smaller. I feel like . . . like my publisher is losing faith in me." He glanced over at Moore. "Aren't you going to make some sort of snarky comment about faith or religion or—"

"No," she said. "I'm not."

Daniel gave an appreciative nod.

"What about you, Sam?" It was Sebastian, in his all-too-appropriate seat at the head of the table.

"What about me?"

"What's your publishing horror story?"

Moore twirled a plastic knife between her fingers. "Haven't you noticed? Sam doesn't like to share. He likes to listen. Don't you, Sam?"

It's safer that way, he thought.

He could feel her piercing gaze from across the table.

"I don't know if you can call it a horror story," Sam said. "They want a book a year from me. Doesn't matter what it is. They just want something to slap my name on."

"So give it to them." Moore shrugged.

"I want to give them something good."

"So write something good," she said. "You're Sam McGarver."

It was the closest thing to a compliment he had ever heard from her.

Sam stared at Moore over the flickering flames of the candelabra between them. Through the window behind her, he could see an orange moon beginning to rise over the trees.

"It's that easy for you? You just sit down and pound out something you're proud of every time?"

"Yes," she said.

"And you're doing that now?"

"Yes, I am. I've started something that I think is going to be the best thing I've ever written."

"More adventures under the sheets with erotic demons, I'm sure," Daniel chimed in.

Moore leveled an icy stare at Slaughter. "You think I'm a joke, don't you? Like somehow I don't deserve to sit at a table with you *masters of horror?*"

"I didn't say—"

"Yes, you did."

Daniel glanced down at his plate. He looked suddenly ashamed, like a little boy who'd spoken rudely to an adult.

Sebastian cleared his throat, once again attempting to cut through the tension. He lifted his wineglass into the air. "Well, I would like to propose a toast," he said.

Sam followed suit, holding his drink high. He watched as Daniel and Moore reluctantly joined in.

"To an eclectic group of extremely talented writers. It is an honor to share this experience with you all. I would trust any one of you to ghostwrite my books when I'm dead."

Sam burst into unexpected laughter at the comment, as did Daniel. Even Moore had to fight a smile.

"No one's going to ghostwrite you, Sebastian," Sam said.

"Oh yes, they most certainly will. My publisher is going to 'Robert Ludlum' my ass."

They all laughed harder.

"The only silver lining is that my ghostwriters will do all the work, but their names will be in little, tiny letters under mine." He swept a hand through the air to imply the print on the cover. "Written by A Dead Man, with assistance from Some Poor Asshole."

The table was shaking with the group's laughter.

Sebastian raised his glass. "Cheers."

Thank God for this man, Sam thought.

Glasses clinked. They drank in silence. The candle flames flickered.

Something rustled in the darkness of the hallway. Only Sam noticed it. He abruptly stopped laughing and turned to stare into the shadows.

A shape was moving there. It was coming toward them.

Sam only had time to think: *It's the house.*

And then Wainwright emerged, carrying two plates of food. Kate followed closely behind him. In her hands were their drinks: a beer for herself and a vodka on the rocks for Wainwright. As usual, her camera was slung over her shoulder, the shotgun mic still mounted on top.

"What did I miss?" Wainwright asked.

Sam looked from Kate's camera to the strange, claylike face of Wainwright. "How long were you there?"

Wainwright set the plates down in the two spots beside Moore. "What are you talking about, Sam?"

"In that hallway. How long were you standing there before you came in?"

"I don't . . . I don't really know what you mean there, mate."

The hell you don't.

Wainwright and Kate took their seats. Kate raised her beer bottle. "Shall we toast?"

She looked at them, confused, as they all burst into another fit of welcome laughter.

But Sam did not laugh. He was watching Wainwright.

For the next half hour, they ate and chatted as darkness overtook the woods outside. Their voices drifted down the darkened corridor, through the brightly lit kitchen, into the foyer, and up the stairs, echoing down hallways and through empty rooms, until finally their words vanished into the very walls.

Sam was the first to excuse himself.

While the others talked, he casually but quickly drank down the last of his beer. He held up the empty bottle.

"Going for a refill. Anybody need anything?"

Wainwright picked up his glass and rattled the ice.

"I could use another. I'll go with you."

He started to push himself up from the table, but Sam moved around to his side. "No, I can get it."

"Thanks, mate," he said, handing the glass to Sam.

Sam could feel Wainwright watching him as he moved into the dark hallway. And then the dining room was behind him, out of sight. Sam stepped into the light of the kitchen.

Wainwright's copy of *Phantoms of the Prairie* was still on the counter.

Sam hurried across the kitchen and snatched up the book. He set Wainwright's glass down next to the collection of liquor bottles, making sure his back was to the hallway, and opened the book.

It looks like a textbook. He didn't read it—he studied it.

The book had been marked up in the same way that his students marked up the books for his class: the corners of pages dog-eared, various sentences and key phrases underlined or highlighted in yellow, random notes scribbled in the margins.

He flipped through the book. The pages came to a hard stop halfway through, and something fell out, fluttering to the floor.

Sam bent down and picked it up.

It was a photograph. An original, by the looks of it. The color was fading, everything taking on a slightly jaundiced tone. In the photo, two women sat side by side, one on a rather uncomfortable-looking couch, and the other in a wheelchair. They both had black hair, although the woman in the wheelchair had her hair pulled back into a tight bun while the other let her dark locks fall like curtains around her face. In Wainwright's penmanship, a name was written above each woman: "Rebecca" above the one in the wheelchair, and "Rachel" above the one on the couch.

The Finch sisters.

Rachel was staring straight at the camera, her dark eyes contrasted by the extreme paleness of her skin. Rebecca, though, was glancing at something to her left, something just out of view of the camera. A curious smile played at the corners of her thin lips.

There was something familiar about them. Sam had heard many stories about them, but this was his first time seeing the sisters. Their faces struck a chord that Sam could not quite place.

Their flesh. It seems too smooth. Artificial. Like clay or rubber. Like . . .

"Wainwright's face."

The sound of his own voice made Sam's heart skip a beat.

Sam slipped the photo into his back pocket and replaced the book on the counter. He was unscrewing the cap from the vodka bottle when he heard footsteps behind him.

Wainwright stood on the edge of the light, a step in from the shadowy hallway.

"Everything okay, Sam?"

Sam conjured up a smile and nodded, hoping he wasn't overplaying it. "Yeah. Fine. Just getting you that drink."

Wainwright nodded. "I think we're ready to move to the living room. The interview will be starting soon."

Sam filled Wainwright's glass to the halfway mark and carried it over to him.

"Thanks, mate."

"No problem," Sam said, but he did not release his hold on the glass.

Wainwright cocked his head curiously. "Something wrong?"

His face. It looks just like theirs.

"No," Sam said, letting Wainwright take his drink. "I'm good."

Wainwright had been quite busy before dinner, arranging the furniture in the living room to accommodate his guests, strategically placing it to encourage conversation. He had also started a fire in the living room's large stone fireplace, which burned brightly as twilight wrapped the outside world in a wine-colored cocoon.

Sam felt a hand touch his elbow. It was Moore beside him.

"Check it out," she said, motioning to the coffee table.

A black iron candelabra sat at the center. Several wireless cameras were strapped to the candleholders, transforming the candelabra into a bizarre metal bug with five eyes, each trained exactly where a guest would be sitting. Hovering over the space was a boom microphone on a long, crooked arm. A cable ran from there to a makeshift command center of external hard drives and a notebook computer near the back of the room.

Sam watched the others as they settled into their seats.

Sebastian lazily swirled his Bordeaux. "So, Mr. Wainwright, when does this little production begin?"

Wainwright checked his watch. "In about ten minutes. Seven thirty sharp."

"And until then?"

"You relax. Enjoy your drinks. Make yourselves comfortable."

"Before the firing squad," Moore muttered, her eyes on that multi-eyed creature on the coffee table.

Ask him about the photo, Sam ordered himself.

Not yet. Wait.

"Something on your mind, Sam?" Wainwright asked.

Sam hadn't been aware he was staring at the young man. He shook his head. "No. Just getting my thoughts together, I guess."

Kate took a position close to her command center but still with a clear shot of each member of the group. She leaned back against the wall and busied herself with the camera in her hand.

From a pile of wood just to the right of the fireplace, Wainwright grabbed two thick logs and set them carefully into the fire. The flames fed greedily, devouring the dry wood and growing higher and higher. The entire room flickered with their gluttony. The group sank deeper into their chairs and their drinks. A heavy sense of inevitability settled over them.

Sebastian checked his watch. "Almost time."

"I'll start with an introduction," Wainwright explained. "Then I'll ask some questions to get everyone talking. Ideally this will be one fluid conversation with everyone participating, everyone sharing."

Everyone but you, Sam thought.

Standing with his back to the fire, Wainwright was nothing more than a shadow. "I'm not interested in serving up the same cold dish of previously told anecdotes. I want to know why you write, what truly drives you, what scares you, how you differ, how you're the same. What pisses you off? What keeps that fire burning? I want to dig deeper. Otherwise what's the point, mates?"

The fire popped suddenly. One of the logs exhaled a breath as the flames found a hollow space to invade.

"This is live. Online. To the entire world." Wainwright settled down into a high-backed chair just off the main circle. "Let's make it bloody count. I'd hate to think we all wasted our time."

Sam looked at the clock on his phone: 7:29. "Here we go."

Daniel drew in a deep breath and folded his hands awkwardly in his lap.

"You're going to be marvelous," Sebastian assured him. Then the old man looked to Sam and winked.

Sam nodded, but his hand was already gripping the scarred flesh of his left arm. He glanced to Wainwright, who was rapidly tapping his leg, his body buzzing with energy.

He's anxious. For this moment. His *moment.* Sam warned himself, *Watch him. And be ready for anything.*

Kate, her face glowing green in the light of her laptop, tapped the space bar.

Sam listened as a short pre-taped intro played. The sounds were tinny through the computer's miniscule speakers, but from the theatrical gravitas in Wainwright's voice-over to the jolting screeches of jump cuts, it was obviously similar in style to the introduction the writers had received at the library in Kansas City. The pertinent information was covered: a quick bio on each author, a few lines celebrating their most famous works, and finally an appropriately creepy description of the unique setting for the interview. The house was, after all, the *hook.*

He knew we'd all four show up, Sam realized. If one of them had dropped out, this pre-interview sequence could have been re-edited, but Wainwright produced it with all of them included. He knew they would not be able to pass up the opportunity.

He has us right where he wants us. But for what? What exactly does he have planned?

Sam slipped a hand to his back pocket and felt the edge of the photograph tucked there.

A discordant note announced the end of the intro.

Kate clicked the trackpad and pointed to Wainwright.

Around the room, a series of red lights blinked on as the cameras went live.

Firelight danced in Wainwright's eyes as he spoke directly to the camera before him.

"Happy Halloween, and welcome to the house on Kill Creek. You are on WrightWire.com, and I'm about to share a bloody sweet Halloween treat with all of you. Because here in this house, the location of one of the world's most famous hauntings, I have gathered four of our greatest living horror authors: Sam McGarver, Daniel Slaughter, T.C. Moore, and the legendary Sebastian Cole."

Sam nodded awkwardly toward the camera facing him, as did the others. It was an uncanny sensation, the camera's red light burning in the blackness to let him know that his image was being broadcast to millions of viewers around the world. And here he was in an old, dark farmhouse somewhere in the middle of the Kansas countryside, about to have a casual conversation with four new acquaintances, the occasional silence broken only by the sound of ice clinking in glasses and the crackling fire. If there were spirits in the Finch House, they had to be impressed with the wonders of modern technology.

Taking a poker from a wrought-iron stand beside the fireplace, Wainwright leaned forward in his chair and nudged the burning logs, stoking the flames higher and higher. Were it not for the fire, the group would have been sitting in almost total darkness.

"You are all incredibly different writers *and* people, but you have one thing in common." He turned to the thin sliver of a man that was Sebastian. Half of Wainwright's face fell into shadow. "Mr. Cole, you first: out of all the genres, why horror?"

Sebastian took a moment to ponder the question. And then in a steady and confident voice, he said, "The goal of the written word has always been to explain to man those things which seem unexplainable. We write to understand the world but, more importantly, we write to understand our place in it. I never set out to be a writer of fantastic fiction; I simply understood the dichotomy of the world. Good cannot exist without evil. Light without darkness. It just so happened that when I first sat down at my old Remington No. 5, my very first typewriter, the darkness interested me most. It wasn't intentional.

"*A Thinly Cast Shadow* began with a simple image: a boy wandering alone in a New England field. He discovers what appears to be a cow skull, but, upon closer examination, he finds that the skull has strange features: protrusions where there should be none, teeth made more for chewing flesh than cud."

"But," Wainwright interrupted, waving a finger in the air, "that's about as graphic as the book gets. It's a classic psychological ghost story, not a graphic tale of man-eating creatures run amuck."

Sebastian clasped his hands and pulled them close to his chest. It was a curious reaction; it appeared he wasn't aware he had even done it, but its intent was unmistakable. It was the motion of a father protecting his child, drawing it to him to keep his story from slipping into harm's way. He was, in a sense, guarding the mystery of his beloved story from the gnashing teeth of definitive interpretation.

"I always keep one thing in mind when I write," Sebastian said. "'The oldest and strongest emotion of mankind is fear, and the oldest and strongest kind of fear is fear of the unknown.' Lovecraft said that, and for good reason. When our fate is uncertain, our minds naturally lead us to the worst possible scenario. Any writer worth his or her salt does not need to titillate the reader with fetishistic bloodletting."

Sam noticed Moore cock an eyebrow. *She thinks that comment was aimed at her.* He couldn't say for sure that it wasn't.

"Think of that skull the boy finds in the field," Sebastian continued. "As he turns it over in his hands, he realizes this is no earthly beast. Whatever power spawned such a creature could not have been the benevolent deity we know as *God.* The boy realizes simply by running a finger over the multiple sets of jagged teeth lining the jawbone that this abomination was capable of unspeakable acts. And the reader suspects that on this land—the land to which the boy's family has just moved, the land on which an unfathomable evil birthed a monster—terrible things await those who trespass." He tapped his temple, just below a few thin strands of white hair fighting a losing battle against time. "All in the reader's mind," he said. "All by the power of suggestion."

There was a reverent beat of silence as they hung on the voice of this literary giant.

This is why he's a legend, Sam thought. *He owns us with every word.*

Wainwright swung his hand around to point at Moore. "And on the complete other end of the spectrum, we find T.C. Moore, a horror writer who, it's safe to say, has never even heard the word *subtle*."

"I'll take that as a compliment, sweetheart," Moore said. Her words curled from her lips like smoke.

"You started in self-published erotica, but each one of your books proved to be darker than the last. Your brand of horror centers around obsession and perversion and fetishes too extreme for something as fragile as the human body. It's no surprise that you've made the leap from novelist to screenwriter; your books are almost disturbingly graphic, leaving absolutely nothing to the reader's imagination. They're also consistently polarizing. People either love a T.C. Moore book or they hate it."

Moore's body tensed at the comment. "I would phrase that another way: they either get it or they don't. People hate what they don't understand."

"Are you saying that anyone who claims to not like your books just isn't intelligent enough to understand them?"

"Yes," Moore said without hesitation. "That's exactly what I'm saying."

Daniel gave a snort and shook his head. Moore resisted taking the bait, but she watched him out of the corner of her eye.

"So," Wainwright continued, "how do you react to Sebastian's take on horror?"

"As a rule, I don't react. I *act*. Sebastian's style is elegant. Quaint. I suppose you could say out of all of us, what he writes is the closest thing to honest-to-god literature. But, no disrespect, the golden days of Beaver Cleaver and Good Humor Bars and 'There's nothing to fear but fear itself' are over. They've been raped and tortured and left for dead. The only thing to fear these days is *everything*. Strangers. Neighbors. Your friends. Your family. Yourself. You think there's nothing subtle about my work? Well, take a look at the world all of us—except maybe Sebastian—live in. You want to see the victims of genocide decomposing in mass graves? Turn on the Nightly News. You want to see a girl blowing a zebra? Hop on the internet. You want a badass bitch in black leather to come over and piss on your face while you jerk off into a pair of panties you stole from the local Wash-O-Rama? Well, that's just a phone call or DM away. Subtlety is dead."

"Goodness," Daniel said under his breath.

This time, Moore did turn to him. She was on a roll, blood pumping, teeth grinding.

"Too much for you, Mr. Slaughter? Good. Welcome to the real world."

She leaned in to stare directly into her camera, to speak to that unseen, phantom audience they had been assured was there. "Horror no longer goes bump in the night. Horror stuffs the bodies of dead hookers in his crawl space and then pulls a twelve-hour nursing shift taking care of your sick mother. Horror sits in his cubicle and fantasizes about sucking the toes of the high school cheerleader he plans to strangle after work. Horror stays awake at night dreaming up ways to hurt you and your family and your pets and everything you hold dear. Horror is perversion."

"And why celebrate that?" Daniel asked.

Wainwright sat back in his chair, thick hair falling around his eyes. He rested the fireplace poker across his lap, his hand gripping its handle and tightening as if he meant to swing it at any moment.

Sam watched this nervously, his body tensing.

"Celebrate it?" Moore scoffed. "Are you honestly that simple? While you look to the heavens and sing hymns about rolling away the stone, I'm lifting up rocks to expose the pale writhing worms beneath. They're there, Slaughter; you just don't want to admit it."

Moore paused to collect herself, running the nail of her pinkie slowly up and down the powerful curve of her jaw. When she spoke again, her voice was even and calm. Paradoxically, this made her more intense than before. "And here's the kicker: we're all sick fucks in some way. Even the morally righteous Daniel Slaughter. Our most deviant desires have been around for eons, regardless of the fact that Sebastian's nostalgia and Daniel's religion have whitewashed a period in history when black people couldn't even take a piss with the white folks and Jews were being marched by the millions to their deaths. That may be the most perverse thing of all: ignoring the horror, even as it happens around you."

Wainwright allowed the uncomfortable moment to hang heavily in the air. And then he sat abruptly forward. The sudden action caught Sam off guard, his hands clenching into fists. But Wainwright went no farther than this. He stated simply and evenly, "This is from the *Washington Post*: 'In the case of a reprehensible pseudo-novel like *Cutter*, Moore is less.'"

Moore's head whipped around so quickly, it seemed in danger of snapping clean off her neck. "Baby, my competition is the most talented writers in the world. Yours is a cat that plays the keyboard."

Wainwright did not look away. Even with Moore's ruptured pupil boring into him, the young man held fast. His finger was tapping his leg again. He had another bullet in the chamber.

"And this is from a review of your previous book, *Flesh Forward*: 'Moore is once again trying too hard to offend in an admirable but misguided attempt to prove a woman can write filth just as well as a man.'"

The sound of Moore's scotch tumbler slamming down onto the coffee table made Daniel flinch. "If Barker or Palahniuk had written that book, if Cronenberg had made the film, no one would've batted a goddamn eye."

"So you do think that horror is a boy's club?"

"I think I'm the only one in this room who has ever been asked to give a blow job in exchange for a publishing deal."

"And did you?"

"Fuck you, Wainwright." Her voice was quavering ever so slightly. She was in danger of losing the cool, steel-trap control she usually had over every moment.

"All right now," Sebastian said. "Let's keep this civilized."

Wainwright slid the fireplace poker from his lap and held it like a cane, his palm pressed down on the top of its metal handle, its tip biting into the wood floor. The crackle of the fire was the only sound.

"Sam, you've been awfully quiet," he said suddenly. "But that's kind of your thing, isn't it? Sitting it out. Fading into the background."

Here we go, Sam thought. *My turn.* He picked up his beer bottle and unfortunately found it empty.

"Just trying to stay out of the crossfire."

"Sorry, mate." Wainwright grinned, perched on his chair, his hand on the poker like a king on his throne. In the harsh light of the fire, his face looked more artificial than ever, like a stranger wearing a Wainwright mask. "You can't hide forever."

Once again, Sam had the unnerving sensation that Wainwright could see straight into his mind.

"It's safe to say you fall somewhere between Sebastian Cole and T.C. Moore."

"I guess."

"You're mainstream. You write *popular* horror fiction."

"I've been lucky enough to find an audience."

"Why do you think so many people respond to your style of writing?"

The red light glowed above the lens of Sam's camera like a one-eyed rat studying him, trying to ascertain his weakness.

He told himself, *It's not an interrogation. It's just like one of your lectures. Stay in your safe place. He only gets as far in as you let him.*

Sam straightened in his chair and imagined himself behind his lectern in Budig Hall, that great Gothic window towering over him like a golden arrow. "I believe that first you have to establish the ordinary before you can invest people in the extraordinary. So I start with the natural world and slowly, methodically, I let the supernatural invade. I don't know. . . . Maybe that's why people like my books. Because they see their own lives in my characters and my settings. I understand and appreciate the way others approach horror. Like science fiction and fantasy, it's a genre that does and should encourage the freedom to experiment, to tell stories in unique and personal ways. My way is to start with something very real, very grounded, and then gradually open some cracks in the façade to let the darkness in. I try to pay homage to those who have inspired me, and there's no one who has inspired me more than Sebastian Cole."

"Thank you, Sam," Sebastian said.

If the room hadn't been so dark, they would have seen Sam blush, more out of shame than embarrassment. He still didn't know how to acknowledge what Sebastian meant to him without sounding sycophantic.

"But," Sam continued, "like Moore, I don't want to shy away from the real damage that evil can do. Evil corrupts. It infects. And an infection is not pretty. It starts slow, but in the end, if left untreated, there's a lot of pain and pus and nasty shit that you can't ignore. That's horror to me, when something bad is swept—"

"Under the rug?" Wainwright couldn't resist referencing the title of Sam's first novel.

Sam gave a tight smile. "That's right. When something bad is swept under the rug, it doesn't go away. It festers. In horror, there's no such thing as 'out of sight, out of mind.' That thing will be back, and it will take over your life. That's the root of all fear: the loss of control. Not being able to stop the evil."

"Like Joshua Goodman watching his beloved murdered in this very house."

"Yes."

"Or your own marriage falling apart."

Wainwright's words may as well have been a slap across Sam's face.

"Excuse me?"

"You are currently separated from your wife, yeah?"

In the fireplace, the wood crackled loudly as the flames flickered higher.

"I don't know why that's relevant—"

"Is that something you're trying to channel into your latest novel? I assume you're working on something new."

The image of the lecture hall in Lawrence vanished from Sam's mind. He wasn't speaking to his students. He was here, at the house on Kill Creek, and Wainwright was in control.

"Of course I'm working on something new."

"I only ask because—and please don't take this the wrong way—since your first novel, your books have gotten less . . . personal. You seem to be embracing your status as a best-selling author. You stick to the mainstream, just enough story and character to satisfy discerning readers, just enough splatter to push paperbacks."

"What's your point?" Sam knew he sounded irritated. He didn't care.

Wainwright's black leather jacket creaked as he shrugged, his hands in the air. "You come off as a nice, well-adjusted Midwestern guy. I'm just shooting from the hip here, but it almost feels like that's how you *want* people to see you. A nice guy who writes easily digested genre fiction. But there must be a reason you write what you write."

Sam tried to swallow and found that he couldn't. Something was blocking his throat. Something that tasted like smoke.

"Your mother died in a house fire, didn't she? When you were a child?"

Sam felt the smoke spread to his lungs, filling them. The others were staring at him. He refused to look at their faces, to see the pity, the hunger for gossip.

Keep him out.

"It's not something I like to talk about," he told Wainwright.

Wainwright's hand bobbed in the air like a conductor's baton. "But you've known pain. You've known tragedy. You said horror is the loss of control. I can't imagine feeling less in control than being a young boy and watching your house burn down with your mother inside. Is that where your stories come from?"

Keep him out.

"No."

"No? You don't try to tap into any of that pain? That suffering?"

Keep. Him. Out.

"No."

"Then is that why your books have become more and more superficial?"

Sam shot Wainwright an incredulous look.

Fuck you! his mind screamed. *Fuck you, you little weasel! You rich little shit!*

Instead, in a voice like a clenched fist, he said, "I don't believe they have."

"Critics do."

Sam opened his mouth to answer, but he could not speak. He could not breathe. For the briefest of moments, he looked to Moore.

Without hesitation, she jumped in. "Critics are sad children who were never picked first in gym class," she said, delivering it like the deliberate sound bite she meant it to be.

Sam drew air into his lungs, the attention no longer on him. His heart was thudding in his chest, but with each breath, he felt his body relax. He nodded to Moore, and she nodded back.

"Daniel Slaughter," Wainwright announced, turning on a dime, "author of, what, almost fifty successful young adult horror novels? At first glance, you and T.C. Moore seem to have zero in common. But the violence in your books, although obviously geared toward a much younger audience, is still pretty graphic."

Daniel squirmed in the spotlight as if trying to work his way around a lump in his chair. "Well, yeah, I guess you could say that. . . ."

"But you're a devout Christian."

"That's right."

"Your books were initially embraced by the faithful, who justified the bloodshed as a means to an end. Anything to bring readers closer to Jesus, yeah? But lately that has changed. Many Christians are becoming uncomfortable with the subject matter."

"Well . . ."

"But *you* are a believer, correct?""

Sam watched Wainwright with a dawning sense of dread. *This was his plan all along. He wants to cut us. He wants us to bleed for his audience. Not enough to kill us. Oh no, it would make him look like a royal asshole if he were too aggressive. He's opening up just enough wounds to give his viewers a taste of blood. He's slicing each of us right where it hurts the most.*

"Are you a believer?" Wainwright asked again.

"Of . . . of course," Daniel said. But there was doubt in his voice. "I mean, look, I'm a Christian who happens to write horror, but there's a clear message in my books. Do evil, and you will be punished. Only the characters that are pure of heart triumph in the end. Evil never wins in my books. Good does, because it's from God."

"But do you honestly think that the kids who read your books get that message?"

"I have a teenage daughter, okay? I learned long ago that kids don't respond to sermons. Even in church, if you can get them to go, they're daydreaming about the dance that's coming up or the boy who asked them out or the car they want when they turn sixteen."

Daniel wiped a bead of sweat from his forehead.

"The fact that my books don't preach is the reason why they're effective. The message is always there: good wins, evil loses. Whether kids make the connection between morality and a higher power, who knows. But I think they do. I think they get it."

"But what about your critics? A growing number of them Christians, who say you're simply taking advantage of a wildly profitable slice of the literary market?"

"I'm . . . I write . . ."

"What about those who say your books aren't suitable for kids?"

"They're for *teenagers*," Daniel corrected him. He looked like a very large mouse being playfully batted around by a cruel cat. "These kids know what the world has to offer, the good and the bad. I'm not telling them anything they don't already know."

"So what is horror, Daniel?"

"I don't know . . . how to answer that . . ."

"What is horror?" Wainwright asked again.

"I guess . . . I'd say . . . losing the things you love."

"And that is . . ."

"Family. Faith. God." The fire dimmed slightly, as if the house were exhaling a long, slow breath. "We're all . . . we're all sinners." Daniel was stammering again. "We . . . Horror is the fear and the guilt and the sin that we try to keep inside us, down in the dark, and as storytellers, it's our job to . . . to sort of bring that into the light, you know . . . it's . . ."

Poor Daniel, Sam thought. *He's got you.*

So help him, his mind ordered.

In the darkness, the red lights of cameras glowed.

Sam was frozen in place.

I can't.

It was Sebastian who came to the rescue.

"True horror is different for every person, Mr. Wainwright," the old man interrupted. "Our job as writers is to find a way to connect with some of those people. Not all of them. No one's that good. Which is why we each have unique approaches to our craft. Different, but valid."

The house once again became filled with a perfect silence. Even the fire seemed to make no sound as Sebastian's commanding words drifted through the open doorway and into other rooms.

"But here's something to consider, something that I believe *is* universal when it comes to horror. If I were to walk you into a dark room, and someone leapt out and yelled '*Boo!*,' you would be startled, perhaps even frightened. But the moment would immediately pass."

His voice floated up the stairs. It echoed down the dark hall, slipping through the cracks beneath doors and into empty bedrooms.

"Yet, if on the way to the door, I were to tell you that in that room a very cruel old woman met her end, and every night at the stroke of midnight she returned, her arthritic hands twisted into claws, reaching out to touch what her dead, cataract-fogged eyes can't see. If I were to then lead you into the darkened room and leave you there, locking the door behind me, you would sit there all night, your mind racing, thinking only of what might be out there, waiting in the dark, waiting to grab you with hands as cold as the grave."

The sound of his voice made its way into the alcove, past the stained-glass window now blackened by night, and up the steep, narrow staircase to the brick wall. Even there, the words slipped through cracks unseen.

"This is the key to true horror," Sebastian said with a confidence none of them could dispute. "If you *believe* it's real, then it's real."

Twenty minutes later, Kate tapped the touchpad on her laptop. Sam watched as the red lights on all of the cameras went dark.

The interview was over.

"Well, that was amazing, really." Wainwright beamed, beginning to rise from his chair. "Thank you all so much for being a part of it."

Sam's hand grazed the edge of the photograph in his back pocket.

"You set us up," he said, his voice a low growl.

Wainwright shrugged. "Honestly, I think I showed some restraint, yeah? I could have gone deeper. I mean, there are nastier skeletons in your closets I could have dragged out for the world to—"

Before anyone knew what was happening, Sam was over the coffee table, the lapel of Wainwright's jacket twisted tightly in his fist.

"You son of a bitch!" Sam roared. "You think this is funny?"

Daniel and Sebastian shrank back in shock, but Moore was on Sam in seconds, pulling him back.

Wainwright stood and yanked his bunched-up jacket back into place. "Christ, mate, they were questions! You never said anything was off limits!"

"Why are we really here?" Sam asked.

Wainwright stared at him, completely confused. "What? For the interview—"

"But why this house? Why did you bring us *here*?"

"Sam, I truly don't know what you're getting at."

Sam pulled the aging photograph of the Finch sisters from his pocket and thrust it at Wainwright's shocked face.

"Why do you look just like them?"

Wainwright struggled to make sense of what he was seeing. "Did you . . . did you take that from my book?"

"Answer me!" Sam yelled. "Why do you look just like them?"

"I don't! I don't know what you're talking about!"

Sam swiveled around and held the photo out for the others to see. "Do you see it?" he asked them. "Look at their faces!"

They all leaned in to examine the photograph. Daniel was the first to respond. "I'm sorry, Sam. I don't see the resemblance."

"But . . ." Sam turned the picture around.

Daniel is right, Sam realized. The faces of the Finch sisters did not have the same masklike quality that Wainwright's did.

Wainwright reached out and snatched the photograph away from Sam. "It's just a picture. I got it off eBay," he explained. "You're out of your goddamn mind."

Sam's chest rose and fell in great, undulating waves.

"Steady now," Sebastian whispered in his ear. "Why don't you go outside for some air? I'm afraid this house is getting to you."

Sam did not move.

"Listen to Sebastian," Moore said.

For a moment, no one was sure of Sam's next move, not even Wainwright, who stood with his chin held high.

Sebastian gave Sam's shoulder a pat. "Go on."

On his way to the front door, Sam caught Kate's eye. She was frightened.

Of you, you crazy son of a bitch.

The front door opened and slammed shut.

Sam was gone.

In the fireplace, the flames surged one last time and then retreated, a glowing orange light waiting patiently within the half-eaten logs.

FIFTEEN

8:15 p.m.

SAM WAS DOWN the front steps in a matter of seconds. He stormed across the gravel drive and past that ridiculous VW bus. Ahead of him, somewhere in the darkness, was the bridge over Kill Creek. There was a moment where Sam was sure he would just keep walking, over that bridge, up the road to the entrance ramp to Highway 10.

He stopped about fifty yards from the house.

Calm down. Breathe. Just breathe.

With the sun down, the temperature had dropped a good twenty degrees. He shivered as the wind picked up, but he refused to give in to the cold. He would stand out there as long as necessary, anything to keep him from going back in and strangling Wainwright with his bare hands.

But you were wrong, he realized. *Wainwright had no dark plan. He has no sinister connection to the house. He just set us up so he could twist the knife into each of us in front of his followers.*

At least Sam had kept his cool until the cameras were off. It would have been a disaster if he had lunged at Wainwright with the entire world watching. The clip would have instantly gone viral, which is exactly what Wainwright wanted.

Don't blame him for wanting that. You all want it to go viral. You just want to look good when it does.

He let out a long, slow breath, his heartbeat steadying. Yes, that was why they were there. They all hoped that hundreds of thousands, if not millions, of people would watch that interview. They all had their reasons for needing it to be a success.

For Sam, it meant some fast cash and a way to keep his name relevant, which in turn would buy him the time he needed to finally finish the damn book.

To start the damn book, you mean.

He closed his eyes and listened to every breath, each one slower and softer than the last. Soon he felt his anger toward Wainwright evaporate from his skin like rainwater in sunshine.

But the photograph . . . Sam was positive the faces of the Finch sisters had looked exactly like Wainwright. He hadn't imagined it, had he?

Of course you did. You're losing it. And it's not because you're here in this house. You've been losing it for a long time. It's why Erin left. It's why you refused to give her the life she wanted. To give her a child. Because it would grow up to be just as messed up as you.

It was so quiet out there. Strangely quiet, like being in a sensory-deprivation chamber.

Sam opened his eyes. Overhead, the night sky sparkled with countless stars. The tallgrass stood waist-high and perfectly still on either side of the driveway.

Walking farther away from the house, Sam heard a faint sound ahead in the darkness.

A chirping sound.

There was a steady rhythm to it.

He could see the shape of the wooden bridge emerging from the gloom, taking shape before him like a materializing apparition.

Sam reached out and touched the end post of the bridge's railing. The wood was splintered and rough.

The sound was coming from the other side of the bridge. Actually, it was coming from everywhere on the opposite side—from the edge of the bridge, from the road, from the grassy shoulder, from the shadowy trees that ran parallel to the creek.

The chirping grew more intense.

Insects. The quick pulse of crickets, the slower undulation of cicadas.

In a few weeks, they would burrow under rocks and logs to wait out the winter, but for now, they were out, still singing their song to the stars.

But not where he stood. It was an absolutely absurd thought, but Sam could not help thinking it anyway:

The insects won't cross the creek. They won't come over to this side.

Ahead of him was the light, rapid beat of night sounds. Behind him, there was a perfect, oppressive silence.

Slowly, Sam backed away from the bridge. He turned and picked up his pace, heading back toward the house. The sound of the insects faded away in the distance.

He was passing the beech tree when he sensed a sudden illumination above. He glanced up at the house.

A light was on in the third-floor window. It burned like a lantern in a black tower. And then it blinked out as quickly as it had appeared.

Still staring at that window, Sam moved beneath the branches of the tree.

A shiny black shoe struck him in the face.

He cried out as he leapt backward, tripping over his own feet and falling flat on his back. He stared up into the tree.

The feet of a woman swung slowly over him. She wore a dark dress and long white stockings. Blood had settled into her pale fingers so that they swelled like sausages about to burst. Over the curve of her breasts, Sam could see a sliver of her bone-white face, her bulging eyes glaring down at him.

It was Rachel Finch.

Sam scooted backward until he was safely away from the tree, and then he hopped up, his heart pounding, his chest heaving.

He was wrong.

That's not Rachel Finch. Not anymore.

The body had changed. It was a heavyset woman in her late thirties. Or it had been. She was charred black, her skin peeling away like bark from a rotting tree. What little hair was left looked as if it had melted into a scalp like the cratered surface of a moon. Heat had caused her eyes to explode in their sockets, and a shiny, jellylike substance streaked down her cheeks like grotesque tears. The weight of her body caused her neck to stretch against the rope to the point that he was sure her head would rip clean off.

"Oh God, no," he moaned.

Mommy.

There was movement beyond the sway of her body.

Her fingers were twitching.

He watched as her hand rose slowly into the air. The inciner-ated stump that was once a finger extended, pointing at him. Her jaw dropped open, and what was left of her lips slid up still-white teeth as she tried to form a word that her tongueless mouth could not speak. A cloud of gray smoke drifted out into the air.

Sam pressed his palms against his eyes.

No. No! It's not her! It's not her!

He pressed so hard that he began to see golden embers floating through blackness.

She's not here. It's not real. None of it is real. It is all in your mind.

Because you've finally lost it. You've gone crazy.

This thought was most frightening of all.

Finally he lowered his hands. He opened his eyes.

There was no body in the tree.

The branches swayed lazily in the breeze.

Kate was in the foyer, sitting at the foot of the staircase, when Sam returned. She quickly rose, pulling an olive-green Army Surplus jacket tightly around her as the cool air swept in from outside.

"Is everything okay?" she asked.

It's your face, he realized. *You look like you've seen a . . .*

He couldn't even finish the thought. It was too ridiculous.

"Everything's fine," he told her. He didn't expect her to believe him. He wasn't even sure he did.

She glanced over her shoulder to make sure they were alone.

"I wanted to talk to ya about what happened. About the inter-view." She kept her voice low, which flattened her usually rich accent.

"It wasn't an interview, Kate; it was an ambush. He used us to put on a show for his followers." The anger remained, but there was no threat of it boiling over as before. His nerves were still frayed by what he had seen outside.

What you thought you saw, he corrected himself.

Kate pinched her bottom lip between her teeth and glanced away. "I know he can get carried away sometimes. He's ambitious. But he's also scared of, ya know, everything falling apart. Of losing what he's built. He feels like he has something to prove."

"Yeah, well, he can join the club."

"Please. He's a good person." She stared up at Sam with pleading eyes. "He's been there for me when I've needed him. And he really does respect you."

He has a funny way of showing it, Sam thought, but saying this to Kate would solve nothing. Instead, he nodded.

"I've already talked to the others," she said.

"And?"

"Sebastian and Daniel seem willing to overlook the, ya know, aggressive moments of the interview."

"And Moore?"

"She asked me if Wainwright ever fucked me as hard as he fucked you guys tonight."

Of course. Classic Moore.

"What did you say to that?" Sam asked.

Kate gave a devilish grin. "I told her if he fucked y'all that hard, your egos wouldn't be walking straight for a week."

Sam offered her a hint of a smile, but he said nothing.

Her grin faded. "I'm sorry," she said. "For the rest of the night, no tricks. No bullshit. I promise."

When Sam and Kate entered the kitchen, the others were talking about the wall.

Everyone paused, waiting to see if Sam had cooled off. Wainwright was back to his usual stance, hands in pockets, legs slightly bent. But for the first time since meeting him, Wainwright looked downright sheepish, almost embarrassed by what he had put them through in the interview.

Sam let everyone stand in silence for what felt like an hour.

Just put it behind you, he told himself. *It was in your head. Don't hold Wainwright responsible for how screwed up you are.*

Finally he spoke. "What wall?" he asked, as if the prior events had never occurred.

The whole group was present. Everyone but Daniel had refilled their glasses with much-needed (and thankfully abundant) alcohol. Sam quickly noted two cameras mounted in opposite corners of the room, their red lights blazing. Intermission was over. The show was back on.

Kate leaned in close to whisper, "They're not live. I'll edit the footage later."

"Make me look good," Sam whispered back.

Wainwright lit a cigarette, waiting to inhale deeply before explaining, "The wall upstairs, on the third floor."

"There's a staircase leading to a brick wall," Kate added.

Sam frowned. "A brick wall?"

"Yeah, I thought . . ." Kate's voice trailed off.

Wainwright shot her a stern look as he blew out a cloud of smoke. "She thought she saw something at the top of the stairs."

Daniel leaned in, suddenly interested. "What did you see?"

"It was a trick of the light," Kate explained, more than a little embarrassed by the attention. "Just a . . . a shape or something."

"Where does the staircase go?" Sam asked.

"To a bedroom," Wainwright said. "When the Finch sisters moved in, it became Rebecca's room. The number three button in the elevator? That goes straight there. Or it used to. If you take the elevator to the third floor now, it'll open to a brick wall, just like the staircase."

Daniel had turned his attention to the plate of cold cuts. He stood over them like a buzzard eyeing the remains of a picked-over carcass. "Why would someone brick up a bedroom?"

Wainwright took another drag and contemplated the question. "No idea," was all he could muster. "Rachel Finch did it after her sister's death."

"Bitch must have been out of her mind," Moore said, running her fingers through the black hair cascading over her shoulder.

"There's a light on up there," Sam told them.

Wainwright shook his head. "No. That's impossible."

"I just saw it. Outside. It was on."

Overhead, the lights suddenly dimmed by half. Then, just as unexpectedly, they shot back to full power, only to dim once more. This time, they did not return to their previous strength.

A thin slice of roast beef slipped from Daniel's fingers. "What's happening?"

"Perhaps the house is waking up," Sebastian teased.

Daniel chimed in, "That's how it happens in these houses. It's always at night. During the day, everything's fine. But at night? That's when everything goes down."

"The only thing going down is a pound of salami down your throat," Moore said.

The lights buzzed as they dimmed further.

Sam shot a look at Wainwright. *No bullshit,* he thought. *Then what's this?*

Wainwright didn't bat an eye. "It's the generator. In the basement," he explained to the group. He marched out of the room, returning a moment later with a large black flashlight. He clicked it on. It emitted a striking beam in the orange glow of the half-light.

"I'll go with you," Sebastian said, already reaching for the basement door.

Sam touched him on the shoulder. "Wait."

"I'm old, Sam, but I'm not that old. I'll be fine." The hinges gave an angry squeak as Sebastian opened the door.

"Kate, would you mind?" Wainwright motioned to her camera.

She nodded. A flick of her thumb and a light mounted atop the camera blasted a pure white beam.

"The rest of you, sit tight," Wainwright said. "This should only take a second."

Without warning, the camera was snatched out of Kate's hand.

"Don't tell me to sit tight," Moore said to Wainwright, looking through the camera lens.

"Moore," he scolded, but Kate silenced him with a wave of her hand.

"It's fine," she said. "Let her go if she wants to." Then, to Moore: "Just be careful with the camera."

Sam watched as Moore marched through the open basement door. Wainwright and Sebastian followed, descending into the darkness.

The basement was freezing.

Moore followed Wainwright's flashlight, adding to it the light of the camera in her hands, creating an orb of luminance with a radius of about ten feet. Wainwright swept his hand slowly back and forth like a searchlight as they reached the bottom step and made their way across the cold floor. The concrete ceiling was uncomfortably low, the height from floor to ceiling no more than seven feet. Like they were being slowly crushed by the house above.

They could see nothing beyond the light. As they moved, objects emerged from the dark. Several bent rusty nails. Broken pieces of stone. The skull of a long-dead rat.

The walls reverberated with the subdued hum of the sickly generator. They tried to follow the sound as they worked their way through the darkness. It was impossible to ascertain the layout of the room. For all they knew, they could have been walking in the wrong direction, away from the generator, toward . . .

Toward what? Moore wondered.

She didn't know. Toward whatever was already in the basement, in the dark.

The edge of the light crept across the floor.

We've gone too far. The basement shouldn't be this big. The voice in her mind was a younger voice. A girl's voice.

Moore felt the pinprick of fear against the back of her neck and scalp. She drew in a sharp breath through her nose, her nostrils flaring.

Keep your shit together, an older, stronger voice ordered.

Their feet shuffled across the concrete. The line of light continued to move before them, revealing an old yellowed cigarette butt. Around the edge of the filter was a smudge of red lipstick.

"Where is this thing?" Sebastian asked.

The irregular chug of the generator was louder now, but still it was impossible to place it. Moore swept the camera's light to the side. The blackness retreated, and her heart rate quickened as she realized she had no idea what she was about to see. But the light exposed only empty space. She whipped the camera to the left, and the darkness reclaimed its ground only to shrink back in the other direction. On the floor was a metal wheel. The spokes blooming from its center were bent and broken. The rubber around its edges was rotting away in uneven patches.

From a wheelchair, Moore realized.

Suddenly the shadows before them began to wash away. The boxy outline of a metal machine emerged from the black.

"There it is," Wainwright said.

"What's wrong with it?" Sebastian asked.

"Don't know. Best-case scenario, it's just low on fuel. Worst case, it's a mechanical problem."

"And if it's the worst case?"

"We'll be in the bloody dark until morning."

Moore shivered, half at the cold, half at the thought of spending any amount of time in the house with no electricity. She steadied the camera's light before the men noticed her unease. The last thing she needed was for them to think the house was getting to her.

The orb of light illuminated the generator and a few feet on either side of it. Otherwise, the room was pitch black. At the top of the wall, Moore noticed an air vent to which the generator's exhaust hose was affixed and a few exposed pipes protruding like steel roots. Jagged cracks split the dusty floor, giving it the impression of a breaking ice floe.

A half-conscious thought stabbed sharply in Moore's mind: *There's nothing beneath us. If the floor gave way and we fell in, we would sink forever. Forever and ever and ever . . .*

"Are you all right, dear?" Sebastian asked her.

Normally Moore would have snapped someone's head off for calling her "dear," but from Sebastian, it was comforting. There was no condescension in his words. The old man was truly concerned.

Moore ignored the question.

"So," Wainwright began as he knelt down to examine the generator. The shadows seemed to wrap around him, pulling him in. His deep voice boomed even louder off the hard surfaces of the basement. It seemed to come from all sides at once. "Here we are. Two generations of horror. In the basement of a haunted house." He nodded toward the impenetrable dark. "What do you think is out there?"

"What do you mean?" Sebastian asked.

"I mean when the lights come on, what do you think we'll see?"

Moore squinted, trying to look past the sphere of light protecting them, but she could see nothing. The basement was an empty void.

"Why don't you tell us what we'll see?" she asked Wainwright, unamused. "You're the expert on this place."

"Come on. You're writers. Hell, Moore, I even heard you were good at it."

I don't like this, Moore told herself, but the hint of fear she felt only made her angry.

"Please? For a fan?" Wainwright asked.

Sebastian sighed. "Well . . . I suppose whatever it is, it's there in the dark right now, isn't it? It must have been here when we arrived. And now it's watching us."

He pointed into the dense blackness. It seemed to stretch on infinitely.

"It would have to have some connection to the house. Goodman, perhaps?" He turned to Moore.

She resisted at first. Then she shook her head and whispered, "No. He's too tragic. It needs to be something crueler, more twisted."

"Right," Wainwright said. There was excitement in his voice.

Moore and Sebastian peered into the abyss. She tried to imagine what shapes might be hiding behind this black curtain.

"The Finch sisters," Sebastian said in a hushed voice. "Yes. Yes, that's exactly who is down here. They watched us descend the stairs. They followed us as we made our way across the basement. They stayed just outside the light so that we couldn't see them. But they're watching us." He cocked his head curiously. "Wait. Do you see that?"

"See what?" Moore asked.

"There." Sebastian pointed into the darkness. "I can actually see them. One of them is in a wheelchair—"

"Rebecca," Wainwright chimed in.

"And standing beside her is her sister—"

"Rachel."

"That's right. They're staring back at us." He leaned toward the edge of the light. His face was in danger of passing into the dark. "They know we can see them. Oh . . . oh, now they're moving. They're coming closer. Can you hear that? It's the sound of the wheelchair. The left wheel, it makes a faint squeak as it turns, as it rolls closer and closer . . ."

Moore listened. She heard only the sounds of the generator and her own slow breaths.

Of course, because nothing else is there.

She breathed in through her nose and winced. There was the scent of the basement, musty and damp, but beneath this was something else. A foul odor of something rotting.

A dead animal. Poor bastard fell down into the basement and couldn't get out.

But the smell seemed to grow stronger, as if whatever it emanated from was moving closer.

She thought she heard the sharp squeak of a wheel as it came to a sudden stop.

"They're just outside the light," Sebastian whispered. He held out a hand, palm up, to Moore. "Give me your hand."

"Why?"

"Just give it to me."

Moore frowned. She could feel her heart beating in her chest. She hoped he didn't notice the sweat on her palm. "Don't get any ideas, old man. Just because I'm down here in the dark with you doesn't mean you're getting any action."

"Oh, honey, on that count you have nothing to worry about," he whispered, making sure Wainwright could not hear.

The camera tilted slightly in Moore's hand, momentarily forgotten, as she realized what Sebastian was implying. "I . . . I didn't know—"

"You've said it yourself, Moore. I'm from another era. And in that era, it was better to keep such personal matters secret. It helped that I was a bit of a prude."

"That's . . ." Moore stopped herself. She had let the word slip out before she knew what she was going to say, an occurrence she rarely allowed.

Sebastian looked to her. "It's what, dear?"

Just say it, she thought. *No need to be clever.*

"Sad," she told him.

Sebastian nodded, considering it. "Yes, in a way, I suppose it is. But I wasn't completely alone. I had one great love."

Moore's voice was uncharacteristically gentle. "Are you two still . . ."

Sebastian shook his head. "He died, almost four years ago. Cancer. He was my editor, in fact. His name was Richard."

Moore heard the sound of a cap being unscrewed. The sharp odor of gasoline stung her nostrils. She looked down.

Wainwright was on all fours, his upper half obscured by the side of the generator. "Good news," he announced. "She's just low on fuel."

He rose to his feet, dusting off his knees as he scanned the area around the machine. The beam of his flashlight fell upon a red five-gallon gas can. He snatched it up and gave it a shake. Liquid sloshed around inside. He quickly removed the cap on the gas can, which, when reversed, became a spout. He tipped the spout into the generator's fuel tank. The gas gurgled loudly as the machine drank it up.

"Are they still there?" Moore asked Sebastian, picking up the game right where they had left off.

Sebastian once again held out his hand. This time, Moore took it without hesitation.

"Yes," Sebastian said. With their hands clasped, Sebastian reached toward the blackness.

Beyond their bubble of illumination, the entire world ended.

"Rachel is reaching for us now." Sebastian's voice was so faint, it was barely audible.

"I can see them now," Moore said. "Rebecca is smiling."

"It's an awful smile. Sinister. She's looking up at her sister and grinning. Her flesh is stretched so tightly, I can see the bone. And those eyes . . ."

Their fingertips reached the edge of the light, and Sebastian paused.

"Do you hear that?" he asked.

Moore listened. She could hear something, like the sound of running water.

"It's the gasoline going into the tank," she suggested. She listened again. The sound was coming from somewhere in that impenetrable abyss. "Is it the creek? Is that possible?"

Sebastian did not respond.

Moore glanced over at him. His face was suddenly slack, his eyes wide and staring.

"Sebastian?" she whispered.

She noticed that his jaw had dropped so that his mouth opened slightly. A glistening star of saliva appeared in the corner of his lips.

"Sebastian."

His eyes were vacant. His hand was heavy and limp in hers. *This isn't part of the game. There's something wrong with him.* "Sebastian," she whispered louder.

The tips of their fingers hovered at the light's end.

"Is that you?" Sebastian asked suddenly.

Moore followed his gaze into the darkness. She saw nothing beyond the light.

Who is he talking to? Moore looked to him again. His eyes were quivering in their sockets.

Because he sees something. He sees something out there!

Suddenly he let go of Moore's hand. His arm dropped to his side. He lurched forward one step, then two. He was walking out of the light, into the darkness.

"Sebastian!"

His face crossed over. He looked like he was dissolving into the shadows.

She grabbed his arm to stop him.

Without warning, the old man gasped loudly and his entire body flinched. He reared back, away from something.

Something in the darkness! Something right there in front of us!

Moore turned the camera's light slightly, and her hand, still gripping his arm, plunged into the dark.

Her fingers touched smooth metal. A handle. She gave it a nudge and felt the object roll slightly.

A wheelchair. You're touching a wheelchair.

A name exploded behind Moore's frantically searching eyes: *Rebecca Finch.*

Something brushed the back of Moore's hand, caressing her. It was cold and spongy, like—

Dead flesh.

A hand clamped down over hers as a roar came out of the blackness.

Moore yelped, the camera's light flashing wildly around the basement's filthy walls as she scrambled away from the sound.

"It's the generator!" Wainwright yelled. The roar had settled into a steady chug. "It's okay. It's just the generator."

A ball of orange light appeared in the abyss, then another, and another. They flickered once, twice, then with a surprisingly loud pop, they brightened to full strength.

Three bare sixty-watt bulbs hung from the ceiling, casting cones of bright light down into the basement.

There was nothing before them. No Rachel Finch reaching for them. No Rebecca Finch grinning madly in her wheelchair. Only an unfinished basement, a bare concrete cube that was much smaller than Moore had imagined.

She turned to Sebastian. His eyes were no longer vacant, but he was staring at the empty room with a look of complete confusion.

"I saw . . ." Then he looked to Moore, and the confusion vanished. He was back. "Moore? What is it? What's the matter?"

She did not know what to say.

Wainwright clicked off his flashlight. It was no longer necessary.

"Let's get back upstairs," he said.

SIXTEEN

10:08 p.m.

THE FIRE HAD nearly died out in the living room. A blackened sliver of wood smoldered in the glowing embers, a trail of smoke snaking its way up the chimney like a dark spirit fleeing to the sky.

Sam dropped another log onto the fire, the impact sending a plume of ash into the air. A single flame leapt up as the dry bark caught. The flame spread, hungrily consuming the fresh wood. Before long the entire log was engulfed. The fireplace roared as the air fed the blaze.

He stepped back, putting distance between himself and the flames. The fire brightened the living room, but it also cast shadows that lurched and quivered in the periphery.

Only shadows, he told himself. *Nothing else.*

He took a deep breath and tried to relax. Kate was upstairs, her camera holstered for the night. Wainwright had gone with her to say good night. Daniel and Moore had also retired to their bedrooms. Daniel had borrowed Sam's phone to try calling his wife and daughter again, while Moore was working on her new book. She let everyone know they would not see her until morning when "this manufactured shit-show is over."

That left Sebastian, now seated opposite Sam on the couch. The old man rested quietly, his eyes fixed on the leaping flames, his drink forgotten on the coffee table. Sam was well aware of how frail the septuagenarian was. But there in the living room, the shadows chiseling away at what little fat still clung to his bones, Sebastian was a living skeleton. He looked brittle, as if the slightest effort could snap him clean in two.

"What are you thinking about?" Sam finally asked.

Sebastian tried to muster up a carefree smile. It was not convincing. "I can't really say. Just off on a journey, I suppose."

Sam stared at the old man, who was watching the flames lap at the shadows.

For a long moment, they sat in silence. Above them, the house creaked. Sam cocked his ear, listening. Waiting. He heard shuffling. Footsteps.

It's one of the others, in their room. That's all.

The footsteps stopped, almost as if they knew they had been heard.

But there was another sound. He had to strain to hear it.

What is that? He tried to place it.

The drawing in of air. A soft exhale. There was a slow, patient rhythm to it. Sam turned and stared into the dark archway that led into the foyer. He could almost feel the air pulling past him, through the foyer, up the stairs, deeper into the house. Then it was pushed back, only for the cycle to repeat again.

Breathing. It's like the house is breathing. But softly. Like it's relaxed. Content.

Content to what? he asked himself.

To be here with us. To listen.

Sam clenched his jaw and shook the thoughts away.

Don't.

But—

Don't! Stop looking for things that aren't there. Stop trying to make every situation worse for yourself!

In the fire, a log popped loudly. Sam flinched. The flames were higher now.

I shouldn't have put on that last log. I should have let the fire die.

The flesh of his left arm felt tighter, like a constrictor around the muscle and bone.

"I like you, Sam," Sebastian said suddenly.

Sam was pulled from his thoughts. He turned to Sebastian, confused by this proclamation.

"I find Daniel pleasant enough," Sebastian continued. "I didn't much care for Moore when I met her, but believe it or not, she's growing on me. Kate is a sweetheart, and Wainwright, well, I don't think he's on any of our top ten lists right now. But you, Sam, I can say that I genuinely like you."

"The feeling's mutual," Sam assured him.

"I've always had a very good memory."

Sebastian was still lost in the fire. He spoke directly into the inferno.

"I can remember things from when I was a small child as clearly as if they happened five minutes ago. I can remember what I wore to my first day of kindergarten. I can remember my father's proud face when I learned to ride a bicycle. I can remember my mother crying when she learned that her father—my grandfather—had died of a heart attack. I can remember Richard's face the day before he learned he was sick, the last perfect day of our lives."

Following Sebastian's gaze, Sam looked into the flames, searching for what the old man saw there. The fire flickered excitedly. The tips of the flames were nearly to the top of the fire box.

Sam smelled the smoke, and his stomach turned.

"Tell me, Sam, what's the most vivid memory you have from life?"

The question was completely unexpected.

"I don't understand . . ."

"Tell me."

An image appeared in Sam's mind, silent yet vivid. He tried to push it away.

"Um . . . I don't know, Sebastian—"

Sebastian shook his head. "No. You thought of something the moment I asked the question. What was it?"

A house on fire. His brother holding him back. Breaking free from Jack's grip. Plunging a hand into the burning rubble. The flames eating his flesh.

A cast-iron skillet, caked with blood. His trembling hand clutching its handle.

He forced these images away and fought for something better.

"Sam?"

"My wedding day," Sam lied. He grasped desperately at this new memory and took hold of it. "I thought of my wedding day. My wife smiling as she came down the aisle. It's cliché, I know. But I can see her perfectly. I can smell the flowers. White roses. Hundreds of them." He was unaware that the memory had made him smile.

"And why do you think that image of your wife on your wedding day remains so fresh in your mind?"

"It was an important day in my life—"

"Beyond that."

"I don't know," Sam said with complete honesty. Then something occurred to him. "Because it was perfect, I guess. A perfect moment. A perfect life."

"And what happened to that perfect life?"

Sam stared deeper into the fire, offering his words to the flames. "I screwed it up. I pushed her away."

"Why?"

"Because I don't deserve her."

"Why?"

"She's too good," he said sharply. He had thought this countless times but never said it aloud. Now here, with Sebastian, he felt safe saying it. "She's a good person, and I'm . . ."

Bad. Because of what I did.

He shook his head. "It doesn't matter why. She's gone."

"And do you remember the moment you realized you had lost her forever?"

There was Erin, her face streaked with tears, standing in the doorway of their home. She was begging him to ask her to stay. And there he was, sitting on the stairs, completely numb, refusing to give her the thing she wanted most, to give her a family, a child. She had put up with his moodiness, had loved him even as he pulled further and further away from her. But this was the final straw. He refused to give her happiness, because he was afraid.

"Yes. I remember."

"Two very different yet equally vivid memories," Sebastian said. "One of happiness. One of pain. Yet they are both important. They are who you are."

"Sebastian, what is this all about?"

Sebastian sighed, crossing his legs and placing his clasped hands on his lap. "I used to worry about many things. I worried that my writing wouldn't be taken seriously. I worried that I wouldn't be able to make a career of it. I worried that my wife would discover that I was a homosexual and, after she did, I worried that the public would discover the same thing."

Sam looked over, but Sebastian did not meet his gaze. Sam had never known this detail about his idol's life. Before Sam could comment, the old man continued:

"And, a few years ago, when my lover, Richard, was diagnosed with cancer, I worried that he wouldn't be able to beat it. He didn't."

"I'm sorry." It was all Sam could offer, and he felt ashamed at the feebleness of the words.

Sebastian picked up the glass of whiskey from the coffee table, but he did not drink. He swirled the amber liquid around and around.

"I feared these things, but in the end, they all made me who I am."

He sucked down a gulp of whiskey and winced at the burn. "Hold on to those memories, Sam. The good and the bad." He regarded the liquor in his glass. "Because someday, much sooner than you think, you may lose them from your life. One by one, they will go. The worse, when it happens, will be the memory of love. Love is warmth. It's like Greek fire; no matter how much others try to dampen it, it only grows more intense. I want to remember love, Sam. I want to remember it forever. Because the thought of losing that, well, there's nothing more terrifying. Not even in this decrepit old house."

The flames flickered as a gust of air was drawn down the chimney.

Sebastian glanced at his watch, then pushed himself up from his chair. "It's almost ten thirty. I'm afraid that's bedtime for this old bag of bones." He carefully shuffled past the fire. As he did, he lightly touched Sam on the shoulder, then continued on his way.

He was almost in the foyer when Sam said, "Good night, Sebastian."

Sebastian paused and smiled. "Good night, Sam."

Sam watched as the old man turned and vanished into the darkness.

Wainwright stood in the kitchen, pouring himself a vodka on the rocks. He sipped as he checked the WrightWire app on his phone. The video was up on the home page for those who hadn't joined them live. He glanced at the viewer tally below the video window and choked on his drink.

Four million. And counting.

"Holy shit," he whispered. "Holy. Shit."

Four million views in under four hours. By tomorrow it would be near ten. This was big. His silly little Halloween event was paying off.

He hadn't really expected it to work. He was sure they would all flake. Or that the house would be uninhabitable. That was the best stroke of luck. For a country house that had been unoccupied for almost twenty years, it was in surprisingly good shape. The cleaning service could take some of the credit, and the Finch sisters had done their fair share of remodeling in the seventies and eighties, but it wasn't all due to their hard work. No, the person who deserved the majority of the accolades was Joshua Goodman, the man who built the place. He obviously knew what he was doing. At first glance, the house was deceptively unassuming. The closer one examined the finer details, though—the hand-carved crown molding in each room, the flecks of color added to the glass of the sunroom windows, the satisfying weight of each door, as if sliced clean from the center of a monstrous tree—it all added up to a house that had stood the test of time.

Wainwright had never built anything like this place.

Sure, he had his career, which continued to climb steadily upward. Despite an increasingly cluttered landscape on the web, he had turned unconventional genre pieces into something of an art form. But it all started with the money his father had given him; Donald Wainwright, publisher of the tabloid trash rags that cluttered supermarket stands from coast to coast. Wainwright's success was never truly his. At the end of the day, he was just a trust fund kid using Daddy's money to meet his famous heroes.

And exploit them.

Yes. That, unfortunately, was part of the formula now. If he hoped to keep WrightWire going, he had to continue to make noise, even if it meant burning a few bridges.

But at quarter to ten, it appeared his Kill Creek adventure had (for the night at least) come to an end. He had to admit, he was a bit let down. Despite his love of horror, he didn't entirely believe in ghosts—although he was hesitant to rule out the supernatural altogether. Still, he had hoped that something big would happen. Levitating furniture, perhaps. Ectoplasm appearing from thin air. Demonic voices ordering them to get out. Whatever Kate saw, that could have been something, but it wasn't *enough*. The Adudel book set the bar high, and yet here Wainwright stood, enjoying a civilized drink in the kitchen while the other guests brushed their teeth and crawled into bed. He came to the house thinking they were entering a gateway to hell, and instead he found himself running a bed-and-breakfast.

Sucking the last of the vodka from his glass, he fished a handful of ice from a bucket in the freezer and poured himself another. He was starting to feel the buzz of alcohol fogging his brain.

He stepped into the narrow hallway that cut down the back side of the house like a spine. The space was alarmingly tight, unlike any other part of the house save the steep stairs leading up to the third floor bedroom. Wainwright was surprised that the Finch sisters had not widened the hallway, if only to make room for Rebecca's wheelchair. She could have gone through the study to get to the kitchen, but it would have been a bit out of her way. If they went to the trouble of installing an elevator for her, why not add two feet to each side of this suffocating hallway?

He wondered if Rebecca was ever envious of her sister's good legs, able to go anywhere in the house she pleased, enjoying the simple pleasures of climbing stairs or taking a shortcut through the back hall.

Wainwright's mind wandered. His feet carried him farther down the hall.

On his phone, he scrolled to the comments section of the Kill Creek video. There were already over a hundred comments. Most were from overzealous fans trying to get the attention of the authors through passionate vows of support. There were words of praise for how raw and intimate the interview had been. But peppered among the positive entries were comments he was beginning to find familiar, a trend that he found troubling.

"Wainwright is full of shit."

"Fucking poser."

"That little bitch Wainwright thinks he's famous."

They're just trolls, he reminded himself. *Pathetic losers who have no lives so they try to tear you down.*

But it's starting to work.

He hated to admit it, but it was true. With each hateful comment, he felt more and more isolated, even as his empire grew.

They're all going to turn on you. You'll be alone.

"No," he said aloud. "I have Kate."

The thought warmed him. He took another drink.

Someone was at the far end of the hall. Through the bottom of his glass, he saw her distorted image.

A woman with black hair.

He quickly lowered the glass.

No one was there.

Pull yourself together, mate. You're letting this place get to you.

Beside him, the candelabra bulb went out like a candle. A second later, the next in the row of mounted wall lights was mysteriously snuffed out.

Wainwright watched as each light went out one by one, darkness engulfing the hallway in two-foot chunks. Soon the entire hall was swallowed by the dark.

"What the hell . . ."

His first thought was that the generator was running low on fuel again. Like a car, it would sputter for a few more minutes before completely kicking the bucket, but it should have had enough juice for the lights to stay half-lit. He peered over his shoulder, toward the kitchen. The lights there still burned brightly.

It couldn't be the generator. That would affect the entire house. So what was it? Bad wiring, maybe. The house was old. But these lights had been on since four in the afternoon. Why hadn't they experienced problems earlier?

From somewhere in the darkness around him, there came a scratching sound, like claws on stone.

Wainwright quickly took a step backward, but the back of his foot collided with something. He lost his balance and tumbled to the floor.

There was a pale light beside him.

My phone.

It was still in his grip. He thrust it forward, shining the light of the phone's touchscreen onto the floor where he had tripped.

There was a woman's black shoe. A long white sock extended up a leg that disappeared into the darkness.

They're standing right over you!

Panic rippled through Wainwright, a million icy pinpricks on his flesh.

He let out a pathetic whimper and desperately heaved himself up. He sprinted through the lightless space. He could see nothing. He was running blind.

The glass of vodka. It was still in his hand. He let it go and heard the glass shatter on the hardwood floor. He sprinted toward the light of the kitchen, and as he reached it, his right knee buckled.

Falling. He was falling toward the light.

Wainwright crashed to the floor, sliding to a stop against the base of the island. He was back in the kitchen, safe beneath the bright recessed lights. His heart thudded wildly in his chest, his lungs filling with desperate breaths.

He sat up and spun himself around on the cool floor. He stared into the hallway.

The lights were on. Every single lamp was illuminated. He could see the archway that opened to the foyer and past that, the doorway to the living room.

On the floor, something sparkled.

It was the tumbler he had dropped, shattered into jagged glass teeth.

Moore stood at the bottom step of the staircase, a half-full whiskey bottle dangling loosely in one hand. She stared up at the third-floor bedroom, or rather the brick wall that blocked it. She assumed the others were asleep; she hadn't heard a peep from them since Sam and Sebastian had come up from the first floor.

She checked her watch. Eleven o'clock, on the dot. She wanted to go to bed, to fall into a deep, dreamless slumber, and wake up in her own bed. But there she was, alone and restless. Moore squinted up at the brick wall. She had known some crazy bitches in her life, but never one who walled off the bedroom of her dead sister.

She set the whiskey bottle on the bottom step and took hold of the rail before very carefully climbing the steep staircase. She reached the top of the stairs and crouched down next to the wall, running a finger over the mortar between the bricks. It was remarkably uneven, the bricks haphazardly thrown on top of each other. It was obviously the work of an amateur.

Did Rachel Finch do this herself?

With the nail of her pinkie finger, Moore scratched at the mortar below the middle brick, expecting the aged material to crumble. It did not.

Screw this. She needed to get some work done. She could sketch out some scenes for her new book in her notebook until either she fell asleep or the sun rose, whichever came first.

Planting her hands on the top step, Moore began to push herself up. One of her fingers slipped between a brick and the wooden step.

She glanced down. There was a tiny hole, just large enough for her slender finger to slip inside.

Twisting her finger slightly, she worked it deeper into the hole until she felt her fingertip break through to open air.

The third-floor bedroom.

She imagined standing in that pitch-black room, staring at the other side of this brick wall. She pictured the tip of her finger protruding from a hole at its base like the head of a pale worm.

The image made her uneasy. What if something were in that room? What if it saw her fingertip and decided to grab hold? What if it would not let go?

Enough, she scolded herself. She was already angry that she had let her imagination get the better of her in the basement; she didn't need to rattle herself further.

Moore went to pull her finger from the hole in the brick, but it would not budge.

It was stuck.

"Oh, come on."

She pulled hard, twisted it back and forth, but the wall would not release her.

On the other side, something scratched against the brick.

Someone's in there! Moore thought, her heartbeat quickening to a gallop.

Stay calm, dummy, her mind commanded. *There's no one there. Just get your finger out.*

She took a deep breath and slowly worked her finger out of the hole. In a matter of seconds, it was free, covered from nail to knuckle in gray mortar dust.

Moore brought her cheek level with the last step and peered into the black hole. Whatever was beyond the wall, it was too dark to see. She leaned in closer, her eye less than an inch from the hole. Her eyelashes fluttered against the mortar.

Something moved in the dark.

"Everything okay?" a voice called up from behind her.

Startled, Moore spun around on the step, her back pressed to the wall.

Daniel was at the bottom of the stairs, his plump body as wide as the staircase was narrow.

"Aren't you a little old for Halloween tricks, Slaughter?" Moore snapped as she hurried down the stairs, her fingers skimming the walls for support.

"Sorry," he said. "I didn't mean to scare you."

"You didn't scare me," she assured him as she reached the bottom step. She snatched up the bottle of whiskey and pushed past him, out of the alcove and into the hall.

Daniel pointed to the top of the staircase. Only half of the last step was visible under the layer of brick. "Why do you think Rachel Finch bricked up the door?"

"Who cares?" Moore snapped.

"To keep someone out? Or maybe . . . to keep someone in?"

Moore was already halfway down the hall. "You tell yourself whatever story you want, Slaughter. Maybe you'll dream up something that scares adults for once."

"Good night," Daniel called out sarcastically.

Without another word, Moore slipped into her bedroom, the door clicking shut behind her.

Daniel gave one last look at the brick wall and then turned back to his bedroom door.

Something squeaked, like the turning of metal wheels.

He glanced down the long hallway and, for the first time, noticed that the elevator car was still parked there on the second floor. The accordion door was open.

The squeak came again, closer this time.

There was nothing before him, nothing that could be responsible for the sound.

Daniel took a step farther into the hall.

The squeak moved closer.

He took another step, his door only a few feet away.

The sound matched his movement, seemingly coming to a stop on the exact opposite side of his bedroom door.

Daniel's heart pounded deep within layers of fat and muscle and bone.

Three fast steps, as quickly as his large body would allow.

Three fast squeaks, the wheels rolling right up to the edge of his bedroom doorway.

Daniel turned the doorknob with his clammy hand and sighed with relief as the latch clicked open. He paused for a moment, leaning in slightly to stare at the empty space in front of him.

There was nothing in his bedroom, nothing in the hallway. Nothing.

And yet that sound, it had stopped *right there*.

Daniel pushed the door open wide and shuffled into the bedroom.

As he closed the door behind him, he thought he could hear the faint, steady squeak of wheels retreating to the far end of the hall.

SEVENTEEN

I:00 a.m.

ALL WAS SILENT. Even the howling autumn wind knew to lower its voice as it gently tossed the naked treetops. The great, pale moon cast a ghostly pallor upon the wisps of cloud skirting below it. Their phantom forms curled from nothingness only to dissipate into the ether moments later.

The nocturnal creatures of the forest went about their early-morning routines. A raccoon trudged beside the ravine that once was Kill Creek with only the faint memory of cleaning its hands in the cool waters of the now-extinct stream. A mother opossum waddled through the woods with her young clinging tightly to her coarse gray pelt. An owl lifted its great wings, catching a gust of air to send it swooping down on an unsuspecting field mouse, its talons snatching the prey with a startled squeal, the darkness swallowing them both in an instant as if neither had ever existed.

Yet none dared cross the boundary formed by Kill Creek. The owl let the breeze carry it safely a quarter mile to the west before settling on a branch to devour its breakfast. The opossum steered its fat body toward a hollowed-out elm tree on the far side of the fifty-acre lot. The raccoon, sensing a shift in the roots beneath its feet, their woody bodies twisting like a bed of snakes, scampered out away from the creek and up a massive oak tree. Casting a glance back at the massive form of the dark house, the animal gave a confused whimper and quickened its pace.

Crickets chirped the last few bars of their nightly song. But Kill Creek circled the house like a moat, and within this keep, this stronghold of silence, nothing stirred. Only the tallgrass made a sound, swaying even when there was no breeze, its dry, husky top bristling like the warning rattle of a viper.

In the house, only the clocks broke the absolute stillness. Their march went unimpeded, hands inching dutifully forward, carrying everything around them onward into the future. It was as if the house were also sleeping, conserving its energy for a greater task, someday down the line.

This was not entirely true, of course. The house dozed, but it had not completely forgotten its crass party of trespassers. And as the hands of the clocks clicked to eight past one, the house awoke to the sudden and definite realization that now was the time.

It had waited long enough.

It was time to play.

The blunt tip of a pencil raced across the yellow page, words spilling out in wild, curving lines.

T.C. Moore held a bottle of whiskey in one hand and the pencil in the other. She sat on the floor, her back against the bed, knees bent, a legal pad propped up on her lap. Her hair was unfurled from its braid. It draped across her lowered face as she hovered over the page.

She was lost in her story, lost in the woman she had named Sid, in the painting that Sid was meticulously uncovering, in starting with that single, staring eye hidden within it. Moore now knew who the eye belonged to: Kubaba, the Sumerian Queen. And yet Sid would soon learn that the painting she had discovered beneath the colored oils of another work of art had been created centuries before Kubaba lived, the creation of a cult that worshipped a woman not yet born.

Not the woman, Moore realized. *A power. An ageless power that would one day transform a tavern owner into one of the most powerful rulers in the world. A power that at that moment was revealing itself to an art history major and newly appointed museum curator named Sid.*

The pencil came to a sudden stop, the graphite tip pressing a tiny indentation into the yellow paper.

It came to Moore, a revelation, as all of the words folded in on themselves like a collapsing black star.

The cult was not to Kubaba at all. It was to Sid. Three thousand years ago they worshipped the being that this modern-day woman would become. The bringer of vengeance. The eradicator of weakness. The rebirth of the power.

Moore lifted the whiskey bottle to her lips and drank. She set the pencil down on the ornate rug upon which she sat and flipped through page after page of prose. Random notes filled the margins. She had managed to write fifteen pages since returning to her bedroom. Her body was still warm with the excitement of creation, but she knew she was done for the night. The puzzle of this novel was nearing completion, the profundity of its image revealed. Yet Moore knew when to press forward and when to let the story alone.

You grow in your sleep, she had once been told. The same was true for a story. She would leave it alone for the night, allowing it to become more fully formed in her psyche. On her flight home, she would attack the novel with a clear head.

After setting the legal pad on top of her bag, Moore pulled her shirt off and then stepped out of her jeans, crossing the room in nothing but her underwear. Her skin was pale in contrast to her black bra and panties, the result of spending way too much time indoors despite living in one of the sunniest cities in the world.

She lifted the whiskey bottle and gave it a swirl. Brown liquid spun at the bottom, enough for one more swig. She swallowed it down.

With the exception of the work she had done in the past hour, Moore suspected this trip would end up being a complete waste of time. What had she been trying to prove? That she could hang with a decrepit old has-been? A mainstream hack? A Christian bullshit artist?

She had nothing to prove to them. What she wrote was unpolished by their standards, but it was pure. It was raw. And this new novel . . . it was something completely unexpected. It was mature and powerful and epic in scope, yet it had all the trademarks of an unforgivingly brutal T.C. Moore story.

It would not be easily dismissed; she was sure of it.

The room began to dance before her eyes.

The whiskey. She had drunk most of the bottle herself.

"Time for bed, girlfriend," she said to herself.

Moore crawled onto the bed, lying flat on her stomach, her arm dangling off the side. The whiskey bottle was loose in her fingers, threatening to fall.

She listened as she drew in slow, steady breaths through her nose. Her eyes began to close.

A floorboard creaked behind her.

"Hello, Theresa . . ."

Moore spun around in time to see the fist coming straight at her face. It collided with her eye and she was thrown back onto the bed, sprawled out stupidly like a tossed rag.

The whiskey bottle crashed to the floor, shattering into a million pieces.

The beast was upon her. The smell of cheap beer on his breath gagged her. The beast's fist smashed down over and over and over, bashing her eye until it began to swell shut.

"You think you're so fucking smart," the man growled. She could see his lips moving, but the words seemed to lag a half second behind them. It was like the sound wasn't actually coming from him, even though she could hear it loud and clear.

"When will you learn to keep your bitch mouth shut?"

The fist came down and her pupil split under its weight. She heard a crack as her orbital bone fractured.

"Please!" Moore shouted. "Stop! STOP!"

A fist slammed into her gut. She folded up, the air forced from her lungs. She wanted to scream—

stop stop stop stop stop stop stop stop stop

—but she had nothing to back the words.

A hand wrapped around her neck. There was no breath to cut off. She had nothing left in her body.

Stop hurting me!

The hand tightened. She heard the tendons in her neck begin to pop like overly tightened guitar strings.

"What do you say to make me stop?" The words were not coming from him, even though his mouth was moving. He was like a ventriloquist's dummy. Someone was speaking through him in a perfect imitation of his voice.

"What do you say?"

A black cloud began to creep into the edges of her vision. She was losing consciousness. She could feel her eyes bulging, desperate to be in this room, in this world.

"Tell me!"

His grip loosened just enough for Moore to suck in a painful breath.

"What do you say to make him stop?"

Him?

"Bitch, do you want to die?" It was no longer his voice. It was something else, deep and bestial. "Say it!"

"I'm nothing!" Moore managed to force the words from her lips.

"Say it again!"

"I'm nothing! I'm a piece of shit! You're everything! I don't deserve you! I'm *nothing!*"

The hands let go of her neck.

She opened her eyes.

He was gone.

She fell back onto the bed. Her hand shot to her eye. No fracture. No swelling.

Leaping up from the bed, Moore rushed over to an ornate oval mirror mounted on the wall. She frantically searched her face for any sign of injury. There was nothing. She was fine. Everything was fine.

She turned her head to the side, studying her reflection.

A woman was standing beside her bed, head cocked, gray eyes staring through flowing black hair.

Moore spun around.

But no one was there.

She scanned the room. It was empty. On the floor, the whiskey bottle lay on its side, still intact.

Her legs began to tremble beneath her. She barely made it to the bed before they gave out.

Moore reached up for a pillow and clutched it to her chest. She began to cry.

She was alone. Completely alone.

Slowly, her tears ceased. Her eyes closed. She drifted off to sleep as if nothing had ever happened.

At the foot of his bed, something stirred.

Sebastian was pulled from a chasm so deep and dark, he felt he would tumble down, down, down forever, his prayers for an end unanswered for all eternity.

He opened his eyes. The shaft of moonlight streaming in through the window lit the room just enough for Sebastian to sense its dimensions, to know that he was no longer trapped in a boundless void.

But someone was there, standing within the shadows beyond the moonlight, a few feet away from the foot of the bed. He could hear the person breathing. Shallow, raspy breaths.

Sebastian sank back into his pillow, staring, waiting for the thing in the shadows to move.

It's not a person, he scolded himself. *It's just a shadow. You're forcing yourself to see something that isn't there.*

He blinked his tired eyes, wetting them in the dry fall air. The shadow person began to take on dimension. Details emerged from the darkness.

A pale face. Smiling. Wide, staring eyes.

A woman.

Sebastian drew in a startled breath. His heart thundered in his chest.

But when he blinked again, the image before him had changed.

The dark shape was now tall, six feet at least. Its outline was of a broad-shouldered man.

Sebastian pushed himself up in bed, the decorative carvings of the headboard digging into his back. He squinted, trying to penetrate the darkness to see who—*Or what*—stood before him.

The dark shape shuffled forward, a lurching step that seemed to take great effort. The ashen glow of moonlight fell upon tan skin, highlighting a pillow of rich brown hair and warm dark eyes.

It took a moment for Sebastian to accept what he was seeing. Something in the back of his brain insisted it could not be. That it was an illusion.

Though there it was, standing before him. If he reached out, he could touch it.

Him, he corrected himself. *Touch* him. *Richard.*

"Sebastian," the man said softly.

It's him. By God, it's his voice.

No, something was off. Sebastian couldn't quite put a finger on it. The man smiled. "It's me. I'm here."

It's his lips. His mouth opened, but his lips barely moved. They didn't form those words. That voice did not come from him.

The man stepped closer. He seemed to radiate moonlight. "It's me, honey. It's really me."

Hot tears began to stream down Sebastian's face. He didn't care how or why this was happening. He didn't care if things weren't exactly right, if this were an illusion or a phantom or a trick of his deteriorating mind. He only wanted this moment, right here in this room, in this house. "Richard?" Sebastian's lips began quiver.

"I want to talk to you," the man said, the words floating from his open mouth. "We can talk all night if you want. I won't go anywhere."

Leaning forward, Sebastian reached out a trembling hand, desperate to span the distance between them.

The man from the shadows reached back.

Sam was dreaming.

He was at a party. Thrown by whom, he couldn't say. The room was packed, and the guests wore festive paper hats of various colors. Some blew into noisemakers as others laughed at the startling sound. Their dress was oddly dated, the men in black ditto suits and top hats, the women in cumbersome gowns draped over crinolines. It must be a holiday, New Year's Eve perhaps, although he could not remember ever attending such a party.

From across the room, he watched Erin laughing uncontrollably as a group of men took turns entertaining her with outrageous stories. They fawned over her, each one more obvious than the last. But Erin's eyes were on him, even as the men began to kiss her, first on the cheek, then on the lips. She did nothing to stop them as they caressed her, their hands aggressively squeezing her breasts, rubbing her erect nipples, fingers worming under her short dress. The men kissed her neck, her legs, her exposed breasts, and still she stared at Sam, laughing harder as the men took liberties without consent.

He cried out, *Erin!*

He wanted her. He needed her. The thought of anyone else having her was unbearable.

He had been wrong to let her leave. It was a mistake. He should have stopped her.

Why didn't I just tell her the truth?

He tried to call out to Erin again, but her name caught in his throat. It burned with a terrible heat. His entire throat was on fire. Dark gray smoke filled his lungs.

He was choking. He was dying. He was burning alive.

He looked down and saw he held an old cast-iron skillet. Dark blood covered the rough, seasoned metal. It dripped from the edge, splatting on the ground.

He blinked and then he was in his house. Erin was crying. The place had been cleared out, not a single piece of furniture, not a single book on a shelf, nothing left to remind him of his old life.

Old life, he thought. *That's what it is now. Gone forever.*

But he was wrong. Erin was telling him that it was okay, that she forgave him. Perhaps this whole, horrible mess was partly her fault. She had neglected him. She had allowed them to drift apart.

Sam shook his head. It didn't happen this way. It was all his doing. He was the one who drank too much, who picked fights, who retreated within himself until she had no choice but to leave. He was the one who refused to give her the family she had always wanted.

She reached out and took his hand.

But it was not her hand.

It was the immolated hand of a woman, flesh burned free to reveal patches of white bone.

It was the hand of his mother.

Sam closed his eyes and began to scream. *No! No! No!*

Smoke filled his open mouth, choking him, consuming him.

Sam woke with a start. The details of his dream were gone immediately.

There had been a sound that woke him, he was sure of it. He lay in bed, perfectly still, trying to listen over the thump of his wild heart.

There it is.

It was faint, but he had not imagined it. He pushed up onto his elbows and turned his ear toward the sound. He strained to hear it.

Scratching. Like something scraping against the back of the wall . . .

A knock on his bedroom door made him jump.

"Christ," he said sharply to himself. He listened. The scratching sound was gone.

Quietly, Sam climbed out of bed, the floor cool on his bare feet as he crossed to the door. He leaned close, his ear inches from the door, and he listened. Someone was on the other side. He could hear the soft pull of air as they breathed.

"Sam?"

The voice startled him.

"Sam, are you awake?"

He quickly yanked the door open. Moore stood in the hallway, wrapped in a heavy patchwork quilt.

"I'm sorry. I don't mean to bother you."

"Is everything okay?" Sam asked.

The edges of the quilt, held tightly around her, were moving slightly.

Her hands are trembling, Sam realized.

"Can I come in?" There was a surprisingly vulnerable quality to her voice.

Sam stepped aside, and Moore hurried into the room. He shut the door behind them and the latch clicked into place.

"Moore, what the hell is going on?"

"I thought someone was in my room," she told him. She was facing away, toward the crumpled sheets of his bed.

"Who?"

She did not respond. "Sorry," she said, moving back toward the door. "It was nothing. I'll see you in the morning."

Sam reached out and touched her shoulder. "Moore. What's wrong?"

Moore paused. She let out a slow breath. "I'm messed up, Sam."

"We're all messed up, Moore."

"No." She shook her head. She was still not facing him. Her long mane of black hair swung back and forth against the quilt. "I mean . . ." She stopped to collect her thoughts. "Has anything ever happened to you that just fucked everything up from that point on? Like your life just took a nosedive and you've never been able to pull up?"

Sam tasted smoke on the back of his tongue.

"Has anything like that ever happened to you?" she asked again.

He nodded. "Yeah."

"What was it?" Without seeing her face, her voice had a strange quality to it, as if it were not coming from in front of Sam but somewhere around him.

"Moore, what's this all about? Did something happen?"

She let out a slow breath, forcing herself to say the words: "I don't want to be alone right now."

Slowly, Sam moved around to face her. She would not meet his eyes. He had never seen her look this way. She looked—

Scared, he realized. *She looks scared.*

"What happened?"

She shook her head. "Nothing happened, okay? I'm sleepwalking, Sam. That's it. I'm walking in my sleep right now so, you know, just forget this ever happened. Can you do that?"

Sam's eyes were playing tricks on him, making it seem like Moore's words did not match her lips. He pressed his eyes shut, trying to rid himself of the fog of sleep.

"I shouldn't have come here, but . . ." Her words trailed away.

Sam reached out and touched the tips of her fingers that held the quilt in place.

"You can talk to me."

She did not respond, but her eyes flashed to his. The fear was back. She curled her fingers around his.

"I don't want to go back to my room" she said, her voice barely a whisper.

"Why?"

"I just . . . Can I stay here?" she asked.

Sam let his hand slip deeper into hers.

"Can I stay here with you?" She slipped up close to him, pulling his hand inside the darkness of the quilt.

His fingers touched flesh. She pressed his hand against her warm body.

"Moore . . ."

He let her guide his hand to the curve of her breast. His fingers brushed her erect nipple, and he heard her give a sharp gasp.

The quilt slipped lower, revealing her bare shoulder. Moore let go with her other hand and let it fall to the floor.

She stood naked before him. Her skin glowed in the moonlight.

Time seemed to stop. Sam was frozen in place, unable to move even if he had wanted to.

But he did not want to move. He wanted to be here, with her.

Her lips brushed against his neck, his flesh alive with every exhaled breath. She was kissing him now, her eager tongue pressing into his mouth. She bit his bottom lip and gave a hard tug.

Time began to move again, faster than before.

She slid his hand over her taut, pale stomach and down between her legs.

Sam blinked, and now they were on the bed, his T-shirt and flannel pajama bottoms in a heap on the floor. Her breasts grazed his erect penis as she pulled off his boxers, and an electric current caused every muscle in his body to contract. He could feel his heartbeat thudding throughout his entire body. Moore straddled him and took him inside her.

They were moving as one, hands grasping each other in a frantic effort to force their bodies even closer together.

The sharp blades of her silver fingernails dug into his back, and Sam felt something warm begin to trickle down his skin. He did not care. She could flay the flesh from his bones and he would still fuck her. He would not stop fucking her for pain or fire or death. He wanted to be in that moment forever.

Sam reached up into the black mane cascading down her back and twisted the hair around his left hand, clenching it in a tight fist. She moaned, burying her face into the crook of his arm, her mouth finding his scars, her tongue tracing the ridges of his hardened flesh.

He thought of her sinking her teeth into his scars, of her ripping the tattooed skin from his muscles and spitting each bloody mouthful into the dark.

He was deep inside her, deeper than he thought possible.

Sam blinked.

Moore was staring straight at him. The pupil of her right eye was a black starless universe before him. It was beautiful. He was falling into the void. There was nowhere else he wanted to be.

Her lips did not move, but he heard her voice, or something close to her voice. It was alien and strange. Layers upon layers of words.

"Tell me," she said.

Her hair fell over the side of her shaved scalp like a waterfall at night. The end of each strand was a tendril, grasping to take hold.

"Tell me what happened to you."

The hair slipped around Sam's neck and tightened. He could feel it constricting like a snake just below his Adam's apple. It pulled him closer, his lips finding the dark chasm of her ear.

"Tell me everything."

And Sam began to speak.

When he opened his eyes, he was alone.

Sam sat up in bed, confused. It was still the middle of the night, and he was dressed in his T-shirt and pajama bottoms. He slipped a hand beneath the back of his shirt. No marks. No blood.

"Holy shit." He exhaled the words in a shuddering breath.

It had been a dream. It *had* to have been a dream.

His body gave a sudden shake in the cold night air. Without thinking, Sam pulled the comforter from the bed and wrapped it around him like a cocoon. For what seemed like forever, he sat in bed and concentrated only on the whisper of his own breathing.

As his senses became more focused, he began to hear the sound of a voice. It was muffled—in fact, at first he could only make out the reverb of its low bass tone—but it was unmistakably the sound of someone speaking.

Holding the comforter around his waist, Sam shuffled across the room, following the voice to the north wall, which separated his bedroom from Sebastian's. He pressed his ear to it, the wallpaper rough against his cheek.

It was Sebastian's voice, soft and steady. Sam's first thought was that Sebastian was talking in his sleep, but the rhythm of his speech was conversational, clusters of words broken up by irregular yet deliberate pauses. Many of his sentences ended on the upswing. Questions. He was asking questions. But to whom?

Maybe he was talking on his cell phone. No, wrong again; none of them had gotten reception since midafternoon. A landline, then. Perhaps he had a phone in his room and was using the house's hard line to call home. That wasn't right either. The house had been vacant for years. The phones couldn't still be in service.

Sam cupped a hand over his exposed ear, pressing the other harder into the wall. It was no use. He could not make out what Sebastian was saying. He held that position for quite some time, oblivious to the passing minutes.

Eventually he gave up, crawling back into bed with the intention of asking Sebastian about it in the morning.

Sleep evaded him. He lay there, staring up at the chipped ceiling, tracing the cracks like an explorer riding a river, following each tributary to its inevitable end.

He could still hear the murmur of Sebastian's voice as he finally drifted off.

This time, he did not dream.

EIGHTEEN

9:15 a.m.

THEIR BAGS WERE packed and set in a neat row by the door. Sunshine streamed in through the windows flanking the front entrance. Dust motes swirled in the light.

Sam had awoken at precisely eight o'clock. He didn't have any concrete memories from his night in the bedroom and assumed he slept soundly for the most part. Yet he went about his morning ritual in a haze, brushing his teeth, combing his hair, slipping into clean clothes wrinkled from his duffel bag. He moved a bit slower than usual, his body weighed down by some unknown burden.

Bad dreams, he told himself. *Nothing more.*

Sam met the others in the living room.

One by one, Wainwright pulled them aside for one last interview. This was their chance to plug their latest projects. This was their true reason for agreeing to spend the night at Kill Creek. Their business. But their hearts were no longer in it.

And then it was done. The cameras went back into Kate's case. The computers were already loaded in the back of the VW bus.

It's over, Sam realized.

In the foyer, the four writers stood quietly while Kate shot video from a few yards away. Sam glanced over at Moore, her eyes shielded behind sunglasses. His brow furrowed as his mind attempted to retrieve a fuzzy image.

Moore, wrapped in a quilt.

But then it was gone. All he could remember was the sensation of thin tendrils tightening around his neck.

Wainwright was the last to join them after making sure nothing of value was left behind on the second floor.

"Well," he said as he descended the stairs, "it looks like we're ready to go."

"Just like that?" Daniel asked. There was a hint of sadness in his voice, as if he were going to miss the place.

"Just like that," Wainwright replied.

Sam snatched up his bag. Wainwright threw his own bag over his shoulder and lifted Kate's two cases, one in each hand. He gave Kate a little nod to let her know that he had everything under control.

"I would say that it was a pleasure," Moore told Wainwright. "But, frankly, this was a complete waste of my goddamn time."

"Once the buzz on all of your upcoming projects quadruples, we'll see if any of you still regret it."

Moore grumbled something under her breath but seemed content with this prediction.

Sam took the doorknob in his hand and gave it a twist. The latch clicked. The door swung open. "One of the world's most haunted places. Kind of underwhelming, don't you think?" He held the door while the others filed out.

"How many times do I have to say it?" Moore said. "It's all a crock of shit."

Daniel exited in silence. The wooden planks squeaked softly as he crossed the porch and moved carefully down the front steps. Reaching the gravel drive, he glanced back over his shoulder.

"What is it?" Sam asked.

"The windows," Daniel replied.

Sam looked up to the third floor. A memory flashed through his mind of a light burning brightly there. But that was impossible. The windowpanes were completely covered by wooden planks.

Daniel frowned. "I swear there weren't boards on them yesterday. But there must have been. They're there, on the inside."

On the inside, Sam thought. *To keep something from getting out.*

Sebastian stepped through the open front doorway of the house and onto the porch. "It's really a shame that interest in this house is waning," he said. He grasped the railing as he descended from the porch, carefully taking each step one by one.

"Someone should buy it," Daniel said. "Bring some happiness back to the place."

Then he turned away from the house and trudged farther down the drive.

Sam stood in the front doorway and waited for Wainwright to follow. He did not. He was a few feet away, his back to Sam, his eyes fixed on the top of the stairs.

"Wainwright?" Sam called out.

"I thought . . ." Wainwright's voice trailed off, replaced by the startling sound of the elevator descending. The chain clanked within the walls as if it were drawn over an ancient pulley. There was an audible jolt as the elevator arrived on the first floor.

Outside, the others had stopped in the front yard and were staring back through the open doorway. "What is it now? One more scare before we go?" Moore called out, her sarcasm ringing loud and clear.

Wainwright motioned to the elevator. "What in the hell caused that?"

Now it was Sam's turn to give an ignorant shrug.

Setting the cases and duffel bag down on the floor, Wainwright started toward the elevator.

"Wait," Kate said suddenly. There was a quaver in her voice. "Don't."

Wainwright ignored her. He stepped up to the elevator and, with a metallic clatter, folded the accordion door open. He stared into the car at whatever had ridden it down.

"What is it?" Sam asked. He was shocked to find himself struggling for breath.

Taking two steps forward, Wainwright disappeared into the elevator. Kate whimpered helplessly as he did.

Sam thought, *He's not coming out. We'll never see him again. He's crossed over into another place, a dark place, a world that devours you whole.*

He was wrong, of course. Wainwright popped back out, a confused grin on his face. "There's nothing here. Must have been some sort
of malfunction."

"Sam, is everything all right?" It was Sebastian, his hand on the
rail, one foot on the porch steps.

A ripple of relieved laughter worked its way through Sam, Kate,
and Wainwright. "Come on," Sam said, pointing through the front
doorway. "Let's get out of here before we give ourselves heart attacks."

Kate did not hesitate. She hurried out the door, smiling apologetically at Sam as she passed.

Wainwright was right behind her. "This place really screws with
your head, yeah?"

Sam stepped out onto the porch and began to pull the front door
shut. He could not quite explain it, but he expected the door to give
him some resistance, to pull back in an effort to keep the entryway
open. Instead, the extra force he exerted caused the door to close with
a slam.

Wainwright jumped. "Jesus!" he shouted.

"Sorry," Sam said. Out of habit, he tested the knob. It was locked.
He didn't remember locking the door from the inside, but what did it
matter? Better to have the house shut tight than to let any Halloween
stragglers wander in to desecrate the place.

The floorboards creaked as Sam marched across the porch and
down the steps. The others were ahead of him, Moore and Daniel leading the way. Kate and Wainwright were quickly overtaking Sebastian,
whose lackadaisical stroll was more an effect of old age than an unwill-
ingness to rush. It did not take long for Sam to catch up with him.

"Sebastian?"

"Yes, Sam?"

"I've been meaning to ask you." He mentally fumbled for the
right words. The question he had was a strange one, but he felt compelled to ask it. "Last night, I thought I heard you talking. In your
room."

"At what time?"

"Little after one, I think."

The corners of Sebastian's mouth curved into a frown as he tried
to recall the incident. "I don't believe I was, Sam. I slept through the
night."

"But I heard your voice. It sounded like you were speaking to someone. Asking questions."

Sebastian shook his head. "Unless I was having a conversation in my sleep, I'm afraid your mind was playing tricks on you."

Sam fell silent. Maybe the old man was right.

"Oh glorious, the cavalry is here," Sebastian said as they neared the edge of the yard.

A police cruiser was parked up ahead. Sam watched as two officers—a large bear of a man and a skinny guy whose uniform appeared to be in the process of swallowing him—spoke quietly to one another. Their faces were dour, the skinny officer looking like he wanted nothing more than to hop in the cruiser and speed off, leaving the house behind.

Daniel and Moore were the first to reach them. Moore muttered something to the large officer, probably something unnecessarily sarcastic, but the officer completely ignored her, instead taking Daniel by the arm and leading him away from the group. Moore and the other officer, whose badge Sam could see read, "Deputy D. Ready," began to get into it, with Moore asking pointed questions and Deputy Ready politely suggesting she "settle it down."

Sam and Sebastian came up behind Wainwright and Kate, who had also joined in badgering Deputy Ready.

"What's going on?" Sam asked.

"That's what I want to know," Moore said.

"Just everybody relax," Ready ordered them with a Texas twang. "My partner needs to talk to Mr. Slaughter alone for a sec."

Instinctively, Kate raised her camera. "What are they talking about?" she asked from behind the lens.

Ready swallowed hard, obviously uncomfortable with the situation. "I'm afraid I can't tell you that, ma'am. It's a personal matter."

The large officer, a man in his late forties whose badge announced him as "Deputy B. Montgomery," had a hand on Daniel's arm. Not around it to keep him from fleeing. Under it to offer support should his legs give out.

The questions from Moore and Wainwright were flying fast and furious, Wainwright taking a cue from Kate and refusing to let a new development in the story slip through his fingers.

"Something is wrong," Sebastian whispered to Sam.

He was right. Deputy Montgomery's demeanor had not changed, but Daniel's face was scrunching up into an ugly puggish expression. His lower lip began to quiver. As Sam watched, Daniel crumpled to the ground. A flood of tears suddenly poured down his cheeks. Deputy Montgomery tried to keep him on his feet, but the overweight man was too much for him. He finally resorted to crouching down on one knee as Daniel's bulk shook with uncontrollable sobs.

Wainwright and Moore halted their interrogation and the group stood in stunned silence. They knew they were witnessing a sacred moment, the unhinged misery of another human being. Even Moore seemed uncomfortable in the presence of such soul-wrenching pain.

"Tell us what happened," Sam told Deputy Ready.

Ready opened his mouth to give them the same old official "no can do," then thought better of it. He shed the cop façade with little effort, becoming, in an instant, a polite country boy, eager to please.

"His daughter was killed this morning," Ready said, his words cracking like ancient yellowed paper.

The revelation hit them like a punch to the chest, the impact stopping their hearts for a full beat.

"How?" Kate asked with a terrible, squeaky voice.

"Car accident. Girl was on her way home from an overnight Halloween party when another car lost control and swerved into her lane. Slammed right into the side of her car. Least that's what we think happened. Impact killed her instantly."

And there it was, sickeningly definitive. There was nothing more to say.

Daniel was wailing, the horrible noise emanating from deep within his throat. It was the sound of a tortured animal, one that knew there was no escaping the terror that awaited it.

It's the worst sound I've ever heard, Sam thought. He fought the urge to clamp his hands over his ears.

Moore took a step toward Daniel, her arms opening wide, and then she froze, suddenly unsure of what she was preparing to offer him. She lowered her arms and glanced to the ground in something that looked awfully close to shame.

Sebastian caught Sam's eye. The old man's face flinched with a collision of emotions. His stare was helpless, regretting that he had to exist in this moment.

Sam felt the sting of tears in his eyes, and he had to look away. He turned to face the house, biting his lower lip in an effort to keep the emotion at bay. There it was, the house on Kill Creek, the Finch House, the old, grizzled monster that stalked the dreams of children, that danced on the tongues of morbid storytellers. It disgusted him, the sight of this tall tale, this fraud, this fake. They had spent the night in the belly of that bitch and nothing they encountered could compare to the horror they were witnessing at that moment.

His heartbeat began to pulse in his ears as his temper flared. He wanted to destroy the house, burn it down. He wanted it to experience the anguish that Daniel was feeling. Because the death of Daniel's daughter was no ghost story. It was no campfire tale. It was real. And they could not just flick on the lights and be safe again.

The first tear spilled over and the rest could not be contained. In the shadow of the Finch House, Sam covered his face and wept, not sure why he was so consumed with a sense of sheer helplessness.

He would know soon enough. For in the months to come, Sam would realize that he had been wrong about two things.

It was a ghost story. All of it.

And he should have torn the bitch apart board by board when he had the chance.

PART THREE

A THINLY CAST SHADOW

Spring

Even now, as I sit hundreds of miles from that lonely patch of forgotten America, I can sense the house calling out to me. It is in my darkest dreams, its emptiness swallowing me, its secrets enticing me with a knowledge no mortal man was meant to comprehend. I cannot forget the house. Because the house has not forgotten me.

—*Dr. Malcolm Adudel*
Phantoms of the Prairie

NINETEEN

THE PRINTER GAVE an irritated beep. Out of paper. Again.

Without looking, Sam reached over and snatched a new ream from a teetering stack. He ripped open the paper wrapping like a lion tearing into its prey. He took out an inch and shoved it into the printer's paper tray. The action was more than second nature now. It was programmed in him, an occurrence so common, he was barely aware of doing it.

There was a moment of hesitation as the printer calibrated. And then the pages began to roll out once more, one upon the other until the inch of blank white space became a thick wedge of words.

Only briefly did Sam's fingers leave the computer keys. He was enveloped by a fever, his skin flushed, his face hot to the touch. He could sense the dank odor of sweat wafting up from inside his shirt. He had not showered in days. Hadn't even changed his clothes. Not that he cared. All that mattered was the book, finishing the book, pounding out the last, perfect words and relishing in the moment when the final page could join the others. So many others. Piles and piles. They dotted the room like tiny paper buildings, carelessly constructed, easily toppled.

It had begun six months ago with a single moment of inspiration. Sam was back in the lecture hall, the seats filled with students anxious to hear about their professor's night at Kill Creek. Most had viewed the original interview on WrightWire and the subsequent videos Wainwright had posted in the following days. The students had also read about the death of Daniel Slaughter's teenage daughter, which now seemed like an ominous punch line, as if the spirits of Kill Creek were getting the last laugh.

The students asked a few questions, but Sam shot them down. He did not want to talk about Kill Creek. When he closed his eyes, he could still see the unbearable pain twisting Daniel's face into something unrecognizable. Sam made it very clear that the class would follow the syllabus, not discuss something they could easily watch online.

He was in the middle of a lecture on the role of Satan in horror—from the Salem witch trials to the Satanic Panic of the 1980s—when, without warning, a simple, pristine sentence slammed into Sam's head:

"The house called to him, and he answered."

He tried to ignore it, but the line would not go away.

Sam returned to his lectern and jotted down the words in a small spiral notebook before returning to his lecture. But then another sentence formed from the ether, and another, and another. Each time, Sam raced to his lectern to scribble down the words until, finally, they started to come to him so rapidly that he abandoned his lecture altogether. Sam dismissed the class with a wave of his hand; he did not want to interrupt the flow of thoughts and images flooding from the tip of his pen.

He went straight home that day, tapped the space bar to wake his computer, and dove headlong into this new tale. When he looked up from the wall of words on the screen, it was past midnight; he had been writing for ten hours. He had not bothered to turn on a single light. Only the glow of the monitor illuminated his face.

The next day, the words came twice as fast. Every now and then, without warning, Sam would leap up from his chair and pace the room just to release the energy building up in his body, the excitement that his fingers could not type quickly enough to expunge. His bout with writer's block was officially over. He had broken through whatever had kept the words from flowing, and now they washed over him in a great deluge.

The day after that, Sam canceled his afternoon class and continued pounding away on the keyboard. The house around him seemed
to disappear, the walls and ceiling slowly evaporating until he sat at the
center of infinite darkness.

Days vanished, then weeks. When he happened to glance out of
the front window of his home, he was shocked to find a heavy blanket
of snow covering the front yard. By then it was December, and Sam
had written over four hundred pages.

Sometime in the middle of that month, his cell phone rang. He
had begun ignoring it after one particularly awkward call in which the
dean of the School of Liberal Arts and Sciences informed him that
the school was handing his class over to an associate professor in the
film department. Sam said he understood and hung up on the dean
mid-sentence. This time, though, the name on the caller ID made him
push away from the computer and snatch up his phone.

It was Erin. She spoke softly and slowly, as one might speak to an
animal they fear they may startle.

"Sam? I've been calling for days. Are you okay?"

They met at the Bourgeois Pig, a coffee shop on Ninth Street. A
light snow had begun to fall when Sam arrived. Erin was sitting at a
table by the front window. She had always been beautiful, yet something about her now seemed even more breathtaking. Her hair was
longer, for one. The stylishly choppy pixie cut of the old Erin—*his*
Erin—had grown out to an inch or two below her ears, the ends curling up to caress the curve of her jaw. She wore a fitted green turtleneck
sweater that he'd never seen before. New hair. New clothes. New Erin.

When she hugged him, though, everything fell back into place.
His hand found the curve of her back, her chin slid perfectly onto the
edge of his shoulder. They were one again, if only for a moment.

They sat in silence, neither sure what to say to the other. It was
Erin who finally spoke.

She wanted to talk. She had been thinking about many things
lately, about why she left, about how over the course of their marriage,
Sam had pulled further and further away, about the love she knew she
still had for him and her inability to shed it no matter how hard she
tried. She wanted a family, she wanted kids, but for whatever reason,
Sam did not feel the same. She said she felt betrayed that he hadn't told

her this earlier in their relationship. She'd been honest with him before they got married about what she expected from life.

"It's like you think you don't deserve to be happy," she told him bluntly.

She's here to reconcile, Sam realized. *She wants to put it all out on the table to see if there's any shred of hope of saving what we once had.*

But the more Erin spoke, the more Sam found his mind drifting back to his book, to the characters he had left at home, saved on the hard drive of his computer. He tried to listen to Erin, but the voices of his characters crowded into his brain. They were screaming at each other, a frenzied moment in his story, as they tried to make sense of the horror that was overtaking their lives.

"Are you even listening to me?" Erin's voice broke through the cacophony.

Sam nodded vigorously. "Yes, yes, I'm sorry. It's just . . . I've been writing something new. I think it's the best thing I've ever written."

He tumbled into a rambling explanation of the plot, leaping randomly from character to character, from beat to beat, spinning a haphazard web of half-thoughts. Erin watched him, her eyelids glistening with a rim of tears, as he became lost in the rhythm of his own voice. He was no longer speaking to her; he was reliving the now six-hundred-plus pages he had written since the first week of November. New ideas spiraled from his lips. He paused to ask a passing waitress for a pen, then snatched up a napkin and hunkered over it, scribbling down notes. When he had filled both sides of the napkin, he looked up for something else to write on.

Erin was gone.

Outside, the snow was falling harder.

By the middle of January, Sam decided he needed a break. He had written almost a thousand pages. It was too long, he knew. The story was threatening to spin out of control. He needed to read through what he had written and make sure it wasn't incomprehensible madness. So he printed out the first three hundred pages, flicked the wall switch to ignite the gas fireplace in his living room, and settled into a worn leather chair with a red pen.

Flames sprang up between deliberately placed ceramic logs.

He was somewhere around page thirty when Sam became aware of a log crackling.

He looked up from his manuscript and found the flames devouring wood—actual wood—as they danced within a large stone fireplace.
Intricate carvings of vines and leaves adorned the fireplace mantel. To
his right, an archway opened to a dark, narrow hall. To his left, the last
of the evening's purple light drifted in through a large picture window,
through which Sam could see the rickety railing of the porch and the
twisted body of a beech tree.

The hanging tree.

The pages fell from his hand and fluttered to the floor.

He was back in the house on Kill Creek.

The fire roared, the intense light casting harsh shadows against
the living room walls. Smoke was drifting not up the chimney but out
into the room. Sam gasped, and that harsh black smoke bit into the
back of his throat. He coughed, trying to force the smoke out, but it
was all around him, burning his lungs, stinging his eyes. Through the
haze of smoke and tears, Sam saw something twist in the fire's belly.

It was not a log.

It was an arm. The charred skin was peeling back to expose
bloody red muscle beneath. At one end, incinerated fingers curled into
a terrible black claw. White bone poked through the fingertips. The
embers beneath the arm shifted, the obscene thing tilting forward. And
then the hand opened, fingers stretching through the flames to touch
Sam, to burn him like it had been burned.

"Sammy?" a woman's voice called from the darkness behind the
crackling fire.

Sam had fallen to the floor, pushing himself desperately away
from the stone fireplace. The house was dark now, the only light coming from the fire and a pale glowing object at the far end of the room.

His laptop.

The cursor blinked steadily at the end of the last sentence.

Something inside him told Sam that returning to his story was
the answer.

"Sammy . . ." the voice called.

In the fire, the arm shifted again, revealing the curve of an elbow.
It was not a severed arm. It was connected to something deeper within
the fireplace.

A face hid in the darkness beyond the fire. Sam could see the light
of the flames reflected in the glistening surface of its boiling eyes.

Sam leapt up and raced toward the computer. As he reached it, he spun around.

He was in his own living room again. The low flames of the gas fire burned steadily above fake logs.

The edge of his little finger touched one of the computer keys. The story he had been writing for the past three months rushed back to him, and with it an overwhelming sense of calm.

A day later, he tried once more to stop. Again, his home began to transform around him. Again, the burned thing called his name.

He drank, but alcohol would not keep his mind from drifting back to that old house in the countryside. He doubled his antidepressants, then tripled them, and still the voice called from behind a wall of flames:

"Sammy. Sammy . . ."

There was only one way to keep his madness from overtaking him.

As long as he was writing, he was safe.

That had been January.

It was now April, and the story was not yet complete.

The sound of fingers on keys rattled like machine-gun fire, sentences racing unimpeded across the glowing computer screen. The scene he was crafting was the most important of all. The climax. It was the reason for his obsession with this story. The instant when his characters would open the door and discover the secret that had been waiting for them for ages, readying itself to be unleashed upon the world once again.

Rarely did a story flow without a moment of hesitation. It was as if every single word was already written in his mind; all he had to do was get the words out:

> *The hammer was a nice one from Buckwood's Hardware Store at the corner of Walnut and Sixth, just south of the Lutheran church where Pastor Charles had led a sermon about the evils of adultery a mere forty-five minutes before. Pastor Charles had tobacco-stained teeth and pit stains on his striped short-sleeved shirts. He had cancer in his lungs and heaven on his mind, and as he prepared*

for the late service at quarter past eleven, he had no idea that a hammer had been purchased from the hardware store around the corner, a hammer that was now pounding into the unshaven cheek of Roscoe Trout.

Ol' Roscoe fought at first, the way simple men did. He balled up an arthritic fist and tried to take a whack at Tommy's kisser. But with each blow of the hammer, Roscoe became less and less interested in landing a punch. He just wanted what teeth hadn't rotted out from years of neglect to stay put in his head.

Tommy couldn't make any promises. He was having way too much fun swinging that twenty-ounce rip claw into the side of the old drunk's face. It made a real pretty window through which he could see the side of the man's exposed jaw and those nasty purple sinkholes where teeth had once been.

It was nothing against Roscoe. Sure, he was a loudmouth who sucked down moonshine like a yellow-bellied watersnake sucks down pond frogs, but most people in town found him harmless enough.

Yeah, Tommy would have left him well enough alone if Roscoe hadn't taken it upon himself to stand in front of the wall.

It was the wall Tommy wanted. It was the reason he bought the hammer in the first place.

There were a lot of people to blame for the messy deed in which Tommy now found himself engaged. There was the man who built the house in the first place. There were the people who owned it after that man died and chose to seal off the door with a nice stack of burnt clay bricks. And, perhaps most of all, there was the little girl with the jet-black hair who thought she could throw Tommy off the scent. But Tommy was a coonhound. Tommy never lost a scent once he took hold.

Pretty soon the hammer drove itself all the way through Roscoe's head and hit brick. The sound made Tommy's heart leap like fireflies shaken from the mouth of an open jar. Roscoe's lifeless body slid down to the hardwood floor, and spatters of blood swept across the far wall as Tommy arced the tool up over his head and down again.

The flat nose of the hammer collided with the wall, and the first brick broke free.

Without warning, the flow of words ran dry.

Sam stopped with a lurch, his joints locking, his knuckles curling his hands into grotesque claws.

"Shit," he said aloud. *What happened? Where did it go?*

Reading back through what he'd just written, he tried to rediscover the path that would lead him to THE END. It was no use. His mind was a dense thicket of thorny vines. There was no moving on. He would have to find another route, or else . . .

Or else what? Quitting was not an option. He would crack it. He *had* to crack it. This was his masterpiece. Everything was riding on it. He had to finish.

Sam shuffled like a zombie into the kitchen, oblivious to the mounds of detritus littering the floor, his eyes looking only inward, searching in vain for that nonexistent train of thought. He grabbed a beer from a barren shelf in the fridge and twisted off the cap. The cold liquid soothed his scratchy throat, and Sam suddenly realized how intensely thirsty he was.

When was the last time I stopped for a drink? Or food, for that matter?

On the kitchen counter, his cell phone buzzed. Another missed call. He punched in his password and saw the number hovering over the Phone app. Forty-two missed calls. Impossible. He couldn't recall the phone ever ringing. Yet it must have. He couldn't remember the last time he checked his voicemail.

He opened the app, tapped Speaker, and pressed Play. The most recent message began:

There was nothing, only the crackle of an open line. Then, from the audible wasteland, the voice of a woman spoke, clearly and loudly, "Sammy?"

Sam froze.

"Sammy, I know you're there."

It was his mother's voice. Her words were slightly slurred. The alcohol was a lubricant for her hate and resentment.

"I can see you, you little shit."

Sam pressed Pause, but the message continued to play:

"I can see you standing in the kitchen, like the dumb little puppy you are!" He pounded his fingers against the phone's touchscreen. There was no response. The phone was frozen, yet the message would not stop.

"You look at me when I'm talking to you!"

His head jerked up. She was no longer just a voice through the speaker on his phone. She was right there in front of him. He knew it.

He glanced frantically around the empty kitchen.

"You're pathetic. How could I make such a worthless thing as you? I should have drowned you and your no-good brother in the pond when you were babies. Put you in a sack like stupid mewing kittens and *sunk you to the bottom.*"

A horrible moan escaped Sam's lips, full of the fear and despair he had felt every day as a child in that little house in the country, outside that blink-and-you'll-miss-it Kansas town. He reached blindly for an object—any object—and his hand found a metal handle. He gripped it and swung the object down with all his strength onto the phone. Plastic and glass shrapnel went flying as the phone shattered. He brought the object down again and again until the phone was a mess of scattered parts. He stepped back, chest heaving, trying to catch his breath. He glanced at the object in his hand, realizing for the first time that he held the handle of a cast-iron skillet. Just like the one in his mother's kitchen. He flinched, his fingers slipping from the handle, the skillet clanking to the kitchen floor and coming to rest beside the crown molding that ran along the base of the wall, that beautiful molding with hand-carved details of leaves and vines.

No. That wasn't in his house. That was in the house on Kill Creek. That couldn't be here.

You're not here. *You're back there. You're in that house because you NEVER LEFT!*

He closed his eyes tight.

Above him, from deeper in the house, came the sound of whispers, of voices collapsing over each other like the churning tide in a pitch-black sea.

"What do you want?" Sam yelled to the house.

He knew what it wanted.

A key turned in Sam's mind, the click of a lock releasing a flood of irrational terror. He had to keep writing, or the thing would come for him. Every time he stopped, it came closer.

Sam opened his eyes. The skillet was gone. His cell phone was on the counter, in perfect condition.

The voice croaked out of the phone's tiny speakers: "I'm sorry, Sammy. Give me a hug, Sammy. Hug your mama. Please. Turn around so I can see your face."

Sam did not turn around. He raced into the living room and threw himself down into the chair at the desk. He placed his fingers properly on the center row of the laptop's keyboard.

"Come on," he ordered under his breath. "Write."

He typed a few words, nothing special, a sentence he had no intention of finishing. The wave of inspiration he had ridden up to this point had broken. He was now simply a kid splashing in puddles. But he had to keep writing. Because that was what kept the thing away.

As he had hoped, quiet settled through the house; the phantom noise, for the moment, silenced.

Sam sighed, trembling. His next thought terrified him:

You're losing your mind.

"No," he said aloud. "No. No, no, no."

Sam's head throbbed. He buried his face in his hands, his elbows planted on the keyboard, sending a constant stream of gibberish across the computer screen.

"What's wrong with me?" he asked, his voice quavering. It was a voice he hadn't heard in weeks. It was his voice, pure and sane. The threat of tears caught him by surprise. "What the hell's happening?"

A new sound jolted Sam to his feet.

Pounding.

This is it, he thought. *It's finally come to take me. It's going to end this right now.*

After a couple minutes, reason came to him.

Someone was knocking on the front door.

Sam peered through the curtains at the man on the porch. From that angle, he could not see the man's face, but something about him seemed frustratingly familiar. The way he stood with his hands in his pockets, his shoulders slumped; the pristinely laundered suit; the way he rolled up on the tips of his toes as if trying to add inches to his short frame.

Without warning, the man cocked his head to the side and his face came into plain view.

"Eli?"

The agent yelped, startled, as Sam threw open the door.

"Hey, Sam."

Eli smiled, embarrassed, as if to say, *I need to stop flying all the way to Kansas just to talk to you*. Then, as he took in Sam's appearance, Eli's lips turned down, and his eyebrows followed. Eli's eyes drew over a rough, patchy beard. The rumpled and stained clothes. The greasy, unwashed hair. The bloodshot eyes that begged for sleep yet never closed.

"Sam, what's going on?"

Don't tell him anything, he warned himself.

"Nothing," he said to Eli.

"Bullshit. You look . . ."

"I look *what?*"

"You look horrible," he said bluntly.

Sam faked incredulity. "Eli, cut me some slack. I've been writing nonstop for days. I'm trying to finish a book. You should be happy."

"Yeah. The book. Actually, that's what I wanted to talk to you about." He tapped his toe as if he really didn't have time for the house call. "Can I come in?"

"Sure." Sam pushed the front door open wider, stepping aside to let him by.

No, what are you doing? Don't let him in!

The moment Eli was inside, Sam knew it was a mistake. His brow furrowed further. His eyes scanned the room with a horrible mixture of shock and disgust. Sam had been so consumed with his novel that he hadn't bothered to take a really good look at the place. Now, through Eli's eyes, he saw it.

Drinking glasses, half-full of unidentifiable liquid, sat perched on end tables, on bookshelves, on the stairs. Dirty plates crusted with food were placed on the floor as if to be cleaned by a dog he did not own. Discarded clothes were draped over the banister, over lampshades, in dank, mildewing piles, a mass grave of unwashed laundry. There was an identifiable trail, clear of debris, leading from the kitchen to the computer desk, then around in a lazy arc to the staircase. Instinctively, Sam began to snatch up the rubbish, knowing he was only making the situation worse.

"What in the hell is going on here, Sam?" Eli's tone was cold, the accusation unmistakable: *What is wrong with you?*

"I told you, I've been writing."

"Looks like that's all you've been doing. Have you even showered lately?"

Sam's skin prickled as a furious anger gripped him. "Eli, what the hell do you want?"

Eli took a half step back. He offered up an apologetic smile, sensing that he was pushing Sam close to the edge. "Let's have a beer," he said.

Sam did not respond.

"Come on." Eli nodded toward the kitchen doorway. "Go grab a couple beers, something local and undrinkable. Let's you and me sit outside and talk."

The spring air was cool with just a hint of the humidity that would weigh down the summer to come. A gentle breeze from the north brought with it the earthy scent of the Kansas River half a mile away.

Sam sipped his beer in silence, trying to keep his attention on the vagueness of the quiet street he lived on.

Eli turned his beer bottle around in his hands. He had yet to take a drink. "You don't return my calls. You don't respond to my emails or texts. Sam, I'm worried about you."

"Don't be," Sam said, running a hand through greasy hair that had sprouted, uncut, into a four-inch mop.

"But look at you. You're a mess. Your house is a disaster area. What's going on, man?"

For a moment, Sam thought he heard a noise. The whisper of voices. The sound of charred hands, twisted by fire into claws, fumbling with the knob of the front door.

Go away, his mind pleaded. *Leave me alone!*

And then that inevitable thought returned to him: *Your mind is the problem. It's all finally caught up to you. You're cracking up, and you can't be fixed.*

"Sam?"

"Everything's fine. I'm just anxious to finish the book."

"Tell me about it."

"I told you this last fall, Eli. I don't have an outline. It's just sort of . . . pouring out of me."

"Then tell me about what you have so far."

His mouth opened, his lips preparing to curve around the words, but the explanation abandoned him. The past six months were a blur; he remembered only the parade of words across the computer screen, pushing blindly forward, forging ahead into uncharted waters. He had never stopped to sum up the plot into anything resembling a pitch.

"It's about a house," he said finally. "A house with a strange and mysterious past. A family moves in, thinking it will be the start of a new life. Only the house begins to feed off of them, manipulating them, forcing them to do drastic and terrible things. Except for one. The youngest daughter. She senses the evil and delves into the house's past, trying to find a way to stop it. Eventually, her search leads her to the bedroom on the third floor. There's just one problem—"

Eli leaned forward in his chair, picking up the thread without a pause. "She can't get in. Because the door has been sealed by a wall. A brick wall. And the more she tries to tear down that wall, the more those around her become affected by the evil."

Sam stared at Eli, mouth agape, head cocked curiously to the side. "That's right." He almost whispered the words. "How . . . how could you know that?"

Eli stood and walked the length of the front porch, his thumb tracing the lip of the beer bottle as he tried to find the perfect words. It was obvious this was the reason for his unexpected visit. "About a week ago, I spoke to Dale Sommers at Kanyon?"

"You called my publisher?"

"No, he called me. Kanyon just acquired Brute Force Press, which you'd probably know if you didn't have your head buried in a Word doc. Brute Force has published the last three books by T.C. Moore. Sommers was worried about Moore. He hadn't heard from her in weeks. She wasn't returning his calls. She wasn't returning anyone's calls. So he wondered if I could ask you to try to contact her. I told him I was having the same problem with you. I asked Sommers what Moore was working on, and, after some prodding, he read me a short outline she'd given him back in November. It's very similiar to yours, Sam."

"How similar?" Sam asked.

"I mean, the characters are different—you deal with a small-town family, whereas Moore's main characters are young and brutal twentysomethings—but for all intents and purposes, the two of you are basically writing the same book."

This can't be happening! his mind screamed.

"How is that even possible?" Sam's voice was barely a whisper.

Eli set the beer down on the porch railing and shrugged. "Look, it makes sense. Obviously, Kill Creek inspired both books. The house. The supernatural legacy. The bricked-off doorway. I mean, it's odd that they're as similar as they are, but it's not impossible that, creatively, you would find yourselves going down the same path. What worries me is how this process is affecting you *personally*. And if Moore has gone off the grid too, I can only assume she's become consumed with her book, just like you."

Sam thought of all the voicemails on his phone, the missed calls. He thought of his lost job at the university, and of the disastrous meeting with Erin.

The gravity of the situation perched on Sam's shoulders, a fat, gluttonous bird digging its black talons into him, all the way to the bone. In his mind, he pictured the small city of paper that awaited him inside the house, towers of eight-by-eleven pages stacked clumsily around every room.

If Moore truly was writing the same book, then all of his work was for nothing.

Sam gave a sharp, humorless laugh. There was nothing to say.

"You might want to try getting in touch with Moore yourself," Eli suggested. "See if she'll talk to you. You have her number?"

Sam nodded and looked down at his beer. Wainwright had given them each other's contact information a few days after they'd returned from Kill Creek. It was given under the pretense of keeping in touch, although Wainwright suggested they might want to let Daniel know they were thinking of him. Sam hadn't bothered to call or email Daniel. He just didn't know what to say. Nothing could make things better for Slaughter.

"I'm sorry, Sam, but I have to fly back this evening," Eli said. He crouched down so that he was at eye level with Sam. "Do me a favor: take a break from the book, shower, shave, clean up the place. And call Moore. Find out if there's any way to salvage what you're working on. Okay?"

"Yeah," Sam replied. "Okay."

Eli gave him a pat on the knee. "Take care of yourself, Sam."

Sam nodded.

He watched as Eli walked down his porch steps and onto the front walk. Halfway to where his rental car was parked at the curb, the agent turned around and called back: "And answer your goddamn phone from now on."

Eli did not wait for Sam to respond. He climbed into the rental car, fired up the engine, and drove away.

Sam closed his eyes and held his head in his hands. He listened to the afternoon breeze blowing through the budding limbs of trees. Somewhere down the block, a child shrieked happily. Sam focused on the sound of his own breathing, the slow draw of breath in and out of his lungs.

Beside him, the doorknob jiggled. There was a pause, and then something dragged slowly down the back of the door, like fingernails scraping against the wood.

Sam sucked in a sharp breath. He could taste smoke. It bit harshly into the back of his throat. Cautiously, he got up from this chair and inched toward the door. He took hold of the knob, wincing when he heard the latch withdraw. With a sharp shove, he threw the door open, fully expecting it to collide with a misshapen form on the other side.

The door swung open, fast and free, bouncing roughly off the adjoining wall. There was nothing there. Only his empty house and the mountains of poorly stacked paper that had come to represent an isolated life.

Sam minimized his Microsoft Word document and opened his internet browser. A wall of favorite sites appeared. He clicked on Facebook and searched for T.C. Moore. If she had a personal account, a simple search of her name did not reveal it. There was, however, an official author page. Sam clicked on it and scrolled down. The images displayed were classic Moore, a mix of sex and violence, meant to disturb. The last post was from November. She had shared the link to the WrightWire video. Sam noted the number of views listed under the video: over six hundred thousand people had watched the video on Moore's Facebook alone.

"Christ," Sam said under his breath. He hadn't even bothered to watch it.

There were a few more posts from Moore after the WrightWire link, random plugs for past novels. The last post was an ambiguous message to her fans: "Working on something new." After this, there was nothing.

Sam opened a new tab and directed the browser to Instagram. A quick search brought up *TheRealTCMoore*. The experience was similar: dark, morbid photos mixed with artistic shots of her books and selfies that sold her power and sexuality. Just like on Facebook, the posts became less and less frequent through the first two weeks of November. Then . . . nothing.

Twitter showed the same results. Even online fights with haters, which apparently had been a favorite pastime of Moore's leading up to October, ceased once her feed hit the middle of November.

Sam sat at the desk for a long time, pondering his next move. He could email her, but something told him he would get the same radio silence as her agent.

His finger moved to the laptop's power button and paused, hovering.

Sam stared at the computer screen. At the bottom, his novel—his thousand-plus page magnum opus—was represented by a small minimized document icon. He could expand it and keep working. He could try to press forward.

Or he could do as Eli had suggested. He could take a break.

It won't like that, his mind warned him. *It won't let you rest until you're back at that keyboard.*

"There is no *it*," he said to the empty room. "*It* is all in your head because you've gone goddamn insane!"

Unless. . .

Unless Eli was right and the same thing was happening to Moore.

Then I wouldn't be crazy. I couldn't be, right? That would be proof. Proof of . . .

Of what? his mind asked. Sam didn't know. Part of him was afraid to know.

The computer gave a final disapproving beep as he pressed and held the power button. The procedure was far easier than he had expected. The hum of the laptop ceased, the glow of the monitor went dark, and that was that.

He took a long, indulgent shower, letting the scalding hot water pour over his weary body.

Once he was in bed, the lamp on the nightstand clicked off, the darkness settling upon him like a dense black blanket, the confusion of the day's events came rushing back to him. His book, the one thing—the *only* thing—that gave him a sense of purpose was in danger of fizzling out before he could even light the fuse.

He had to be sure, which was why, in the morning, he would book a flight to Los Angeles. He would go to see Moore in person. The only way for Sam to put this beast to bed would be to see the pages of Moore's manuscript with his own eyes.

And if they're the same?

He wasn't sure what he would do. He was too invested in his book. He couldn't just scrap it. Maybe there was a way to salvage what he had.

In the meantime, Sam would put the book on hold. He would stop writing. Cold turkey. Just like that.

No sooner had this thought flitted through his mind than the scent of burning flesh filled his bedroom.

Sam's flesh prickled. He held his breath, refusing to acknowledge the smell. For a moment, only the steady tick of the clock on the wall filled the room.

Then came the sound, a wheezing sound. Someone having trouble breathing. Someone in pain.

It's coming for you! his mind screamed. *Because you stopped. Because you've given up on the story.*

Sam trained his eyes on the open doorway, peering into the blackness.

A shape slipped through, dark and hunched. Every now and again it caught the moonlight, and in those horrible, brief moments, Sam imagined he could see a face, its mouth pulled tight in a jagged sneer, its eyes wild and mad. And then the black of night would wash over the image like a midnight wave, lost to darkness.

Something snapped, like a fingernail bent quickly backward. The shape began to drag its bulk toward his bed.

The odor of burning flesh was overpowering.

It's her, his mind told him. *It's her. She knows what you did.*

"It's not real," Sam said under his breath.

He rolled over to the edge of the mattress, propping himself up with one hand while reaching for the lamp with the other. His entire being cried out for him to stop, to not look at what was waiting for him in the dark, to not shed light on a thing he could never forget.

It's all in your head. It's all in your head.

It's NOT REAL.

The wave of night receded once more and the face was staring up at him, body hunched down on the floor, head cocked, sunken cheek pressed against the side of the mattress, teeth clenched in a lipless grin.

He clicked on the lamp. In an instant, the sixty-watt bulb pushed back the darkness, an orb of luminance warming the room.

The creature did not vanish in the light. The face peered up, burned beyond recognition. The back of its skull was caved in. It reached up with a charred black finger.

"You did this! You did this to me! YOU DID THIS!"

Sam pressed his eyes shut.

"No! Stop!"

"YOU DID THIS TO ME!"

"Stop stop stop stop STOP! YOU'RE NOT REAL!"

Sam opened his eyes.

There was nothing there.

A shaky sigh worked its way from his mouth, and Sam fell back onto his pillow, trembling.

Around two in the morning, he finally drifted off to sleep. When the sun rose shortly after six in the morning, the bedside lamp still burned brightly.

TWENTY

MOORE STOPPED AT the bottom of the stairs and took a deep breath.

Get back on track, she told herself. *Gotta push through.*

Her shoes clicked softly on the glazed concrete floor as she passed under a grand arch and into the kitchen. Like the rest of her house, the kitchen was cold and sleek, all stone and metal.

She opened a cabinet, quickly scanned the labels of the numerous high-end liquor bottles and reached for a thirty-year-old Balvenie.

One drink to clear the cobwebs, and then you have to kick this thing's ass.

Just as her hand grasped the bottle's neck, a whisper came from the other room.

"Theresa."

Moore spun around.

The archway was empty. Beyond this, a single shaft of light cut through the darkened room.

For a moment, she stood perfectly still, listening.

There were no sounds, save for the occasional muffled whir of a police helicopter flying over the city below.

Slowly, she edged toward the archway.

Breathing. I can hear breathing.

Someone's there.

You know who is there, her mind insisted.

Fear prickled her skin like a gust of icy winter air, and the sensation enraged her. She grasped the wall of the arch for leverage and stormed into the room.

The sunlight blinded her. She flinched, blinking, and held up a hand to shield her eyes. Quickly, she backed out of the shaft of light and into the shadows that clung to the edges of the room.

He's here. In the dark.

She took another few rapid steps backward and collided with something behind her. Instantly her fists clenched as she whipped around, ready for a fight.

The wall. You ran into the wall, you pathetic, scared little girl.

She unclenched her fists and leaned in closer to the wall, peering into the shadows. Her eyes adjusted to the darkness.

Something wasn't right.

Reaching out, she ran a hand over the wall's surface. It was not the smooth plaster of her house. This was brick, decades old, and haphazardly stacked, as if it had been constructed quickly.

This was the wall in the Finch house.

Moore jerked her hand away, not wanting to touch the brick for another second.

You're not really there. You're in your house, in Los Angeles. You are not there!

From behind the wall, something scratched frantically at the bricks. It began to scream, desperate to be let out. The sound was faint, echoing over distance, as if past this wall were not the Hollywood Hills but an immense empty room.

Moore backed slowly away, her entire body clenched to keep from shaking.

"Go away," she ordered.

The screaming grew louder. There was a rhythm to it, a strange, uneven flow of starts and stops. It was no longer behind the wall. It was all around her.

"Go away!" she roared.

She blinked, and the bricks were gone, replaced by the plaster wall that had always been there.

Yet the sound remained. It was coming from somewhere above.

Moore cocked her head, listening.

It was the barking of a dog.

The pit bull nearly ripped off Sam's face.

Sam quickly scrambled up one of the several brick lampposts dotting the yard. The dog snapped its powerful jaws at his heels. He wouldn't be able to hold on much longer.

"Moore!" Sam called out. "It's Sam McGarver! The writer! Remember, we met last fall at . . ." His voice trailed off. Somehow saying its name made it all too real, recognition that the house was what bound them.

The dog was barking wildly, inches below his feet. Thick white spittle splattered his shoes.

Sam's fingers were slipping. In another minute, he would fall to the ground and have his flesh torn away in warm bloody mouthfuls.

Just that morning, Sam had thought getting on a flight from Kansas City to Los Angeles would be the most difficult part of his spur-of-the-moment adventure. Finding Moore's house wasn't a problem; Eli was easily able to obtain her address. When no one answered the buzzer at the gate, scaling the fence that surrounded the gorgeously landscaped estate also turned out to be a surprisingly effortless feat. A low, thick hedge held Sam's weight long enough for him to reach the fence's top crossbar. There was a tense moment when Sam thought he might lose his balance and impale himself on the large black spikes that dotted the fence. An image flashed through his mind, of lying on the lush lawn, clutching a bloody handful of ripped scrotum while waiting for the screaming siren of the paramedics to reach him. And then he hopped to the other side, down onto the yard where he casually strolled up the steep drive toward the front door.

That was when he saw the hulking pale creature round the corner, and Sam ran for cover.

Sam peered over the lawn to the front porch. He took a breath and tried one more time. "Moore, just let me come in! I'll explain everything!"

"McGarver, what the hell do you want?" It was T.C. Moore all right, that unmistakable mixture of aggression and sarcasm.

"I just need to talk to you," Sam said again.

"About what?"

"Your book." Sam knew this wouldn't be enough to earn face time with Moore. He thought for a moment, then added, "Your book about the house."

There was a pause, an eternity it seemed, although it could not have been more than a minute or two. And then the silence was broken by the squeal of door hinges. Sam heard a whistle, and Moore called out:

"Lilith!"

The pit bull instantly obeyed, skulking off around to the back of the house.

Moore was standing just outside the front door, her slender form draped in a sleek silk kimono. The front was loosely tied, the edges barely concealing her breasts. She was thinner than before, less toned, muscle giving way to bone. In her right hand, a pistol dangled loosely.

"You've got ten minutes," Moore announced with a stunning lack of emotion. Then she turned and marched back inside, leaving the door wide open for Sam to enter.

Ten minutes would turn out to be nearly two weeks. But, of course, neither of them knew that at the time.

Moore's house was exactly what Sam had expected—cold, hard, purposely uncomfortable and uninviting. It was like a cinder block encased in glass, with only the breathtaking views of the city from high in the Hollywood Hills to soften the experience.

As she led him through the foyer and into the spacious living room, Sam took notice of the lack of clutter. It was nothing like his place.

I was wrong. I shouldn't have come here. She'll laugh me out of the house and tell me to take a flying fuck.

But Moore did not laugh. She did not even offer so much as an apology, snide or otherwise, after the near mauling in her front yard. Sam had found her standing in the foyer with a tumbler of whiskey in one hand and the gun in the other. She set the revolver on the concrete counter of a nearby credenza and wandered off into the next room.

They stood in Moore's cavernous living room, metal shelves running the length of the light gray walls, dark oak floors beneath their feet, a grand picture window framing the smog-shrouded city beyond. Moore stopped in front of a leather chair, but she did not sit. She stared at Sam, exhausted, black bags cupping her tired eyes like crescent moons.

"What do you want, McGarver?" she asked.

Sam shuffled nervously, not sure how to begin. "Tell me about the book you're writing."

She gave a harsh chuckle. It sounded more exhausted than defiant. "Not a chance. You can read it with everybody else when it's finished."

"How long is it?"

"I don't know," Moore said. "It isn't *finished.*"

Sam pushed back. "But how long have you been working on it?"

Moore stared at him curiously, not sure of Sam's endgame. Then she attempted what she obviously hoped was a dismissive shrug. "All right, I'll admit, the book's gotten a bit . . . out of hand."

"When's the last time you slept?" he asked.

Moore gave a long, gruff sigh, as if her chest were filled with leaves, the air rustling them as it exited her lungs.

"You seriously flew all the way to LA to ask me how I'm sleeping?"

"You know why I'm here."

"I was just about to get a drink," she said. "You need a drink?"

"Moore. Please."

She started toward the spiral staircase that led down to a walk-out basement, then stopped mid-step.

"What's the matter?" Sam asked.

Moore shook her head, her eyes still on that staircase. "Nothing. Be right back."

She disappeared into the depths of her home.

Carefully, quietly, Sam rose to his feet. He quickly moved down a narrow hallway lined with framed black-and-white photographs. They were all close-up shots of men and women, a somewhat disturbing mixture of sex and violence—a split bottom lip; a penis gripped in a fist, then both wrapped in barbed wire; a knife resting on a perfect triangle of matted pubic hair.

At the end of the hallway was a door. Sam reached for the knob. He carefully turned it, his heart leaping as it clicked open.

He stared into the room, and his heart sank.

Here it is. The mess.

Unlike the rest of his house, Moore's study was a shaken jigsaw puzzle of papers and books and yellow legal pads. At the center of the storm was a desk, upon which sat a laptop computer, its screen displaying the absurdly awful image of a child staring curiously down the barrel of an assault rifle.

He found several pieces of paper still in the printer. He picked up the last two pages.

Under the bridge at Walnut Creek or in the crowded basement of the house on Sixth Street, she called him "Pretty Boy" or "Pretty Boy Tom," but when it was just the two of them alone, she called him Tommy, and he called her Charlie. His Charlie. His one and only.

She knew he was full of shit. He was pounding plenty of strange on the side. But he always had two-day stubble that rubbed her cheek raw and a dumb eyebrow ring with a turquoise stone and that same pit-stained short-sleeved shirt that he never washed, and when he called her "Charlie," her heart melted and her pussy did a backflip.

Today he called her "Pastor Charlie." Her holiness. She told him it wasn't funny. He said it wasn't a joke. She was something greater now. Bigger and deeper and brighter than the goddamn stars. He kissed her hard with his tobacco-stained teeth and their tongues were mating snakes as they curled around each other.

"Do it, baby. He wants you to do it."

Charlie had a hammer in her hand. A "carpenter's hatchet" is what Buckwood called it when he'd loaned it to them. Hammer on one side, hatchet on the other.

Charlie's nails were painted black like that door in the Rolling Stones song. She smiled. "Hey, R.T., you ready to do us that solid? Remember, you owe us, you weed-bumming bitch."

R.T. nodded, but then again, that's all he could do. His hands were tied at the wrist, his feet at the ankles. He was completely naked. His back was to the wall.

"Play with my cock when you do it," he said.

Tommy said, "It's fine, girl. I don't mind." And he meant it because he was a stand-up guy with a job and a car and love in his heart.

Charlie took R.T.'s sad little prick in her hand and worked it up and down.

Her black nails grazed his scrotum. His dick was on fire now. He wasn't going to last long.

"Do it," R.T. moaned. "Do it right when I go." He pressed the back of his head up against the wall.

Tommy whispered, "This is gonna work, right?"

Charlie raised the half hammer in one hand, blade side down. In the other hand, she felt the first wet kiss of R.T.'s cock against her palm.

Now!

She slammed the blade down into his skull as his body shook. She couldn't tell if it was from the shock of the blow or the ecstasy of orgasm. R.T. was a sticky, quivering mess from head to hog.

"It's working." Tommy slid a hand around her waist and pulled her close. "It's working!"

The wall was opening. The first brick broke free.

"What the hell do you think you're doing?" Moore cried as she rushed into the room. Scotch sloshed over the rims of two tumblers as she slammed them down on the desk. She snatched the pages from Sam's hand.

"I'm sorry, I . . ."

"You're fucking right you're sorry!" She shoved him, hard, and his hand hit the keyboard of her laptop. The screen woke, revealing a Microsoft Word document. Several terse paragraphs filled the upper part of the page, but the cursor blinked midway down. Just as Sam's had. Blink. Blink. Blink. Waiting for the flood of words.

"Why did you stop?" Sam asked after a moment of silence.

"What?"

"Why did you stop?"

Moore drew in a deep breath, her heartbeat slowing, her anger subsiding.

"Because some asshole was trespassing on my property," she said. Her tone was less than convincing.

"But what stopped you before that?"

Moore's bottom lip trembled. Here was the truth. Here was everything she had feared for the past six months. She bit her trembling lip between her front teeth.

"McGarver, don't do this."

"You've been writing since we got back, haven't you? Like you *have* to? Like something is making you write?"

A light flickered behind Moore's dark eyes, across the surface of that broken pupil like the rainbow sheen of oil on water.

Sam thought with a sudden sense of relief, *You're not crazy. This is happening. It's really happening!*

And then relief turned to dread: *You're not crazy. This is really happening.*

"Tell me what's going on," he said.

She wrapped her arms around herself like armor. She said nothing.

"When I would stop writing," Sam explained, his voice soothing and honest, "I would think I was in that house again."

Her eyes flashed up to him. He had clearly struck a nerve.

Sam continued, "I thought I was going crazy. I was forgetting to take my meds, for depression, and at first I thought maybe it was some sort of withdrawal. So I started taking them again, but it didn't help. I even bought a carbon monoxide detector because I read that a leak could cause hallucinations. But now I know I wasn't hallucinating, and I'm not crazy. Because it's happening to you too."

Moore clenched her jaw. She was fighting tears. Sam had never seen her so vulnerable.

It terrified him.

"It's happening to you," he repeated. "Isn't it?"

Moore stared at him intensely. And then she gave a small nod.

Sam motioned to the blinking cursor on the computer screen. "But you stopped."

She sighed and picked up a few papers from a stack. "It was flowing until—"

"Until you got to the part where someone tries to break through the wall. The wall that will unlock the house's secrets."

Her head whipped around to glare at Sam with that awful eye. He noticed for the first time that the once shaved sides of her head had grown out. Her hair was not the stylish mane it had been. Now it was starting to resemble the world's longest mullet.

"How did you know that?"

"Because it's exactly where I stopped," Sam said. "In the book I'm writing. The book I've been writing for the past six months."

Moore's eyes narrowed, scrutinizing Sam.

"What's it about?" she asked. "This book of yours?"

There in Moore's study, in that cinder block of a house high on a hill above Hollywood, California, Sam revealed something even his publisher didn't know. He told Moore the plot of his new novel. Not just the logline, as he usually did when asked about a new project, but the entire thing, from beginning to end, twists and turns and plot points that critics would preface with a blinking neon sign: SPOILERS AHEAD!

He told it all.

"It begins with a house. Not a Gothic mansion but a house like any other, in the middle of a small Kansas town. A family moves in. A husband, a wife, and two kids—a daughter, Alex, fifteen; and a son, Jake, ten. At first everything is just fine. Dad gets a new job. Mom joins the local PTA. But something's off. Alex senses it at first but quickly dismisses it. Jake can't shake it though. At night, there are sounds from the wall at the end of the third-floor hallway, just past what is apparently the only room up there, a sewing room.

"Then things start to go south. Dad has a pretty young assistant at work and he can't stop thinking about what it would be like to fuck her, even though his family is the most important thing in his life. Not just sleep with her but *fuck* her, whether she liked it or not. Mom, a staunch pacifist, is starting to have terrifyingly vivid daydreams about brutally murdering the loudmouthed rich bitch mother of one of Jake's schoolmates. And Alex, once an honor student, athlete, and all-around outgoing girl, has become reclusive, a teenage Renfield, collecting dead bugs and birds and eventually hiding something far, far worse beneath a cover of leaves in the basement.

"Jake senses the changes, not only in his family but in himself. He's ten years old, experiencing for the first time the brutal social Darwinism that will make junior high and high school a living hell.

He finds himself reveling in the cruelty he can inflict on weaker kids, relishing the cheers of the popular crowd. One day, he shoves a stick into the spokes of a classmate's bicycle. The poor kid goes flying, breaking his leg. And as the cool kids watch, Jake reaches down to his fallen classmate and gives that fractured tibia a little twist, just to hear the bones grind together. It isn't really the fact that Jake enjoys doing this that scares him; it's that he knows what he's doing is completely wrong and still he does it, as if he's standing outside of his body and watching some other kid named Jake, a stranger with his face, carry out these sadistic acts."

Outside, a cloud seemed to pass in front of the sun, even though the sky had been clear and blue for miles when Sam arrived. Moore shuffled her bare feet, placing one behind the other as if she meant to run away at any moment. She gripped the edges of her kimono and pulled them tight. A darkness was creeping up behind her. A coldness had invaded the house.

"So Jake begins to suspect the house," Sam continued. "He delves into its history, first uncovering what seems like a series of random mishaps involving previous owners. And then a pattern begins to emerge. Each occupant only inhabited the house for one year before something in their lives went terribly, inexplicably wrong. One man walked a mile barefoot in the snow just to shoot his neighbor. A son locked his little sister in an abandoned refrigerator and left her to die, gasping for breath and crying for her mother. And at the beginning of this trail of death sat one incident in particular—a man was murdered by thieves and his girlfriend strung up by her neck in the tree out front."

Sam paused here, reading the recognition on Moore's face. "I know," he said. "That one sounds familiar."

Moore simply gave a nod. She was, for possibly the first time in her life, speechless.

Sam took a breath and continued. "Anyway, the more Jake researches the house, and the more he fights its influence, the louder those sounds grow behind the wall of the third-floor hall. It's as if something is trying to get out. But he is the only one who can hear it.

"Then, while he's in the yard, Jake makes a startling discovery. The exterior of the house seems to extend a good eight feet farther than the third-floor hallway. He gets to thinking—what if there's a room behind that wall? So as his family falls apart around him, taken over by the evil within the house, Jake chips away at that wall, trying to gain access to the room beyond and what he hopes will be the secret to the omnipotent terror.

"And then there's Tommy."

"Tommy," Moore said, the words little more than an exhaled breath.

"He knows the power that lies behind the wall. And Tommy wants it all for himself."

It seemed as if Moore had stopped breathing. She stood frozen, paler than he had ever seen her, bloodless flesh against her pitch-black hair.

"It all comes to a head one night near the end of their first year in the house, the same night that Dad rapes and nearly murders his assistant, the same night that Mom follows that rich bitch mother home with the plan to bash her Botoxed brains in, the same night that Alex lures a classmate into the basement to show him the surprise that is now rotting beneath that mound of dried leaves. That night, Tommy—a local handyman in my story—slips into the house and breaks through the wall to peer into the absolute darkness on the other side."

Sam's tale came to an abrupt end. At first Moore simply stared at him, blinking, waiting for the story to continue. When it did not, she cleared her throat, readying it for the first word she would speak in a quarter of an hour.

"What does he find?" she asked, her voice barely a whisper.

"I don't know," Sam replied. "That's where I hit my first bout of writer's block since I'd started writing, like inspiration slammed on the brakes and my novel skidded to a dead stop." He pointed to the screen of the laptop computer, tapping it where the cursor steadily blinked. "And I'm guessing that's where you stopped too."

Moore sucked in a trembling breath.

It's happening to him.

For the first time in six months, there was someone she could talk to, someone who might understand what she was going through.

She looked into Sam's eyes and said, "I feel it too, like I'm back there. In the house. Sometimes I'm not sure I ever left."

He reached out and touched her hand. She did not pull away.

"I know," Sam said. "I know."

Just tell him, Moore thought.

But I don't know if I trust him, a second voice said. It was the voice of a younger Moore. Of a girl everyone called Theresa.

You don't have a lot of fucking options right now, do you?

Moore swallowed hard and began to describe her novel.

Some of the character names were different, their backstories and relationships less family oriented, their horrible transformations much darker and sexually perverse, but as Moore laid out her own tale, from the discovery of the house to the moment where the bite of the hammer (or in Moore's case, a hatchet) slams into a man's skull in hopes of opening that third-floor wall, she realized what Sam said was true.

They were writing the exact same novel.

Perhaps even more surprising than this discovery was how Moore reacted. Even she expected herself to go off into a classic Moore temper tantrum, throwing objects and expletives wildly around the cluttered room. Instead, she gave a long, deep sigh, her shoulders drooping as every muscle in her body relaxed for the first time in almost a year.

You're growing up, girl, she chided herself.

"I wrote nearly a million and a half words," she said after a prolonged yet welcome silence. "Three thousand pages. I just couldn't stop. Not to answer the door or the phone. Barely long enough to eat and piss. I even abandoned the book I'd been working on before we went to the Finch House. I was insane about that book before I went to Kill Creek, and then . . . I just didn't care about it anymore. Only this story mattered."

"I was up to twelve hundred pages," Sam admitted, angry that part of him felt this wasn't nearly enough compared to Moore's output. "I was overwriting everything and I knew it, but as long as I was writing . . ." His voice trailed off.

"This is ridiculous," Moore said suddenly, crossing her arms tightly over her chest, her eyes searching the room, looking for an answer that wasn't there. "I mean, we went to Kill Creek. We were inspired by it. And now we're writing about it, that's all. That's why this is happening."

Sam shook his head. "I don't think so."

"It's not real. It can't be real. It's a delusion."

KILL CREEK   233

"A delusion that we're both experiencing, almost two thousand miles apart?"

"It's not unheard of." Moore was speaking rapidly now, anxious to find a rational explanation. "There have been countless examples of mass hysteria throughout history. Nuns in the Middle Ages who suddenly began yowling like cats. A dancing plague in the fifteen hundreds. The Salem witch trials. The Mothman sightings in West Virginia. People felt compelled to do irrational things. They believed they saw things that weren't there. People who had no connection to one another. The delusions spread like diseases."

Moore could see the anger boiling up in Sam.

"This is not a delusion!" he cried. "This is happening. This is real."

"No. No, I can't accept that."

"You don't have to accept it," Sam said. "It's *happening*. To you. To me."

Something occurred to Moore. She looked up at Sam with a new sense of purpose. "What about the others? Maybe they're fine. Maybe it's just us."

Sam considered this for a moment, then took out his phone.

"What are you doing?" Moore asked.

"Calling Daniel." Sam opened his contacts and scrolled down to the *S* section. There it was, the phone number he had gotten from Wainwright last year.

Sam tapped the number, then Call. He put the phone to his ear.

On the other end, it began to ring.

TWENTY-ONE

DANIEL SAT WITH his palms pressed flat against his closed eyes, losing himself in the tranquility of his study. His cell phone, which had been ringing off the hook for nearly a day now, had finally fallen silent. He was thankful for this. He did not want to answer it. He did not want to be forced into mundane conversation.

He could hear his wife shuffling around in the hall, her footsteps light as she passed. She wanted him to come out, he knew this, and he would in time, but not yet. Not until he cleared the unexpected hurdle before him, that blinking cursor on the computer screen, marking the moment when his story had abandoned him.

In the absence of writing, Daniel had allowed his mind to wander, to imagine what it would be like when his publisher read the new manuscript. They wouldn't print it. It was too dark, not at all the kind of self-righteous trifle to which his Christian audience was accustomed. This was no slim volume of teen-friendly carnage, served medium rare with pipin' hot sides of judgment and salvation. This was a dense work that weaved through the shadows of the soul, morally ambiguous without even the faintest glimmer of a light at the end of the tunnel. It was real. It was life.

A year ago, Daniel would have scoffed at such pessimistic thoughts. That was before Claire was snatched away from him. In that moment, standing with the deputy sheriff before the house on Kill Creek, a single sentence was uttered—

Your daughter, she's been in an accident

—and Daniel sensed something snap within him, actually felt it break like the dead branch of a diseased tree, and all the hope, all the peace, all the God-given calm that had once filled his heart began to drain free.

Once, years ago, Daniel and Sabrina were out for a walk, their new daughter snug under a blanket in the stroller, when they came upon an apartment fire. It was an ancient six-story complex on the northeast corner of the intersection. Black plumes of smoke poured from the uppermost windows. The firefighters appeared to have the blaze under control, the powerful streams from their hoses extinguishing the flames.

The residents of the building huddled on the very edge of the sidewalk. It was obvious they would not be returning home. The fire had done too much damage. Some coughed, some stood silent, most watched the inferno with tear-streaked faces. At the far side of the group stood a mother with her son. She was not crying. She smiled warmly at the boy, raking a hand gently through his hair.

"Why are you smiling?" Daniel could not help but ask. "You've lost everything."

"I've lost nothing," she replied softly. "My son is everything, and God has spared him. God has spared us both. I have everything I need."

It was a profound moment. Coupled with his safe passage through the tunnel of spiders as a child, the words of this humble woman shone a Promethean light on the dark road of life.

No more. The warm glow had been extinguished. Salvation was not a blessing but an absurd joke, plucked cruelly away like a dollar bill at the end of a long stretch of twine.

Again he heard the floorboards creak as his wife approached his office door. This time, she did not move on. A moment passed, and then there came a light knock.

"Daniel?" Sabrina called out sheepishly.

"I'm working."

"Can I open the door?"

"I'm working," he said again, more forcefully.

Another pause, but her footsteps did not recede. Finally, she spoke again.

"Pastor Charlie is here."

Daniel sighed, irritated. Sabrina had threatened several times to bring their minister to the house. She had made good on that threat. Why couldn't she just leave him be?

"Daniel?" This was a man's voice, deep and soothing. "Daniel, why don't you open the door so we can talk about it?"

"What's there to talk about?"

"You tell me," the man replied.

Sabrina's hands shook as she poured coffee, the lip of the pot clinking loudly against the delicate porcelain cup.

Pastor Charles Norland sat perched on the edge of the couch, his hands folded humbly on his knees as if in preparation for prayer. Physically, Pastor Charlie was not an imposing figure. His dark suit hung limply from his wiry frame, the top button of his white dress shirt undone to allow tiny threads of black hair to peek through. He tanned easily; even with the majority of his days spent inside the First Lutheran Church on the corner of Sixth and Walnut Streets, his skin retained the bronze sheen of summer. At forty-two, his hairline was finally beginning to recede, cutting a widow's peak. Pastor Charlie was six feet tall and no more than one hundred and sixty pounds. His voice was slow yet deliberate, understated yet powerful. Like water seeping through the fractures of a seemingly impervious boulder, Pastor Charlie's voice had a way of working its way into your very bones, until you suddenly found yourself broken open before him.

Daniel waited while Pastor Charlie took a hesitant sip of the steaming coffee. He looked to Sabrina, who quickly glanced away.

Pastor Charlie swallowed and asked, "So what's going on, Daniel?"

"Nothing. I'm working on a new book."

"And do you usually lock yourself in your office for days when you're working on a book?"

Daniel shook his head. "No. But this . . . this is a different kind of book."

Pastor Charlie drew in a long breath, the air whistling in his nostrils. "You haven't been to church in quite some time, Daniel."

"Don't take it personally." A smirk played at Daniel's lips. He never used to smirk. Not before.

For the next five minutes, Pastor Charlie backed off a bit, spinning lackadaisical tales of his congregation, how Minnie Conrad caused a bit of a stir with the church choir when she chose a pop song for her solo ("Roar" by Katy Perry), how sixteen-year-old Shelly Ellerman interrupted Charlie's Memorial Day weekend sermon by throwing up in the second pew (it seems Shelly was battling her first hangover), how the church had finally raised enough money to restore the chapel's oldest stained-glass window, the one depicting Jesus's ride into Jerusalem on Palm Sunday (work should be completed by late September).

Daniel felt himself being pulled bit by bit by the calm, steady sound of Pastor Charlie's voice. He glanced subtly around the room for any conceivable distraction, something to focus on in an effort to break the spell. The coffee table with its neat stacks of appropriately thick books. Charlie's shoes, recently polished black yet bearing smudges of rough leather where his rag had missed. The hump of Daniel's own belly, much smaller than it had been six months ago, rising steadily up and down with each breath. "I'm beating it," Daniel said suddenly, interrupting the pastor's rambling.

Pastor Charlie paused, confused. "What?"

"My 'Dunlap Syndrome.'" Daniel pointed to his shrunken paunch. "When your belly *done lap* over your belt."

He chuckled, amused by his own cleverness.

Sabrina put a hand on her husband's shoulder. "Daniel, please."

Daniel looked to his wife's face, pained and fearful. She was going to be thirty-eight in a couple months. She was far from old. She still resembled the pretty little wallflower he had fallen head over heels for in high school. But her eyes had aged, fine wrinkles creeping around the edges like spiderwebs. She looked tired.

Daniel and Sabrina had been so young when they met, marrying shortly after graduation, both only eighteen. They didn't know it at the time, but Sabrina was already pregnant. Far from planned, the predicament had been just that at first, a situation neither was prepared to deal with. Terminating the pregnancy was not an option. Their fear and anxiety was no reason to end a life. Before they knew it, one spring day, they had a daughter, a beautiful, insanely perfect baby girl. They named her Claire after Sabrina's mother's favorite piece of music in

the whole wide world, Debussy's "Clair de Lune." Daniel had hoped
that their child would take after Sabrina, so he found it breathtakingly
remarkable to see hints of himself in her angelic face.

Then a strange thing happened. Sabrina never got pregnant again.
They tried, Lord knows they tried, but it just wasn't in the cards. Claire
was their miracle baby, a fateful occurrence never to be repeated. So
Daniel and Sabrina put all of their love into this one child, this flawless
combination of their separate souls.

It was an indescribable sensation, to one moment be a parent and
the next, not. If they had been able to have more children, perhaps the
loss would have been easier to sustain, the pain spread over the collective shoulders of a grieving family. Instead, there was no longer a family
at all. They were a couple again, as they had been in high school, as
they would be when they died. No generation to carry on their name.
Nothing to represent the merging of their hearts.

This made Sabrina very sad, and rightfully so. But Daniel was
experiencing something he had never truly known before. Daniel was
filled with rage.

"What?" he snapped at his wife.

Sabrina took a step back, alarmed by his tone. "Nothing, Daniel.
I just . . ."

Pastor Charlie, sensing that the moment was about to spin out of
control, leaned back on the sofa and said, "Sabrina has told me about
the . . . other things that the two of you have been experiencing."

Again, Daniel's accusatory scowl flashed to his wife. She dodged
his stare, lowering her head and fumbling with an errant thread
dangling from her blouse.

"Daniel," Pastor Charlie continued, "whatever's going on, you
can talk to me. You know that."

"Nothing's going on," Daniel insisted. He did not care if the
words rang true.

"So you haven't heard noises?" the minister asked. "You haven't
seen anything strange in the past few months? You haven't felt as if
something is in the house with you?"

"No. Nothing. We've been completely alone."

"Is that how you feel? Alone?"

No response.

"Have you prayed?"

"Why would I?" Daniel asked coldly.

The concern on Pastor Charlie's face was clear. He was not used to hearing such bleak thoughts from this once happy-go-lucky man.

"Because you're in pain," Pastor Charlie suggested. "Because you've experienced a great loss."

"And what is God going to do about that?" Daniel asked. His palms were beginning to sweat. He wiped them on his pant legs as he inched forward in his seat. "Is He going to give her back? Is He going to take my daughter and uncrush her skull? Unbreak her bones? Take her beautiful face and patch it back together like a goddamn quilt?"

Sabrina made a small, pitiful whimpering noise, and the sound of it infuriated Daniel. His pale, doughy face was flushed with the flow of hot blood.

He turned to his wife. "Oh, and what? I'm supposed to mourn like you? I'm supposed to shove my sadness down into some deep, dark hole and pretend like nothing has happened?"

"I'm not pretending like nothing happened!" Sabrina screamed.

Daniel ignored her. He turned to the stunned face of Pastor Charlie. "Well, I can't hide how I feel. Not anymore. I'm mad. I'm *furious*! I want things, Pastor. I want the respect that other authors get. I want a bestseller. I want a goddamn hardcover. I *covet* these things. That's a sin, right?"

Pastor Charlie nodded dumbly.

"I want another child. I want a wife who can give me another child."

Sabrina shrieked, "Oh God, Daniel! Stop!"

But Daniel did not stop.

"But most of all, the one thing I want is my daughter back! WHY WON'T GOD GIVE ME MY DAUGHTER BACK?"

Pastor Charlie took a breath and attempted to remain calm. "God didn't take Claire to hurt you, Daniel. God is merciful. He shares the pain you and Sabrina are feeling."

"Bullshit!" Daniel roared. "How could God know?"

"Because He, too, lost a child," Pastor Charlie explained. "He sacrificed His only son so that we may be saved."

Daniel nodded, a bit too enthusiastically, his head bobbing as if it were on a spring. "That's right. That's right, He *sacrificed* His son. *He* made the call. He gave the okay on that one." Daniel jammed a finger into his own chest. "But I didn't. I didn't have a say in my daughter's death. I didn't give the old green light for a car to hop the median and broadside her. He did! God did! So fuck Him!"

"Daniel!" Sabrina's mouth hung open, not even a breath to fill it. Daniel spun on her, eyes wild. "What?"

Fat tears spilled from Sabrina's eyes. They coursed down her cheeks like rainwater, carrying with them streaks of black mascara. She took a step away from him, holding one trembling hand out in front of her as if she expected him to lunge her way. Her left heel settled on the plush cream carpet, and Sabrina slowly spun on it, allowing the momentum of the movement to point her toward the hall. A moment later, she was hurrying up the stairs to the second floor, the sobs suddenly too powerful to contain.

Pastor Charlie remained on the couch, stunned by the uncharacteristically hateful show Daniel had just put on.

There was nothing more to say.

A sudden odor filled the room. The scent of decay, of rotten things in darkness.

The scent of the well.

Daniel winced and looked to Pastor Charlie. The long-faced man was fixated on his clasped hands, lost in a silent prayer. He did not appear to notice the foul smell.

The odor brought another moment rushing back to Daniel.

Standing at his daughter's open grave, watching as the coffin was lowered down into the ground. He had noticed the scent then, too, although his grief had kept him from fully recognizing it. Now he remembered, standing at the edge of that hole, an inexplicable gust of air rising up and with it, that awful smell of decay. He remembered seeing shadows in the hole. Now, in the theater of his mind, he saw them again. Yet this time they moved, swaying like sea anemones. They were arms waving, hands reaching to welcome his daughter into the darkness.

"She's in hell," Daniel whispered.

From somewhere above in the house, he heard a faint squeak, like the turning of a wheel.

A tear slipped free and ran down Daniel's cheek. "I have to go," he said.

Pastor Charlie stood into a shaft of light, his face lit from above, creating huge pools of shadow that obscured his eyes.

"Please, we need to talk about this," the pastor said, reaching out a hand.

Daniel gave a helpless whimper and raced up the stairs.

Sam ended the call. He had left nine messages for Daniel, and now, on the tenth attempt, an artificial voice told him that the mailbox was full.

"Maybe he doesn't have his phone on him," he speculated.

"Or maybe he's just not answering," Moore replied. She was standing at the large picture window in her living room, her back to Sam. The knobby green hills beyond were bright with the perfectly even California sunshine. She was a sleek, powerful silhouette against them.

"He could be out of town, on a trip. Out of cell phone range," Sam offered.

Moore shook her head. "How many times have you gone out of town since we left Kill Creek? Better yet, how many times have you left the house?"

Sam gave a knowing nod. "This is the first."

"Exactly. No, Slaughter's there. He's just not answering his god-damn phone."

Sam had spent the night at Moore's house, crashing in the sparsely furnished guest room. With one duffel bag packed with only two changes of clothes and essential toiletries, he was unprepared for extended travel. He was beginning to realize how spur-of-the-moment this trip had been. He'd never asked himself what would happen if he stayed longer than a day.

He had showered in the extravagant bathroom downstairs, letting the water fall like rain over his body. He emerged from the shower, a towel wrapped around his waist, to find Moore at a large vanity. She was running a pair of electric clippers over the sides of her head. Clumps of short black hair fell into the sink below. When she was done, Sam held out his hand. Without a word, she handed him the clippers. He adjusted the guard and began to mow strips through his overgrown hair. Then he removed the guard entirely and shaved off the beard that crept across the lower half of his face and down his neck. In a matter of minutes, he was done. He ran a hand over his buzzed hair, enjoying the sensation against his palm.

The night before had passed without incident. No strange noises. No scratching from the ceiling above. Once he thought he heard Moore stir, footsteps in the hall, but they quickly receded and were gone.

Sam was back on the phone in an effort to rouse Daniel, but he knew that if they wanted to check in with him, they would need a new plan of attack.

Sam plopped down on a sleek leather couch, picking up a small ivory statue from the coffee table to inspect the outrageously large phallus protruding from it. Classic Moore décor.

"So," he said, "what now?"

"We go to him," was her answer.

"Go to Chicago?"

"Why not? You came here to see me, to see if I was going through the same thing as you."

"I came here to make sure I wasn't crazy."

"And I'm still not convinced we're not," Moore offered, turning away from the window to face him. "Maybe we're both crazy and Daniel Slaughter is just really bad about checking his voicemail. There's only one way to find out."

"Go to him." Sam sighed.

Somewhere in the sky overhead, thousands of miles above them, a jet screamed by.

TWENTY-TWO

FRIDAY, APRIL 2I

THE FIRST RAYS of dawn began to filter through the lopsided venetian blinds, but Kate had not slept a wink all night. She stared into the fuzzy orange light with bloodshot eyes, the shadows from the blinds cutting across her face like black prison bars. Normally—that is, back when her life was her own—she would have been furious at not getting any rest. She would have dreaded the sound of her alarm clock buzzing, of dragging herself from bed, of trudging to the shower with invisible weights pulling her down.

That scenario now sounded like an absolute pleasure, a welcome respite from her current situation. Exhaustion did not even begin to describe it. Her days and nights had begun to blur with only these moments—staring into the growing sunlight—to remind her of the difference between the two.

For the first few weeks after the madness had begun, friends and concerned neighbors would stop by unannounced, knocking on her door and calling out, "Kate? You in there? You okay?" She told them she had the flu, and after that excuse wore thin, she simply ordered them away. Wainwright had been the most persistent, showing up around seven p.m. every night after work. But she managed to discourage even him, and soon they all stopped coming, leaving Kate to the absolute silence of her tomblike studio apartment.

She lay in her bed (a mattress, really, the blankets crumpled in a pile on the floor), her head cocked to the side on her rumpled pillow, her face slack. A few blocks away, church bells chimed. They went through their automated tune with the precision of a Swiss watch, making an artificially joyous sound.

There was the distant feeling that she was late, that she should hop out of bed and scramble to get dressed, but this sensation quickly dissipated. She had nowhere to go. No job. No friends. No life. Only this. Only the claustrophobic isolation of the world behind her locked door.

From somewhere outside, drifting in like echoes from an alternate universe, came the sounds of waking life. A car honked. A dog barked. A man yelled curse words at no one in particular. Kate recognized these individual noises for what they were, but they no longer held the resonance they once did. They were sounds from the past, heard through a tear in time.

In twenty minutes, the sunlight had crept from the uppermost corner of the room to halfway down the wall, illuminating a spread of overlapping photographs as it traveled its daily journey. Each photo was a five-by-seven print, some color, some black and white, most from Kate's Hewlett Packard PhotoSmart printer. It was a mosaic of random frames from various video shoots. A few were of celebrities, a mixture of staged scenes and candid shots. Others were personal pics, various street scenes, life as she once knew it. These were the most recent additions, photos she had taken as a dark experiment, to make sure that what was happening really was happening.

Now she knew it was. There was no doubt.

In the beginning, she thought it was a fluke. A camera trick. A malfunction within the machine. The first anomalies were present in her footage from the Kill Creek shoot. Most people wouldn't have noticed them as they flashed by at one-thirtieth of a second. But Kate did. She tracked them down, frame by frame. A shadow that seemed to go against the falling light. A wisp of white in the corner of a dark room. Then they began to take shape. A body. A head. A face staring out from the shadows.

Her first thought was that the entire shoot was marred by distracting flash-frames. But as soon as she showed the video to Wainwright, the aberrations—a blob of light, a faintly human form—disappeared completely. When a colleague played back the footage that now resided eternally on WrightWire and YouTube, she was stunned to see that the images were flawless.

Her mind tried to replay that moment in the second-floor hallway, when she thought she saw something on her LCD screen.

For one split second, the wall was gone, she remembered. *And there was an old woman. Not Rebecca Finch in her wheelchair. This woman was standing. Black hair billowed around her head. She was clawing the air as if scraping desperately at the other side of the invisible wall.*

But Kate refused to let the image take root in her brain. The shadows and wisps of white in her footage were flukes, she assumed. Her files were corrupted. What the world had seen that night contained none of the deficiencies she now obsessed over.

Her next shoot was for an up-and-coming indie band, the next big thing, straight outta Iowa. Four mopey white guys in dirty jeans and vintage rock tees. It was late when she returned to the WrightWire offices. The sun was setting, cutting strips of gold through the towering black forms of lower Manhattan. Kate plugged a USB cable into the base of her camera, connecting the other end to the port on the side of her laptop. The footage downloaded in a flash. She scrolled through it, pausing when something odd caught her eye.

It was there again. From take to take, she could follow its transformation like a digital flip-book. A fuzzy pale cloud in the first minute of footage. A vertical oval by the middle of the session. By the final frame, the object had taken human form, like a ghostly fifth member of the band. Its hollow black eyes stared out at her, its jaw drooped slightly as if about to scream, its dark hair suspended in air by a phantom wind. While the rest of the group did their best to look aloof, staring off into space to suggest deep thoughts, this horrible wraith looked directly at the camera. Its curled fingers dug at the open air. It wanted out. It wanted *through*. To her.

She had to tell Wainwright. She could trust him. She needed him to assure her that she was not imagining it, that she was not crazy.

Kate's foot tapped nervously as Wainwright flipped through the printed screenshots. She watched his face, but his expression gave no hint to his thoughts. And then he simply shrugged, holding the stack of photos out to her.

"I don't see anything, baby," he said. "I'm sorry."

She stared at the pictures in his hand. She did not want to take them back. She was afraid of what she might find.

That night, behind her locked apartment door, the thing returned. Not just to the band footage but to the Kill Creek shots as well. Kate raced to her computer, frantically clicking on the file that contained the bulk of her video. Her entire library blinked open on the screen, a mammoth window showcasing thousands of thumbnails. She scrolled through them, her fingers leaving wet streaks of sweat on the mouse. It was there. Floating next to her famous subjects. Hovering above a subway stop. Lurking in the background of her family's Thanksgiving dinner.

A pale woman with hollow eyes, standing just behind her happy, oblivious family.

One after another, Kate printed the pictures. She mounted them on the wall in haphazard rows using anything she had—pushpins, tape, glue, rubber cement, chewing gum, nails, screws. She finished late the next morning, the harsh sun of early summer already baking the city outside.

On the wall before her was a mosaic of random images, a crudely assembled overview of her collection. For a moment, Kate had simply stared at them, not breathing, mouth open. And then she crumpled into the corner, her body trembling uncontrollably as she shook her head.

No, no, no.

Together the ghostly images in each photograph formed one monstrous face, spanning from wall to wall, from ceiling to floor. Its pale form flickered in and out like a dying bulb, but it was there, towering over her, staring into her soul with empty sockets: that woman with the flowing jet-black hair.

Nearly two months later, Kate was curled up on her sweat-stained mattress, knees pressed tightly to her chest, the rising sun painting her apartment with the colors of dawn. Her eyes tracked the room, hopping from photograph to photograph. For the moment, it seemed the invading spirit had been exorcised from the images, but she knew this was only a trick. It would return. It always did.

She gave a tiny, frightening giggle, the sound of sanity escaping like air from a punctured balloon.

Her gaze fell upon a wooden handle on the kitchen counter. Oh yes. Now she remembered what she had been up to the night before. It had seemed like such a cold, cruel thing in the darkness, but now . . . now she welcomed the idea.

She pulled herself across the mattress, over the edge and onto the floor. The polished wood was cold against her bare knees. Her skin squeaked as she scooted her body toward the kitchen.

In the hallway outside of her apartment came a squeaking sound, like a wheel in need of oil. It moved slowly down the hall, toward her door.

Kate did her best to ignore it. She had heard it before, late at night, before she drifted off to troubled sleep. It usually stayed at a distance, a faint sound she could not be sure was even there.

Now it was coming closer.

She stared at the far wall, wishing she could see through it. She tracked the progress of the sound as it inched its way down the hall.

Just outside her door, it stopped.

Her fingers touched the base of the kitchen cabinets. She slid them up to the counter, grasping blindly. They found a wooden handle of a knife. She clutched the object to her chest. She was surprised to find that she was not at all frightened. Just the opposite, in fact. She had not felt this confident in months.

Outside her door, there was silence. And then the doorknob began to turn. Slowly, testing. It was locked.

The knife's blade was cold against her skin.

"Hello?" a voice called out. It was a woman's voice, thin and brittle, like ancient paper. "I know you're in there," she said.

It's not really a woman, Kate's mind screamed. *It wants you to think it is, but it's not.*

Kate knew the voice of the thing behind the door was that of a deeper sound being forced up into the higher register of an elderly woman.

"Why don't you open the door, dear?"

With one hand gripped tightly around the wooden handle, Kate pressed the tip of the knife against her wrist.

The doorknob began to twist violently as the thing behind the door tried to force its way in. Once again, it stopped. Once again, there was silence.

"We just want to talk to you, Katie," the voice said.

Kate shivered at hearing the thing say her name.

"I won't let you in," Kate growled through clenched teeth.

The thing behind the door gave a raspy chuckle. "Oh, sweetheart, you already have."

A new sound got Kate's attention. It was coming from the collage of photos covering her wall.

Hadn't she torn those down? She was almost certain she had. She remembered ripping them from the wall in a panic, desperate to be rid of that staring hollow-eyed face.

Yet there they were. And something was behind the photos, scratching against the back of the wall as if trying to dig through it.

A finger broke through one photo. The pale digit poked into the light and squirmed like an unearthed grub.

Kate held the knife steady. The tip bit slightly into her skin. She sucked in a breath, her entire body shaking.

"That's my sister," the old woman behind the door said. "She wants to make sure you help us."

"I'll never help you," Kate sobbed.

"You will," the voice assured her.

Another finger tore through. Photos began to fall, fluttering to the floor as first an arm, then the edge of a shoulder pushed its way into the room.

"Katie Ann. That is your name, isn't it? Katie Ann?" the woman-thing behind the door asked.

It began to repeat her name in an awful singsong voice: "Katie Ann. Katie Ann. Katie Ann."

Kate closed her eyes.

The wall of photos dropped away as a pale form burst through. It tumbled through shafts of morning sunlight and crashed to the floor, stopping in a heap only a few feet from where Kate sat crouched, the knife to her wrist.

The pale form twisted its head, and jet-black hair fell away, revealing a rotting face stretched over bone. It stared at her with hollow eye sockets.

And Katie put her weight into the knife, driving it downward so quickly that the tip broke through to the underside of her arm. Her mouth opened and a shocked gasp escaped. She hated the sound of it. Fear and regret and weakness. And yet there was no other choice.

"Ka-tie Ann . . ." the singsong voice called from behind the front door.

Kate was not even aware as she dragged the blade up her arm, all the way to the elbow, forcing it past the indentation of that groove and into the thick muscle of her bicep. She felt nothing as she twisted the knife around and dragged it back down her arm. A strip of flesh fell free, dangling like the meat of filleted game.

Darkness began to creep into the edges of her vision, overtaking once-pretty eyes that now bulged wildly from her face.

Something warm was rushing down her wrist and into her lap. It began to spurt. Specks of warmth hit the base of her neck.

Her eyes stared straight ahead, into the hollow eyes of a Finch sister.

I beat you, she thought as her mind clouded over.

The pale thing smiled curiously at her, as if to say she were mistaken.

TWENTY-THREE

SATURDAY, APRIL 22

WE CAME ALL this way for nothing, Moore thought.

She looked up at the suburban house as the cab pulled to the curb. It was a quaint two-story Colonial, white with black shutters, on an elegant, meandering street in Chicago's North Shore. The glow of meticulously landscaped, upscale homes warmed several streets to the east. Beyond these cul-de-sacs and winding lanes, the world was swallowed by the black abyss of Lake Michigan. To their south, the blinking lights of downtown skyscrapers bit into low-lying clouds.

"People actually live like this?" she asked.

"Some people don't care about a view," Sam said.

The back door of the cab swung open, and Moore got out. Sam followed. They moved hesitantly up the walk to the front porch. Moore reached out to push the doorbell, then paused, her finger hovering in midair.

"What do we say?" she asked.

Sam didn't respond.

Moore pressed the button.

From inside, they heard a series of pleasant chimes.

No one came to the door.

Moore raised a fist and pounded loudly on the door.

"Slaughter! Open up!"

Silence.

Come on, she thought. *Be home. We have to know what's happening. We have to be sure.*

Without warning, a shiver ran through her body. She suddenly hoped no one answered the door. She wanted to leave.

If you leave now, you'll never have to know the truth.

There was the sound of a hand on the knob, and the door swung open. A plain, sad-eyed woman stood before them.

Daniel's wife, Moore realized. *What is her name? Sabrina. This is Sabrina.*

She was probably in her late thirties, although life had recently added countless years to her.

A random thought flitted into Moore's mind: *Grief eats your youth.*

"Yes? May I help you?" Sabrina was forcing a pleasant tone, trying desperately to hold on to a shred of the decorum she once knew.

Sam did his best to offer a smile. "Is Daniel home?"

"And you are . . ."

"Sam McGarver. This is T.C. Moore. We're—"

Sabrina's expression darkened.

"I know who you are," she said.

"We need to talk to Daniel. It's important."

She stood motionless for a moment, looking from Sam to Moore and back. Finally she took a step back, clearing the way for them to enter.

"Come in."

Sam took a step forward, but Moore pushed past him, entering first.

They stood side by side on the beige tile floor of the foyer as Sabrina closed the door behind them.

"Is he here?" Sam asked.

"Oh yes, he's here." Sabrina looked up at the ceiling. "He's up . . . there. He's always up there."

Moore shot Sam a look. She knew where *there* was: Daniel's office. He was holed up behind his computer, just as they had been for half a year.

"Well, can we talk to him?" Moore was losing patience. She hadn't traveled all this way to be stopped by a skittish housewife.

From above, there came the sound of several footsteps as someone moved across the length of a room.

Then, once again, silence filled the house.

"He's not the same, you know," Sabrina said. It was not so much a statement for them, but for the universe at large, and whatever being may be turning its gears.

Write. Just write.

It had been there before. It had flowed from his fingertips like electricity. And now it was gone. Cut off. Extinguished like a candle whose wick had burned too low.

You can get it back. You have to.

You have to keep writing.

Daniel rubbed his sweaty palms on the legs of his jeans and placed his fingers on the keyboard. He stared at the last sentence he had been able to write:

The first brick broke free.

He tapped a key with his right index finger. His nails were too long. He usually cut them when they got long. He hated the feeling of long nails against the keys of a computer keyboard.

The cursor blinked at the end of that sentence, begging him to move it forward.

The first brick broke free.

Behind him, a dark shape moved into the edge of his vision.

He became aware of raspy breathing.

Daniel didn't know what frightened him more: the thought of it being gone as it was every time he spun around to look, or the thought of it remaining, of it standing there before him.

It wheezed as it drew breaths into wet lungs.

An image suddenly filled his mind: a creature born prematurely, sitting on trembling stalklike legs, a slick sheen of afterbirth glistening on its gelatinous skin, its paper-thin lungs threatening to tear with each raspy breath.

It has no eyes. It has no eyes and yet it sees.

Beneath his motionless fingers, the keys began to click all on their own.

Letters tumbled across the computer screen.

We have her.

An invisible hand reached up into Daniel's chest and gripped his heart, ripping it free and pulling it down, down into hell below.

He should have known all along what the thing at the edge of his vision looked like, a twisted shape, blond hair matted to its crushed skull with thick black blood.

He jerked his hand away from the keyboard, yet the words continued to race across the screen, over and over and over:

We have her We have her We have her We have her We have her

"Stop it," he whispered.

We have her We have her

"Please, stop."

We have her

Without warning, he grabbed the keyboard and yanked it, hard, pulling the cord free from the back of the monitor. He flung it across the room. It smashed into the wall and plastic keys rained down on the floor like hail.

Still the words streaked across the computer screen, faster and faster:

We have her We have her

The eyeless thing was right behind him. He could see it without even turning. It was standing directly over his right shoulder.

Not a thing. It's not a thing. It's your daughter, goddammit.

Cold, lifeless fingers grazed Daniel's neck.

And he screamed.

Sam and Moore heard the muffled shriek from above. They were half-way up the staircase when Daniel came rushing down. He slowed at the sight of them, his fear momentarily overtaken by confusion.

"Sam? Moore? What are you . . . ?"

God, he looks so thin! Sam thought. *He's wasting away!*

He wasn't thin, exactly, but compared to the massive man he had been last year, this may as well have been a living skeleton.

"What happened?" Sam asked. "What did you see up there?"

Daniel shook his head, unable to put it into words, and he pushed past them.

Sabrina was waiting at the bottom of the stairs.

"You brought this into our house!" she yelled as Daniel pushed past her too. There was such anger in her voice, months of obedience cast aside as she unleashed her fury. "You did this to us! I told you not to go! I told you not to go!

Daniel threw open the front door, and the humid Chicago air grabbed him in its fist.

They met in the middle of the front yard. Daniel was sucking in great, desperate breaths.

"I'm sorry. I'm sorry about all that." He shook his lowered head like he was apologizing for an unruly dog or misbehaving children.

"What happened, Daniel?" Sam asked.

Daniel's clothes were too baggy. He was still much larger than Sam, but he had lost an alarming amount of weight in the past year.

"There was . . ." Daniel began, and then he fell silent.

They waited.

After a moment, he continued. "Upstairs, in my office. There was a girl."

An image appeared in Sam's mind. The burned woman. The thing that crept through the empty halls of his house.

The last shred of hope that he might be losing his mind was ripped from Sam.

This was not the result of childhood guilt. This was not mental illness or a delusion.

It's visiting Daniel too. But as something different. Something just for him.

Sam pushed closer, up the front steps. "What did the girl look like?"

"I don't know."

"Daniel? What did she look like?"

He paused.

Across the street, a middle-aged couple exited their house and paused on their way to the SUV parked in their driveway. They stared over at Daniel's house in confusion.

"Mind your own fucking business!" Moore yelled.

They could clearly see the couple flinch. And then the couple hurried to their car, backed out of their driveway, and drove away at top speed.

Sam put a hand on Daniel's shoulder.

"What did the girl look like, Daniel?"

He exhaled a trembling breath. "She was a teenager. She . . . she looked just like our Claire except . . ."

"Except what?"

Daniel swallowed hard. "Except she didn't have eyes. She didn't have . . ."

Daniel crumpled to the thick green grass, tears running hot streaks down his face.

"What is this?" he asked them. "What's happening?"

"I don't know, but it's happening to us too," Moore said. There was no malice in her voice. In fact, there was something very close to compassion.

Daniel stared up at them. He looked tired, beaten down, cut off from the Zen-like peace he had once projected. The detachment in his eyes was profoundly unsettling.

He must have read the concern on Sam's face, for he turned to him and struggled to muster a trace of conviction.

"What are you two doing here, Sam?"

"We need to talk," Sam told him.

"And then?"

"And then we figure out how to stop this."

TWENTY-FOUR

SATURDAY, APRIL 22

THE WAITRESS, LONG and crooked like a bent cigarette, refilled their cups one by one with coffee as black as river mud. They offered polite smiles, waiting until she had moved down the line of booths before anyone broke the silence.

"What's the situation, then?" Daniel asked them. He had ordered a mound of burned bacon, scrambled eggs, and hash browns smothered in ketchup—just to show them that he was fine, that he was eating, that there was nothing to worry about. But he took one bite of the bacon and set it back down.

Look at us, Sam thought. *We're not sleeping. We're not eating. I weigh less than I did in high school. And Moore, she's lost her definition. She looks exhausted. But Daniel . . . he's wasting away. He's being devoured from the inside.*

Sam watched him push the hash browns around on the plate with a fork.

People must think he's sick, that he has a terrible disease.

In a way, he did. They all did.

"Well?" Daniel was growing impatient.

Moore turned to Sam, one eyebrow raised. "Do you want to tell him or should I?"

"I'll do it," Sam volunteered. He took a breath.

Begin at the beginning.

And so Sam told Daniel about the events that had transpired since their trip to Kill Creek. He told of the insatiable need to write that had pushed him to the breaking point of sanity; of the inspiration that had become oppression; of the sense that he was back at the Finch House every time he stepped away from the computer; of the visit from Eli, from which he learned the details of Moore's latest opus; and finally of visiting Moore in Los Angeles and discovering that their books were impossibly similar.

As Sam recounted his tale, Daniel sank deeper and deeper into his seat. It was the first time he hated—truly hated—being captivated by a story.

Daniel looked to Moore, a thought occurring to him. "You haven't insulted me once since you guys got here."

"Sorry," she said.

"That worries me," Daniel explained. "Anything that can take the piss out of you worries me." He shoved away the plate of food.

"I take it you've been working on a new book too," Sam said.

"Yeah."

"Is it similar to your other books?"

"Not even close."

"Describe it to us."

Daniel did. The plot was no surprise to Sam. The specifics were different—character names, location, motives—but the basic structure was exactly the same as his and Moore's, right down to the moment when the first brick fell from the wall.

"How many pages have you written?" Sam asked.

Touching his thumb to his fingers, Daniel did a quick mental count. "At least two thousand. Maybe more."

"Double- or single-spaced?"

"Single."

"Jesus fist-fucking Christ," Moore exhaled from low in her throat. "That's not a novel. That's a monster."

Snatching up a thin paper napkin, Daniel wiped away the dots of sweat that had sprouted on his brow. "This has to be a coincidence, right? I mean, it's impossible, the three of us writing similar books."

"Except they're not similar," Moore said. "They're the same. Exactly the same. Beat for beat."

They all fell silent. Around them were the sounds of the diner: silverware clinking on plates, coffee cups being refilled, the murmur of voices. It was late, the day already a distant memory. For everyone else in the diner, it was just another Chicago night.

But for us . . .

"There was something with me in my house," Sam told them.

"What was it?" Daniel asked.

They don't need to know. Not yet.

Sam shrugged. "I don't know. A presence."

"I saw it too, in my place," Moore admitted. Her voice was low, as if she were afraid someone outside of their table might hear. "When I would stop writing, it would call to me. It would say my name."

Sam offered her a sad smile. "Still think it's just a mass delusion?"

Moore thought for a moment, then shook her head.

Daniel rubbed his forehead so hard, he left red streaks across his skin. "We never should have gone to that house. None of this would be happening if we hadn't gone there." Then something occurred to him, his eyes wide. "What about Sebastian?"

"We haven't spoken to him," said Sam.

Daniel's face brightened. "Well, we should. Maybe he's not experiencing it. Maybe he's all right."

"So? What if he is? What does it prove?" Moore asked.

"Nothing," Daniel admitted, "but it would at least mean that whatever's happening to us, stops with us. It would mean it's contained."

Contained.

The word did not sit well with Sam. It conjured up images of a virus run amuck, of men in hazmat suits working feverishly over doomed patients as dark rivers of blood poured from every orifice. The word made him feel as though they were infected with something unknown and therefore incurable. Three more bodies to throw on the fire.

"We have to go to Sebastian," Daniel insisted. "We have to check on him. See if he's okay."

Moore ran chipped fingernails over her face and let out a slow, irritated groan. "This is just fantastic. We spend one night in that house, and now we're on a goddamn supernatural scavenger hunt."

Daniel shook his head. "But it's obviously not just going to go away. We have to do something about it."

"I know we have to do something! Just give me a goddamn moment to express my fucking feelings!"

Moore shoved her coffee cup away with a clank, a bit of java spilling over the lip and onto the saucer beneath.

Daniel smiled a small, pleased smile. "That's the T.C. Moore I remember." And then, as quickly as it had appeared, the smile faded, his face regaining its previous slackness. It was a transformation that happened much too easily, as if this were the first smile Daniel had allowed himself in a long time.

The three sat quietly, Moore tapping a fingernail on the rim of her coffee cup, Daniel poking at his breakfast with disgust.

"I'm sorry about your daughter," Sam said suddenly. "I don't think I ever told you that."

Daniel paused, not looking up from the red traces of ketchup that cut through the sea of grease on his plate. "Yeah . . . well . . . shit happens."

Sam had expected, "The Lord works in mysterious ways" or "Everything happens for a reason," but not "Shit happens." This was the death of Daniel's only child, after all, his flesh and blood, not a blown tire, not a stain on a freshly laundered shirt. "Shit happens" just didn't cut it.

The waitress came around, warming their cups with piping hot coffee.

Sam peered out the window that bordered one side of their booth. The parking lot was out there somewhere, cars in a neat row, snug between white lines. A sign featuring the name of the diner, Bailey's, surely spun at the side of the road, a neon arrow directing hungry travelers to the cozy comfort of the greasy spoon. Traffic must be rolling quietly down the street, anonymous drivers fighting sleep as they made their way to destinations unknown. It was all there. It had to be.

But Sam could not make it out. He stared through that window, and all he saw was darkness.

TWENTY-FIVE

SUNDAY, APRIL 23

THEY PLANNED TO fly to Ithaca, where they would check on Sebastian. There was still the chance that whatever was happening to them had, for some reason, left him alone. But they all doubted this was the case. They expected to find the old man in a similar state.

Unfortunately, Sebastian Cole was somewhat of a recluse. There was no listing of a home address online. There was no official Sebastian Cole website; all sites dedicated to the literary legend were managed by fans, who kindly supplied the information on their "Contact Us" pages that all correspondence was to go through Cole's agent.

The agent turned out to be a crusty bastard in New York who was equally tight-lipped about Sebastian's home address. "All correspondence must go through me," he told them. Hail-Mary calls to local bookstores in Ithaca also turned out to be dead ends. "Mr. Cole keeps to himself," one shop owner said. "See him at Pat's Diner now and again, but can't tell you much about where he lives except that I've heard it's off Ridge Road. Or is it Taughannock? I know it's near the lake. . . ."

They were trying to plan their next move when Sam got a call on his cell phone.

"She's dead."

The voice was familiar. Sam tried to place it.

"Who's dead?" he asked, confused. "Who is this?"

"It's Justin."

The name meant nothing to him.

The caller must have sensed this, for he immediately followed it with, "Wainwright. It's Wainwright."

Justin Wainwright.

It was strange to think of this odd young man as having a first name.

It was almost eight in the morning when he called. The three of them had stayed at the twenty-four-hour diner until dawn, talking and drinking coffee. After the early-morning call to Sebastian's agent, Sam and Moore had accompanied Daniel back to his home so that he could pack a bag. Thankfully, his wife was at church, allowing Daniel to go about his business without a messy confrontation.

When Sam's cell phone rang, he stepped out the back door and onto a semicircular slab of concrete that served as the Slaughter family's patio. A five-burner, stainless-steel grill was positioned on one side, a wicker couch and two outdoor chairs on the other.

"Who's dead?" Sam asked again.

Careful. This is Wainwright. You don't know what he's up to.

Wainwright cleared his throat. "Kate. You know, my . . . my . . ."

I know who you're talking about, asshole. But . . . dead? Kate's dead?

Sam could no longer feel his legs. He let his body slip down into one of the chairs, his eyes darting back and forth but focusing on nothing. "How?" he finally managed to choke out.

"*Killed* herself." Wainwright practically screamed it. He cleared his throat again, attempting to keep his emotions under control. "She slit her wrist, Sam. No, *slit* isn't right. She savaged herself. Cut her bloody arm to shreds. Last Thursday. Her landlord found her on the floor of her apartment, lying there. Oh my God. Why would she *do* that?"

Why the hell's everyone asking me like I know what the hell's going on? Sam wondered.

Eventually Wainwright admitted to Sam that Kate had changed over the past few months. She had grown increasingly paranoid, claiming at first that someone was tampering with her footage. She began arriving late to shoots, then not showing up at all.

At the same time, their personal relationship was suffering. She wouldn't return his calls. She stopped coming over to spend the night. At first, he thought she was blowing him off, that she had tired of him. But Kate had always been so kind and understanding. She had seen past his money and his pathetic quest to prove his worth to the world. She had truly liked him for who he was.

"There aren't a lot of people who like me, Sam," he admitted.

No kidding, Sam thought.

Ultimately Wainwright had no choice but to let Kate be, both personally and professionally.

Then, one night in late March, he spotted her crossing the street in SoHo. Her appearance was shocking, her face slack, thick shadows under her eyes, clothes and hair unwashed. He called out to her, but she quickened her pace and disappeared down the crowded sidewalk. A week later, he stopped by her apartment and knocked. He was sure she was home, he had heard shuffling from inside, but she never answered the door.

Now she was dead.

"Sam?" Wainwright asked hesitantly. "You there?"

"I'm here," Sam assured him.

Wainwright lowered his voice, as if he were afraid someone might overhear. "Look, I know you think I'm a piece of shit. That interview last year, it wasn't exactly above board. I get it—that's on me. But I swear it was supposed to be good for all of us. It wasn't supposed to be . . . whatever this is. Whatever started after we got back from Kansas."

Sam felt the world fall away from his feet, leaving him floating in empty space. "What do you mean?"

A sharp breath from the other end of the line.

"What's happening to you?" Sam asked.

"Nothing."

"Bullshit."

"It's probably just my imagination but . . ."

"But what, Wainwright? Damn it, tell me!"

Another pause. Then, "I've seen things. Usually just out of sight, you know? Sometimes at night, moving in the shadows. At first I thought it was my eyes playing tricks on me, until the other night. After I found out about Kate. I was alone in my apartment, and I had been crying, and . . . I heard someone laugh. Right behind me. Like,

like a chuckle, you know? Raspy. Like an old woman. It was right there behind me and it was damn well enjoying seeing me in pain."

Sam's flesh prickled at the thought, icy fingers tracing his spine.

"I couldn't turn around," Wainwright continued. "I tried, but I was terrified, Sam. Something told me that whatever was behind me, I didn't want to see it. There was another chuckle, and then it reached out and tapped me on the shoulder. Just one finger, tapping me. Asking me to turn around. I closed my eyes and muttered something under my breath."

"Muttered what?"

"A prayer, I guess. I don't know; I tried to wish it away. I knew that if I turned around, if I did see it, I would go crazy. I knew I would be looking at something that shouldn't exist. Something . . . unnatural. I must have stood there for at least ten minutes." Wainwright's words were slower, his voice steady. "Finally, I couldn't stand it anymore. So I took a breath and spun around. And there was nothing there. Absolutely nothing. I was alone, like I had been all day." He gave an embarrassed laugh. "God, it sounds so silly when I say it out loud. You must think I've lost it, mate."

He's not messing with you, Sam told himself. *He's scared. Really scared.*

As Sam leaned back in the patio chair, Daniel's house seemed to loom over him, blank windows reflecting the sun and sky, taking on the appearance of multiple eyes, like those of a spider, motionless, waiting for the perfect moment to strike. He hadn't noticed it before, but the two-story structure had an attic window, perched slightly higher than the rest, a single pane that gave the house the illusion of a third story.

"Sam?" Wainwright called from almost a thousand miles away. "Sam, are you there?"

Wainwright met them at LaGuardia Airport. He did his best to fake a smile. "It's good to see you," he said. Sam knew that he meant it.

That uncanny, rubbery look to Wainwright's flesh was still there, but his hair was greasy and flat. What had seemed like purple streaks in his eyes when they'd first met were now gone.

It was one o'clock by the time they drove into the city. Harsh rays of sunlight cut through the towering black forms of skyscrapers. Even though it was only April, it was a scorcher of a day, the heat shimmering off the asphalt in spectral waves. New York City smelled like a foul, musky beast, the very sidewalk sweating in the blazing sun.

They rode mostly in silence through the heavy traffic. Half an hour later, they pulled into a parking garage on the Upper East Side. Wainwright called it an *apartment,* but in reality it was the entire top floor of a fifteen-story building overlooking central Manhattan. Multiple walls had been taken down to create an expansive loft with floor-to-ceiling windows. In the distance, sunlight glinted off the surface of the reservoir in Central Park. It was exactly the kind of bachelor pad one might expect from Wainwright—hardwood floors stained black, stainless-steel appliances, monochromatic furniture. The few punches of color were from pieces of framed artwork by unknown artists and vintage grindhouse movie posters. Dividing the loft were bookshelves packed with vinyl records, tattered paperbacks, and countless Blu-ray discs of obscure genre movies.

Wainwright did not say a word as he hurried across his loft to the kitchen. Rising up on his toes, he fished a bottle of whiskey from a high cabinet above the refrigerator. Ice clinked as he dropped a handful of cubes into a tumbler. He unscrewed the cap and clumsily sloshed three fingers of hooch into the glass. He took a long, desperate sip.

Sam glanced around at the impeccably clean space, so different from all of their homes, free of filthy plates, empty bottles, and stacks of printer paper, the detritus Sam had found almost comforting during the past months.

Seeming to sense Sam's thoughts, Wainwright motioned to the room with his tumbler of scotch. "Cleaning lady. Comes twice a week."

He gulped down the rest of his drink, sucking the alcohol from the ice cubes. He held up the glass.

"Anybody?" he asked.

Moore raised her slender hand.

Aw, what the hell, Sam thought, holding up a hand.

Daniel sank down into a white leather chair without a word. He rubbed his sweaty hands across the legs of his khakis. He may have been thinner by comparison to last year, but the summer heat was still no friend of his. Sam watched him closely. This new, gaunt Daniel made him uneasy—the way the skin hung loosely from his cheekbones, the droop of his shoulders, the sag of his oversized clothes. It was like his skeleton was shedding everything from its bony frame, like a thing of complete yet ghastly simplicity existed within him. It yearned to be free of the weight it carried.

After Wainwright had poured two more drinks and handed them to Sam and Moore, he leaned over the granite kitchen counter and glanced around at his guests with darting eyes.

"Something is happening, right?"

Their silence confirmed it.

Wainwright whistled shrilly over his glass, sucked down the whiskey in a single gulp, and quickly tipped the bottle for a refill.

"I knew it; I bloody knew it," he muttered. "It followed us. Whatever was in that house, it followed every one of us."

"Just take it easy." Sam sipped at the whiskey. He really didn't feel like drinking; he'd had too little food and sleep in the past few days. But he welcomed the alcohol's promise of reprieve. He just wanted to numb his nerves a bit.

"Take it easy? Take it *easy*?" Wainwright stepped out from behind the kitchen counter. "Why the hell should I take it easy?"

"Because whatever it is, it hasn't hurt us," Moore said. Her tone was steady yet unusually soft. She was approaching Wainwright with a gentleness none of them had seen from her before. "It's messing with our heads, but that's all."

Wainwright's mouth turned down in disgust. "Hasn't hurt . . . ? What about Kate? She's dead, for Christ's sake!"

"Kate killed herself," Moore explained. "It didn't do it. She did."

"But it made her do it!"

"Okay, okay," Sam said calmly. "All we're saying is that if it wanted to shove us down the stairs or push us in front of a bus or just beat the hell out of us, it would have done it. But it hasn't. It hasn't touched us."

Wainwright's brown eyes reddened as they filled with tears.

"I could have helped her," he said, his throat suddenly thick with mucus. His entire body began to tremble. The ice rattled in his tumbler. Tears flooded down his cheeks in a great deluge that stunned them all. He set the tumbler down on the counter with a loud smack, covered his face with his hands, and sobbed.

Sam went to Wainwright and hugged him tight. The young man buried his head in Sam's shoulder and wept.

"I loved her," he said, his voice muffled and shaky.

"I know."

"She didn't deserve this," Wainwright whispered.

"None of us deserve this."

They all turned to the sound of the voice. It was Daniel, now sitting on the edge of his chair, his hands on his knees.

"None of us deserve this," he repeated.

Wainwright wiped his palms across his wet face. He seemed embarrassed by the show of emotion. He took a series of deep breaths, retreating further into himself with each one.

He was once more in control.

"What do you think it is, Sam?" he asked, his voice level.

He's not the expert on Kill Creek anymore. He's just as in the dark as we are. The thought made Sam feel even more helpless.

"I don't know." Sam shrugged. "Only thing I do know is that it was at Kill Creek when we arrived, but it didn't stay there when we left."

He put his glass to his lips and gave it a steep tip, but no whiskey touched his mouth. It was gone. He had finished his drink without knowing it.

"We're going up to find Sebastian," he explained, his words steady and clear. "If this is happening to us, it must be happening to him too."

"Then what?" Wainwright asked. There was judgment in his voice, as if he were setting Sam up for something.

"We make sure Sebastian is okay, and then we think of a plan. Together."

"Won't work."

"And why's that?"

"You said it yourself. We don't know what we're dealing with," Wainwright said.

They watched as Wainwright crossed to one of the bookshelves and ran a finger over the tops of the paperbacks that filled it, stopping on a book near the middle. He pulled it free and tossed it to Sam.

Pages fluttered like the wings of an injured bird. Sam reached out and caught the book. He looked down at it, his thumb running over the cover. At this point, Sam knew it well. It was Wainwright's copy of *Phantoms of the Prairie: A True Story of Supernatural Terror*, by Dr. Malcolm Adudel.

"We're all familiar with this," Sam reminded Wainwright. "There's nothing in here that comes close to what we're experiencing."

Wainwright motioned to the book. "Turn to the last page. The author's info."

Sam did as he was told, tucking his thumb behind the back cover and opening the book to the final page. He read the words aloud:

About the Author

Dr. Malcolm Adudel holds a PhD in parapsychology from the University of Southern California. He is one of the world's leading experts on psychical research and the author of over forty books on the supernatural. He currently resides in New York City.

Sam lowered the loosely bound paperback. "Adudel lives here. In New York."

"Yes," Wainwright said. From his pocket, he fished out a folded strip of paper. "And I know where."

The brownstone was just across the river, in Brooklyn. Wainwright found a metered parking spot on Washington Avenue, and the four of them climbed out to the shriek of a city bus coming to a stop half a block north. They trudged down the busy sidewalk, past an eclectic mix of stores and restaurants, before coming to a sharp angle that marked the beginning of Adudel's street. They moved down a quiet line of redbrick apartment buildings and brownstones, all of which had seen better days. Great shadows fell on the row of buildings, dark stalks of weeds bursting through the cracked, buckled sidewalk.

On the far corner, a group of kids, the oldest no more than fourteen, sat on a stoop, their voices melding into an odd echo of indiscernible words. At the sight of the approaching adults, they stopped talking, eyeing the intruders suspiciously.

Sam nodded at the boys, but they only stared blankly at him. He glanced back at the others, slowing so they could catch up. Moore and Wainwright were close behind. Daniel, as usual, was hanging back by himself.

He's been so quiet, Sam realized. On the plane to New York, Daniel had kept to himself, his face expressionless.

When they neared the center of the block, Sam asked Wainwright, "What's the address again?"

Wainwright unfolded the slip of paper on which he had jotted down the street number. "Twenty-six forty-six."

Sam shielded his eyes from the glow of the sunny blue sky with his hand and searched the metal numbers affixed to the buildings. "There it is," he said, pointing two doors down.

The name printed on a metal strip above the buzzer was "DeLaud."

It took Moore only a few seconds to solve it. "It's an anagram," she told the others, "for Adudel."

Sam nodded and pressed the button. From somewhere above, they heard the faint chime of a doorbell. He glanced over to the street corner. The kids were gone from the stoop. The street was eerily vacant.

A voice crackled through a dented speaker. "Yes?"

Sam hunched over and spoke loudly into the intercom, "Dr. Adudel?"

There was no response, only the buzz of static.

"We need to talk to you."

Still nothing from the other side.

Moore abruptly pushed Sam aside. She pressed her lips up close to the intercom as if she expected Adudel to feel her hot breath on the other side. "It's about Kill Creek," she said impatiently. "Open the goddamn door."

A long moment passed, the four of them fidgeting nervously on the front steps. Then a loud buzz signaled the front door unlocking. Even Moore jumped at the sound.

The short hallway led to more stairs. They called out, but there was no answer. Light spilled down from a skylight above, giving the act of climbing the steps a sense of literal ascension, as if they were all being lifted from the darkness below. Harsh atonal music tromped through the air, an odd mixture of instruments—a tribal drum, a synthesizer, a trumpet. It made for an ominous fanfare as they reached the top of the stairs.

What the hell are we walking into? Moore wondered. *We know nothing about this man. And here we are, in his home.*

Another hallway stood before them, its walls paneled in rich walnut below, bloodred fabric above. In stark contrast, the cocoon-like tunnel opened to a brilliant, sunlit room. Even from where she stood, Moore could see that the walls were white and pristine, adorned with countless black-and-white photos in ebony frames.

"Dr. Adudel?" Sam called out as he took a few hesitant steps down the hall.

Moore stepped up beside Sam. She reached out and touched his hand.

"I don't like this," she said, not caring if he found the comment weak. It was the truth.

"Neither do I," Sam said.

"Hello?" a voice drifted down from the white room. "Please, come in. I'm in the room at the end of the hall, yes?"

His words were tinged with the hint of an accent, something vaguely Eastern European.

Moore followed Sam down the red hall. The others were close behind them. The light at the end of the hall grew brighter as they moved slowly closer.

They entered the white room, the group squinting, the intense sunshine momentarily blinding them. Moore could make out a human shape sitting across the room. She blinked, and the form came into focus. It was a man, late sixties, thin patches of silver hair dotting his otherwise bald head. He wore pressed tan slacks and a plaid dress shirt, tucked in with a brown leather belt. His tiny eyes stared out from behind oversized frames, the lenses of his glasses so thick, it seemed as if he were peering up from the bottom of a deceptively deep pond. Leaning against his chair was a wooden cane with a silver handle in the shape of a lion's head. He offered them a strange, crooked smile but no greeting, his mouth half-open, expectantly.

"Dr. Adudel," Moore said.

The man nodded curtly but still said nothing. He looked from guest to guest, as if he were absorbing the sight of long-forgotten friends.

Wainwright stepped forward. "We're sorry to just crash on you like this. Unannounced, I mean."

"No bother," Adudel said. His head continued to twitch slightly, silently accepting them. He looked a bit like a rooster pecking the air in anticipation of feed.

Moore quickly scanned the numerous framed photographs on the walls. Most of them appeared to be of Adudel on his globe-trotting adventures into the unknown. As a younger man, he proudly sported a thick head of hair but insisted on those absurdly large frames, like two magnifying glasses over his eyes. There was Adudel at a séance, the hint of ectoplasm streaming from the medium's fingertips; in an ancient stone cellar, mysterious orbs flitting about him like fairies; with the tribesmen of an Amazonian village, beaming proudly at his own courage among these so-called savages; leading a student team into the abandoned room of an empty house, one hand on his cane, the other raised to let the resident spirits know he meant no harm; standing with Rachel Finch at the house on Kill Creek, her hair tied tight in a bun; Adudel alone before the Finch House, dwarfed by the building behind him, the structure looming even from a distance.

This particular photograph gave Moore pause. She leaned in toward it, inspecting the finer details of the print. Something about the picture troubled her. It took her a moment to place it, and then she realized it was Adudel himself. The ghost-chaser was not smiling. He was not standing tall and confidently like in his other photos. Quite the contrary. Adudel looked scared, shaken to his very core.

Because this is real, Moore thought. *This is not a delusion. This is not coincidence. Even Adudel knew there was something real at Kill Creek. And now it's after us.*

Sam watched as the doctor grasped his cane by the handle and gave its tip a solid thump against the wood floor. It had the desired effect, causing the entire group to turn suddenly toward him.

"Now isn't this an interesting surprise?" he said. He spoke in an odd staccato rhythm, dragging out the last word of every sentence. His beady eyes darted randomly from person to person. They never seemed to blink, always open behind those massive lenses.

Sam stepped forward and offered a hand. "Thank you for seeing us. I'm—"

"Oh, I know who you are."

Adudel reached out and grasped Sam's hand, not in a traditional handshake but with his fingers over the palm, his thumb slipping around the back of the hand, forcing Sam's fingers to close over his.

"Yes," the strange little man said, "I know who all of you are." He locked eyes with each of the writers as he spoke their names:

"Sam McGarver. T.C. Moore. Daniel Slaughter."

He kept his grip on Sam's hand, refusing to let go. The man's fingers twitched with excitement.

"I am in awe of every one of you. The respect you command, the power your words hold over your readers. It must be a thrill to know you possess such talent, yes? I have become somewhat of an expert on you these past few months. I have read everything each of you has ever written."

"Bullshit."

Sam turned to Daniel, surprised that the curse had come from him and not Moore.

Adudel's crooked smile stretched wider. "Oh no, Mr. Slaughter, I certainly have. Even by you, and that is, what? Over forty books? Slim volumes, but an impressive body of work nonetheless.

"And, Mr. Wainwright, well, I am a *big* fan of WrightWire. The power you wield, the way you turn people on to even the most obscure works of art. It's very, very impressive."

Have they met before? Sam wondered. The way Adudel was looking at Wainwright gave the impression that they had. There was a familiarity there that gave Sam pause.

Wainwright's expression betrayed nothing. In the harsh light of the white room, his face looked even more artificial, a man-made machine passing as human.

"Then you saw our project last fall," he said. "And you know why we're here."

Adudel's jagged smile began to twitch, much like the fingers still held in Sam's hand. Adudel did not want the idle chitchat to end. He was thoroughly enjoying this moment.

"You're here . . . Well, you're here because you believe I know things about that house that others do not, yes?"

Yes, Sam thought. *Yes. Holy hell, yes, I hope so.*

Grasping Sam's hand tighter, Adudel grunted softly and pulled himself up from his chair. His face was only inches from Sam's.

"I believe I can bring some clarity to this situation," he said. "But first, tea."

Adudel poured them each a steaming cup of oolong tea in ornate hand-painted teacups. He stared at them with those unblinking pin-prick eyes, not bothering to glance once at the teapot in his hand or the cup into which he poured.

Sam sipped the amber liquid, earthy hints of roasted wood rolling over his tongue. "So?" he asked, intentionally letting the word hang in the air.

Grasping his own cup in both hands, Adudel blew a couple cool breaths over the surface of his tea before taking a hesitant sip. Steam rose from the cup and curled around his face like smoke.

"The house," he began, "was nothing more than that. A house. I'm sorry to disappoint you."

Is he serious? Sam thought. *Did we come all this way for nothing?*

He looked around at the group, all exchanging confused glances.

Sam spoke for the others. "Then how do you explain—"

"The experiences?" Adudel grinned into his tea. "Perhaps I should elaborate, yes?"

"Fucking yes, yes, elaborate," Moore spat, reddish irritation rising to her cheeks.

Adudel's beady eyes shrank behind his saucer-like glasses. Holding the teacup in one hand, he reached out for his cane and shifted his weight to it. "In the beginning. That's how all great stories start, yes? The first line of the Gospel of John reads, 'In the beginning was the Word.' In our case, the word came second, for our tale starts, 'In the beginning, there was the house.' May I ask . . . have you read my book?"

All in attendance nodded.

"Then you know the general history." He drank his tea. "Joshua Goodman settled the land in the mid-eighteen hundreds, built his dream home a stone's throw from the thriving town of Lawrence, and he and his secret love, Alma Reed, settled in to live out the rest of their lives in peace. Only one problem: Alma was black. A former slave. Not the best time in history to be a woman of color, not that there's ever been a *best* time in our nation's history. So while Quantrill's men stormed and burned Lawrence, a band of five rode out to the Goodman estate, shot Goodman in the gut, and dragged Alma from the house. Now, if you've read up on your pulp crime novels, you'll know that a shot to the gut is not an instant kill. It's a slow and miserable death. Buoyed by the need to protect his love, Goodman probably could have hobbled into the yard and put up a fight, which is why his attackers made sure to put a bullet into each of his knees. So there lies Joshua Goodman, staring through his open front door as that rogue band of William Quantrill's men first raped his beloved Alma, then strung her from a branch in that twisted old beech tree. You can imagine his view—her legs kicking beneath her, desperately trying to plant themselves into open air as the sweaty brutes stood around her, laughing their horse laughs and patting one another on their hairy backs. 'Good job, Enis. Good job, Clyde. We done killed ourselves another slave. Long live Lee and the South' and all that pickled horseshit."

"I thought she was already dead when they hung her." The voice belonged to Daniel.

"Yes, well, that's one story. But it's not the truth."

Adudel paused to take another sip of tea. No one spoke a word. They waited patiently until he continued. The rhythm of the old man's voice was intoxicating, the pinpoints of his eyes captivating. For the moment, he owned them all.

"As you may remember, days went by before the bodies of Joshua Goodman and Alma Reed were found. A solid week, in fact. You can imagine the horror as that lone rider trotted down Kill Creek Road to find the dark, bloated body of Alma Reed swinging in the breeze, that horrible mixture of honeysuckle and rotting flesh blowing on the wind.

"Even in those days, word traveled fast, and soon every neighbor within ten miles descended upon that house. There was Alma, cut down from the branch, the noose still tight around her swollen neck. There was Goodman, knees a shattered, bloody mess, gut a sopping hole, facedown in a pool of his own blood.

"There are two kinds of ghost stories, as those in your line of work must know: tales of revenge and tales of love cut short. In a way, this was both. So it was destined to become a local legend. The Goodman house, the site of that senseless massacre, where those two poor souls had died gruesome deaths. The details were told in whispers by firelight, first to concerned adults, then to trembling children. The reality of the murders quickly became the stuff of tall tales.

"In the beginning, there was the house. But next, like our good friends in the latter Testament, we encounter . . . the word. Gossip, my friends. Goodman's sad fate became the talk of the countryside as the *word* spread. It wasn't long before the word became sinister. As that house sat alone and abandoned on the banks of Kill Creek, passersby with overactive imaginations began to tell stories of eerie lights in the windows and wails in the night, of specters skulking the grounds and a woman swinging by her neck from a limb in the old beech tree—"

"So they were only stories," interrupted Wainwright. The illumination from the skylight above made his smooth flesh seem to glow.

"At first." Adudel leaned harder on his cane. The wooden rod croaked beneath him, a minor threat. "Though gossip has a funny way of becoming fact. Everyone, it seems, had their ghost story to tell. And pretty soon, people started to believe. Lawrence rebuilt itself, but the Goodman estate did not. It fell into disrepair, an abandoned patch of land, an oft-avoided detour on the way to Kansas City.

"Of course, the house did not remain empty forever. Eventually some rube was tricked into buying the place. But it just didn't feel right. It was cold within those walls. Not the way a home should feel. And then the true sightings began. Apparitions in the night. Wisps of white wandering the halls."

Sam cocked his head, his brow furrowed as he tried to guess where the strange little man was going. "So the place was haunted after all?"

With a sharp laugh, Adudel set his empty teacup down on the kitchen counter. He tapped his cane against the edge of a lower cabinet, knocking out a perfect, steady beat. "Allow me to digress," he said, collecting his thoughts.

Behind him, Sam heard Moore let out a long sigh. The irritable writer was losing patience. Sam held up a finger, signaling her to hang on for just a little while longer.

After a solid minute, the rhythmic tap of his cane ceased and Adudel spoke. "Years ago, a good friend of mine, my lawyer, in fact, was happily married and enjoying a thriving career with a well-respected firm in Manhattan. One day his paralegal retired, and my friend went about the business of hiring someone new to assist him. After weeks of interviews, he settled on a pretty, young girl, fresh out of law school.

I'm not saying that her looks didn't factor into his decision; he was only human, yes?"

Moore arched an eyebrow. "You mean he was a *man*, yes?"

"A good man," Adudel insisted, "and I believe his intentions were pure. But that didn't stop his colleagues from running off at the mouth, especially after he and his pretty, young paralegal spent several weeks working alone, after hours. Word around the firm was that they were sleeping together. He vehemently denied it. He was telling the truth; nothing salacious was occurring. But then his wife began to voice her concern, hounding him when he came home thirty minutes late, interrogating him, scrutinizing his every move. And you know what happened? He ended up sleeping with his pretty, young paralegal. 'To hell with it,' he told me. 'They all said I was doing it, so I figured, why not?' He got divorced, his pretty, young paralegal moved on to another job, and that was that."

Adudel took off his glasses and pulled his shirtsleeve over his hand and gave the monstrous lenses a good wiping. "Do you understand what I'm saying?"

"Not a word," Moore snapped.

"You're saying that the house on Kill Creek wasn't haunted until people believed it was haunted." This was from Daniel, his words flat and distant, an obligatory answer.

Adudel slipped his glasses back on and pointed a bony finger at him. "Precisely."

"Okay, look," Sam interrupted. He knew his friends were growing annoyed with the good doctor. But Adudel had been in that house. He had spent time with Rachel Finch. He had written a best-selling book about it. He was perhaps the only person on the planet who could offer them some shred of assistance. "Let's cut the shit. Something is happening to us."

Adudel did not respond, only offering Sam a curious smile.

"I get it," Sam said. "You live for this type of thing. It's your line of work. But for us . . . we've only written around it. It's never been real. It's always been fiction. Until now."

Moore capped this with an "Amen."

Dr. Adudel gave another throaty chuckle, his amusement with the group boundless.

"Something funny?" These two words from Daniel sent a shiver through Sam. There was menace in them, dull and metallic. It sounded nothing like the man Sam had known last October.

Adudel shook his head, retaining his aloof grin. "It's just that . . . my book? *Phantoms of the Prairie?*" His playful smile widened. "It, too, is fiction."

At first the statement meant nothing. And then the razor-thin blade of its profound simplicity tore them wide open.

I knew it. I can't believe I thought for one second this little freak could help us, Moore thought.

"I told you all that it was bullshit," she said loudly. "He's just jerking us off. He's wasting our time."

"Moore—" Sam began.

She cut him off. "No. No, we're done here. We're leaving." She looked at Adudel, not bothering to hide her disgust. "This might be a game to you, but it's real. For us, it's real."

Moore marched toward the hallway, but no one else moved.

"Let's go," she ordered. The others were still staring in confusion at Adudel.

Daniel leaned closer to the doctor. "How can it be fiction? You wrote it. You experienced these things. It says it right on the cover: 'a true story.' Why would you lie about that? How could you *lie?*"

Wainwright was slowly shaking his head. Watching him refuse to process what Adudel had said, Moore realized this was how she had felt since the day she'd returned from Kill Creek. No matter how much the inspiration of a fresh story had blinded her, somewhere deep within her, she was shaking her head, thinking, *This cannot be. This should not be.*

"Why would I lie?" Adudel repeated Daniel's question. "That may be the most important thing you've asked since you arrived. It is, in fact, what your colleague asked me when I first admitted the truth to him."

Moore frowned. *Colleague? What the hell is this crazy bastard talking about?*

Behind her, there was the sound of footsteps entering the room.

Moore heard Sam gasp.

Her first thought was, *It's Adudel. He's messing with us again. It's another one of his tricks.*

She spun around.

This was no trick. This was not an apparition or a delusion.

Sebastian Cole smiled warmly at the group.

"Hello, my friends," he said.

The moment of silent shock seemed to last forever.

"What . . ." Sam began, unable to make sense of what he was seeing.

He's okay, he thought, and an overwhelming feeling of relief rushed through him.

Sam hurried over and embraced the old man. Sebastian tentatively returned Sam's hug, and then pulled away without a word.

"What is it?" Sam asked, his brow furrowing in confusion.

Sebastian opened his mouth to speak, but Adudel cut him off.

"He contacted me several weeks ago, asking if I could discuss the house on Kill Creek. It's suddenly become a hot topic." He rolled up onto the balls of his feet, bouncing slightly with excitement. He was staring at Wainwright again with that same expectant look, those river pebble eyes seeking some acknowledgment that Wainwright had yet to give.

He turned to Sebastian. "Mr. Cole has been coming down from upstate to see *me*," Adudel explained. He seemed to underline the word *me* with unmistakable pride.

Sam looked at Sebastian—*really* looked at him. The old man's once deathly pale skin was vibrant and alive. He was dressed in a three-piece suit, his face cleanly shaven, his white hair swept back. His eyes were alert and bright. He looked twenty years younger than when Sam had last seen him.

Has he been here this whole time? Sam wondered. *Why wouldn't he come out when he first heard us?*

Unless he was waiting to find out why we were here, his mind suggested. The thought did not sit well with him.

Wainwright was staring at Sebastian as if he thought the man were some sort of illusion. "Why have you been coming here, mate?"

"Research," Sebastian said, the single word meant to explain everything.

"Research?" Sam asked. "For what?"

Sebastian hesitated, unsure of exactly how much information he should share.

Once again, Adudel chimed in before Sebastian could speak. "About the house, of course, same as all of you."

"And what has he told you?" Moore asked Sebastian. The suspicion in her voice was loud and clear.

"Not enough." Sebastian blushed, as if he were embarrassed to admit it.

Adudel tapped the bottom of his cane hard against the floor. "But now you're all here. Together. No reason to keep you waiting any longer."

Off the kitchen was a short hallway with three doors—the first to a bathroom, the second to a small bedroom, and the third to a miniscule study, no bigger than a walk-in closet. It was a cluttered mess, towers of books threatening to topple, mounds of yellow legal pads covered in chicken-scratch notes, an ancient IBM computer at the center of the storm. Adudel led them into this room—Moore at the front of the line, followed by Wainwright, then Sam and Sebastian, and finally Daniel. The six of them cramming awkwardly into the tight quarters.

Wedged behind one particular stack of papers on the top of a battered metal file cabinet was a photograph housed in a dusty wooden frame. Adudel pulled this out from its hiding place and held it up for the others to see. Like the others in the living room, it was black and white, yet this one featured two elderly women, both at least in their sixties, the woman on the right tall and slender, her straight black hair hanging like a curtain around her shoulders; the other confined to a wheelchair, her body slightly bent, her jet-black hair pulled into a painfully tight bun. Both had nearly translucent skin, as if the sun rarely touched them. Their eyes were wormholes, dark and winding. Their faces were as set as stone, expressionless, yet those eyes hinted at something more, some secret knowledge purposely kept from the photographer.

"The Finch sisters," Adudel announced. He tapped an overgrown, yellowing fingernail on the woman standing. "Rachel." He tapped the crooked body in the wheelchair. "Rebecca."

"You met them both?" Wainwright asked, confused. "I thought . . ."

"Rachel gave me this picture. By the time I was granted access to the house, Rebecca was . . . dead."

Something about that pause troubled Sam, although he could not say why.

Shuffling uncomfortably on his feet, Daniel inadvertently sent a ripple through the closely huddled group. He took a step back, into the doorway, leaning on the frame for support. He appeared tired, drained.

Wainwright took the picture frame from Adudel, inspecting the women more closely. From the wallpaper behind them, it appeared they were standing in the house's living room, the very same place where they had all gathered around a roaring fire so many months ago. "So you made it all up." His tone was bitter, as if he had been betrayed. "Nothing happened while you were there."

"Oh, now, I wouldn't say that," Adudel said.

Adudel put a finger to his dry, cracked lips and glanced around the room in an attempt to remember the location of some long-lost item. After pulling out several file drawers, he found what he was seeking: a battered memo book, its cover half-torn from its black spine. He held it out to Wainwright, a peace offering of sorts. "Read it."

Sam glanced over at Sebastian, who was standing off to the side of the group, his arms crossed.

Has he seen this? he wondered. He felt the pang of guilt. This was his idol, the man whose writing had salvaged what was left of Sam's childhood. And now Sam looked at him suspiciously.

But he was here. He's been visiting Adudel. What does Sebastian know that we don't?

Opening the memo book to the first page, Wainwright found a series of notes printed in cramped block letters, Adudel's preferred writing style.

There was a header: May 13, 1983. Along the right margin were a series of times. Wainwright began with the first entry:

9:15 a.m. – Arrived at Kill Creek. Greeted at door by Rachel. Waited for me to step into house before address-ing me. Strange. Not very friendly. Woman of few words. "We are pleased to have you here." Her words. We.

*10:43 a.m. – Just concluded a tour of the house. Much
renovation done by the sisters. Not quite sure why, place
is in the middle of nowhere. No strange activity. No C.S.
felt. No O.A.*

Wainwright paused. "C.S.?" he asked.

"Cold Spots," explained Adudel. "And O.A. is shorthand for
Optical Anomalies. My own term. Anything supernatural that you can
see. Orbs, shadows, ghostly lights."

"Right," Wainwright said. He continued:

*11:32 a.m. – Conversation in the study. I asked about
Rebecca. Rachel reluctant to speak of her. Get the feeling
she's hiding something. Maybe just being protective? A
sister's love? Shown scrapbook, pictures of the construc-
tion done to the house, a few childhood photos of R&R.
Only one picture of them together in house. Rachel gave
it to me. Odd. She has no other copy. Why let me have it?
Noticed that Rachel now wears her hair like Rebecca's,
tied back. Asked about this. She says it is her way of
honoring her sister.*

*1:14 p.m. – Lunch. Rachel made sandwiches. Ate in
sunroom. Rachel pointed out well in back, trail leading
to Kill Creek. Have to go check that out.*

*Still no unusual activity. House a bit cool, but day
is overcast.*

*3:05 p.m. – Something has happened. Asked Rachel
about third-floor bedroom blocked off by brick wall.
She told me it was "none of your concern." While she
was in bathroom, snuck upstairs to third-floor bedroom.
Inspected brick wall. Not done by professional. Not same
level of craftsmanship seen in rest of house. Did Rachel
build this wall herself?*

5:28 p.m. – Spent rest of afternoon asking Rachel about their experiences in house. She spoke freely re: renovation but clammed up when I pressed on supernatural matters. Why won't she talk? Maybe house isn't haunted? Maybe one big hoax?

7:30 p.m. – Witnessed first O.A. After dinner, decided to explore the basement.

Nothing at first. Dark. Dirty. A single bulb to light the room, plus my flashlight.

Was heading back upstairs when shadow in corner seemed to move. Seemed to step forward, away from the wall, then back into darkness. No C.S. during encounter.

9:00 p.m. – Rachel has proposed a curious thing. Over wine, she suggested we "elaborate" a bit. I was confused at first. If house really is one of country's most haunted, why embellish? She would only offer another cryptic answer: "For strength." What does this mean?

9:45 p.m. – Have reluctantly discussed details of my supposed "encounters" in house. Feel like a fraud. But Rachel has made an attractive offer. Too much to pass up. What's one book? Enough true backstory to create "non-fiction novel" as Capote would say. No one can know about this. Enough nonbelievers already. If this one aberration in career can help parapsychology as whole, then it's worth it. Can use R's $$ to fund future investigations. Real investigations. Is that so wrong?

1:00 a.m. – Story complete. Feeling better about this. Not that much different from what really happened. Only . . . more vivid, more detailed.

Maybe just talking myself into it. But it is a believable story. Rachel insists it is the right thing to do.

2:30 a.m. – Heard footsteps in hall. Went to investigate. Saw Rachel turning the corner. Careful not to be seen,

I followed her. Watched as she went upstairs to wall at third-floor bedroom. She sat by wall. I was able to listen. She spoke to wall: "I'm sorry. You understand. You understand." Swear I could hear TWO voices—Rachel's and another. Who is she talking to? Rebecca? Alive? Or her spirit? Could spirit of Rebecca still be in that room?

Wainwright lowered the memo book and looked from Daniel to Moore to Sebastian to Sam, finally settling on Adudel, the man who had written the notes over two decades ago, the man who had transformed this humble experience into a farce of a book, a best-selling lie. He held out the notebook in disgust. "Take it," he said.

Adudel did, tossing it onto the desk. The sunshine streaming through a tiny square window above was beginning to fade, the study suddenly cloaked in gloom.

"So now you know what I know, which is not much, yes?"

"You must have theories," Daniel said. It sounded like an accusation.

Adudel's only reply was a playful grin. He was enjoying the moment. He was not ready to lose them all just yet.

Sam turned to Sebastian.

"What has he told you?" Sam asked him.

Sebastian reluctantly met Sam's gaze. "Not much. Bits and pieces," he said softly.

"But now all of you are here," Adudel explained.

As if he expected it, Sam realized.

Or, at the very least, it wasn't a surprise. The eccentric little man had welcomed them in as a group, had looked at each of their faces like separate parts of a whole, a necessary union.

Adudel pushed down on the top of the silver lion's head, once more lifting to the toes of his feet. It was the action of a showman eager to continue with his act. "This is what I believe. The house became home to an entity because people believed it was haunted. I can't be positive what it is exactly. A wayward spirit that took root in the house, although I highly doubt this. A concentration of psychic energy, perhaps. Whatever it is, it resides there now, and has for over a hundred years. But it grows weak from time to time. As people forget, as the name 'Kill Creek' leaves the public consciousness, the power within the house loses strength. That's what I think Rachel meant when I asked her why we should make up a story. 'For strength,' she said."

He looked to Sebastian and repeated the words: "For strength."

Sam thought he saw the old writer give a nod of acknowledgment, an understanding that was lost on the rest of the group.

"Only the locals remembered the house at that time," Adudel continued. "Rachel needed some way of reminding people that the house was a thing to be feared. I served that purpose. My book gave it strength."

"But your book stopped selling," Moore said. It was not meant to be an insult. It was merely a statement of fact.

Adudel nodded, his jagged grin faltering. "Eventually. People lost interest, yes? It's what we all fear as writers, I suppose, our readers no longer caring about the stories we are compelled to tell. Bookstores stopped stocking it. My publisher stopped printing it. Only used copies existed. And once again, Kill Creek became an obscure legend. It was a name whispered by curious college students but few others. The entity in the house, the thing that Rachel and Rebecca Finch had been so strangely protective of, became dormant once more. Hibernating. Waiting."

"Until we came along," Sam said.

The polished black stone of Adudel's eyes shimmered beneath his thick lenses. "Well . . . that was not entirely by chance. I haven't been completely honest with you. You see, Mr. Wainwright did not come upon my book on his own. I sent a copy to him."

All eyes flashed to the young internet mogul, in his slim-fitting suit, his shirt unbuttoned, his dress casual even as the stress of his situation squeezed him in a vice.

Wainwright's mouth opened slightly, just enough to allow one whispered word: "You?"

The doctor nodded proudly. "The paperback, the one you own. Didn't you ever wonder where it came from?"

"People send me things all the time. Books. Movies. Music." He was searching, attempting to justify the past.

"That's how you chose the house?" Moore spat. "Someone sent you a book and you didn't wonder for one goddamn second *why*?"

Wainwright shook his head in confusion. "It was just the book. No note. Nothing."

Sam turned to Adudel. A thin layer of cold sweat had broken out over Sam's skin. "Why did you send it to him?"

"The same reason you all would agree to such an absurd interview with WrightWire," Adudel replied. There was an irrefutable calmness in his voice. "Because Mr. Wainwright is in the business of putting things back on top."

A pained groan escaped Wainwright's lips. "I made it famous again."

Notebooks and papers flew from the desk as Moore swept them away with a furious hand. She was immediately in Adudel's face. He looked up into her eyes, staring into her broken pupil, and the confidence he had relished was stolen from him.

"What's after us?" she demanded. "What are we dealing with?"

"I-I told you," Adudel stammered.

"But what *is* it? A residual haunting? A remnant?"

"It can't be," Sam chimed in. "It's calculated. It's intelligent."

Intelligent. The thought made his entire body quiver.

Moore spun around to Daniel. "Demonic, then? Is that possible?"

"Why are you asking me?"

"Because you're the goddamn Jesus freak in the group!" she roared.

Adudel chimed in, "I don't believe it's demonic. At least not in the way we think of a demon, as an ancient thing, as a corruption of God's love."

"A portal, then, some kind of doorway to another world," Sam suggested. He suddenly became aware that they had all formed an ever-tightening half circle around Adudel. All but Sebastian. He was standing with his back to the wall, purposely removing himself from the group.

He's barely said a word, Sam realized. *Why is he being so quiet?*

Adudel took a step back, nearly falling as his cane caught on a stack of old leather-bound books. He was trying to put distance between himself and the group.

"Possibly . . . possibly a portal, but I don't believe it was there when Goodman first built the house."

Moore lunged forward and grabbed Adudel by his shoulders. The doctor made a sound like a frightened child.

"Then where did it come from?"

"I . . . I'm not sure . . ."

"Where did it come from?" she repeated.

"It came from us! We created it, yes? All of us. Everyone. From the day Goodman and Alma were killed. Believing the house was bad actually made it bad."

The skin on Sam's left arm screamed, and he realized he was gripping his scarred flesh tightly, wringing it.

"So you wrote your book to give the house power? To make it stronger?" Moore asked incredulously.

Adudel's voice was barely a whisper. "It wanted me to. Rachel . . . she said I would get something in return. She said that's how it worked. And I did! I got what I wanted. My book, my field, my entire life's work was taken seriously. *I* was being taken seriously!"

The parapsychologist's cane trembled in his unsteady hand. "It was here in this house with me back then. I could sense it watching me as I wrote. And then the book was done and people were buying it, people were reading it. And for a few years, it was exactly as Rachel promised. You see, the house needed a storyteller."

A storyteller. Sam looked to Sebastian. The old man would not meet his gaze. Sam thought he saw a grimace tugging at the corners of Sebastian's lips.

Or is it a smile?

"It needs someone to share its legacy with the world," Adudel continued. "But I failed."

"People started to believe you were a fraud," Sam said.

Adudel drew in a shaky breath. Somehow his eyes appeared even smaller behind the large lenses. "The house used me. Just like it is using all of you now. And when you have served its purpose, it will cast you aside. It will forget you. It happened to Rachel Finch. It happened to me."

"It won't happen to us," Wainwright's deep voice boomed in the cramped study.

"It will," Adudel assured him. That crooked smile crept across the old man's face like a fault line opening in the earth. His cheeks struggled to hold the expression as decades of fear and regret fought their way to the surface.

"And then you, too, will be forgotten."

The street was almost completely dark now, even as the sky above retained its cool blue glow, touched here and there with pink patches of sunset. The buildings on either side rose in great black walls, creating the sensation of being at the bottom of a narrow chasm, the reassurance of light so far away.

Sam checked his watch: seven thirty p.m.

How long were we in there? he wondered.

Stepping down onto the sidewalk, Same felt as though they had lost days, a week, even. Their visit couldn't have lasted more than two hours, yet here they were, shuffling back toward Washington Avenue like a pack of brain-fried junkies, unable to comprehend the information they had been given. Sebastian joined them, eager for the fresh air.

Sam should have laughed the parapsychologist's theory away as a ridiculous, overcooked ghost story.

But he didn't. He couldn't.

Sam was the one to tell Sebastian about Kate. The old man didn't want to believe it; he refused to accept the hypothesis that the house had been responsible. The more Sam insisted, the more Sebastian pushed back.

It's only natural. We all tried to rationalize it at first, Sam told himself.

But this is different. Sebastian isn't refusing to believe; he just doesn't like what he's hearing. It's like he's . . . like he's defending the house.

Sam hated the thought. That damn house. The thing that had infiltrated their lives. The thing that would not stop until it had completed its mysterious plan or all of them were . . .

Dead.

Sam tried to swallow, and found that his throat had clenched like a fist.

What do we do? What the hell are we supposed to do?

The answer came to him without warning.

"We have to go back to the house," Sam told them there on the sidewalk in Brooklyn as dusk swept over the borough like a hungry purple shadow.

The group exchanged confused glances.

"To Kill Creek?" Moore asked.

Sam nodded.

"For what?" Sebastian asked incredulously.

"Sebastian, whatever this is, it's reaching into our lives over thousands of miles. We'll never be free of it unless we find a way to stop it."

"How? What do you think we can possibly accomplish by returning to that house?"

"We don't know." Sam turned to find Moore, her hands buried deep in the pockets of a fitted black trench coat, the wind blowing her long black hair back and forth like a pendulum. "But Sam's right. We have to go. And you're coming with us."

The old man scoffed. "And why on earth would I—"

"And the first brick broke free," Sam said.

A breath caught in Sebastian's throat. "How do you know about that?"

"It's where you stopped writing, isn't it?"

Sebastian did not reply.

"It's the last line all of us wrote," Sam continued. "All of our stories were stopped by that brick wall, a wall exactly like the one at Kill Creek. We have to get into that room, Sebastian."

"For what? What's inside?"

Sam shook his head. "I don't know," he admitted, wishing he had some answer, any answer.

"You heard what Adudel said," Moore told Sebastian. "The house needs a storyteller. That's what it's been doing since last November. It's been forcing us to tell its story."

A thought flashed through Sam's mind: *It's been testing us, to choose one of us.* He stared at Sebastian, so alive, body and mind rejuvenated, and he couldn't help wondering if the house had made its choice.

Moore reached out and took the old man's hand in hers. "We can't ignore this any longer, Sebastian. This isn't in our heads. Something is after us."

The great Sebastian Cole, legendary author of hundreds of books and short stories, influencer of countless other writers, looked down at the hand of T.C. Moore and gripped it tight. He ran his thumb over the tops of her smooth fingers.

"Your nails are a mess," he said.

Moore smiled warmly. "A lot of things have gotten neglected lately. You should see my bush."

An unexpected laugh caught them by surprise, but they welcomed the brief reprieve. For that fleeting moment, they felt free.

Only Daniel wasn't laughing. His hands were balled into tight fists.

"Okay. I'll go," Sebastian said, giving Sam an odd hint of a smile. *A knowing smile.*

And then he let Moore lead him away.

They reached Washington Avenue. Horns honked. Engines revved. Headlights flashed by on the busy street. They waited at the corner until the light turned green, then crossed in a jagged line, Wainwright leading the way.

Daniel brushed past Sam, forcing Moore and Sebastian to the edge of the crosswalk as he passed. He was clenching and unclenching his fists, over and over. His face was redder than usual, a bulging vein running like a tributary of hate down the length of his neck.

"Daniel," Sam called after him.

He did not respond.

Wainwright was digging into his pocket, searching for his car keys. He had no idea that Daniel was storming up behind him.

Sam opened his mouth to warn him, but he was too late. Daniel pounded Wainwright square in the back. The force sent Wainwright stumbling, arms waving widely as he tried in vain to regain his balance. He hit the sidewalk hard, his knees driven painfully into the buckled concrete. Twisting his head at an awkward angle, he peered up at the heaving form standing over him.

"This is all your fault!" Tears were streaming down Daniel's cheeks. "You made us go there! You made us wake it up!"

Wainwright stammered, a jumble of sounds trying desperately to form an explanation.

"She's dead!" Daniel screamed. "She's dead because of you!"

His tongue found its footing, and Wainwright pushed out the words. "I know she's dead! Kate was—"

"Not Kate!" Daniel leaned down to give Wainwright the full force of his voice. "Not Kate! Claire! Claire, you son of a bitch!"

The name meant nothing to Wainwright. He stared up at Daniel, his face scrunched up in confusion.

But Sam understood. He glanced over at Moore. Her expression confirmed what Sam feared: *He's lost it.*

Daniel reared back his fist, readying another punch. Suddenly Sam leapt forward, hooking his heavily tattooed arm around Daniel's and yanking him back. Even though Daniel was still a good seventy pounds heavier, Sam was able to drag the blubbering man off the sidewalk and out into the street, slamming him roughly against the back of Wainwright's car. "He didn't kill your daughter," Sam said in Daniel's ear. "That was an accident."

It was all boiling over now; the deluge of tears that Daniel had held back for months coursed down his face.

Someone was pushing Sam aside. It was Moore. She slipped in front of Sam and took Daniel's large face her in hands. Her eyes glistened as she held his gaze.

Daniel's entire body began to quiver. Tears raced down his cheeks. But he did not look away from Moore.

"She's trapped," he whispered. "It has her. It won't let her rest."

Moore loosened her hold, resting her hand on his cheek. The rivulets of tears changed course around her fingertips.

Sam stepped back. He held out a hand to Wainwright. "Let me help you up." But the young man simply stared up at him, his eyes wet with his own fresh tears, his lips trembling.

"Is that Adudel?"

Sebastian squinted as he looked across the street. On the other side, a man stood at the curb, leaning his weight on a wooden cane.

Wainwright and Daniel both got to their feet, their altercation momentarily forgotten.

"What's that crazy bastard want?" Moore asked.

Adudel was yelling something, his head tilted back as he attempted to project his voice over the sound of the traffic.

Sam frowned. "What's he saying?"

"I don't know," Sebastian replied. He cupped his hands around his mouth and called out: "We can't hear you!"

A cluster of cars whizzed by, and then both lanes cleared in a sudden break in traffic. The wind, still carrying the last chill of winter, swirled around them and then it, too, died down.

Adudel's words found their way to the group: "You belong to the house now."

Sebastian waved a hand, motioning toward the other side of the street. "We'll come back over!" he yelled. "Stay there. We'll come to you."

Adudel let go of the silver lion's head, and his cane fell to the sidewalk like a toppled tree. He seemed to take a large breath, as if preparing for a deep dive.

"You will always belong to the house," he said.

Adudel stepped off the curb.

"Oh Christ." Wainwright gasped.

The bus hit Adudel at full force. One second he was there, staring at them through those ridiculously large eyeglasses, and the next he was gone, slammed to the street and dragged under the bus's front bumper. The brakes screamed as the bus tried, too late, to come to a stop. The crumpled form of Adudel tumbled out from behind the bus, arms and legs flailing as his body bounced along the street before coming to rest.

He lay on his stomach, his cheek flat against the asphalt. His glasses were still on, but one lens was shattered, the other missing entirely. His eyes were bleached stones with a speck of black at the center. Half of his head was caved in. White shards of skull poked through hair matted with dark, thick blood. His right arm was twisted over the top of his body at an unnatural angle. A stalk of pale bone sprouted from his forearm. His hand was curled into a limp fist, but one finger was extended.

Sam felt that finger pointing directly at them like the barrel of a gun.

Nearby, someone screamed. Voices cried out. The street was filled with slowing cars and frantic pedestrians.

Sam did not move, nor did Wainwright or Moore or Sebastian or Daniel. They watched in stunned silence as the mangled body of Dr. Malcolm Adudel was engulfed by the crowd.

From a rooftop above them, a flock of pigeons scattered, black bodies disappearing into a sky bruised by dusk.

They could flee, they could fly far, far away, but they could never escape.

PART FOUR

THE PHANTOM LIMB

April 25

What would I give to prove to you that the force within that house is real? What deal would I gladly strike if only I could convince you, dear reader, that what I experienced within those walls was not a figment of my imagination? Nothing. I would give nothing. Because I know in my heart that it is true. And if you still refuse to believe in the power of the house on Kill Creek . . . well . . . I can only urge you to visit it yourself. Once you have, once you've stepped through that doorway and walked its shadowed halls, you will believe. You will believe.

—*Dr. Malcolm Adudel*
Phantoms of the Prairie

TWENTY-SIX

9:15 a.m.

SAM STARED OUT the window and watched as, thousands of feet below, a commercial airliner seemed to hang motionless in air. The world was a patchwork of roads and fields stretching out to the curved horizon.

He closed his eyes.

I'm safe up here, he thought.

It felt true. Rocketing through the air at over five hundred miles per hour, forty-five thousand feet above the earth, he could not feel the pull of the house. It was a speck among specks somewhere far below.

But eventually we have to land. We can't stay up here forever.

He tried to push that moment as far away from him as possible.

No one had noticed when they left the scene of the accident in Brooklyn. Traffic was already backed up for several blocks in either direction. Horns bleated in a harsh, uneven rhythm. The street was filled with people, some comforting the ashen-faced bus driver, others forming a circle around Adudel's mangled body. Faces peered out of the back windows of the bus, a wall of wide eyes and open mouths. In the distance, sirens wailed.

It was Moore who said they should leave.

At first, Sebastian refused. "We have to stay," he insisted. "There must be something we can do! Something . . ."

The sirens were getting closer. Wainwright and Daniel were already climbing into the car. Sam put a hand on Sebastian's arm and said, "We have to go."

Wainwright took the first right. Sam glanced back and saw the flashing lights of a police car arriving, and then Wainwright took a quick left, and the horrible scene was gone from sight.

For ten minutes, they rode in silence. There did not appear to be any rhyme or reason to where Wainwright was taking them, just a desire to put what had happened far behind them. Even Wainwright seemed surprised when, somehow, they made their way back to his apartment. They would spend the night there. They would try to get some sleep.

They would talk in the morning. They needed a plan.

To charter a private jet from LaGuardia to Kansas City International was over twenty thousand dollars, but none of them could stomach the thought of being crammed onto a commercial flight with the weight of their situation pressing down on them. Wainwright had a service he used, mostly for international travel. Luckily the company was able to accommodate their last-minute request.

It was Sam's first time on a private jet. He had always imagined he would be intimidated by the extravagance of the experience, but now he sat in a lush leather chair, staring out the small window at the world far below, and the entire situation sickened him.

He glanced over at Sebastian in the opposite seat. The old man was staring straight ahead, but it wasn't the vacant look Sam had seen in his eyes last October. Sebastian's brow was creased, his eyes fixed on the open space before him. He was not adrift in a mental fog; he was lost in deep thoughts.

"Sebastian?" Sam called over.

"Yes, Sam?" Sebastian tried to muster up a friendly smile.

Sam looked around the cabin. Daniel and Wainwright were in the next row. Wainwright was cradling his head in his hands, his eyes closed, while Daniel had fallen into a shallow sleep, the exhaustion of the ordeal finally too much to fight. His body flinched slightly as unwanted dreams attempted to overtake him. Toward the rear of the plane, there were four seats, two side by side and facing the tail, and another pair opposite those, facing forward. Sam could see the back of Moore's head, the ridge of her black hair rising up over the seat like a shark's fin.

Careful to keep his voice low, Sam leaned over closer to Sebastian. "What do you think we're going to find?" he asked.

The question seemed to catch Sebastian off guard. "At the house?"

Sam nodded.

Sebastian pondered this for a moment. "I truly do not know."

"But you talked to Adudel several times. He must have mentioned something—"

"I know as much as you," Sebastian insisted.

I want to believe him. But I don't.

Careful not to draw the attention of the others, Sam quietly rose from his seat and crossed over to crouch down in front of Sebastian. The old man could not look away now.

"What aren't you telling me?" Sam asked.

Sebastian opened his mouth to say something, then thought better of it. He reconsidered and began again. 'And the first brick broke free.' The books you've all been writing, you said they stopped cold with that sentence."

"That's right."

"That exact sentence is in my book as well," Sebastian admitted. "I remember writing it."

"Because it's where you stopped too?"

Sebastian shook his head. "It was like the phrase exploded out of my mind, and the sheer force of it propelled me forward."

Sam cocked his head, confused. *Forward?*

"I've always been a bit of a pokey writer," Sebastian continued. "Not the 'slam, bam, thank you, ma'am' type like Moore. But this was different than anything I had ever written. Since November, the story had chugged nicely along."

Not how I would describe my writing experience the past few months.

Sebastian held his hands out flat to mime pushing some unseen object. "But when I wrote that sentence, it was like something gave me a hard shove, and then I was racing to the finish line."

"The finish line," Sam repeated. "Wait, are you . . . are you saying . . ."

The old man did not need Sam to complete the thought. "My novel is complete," he said. "I finished it a week ago."

The same time my story came to a sudden stop. When all of us stopped writing. Because it wasn't necessary anymore, Sam realized. *He beat us. Because the house had chosen him.*

Sebastian's words echoed in Sam's mind: *the finish line.*

"How does it end?" Sam asked, his voice barely audible over the steady roar of the jet engine.

"It doesn't matter how—"

"Sebastian, how does it end? How does your story end?"

The plane arced softly just then, and the morning sunlight fell upon Sebastian's face.

"The evil wins," he said, peering out the window at the field of clouds below. "They can't stop it and the evil wins."

The leather chair gave a soft squeak as Sam sat down.

Moore did not bother looking over as she said dryly, "Please, have a seat."

Sam glanced back to where the others sat. They had not noticed him moving to the rear of the plane.

Good. I don't need Daniel and Wainwright hearing this, Sam told himself. *Not yet.*

His face must have betrayed his thoughts, because Moore turned to him, suddenly concerned.

"What is it?" she asked.

"Sebastian finished his book," Sam whispered, his mind still reeling.

Moore straightened up in her chair. "What?"

"It's done. He finished it on the same day that the rest of us got . . . whatever we got. Writer's block."

"Did he tell you anything else? What happens in the story? What's behind the wall?"

"He doesn't know," Sam said.

Moore stared at him, mouth agape. "He doesn't know? He wrote the damn thing."

"He says that the wall falls free and whatever is there is so strange, so foreign, that the main character can't make sense of it."

Moore snorted, annoyed, and looked back out the window. "Classic Sebastian Cole cosmic horror bullshit. Well, that's convenient. Did he say anything else?"

"Only that the evil . . ." Sam paused, afraid to say it himself, to make it true. "Let's just say the good guys don't exactly come out on top."

Moore sucked in a sharp breath.

She's scared, he realized.

T.C. Moore, scared. Six months ago, he wouldn't have thought that was possible.

The jet turned slightly, and the sunlight that had been shining on Moore's face shifted, a deep shadow cutting across her cheek. "I keep thinking about that night, at the house," she said, her voice surprisingly faint. "I have this feeling like something happened there. But I can't quite remember what it was."

Suddenly Sam could feel Moore's body pressing against him, his fingers on her skin, his lips on her lips.

A dream, he realized. *I had a dream that night. About her. About us.*

It all came rushing back to him, sensations cascading out of the darkness. The taste of her mouth. The smell of her skin. His fingers sliding along her sweaty flesh as he fell deeper and deeper into the absolute blackness of her eye.

And you told her. You told her everything. In that dream.

In the house.

His heart began to thud in his chest, like a wild beast in a cage.

"How did it come to you?" she asked.

Sam drew in a sharp breath. "How did what—"

"When you would stop writing. What did it look like? I mean, when you actually saw it."

Tell her.

She won't understand, his mind warned.

Yes, she will. You want to tell her. You need to tell her.

Leaning forward, Sam clasped his hands. He took a deep breath but he did not speak.

Not yet.

She'll understand, he assured himself. *Because she's known pain, like you.*

He stared down at his clasped hands. He used to hold his hands like that when he prayed, when we was a little boy, back when he believed.

Tell her.

"It looked like my mother."

Moore turned away from the window. She was watching him, her expression intense. "Your mother? She died in a house fire, right?"

He did not immediately answer. Slowly, he began to nod. "Yeah. There was a fire, but . . ." He swallowed hard. "She didn't die in it."

"What do you mean?"

There was ten-year-old Sammy McGarver, standing before the inferno that had once been their simple country home. His mother's body was inside, but the fire hadn't killed her. She was already dead.

And there was Jack, by his side. "We can't tell anyone," Jack was saying. "Not even Dad."

That was when Sam had broken away from his brother and run toward the flames.

Sam rubbed his hand over the burned skin of his left arm.

"My mom hated us, my brother and me. She blamed us for all of the unhappiness in her life. She wished she had never had us; she felt trapped, in a family she never wanted. So she drank and she yelled and she called us names. She called us 'worthless.' She called us 'ungrateful little shits.' And when that didn't make her feel good enough, she would hit us."

Moore leaned forward, her face level with Sam's. "What about your father?"

"He was weak. Honestly, I think he was afraid of her. He would try to calm her down, to talk reason, but . . ." Sam gripped his arm harder, rubbing his thumb over the folded flesh. "I knew that my dad wasn't going to save us. Even as a little kid, I think I knew eventually it would have to be me or Jack who stood up to her."

Sam's eyes flashed to the front of the cabin. The others had not moved. Between the distance and the sound of the engines, there was no way they could hear him. Yet he felt as if everyone were listening—Sebastian, Daniel, Wainwright. Even the house, so far below, was hanging on his every word.

Stop. Don't let them in, his mind warned.

Moore must have sensed that he was retreating. She reached up and pulled her black mane over her shoulder, clutching the end in one hand like a rip cord, as if she could pull it should things get too real.

"For me, it was my ex-boyfriend," she said, her voice intimate, almost a whisper. "His name was Bobby. I was young, barely out of high school, living in a shithole house in a shithole desert town northeast of Los Angeles. Back then, I wasn't T.C. Moore. I was just a good Catholic girl named Theresa Catherine, and Bobby was everything. Until he did this."

She pointed to her ruptured pupil.

Sam felt his mouth open to speak, but he had no idea what to say. "I'm sorry," he offered finally.

"I'm not," Moore said. "I was used to Bobby kicking my ass. It'd just become a part of my life. But when I saw my eye in the mirror for the first time, when I saw how that darkness had opened up, it was like staring into another universe, one where I didn't have to be good, obedient Theresa anymore. So one day I just left him. I moved to LA and 'T.C.' Moore was born. And I never saw Bobby again."

"Until now," Sam said.

Moore nodded. "I started hearing his voice, calling from somewhere in my house. 'Theresa. Theresa.'"

She said the name in a lilting, singsong way, and the sound of it made Sam's skin crawl.

"When I wrote, the voice would stop. But a few times, I tried to quit on the novel—to stop because I knew that it was taking over my life—and that's when he would find me."

The edges of her eyes glistened with tears.

"It felt real, Sam. Exactly like the way it did back then. The pain. The fear. It even knew what I had to say to make him stop. I had to tell him how worthless I was. I had to make him feel like a big man."

A single tear escaped her eye and raced down her cheek. She angrily wiped it away.

"It wasn't just the feeling of being back at Kill Creek that made me keep writing. I did it to keep him away."

He reached out and took her hand. It felt strangely familiar, her fingers folded into his.

Because it happened before. At the Finch House. In the dream.

"But it can't really be Bobby," Moore was saying. "He's alive. Last I heard, he was living in Arizona. He's an abusive asshole, but he's not a goddamn ghost."

"It's not him," Sam told her, "just like it's not my mother. It's the house using those things to get to us, to break us down."

"How could it know?"

Because she told it. Just like I told it about my mother. When I told Moore that night. When she came to my room.

But she wasn't really there.

That wasn't Moore. That was the house.

Sam felt as if the floor of the plane had vanished. He was plunging through the open air, spiraling toward the earth.

"It was listening," he said.

"What are you talking about?"

"The house. When we were there last fall. It was listening. To our conversations. To our *thoughts*. We told it everything it needed to know to break us down."

"That's . . . that's impossible," Moore said, but there was doubt in her voice.

Because she knows you could be right, Sam thought.

"It used my ex because he beat me, and your mother because she, what, resented your very existence?"

Sam remembered the dream in the house, and the relief he felt when he whispered those words in her ear.

You can feel that again, he realized.

No. Stop talking. It was a mistake the first time.

Because it was the house. This is Moore. The real Moore.

Tell her.

"Sam?" she asked, confused.

"That's not the only reason," Sam said.

He swallowed hard, searching for courage.

Keep going.

"Sam, you don't have to—"

Yes. You do.

Tell her.

"I killed my mother," he said. They were the hardest four words he had ever spoken aloud.

Shock rippled across Moore's face, like the gently disturbed surface of a pond, her eyes widening, her brows arching, her lips parting to suck in a breath. And then her entire expression flattened, the gravity of Sam's confession pulling her closer. Sam did not seem to see her there. He was lost in a memory.

"She was hurting my brother. She was slapping him, she had him on the floor, and her hands . . . her hands were around his neck. She was squeezing. He couldn't breathe. His face was red and then purple and I was watching him die. I was watching my brother die. So I picked up a cast-iron skillet and I hit her with it, to stop her and—"

Moore touched his arm, her hand resting on his scars. He looked up into her eyes.

"She burned in that fire. But she didn't die in it."

Sam watched as tears began to slip down Moore's cheeks, and then his own tears came, spilling over, dripping off the edge of his jaw and splashing onto the deformed flesh of his left arm.

"And it knows. Whatever this thing is, it knows."

Sam thought of his mother's corpse, motionless on the kitchen floor. He thought of the salvation he found in a novel by Sebastian Cole, third paperback from the top in a stack on a pawnshop shelf. He thought of the life these two things created, a life of stories and secrets, a life that had driven Erin away and left Sam desperate enough to accept Wainwright's invitation to the house on Kill Creek.

And suddenly this moment in which he found himself felt inevitable, fated.

The plane dipped sharply. They were starting their descent.

Soon they would be on the ground.

TWENTY-SEVEN

II:32 a.m.

THE HARDWARE STORE was on Quivira Road in Lenexa, Kansas, a rare mom-and-pop joint that refused to be killed off by the many chains that populated Kansas City and its suburbs.

Sam led the way.

He's on a mission, Moore observed as she walked faster to keep up.

Sam was, after all, the one who came up with the plan. As the plane descended into Kansas City International Airport, he had gathered them all together. Each of their novels had led them to a wall. A brick wall. Exactly like the one that kept anyone from entering the third-floor bedroom in the Finch House. There had to be a reason for that, Sam insisted. The key to truly understanding the house and its power could be behind that wall. And if they understood it, they might be able to stop it.

Wainwright was skeptical, and he wasn't afraid to voice it. "The house was forcing you to write those stories. It might want you—*us*—to go back. It could be a trap."

"So what do we do?" Sam's question wasn't just to Wainwright but to the entire group. "Go home? Let this thing drive us crazy? Or worse? We know what it did to Kate. We *saw* what it did to Adudel. There's no one to turn to. Who's going to help us? The police? The church? The one man who knew the most about that house stepped in front of a goddamn bus."

He had paused, waiting for any of them to protest. They had said nothing.

"If anyone else has a better idea, trust me, I would love to hear it."

The screech of the jet's tires hitting the runway had been the only reply.

So, like Wainwright, Daniel, and Sebastian, Moore followed Sam as he pushed a shopping cart through the narrow aisles of the hardware store.

Their private conversation on the plane appeared to have freed Sam of a weight he had carried his entire life. Moore could see that, for the moment, he was enjoying a slight reprieve from the crushing burden of keeping the secret. There was momentum, and for that, Moore was thankful. Six months of stasis, of keeping herself secluded while she pounded out a never-ending book, had left her feeling something she had not truly felt in two decades: helplessness. Now they were charging forward.

Toward what?

She didn't know. None of them did. They had no idea what to expect once they arrived at the house.

But Sam's right. We can't just go home. We know what's waiting for us there.

Along the back wall of the store were hammers of various weights and sizes. Sam grabbed the heaviest of the sledgehammers, a twenty pounder. He tested its weight in his hands and, apparently satisfied, set it carefully in the cart. He then added a sixty-four-ounce blacksmith hammer, a forty-eight-ounce dead-blow hammer, and a standard milled-face framing hammer with a smooth hickory handle. Finally, he found a twelve-inch concrete chisel and tossed that into the cart.

"That should do it," Sam said.

"You sure you don't wanna just rent a jackhammer and call it a day?" Moore asked.

Sebastian peered into the cart. "She does have a point. It's an old wall of eight-inch clay bricks, Sam. I assume the sledge would do."

Sam's response to the old man was flat and emotionless. "I'm not taking any chances. I want to get that wall down as quickly as possible."

Sebastian gave a small nod and looked away, oddly cowed.

Sam doesn't trust him, Moore realized.

They moved down the next aisle, toward the front of the store. Moore sidled up next to Sam, her hand on the side of the cart.

"What are we hoping to find behind the wall, Sam?" she asked him.

"Rebecca's bedroom," he said, a bit too quickly. "Maybe something that can help us understand what's happening."

Moore eyed the other customers as they passed, people going about their lives, oblivious to the torment she and the others were suffering.

"I've been thinking about what might be in that room," she said, her voice low. "The ghost of Rebecca Finch. Or Joshua Goodman. Or the things it sent to each of us." The thought made her shiver.

Sam let out a slow breath. "Or maybe it's something else, something that never lived," he suggested.

Or it's just a room, Moore thought, *and we're all out of our goddamn minds.*

They reached the end of the aisle. A single register was straight ahead, the line of customers long and moving slowly.

Moore leaned in closer to Sam, her words only for him. "If we break down that wall and the spirit of a Finch sister possesses one of you guys, I will not hesitate to take that sledge and turn your head into brain pudding." She grinned devilishly. "Is it wrong that I hope it's Wainwright?"

A smile broke through Sam's serious expression.

That's good, Moore thought. *It's almost like everything's normal again.*

As quickly as it appeared, his smile faded.

She watched as Sam pushed the cart up to the end of the line, Sebastian falling in silently behind him. Daniel, his hands in his pockets, shuffled after them. There was no warmth among these men, no camaraderie. Only sadness and suspicion.

Wainwright stepped up next to Moore.

"Do you think this is going to work?" he asked, his once-booming voice now thin and weak.

"It'll work," Moore said sharply.

It has to work, she told herself. *We'll beat that wall to hell until it comes down. And whatever the house throws our way . . .*

You'll what? her mind questioned.

We'll deal. We'll improvise.

Even as she thought it, she hated the sound of the word: *improvise.* It suggested a sudden change of plans, a desperate attempt to regain control. It meant that things could go sideways and they'd be taking swings in the dark.

The wheels of the cart rumbled wildly as Sam guided it toward the rental SUV parked at the curb. Wainwright pressed a button on the key fob, and the tailgate rose gently into the air, revealing their hastily packed bags and just enough cargo space for the tools.

Sebastian unzipped a dark canvas bag he had found near the front of the store and opened it for Sam and Wainwright to fill with the smaller hammers. It was then that Moore spotted something a few doors down.

Don't bother, her mind told her.

It will only take a second. It can't hurt.

It's a waste of time, her mind insisted.

She ignored the thought and turned to the others.

"Be right back," she told them.

"Now where is she off to?" she heard Sebastian ask as she hurried down the sidewalk.

A bell above the door gave a friendly ding as Moore entered the used bookstore. She was instantly greeted by the glorious scent of pages—hundreds of thousands of pages—aging silently between their respective covers.

A plump woman smiled warmly. "Good morning. Can I help you find anything?"

"Where's your religion section?" Moore asked impatiently as she glanced over the cluttered shelves.

"Oh, well now, are you wanting Eastern or Western religion? Because if you're interested in Buddhism, I have a beautifully illustrated copy of the—"

"Lady, just hold out a finger and point," Moore snapped.

The woman's smile vanished. She did as she was told, pointing to a section at the top of a nearby bookshelf. Moore quickly scanned the titles and found what she was looking for. As she pulled the book down from the shelf, a young girl's voice spoke from the recesses of her mind, words echoing from decades ago, back when she believed in such magic:

She girds her loins with strength, and shows that her arms are strong.

That's right, Theresa, Moore thought. *Stronger than you were. Too strong to ever go back.*

Moore dropped the book onto the counter and fished out a twenty, more than enough to cover the handwritten price displayed on a small yellow sticker. She held out the bill.

"Here."

The woman did not move.

A low growl came from the far corner behind the counter. "Jasmine doesn't like you," the woman said.

Moore sighed, irritated. "Who the hell is Jasmine?"

From around a stack of paperback romance novels, a long-haired cat the color of dirty dishwater peered out with yellow eyes. It stared straight at Moore as it growled from deep within its chest.

"Jasmine thinks you're very, very rude."

The cat lowered its head but kept its eyes on Moore as it issued another warning, louder than the first two.

Moore dropped the twenty onto the counter and snatched up the book. "Yeah, well, Jasmine looks like a real bitch."

The ring of the bell seemed much less friendly as Moore hurried out of the store.

The others were already in the SUV. Wainwright was behind the wheel. He rolled down the driver's-side window as Moore approached.

"What was so important?" he asked.

Moore held up her find: a leather-bound copy of the Holy Bible.

"I didn't think you were a believer," Sebastian called from the backseat.

Moore shrugged. "I'm not. But I also don't feel like taking any chances."

For a brief moment, she caught Daniel looking at the book in her hand. There was no emotion on his face. He no longer had any connection to it.

"Get in," Wainwright said to her. "It's time to go."

Moore rode shotgun. Her hair was now knotted in a high ponytail. Sam and Sebastian rode in the next row and Daniel sat alone in the far backseat. As he had done last October, Wainwright steered the ship. Kate's absence was felt by all but mentioned by none.

Wainwright steered the SUV onto the off-ramp that would swing them around onto Kill Creek Road. Before they knew it, they were leaving the paved path behind for the noisy clatter of the gravel road, tiny chunks of shale hitting the undercarriage like inverted hail.

The route was much darker than last time, the barren tree branches now overgrown with leaves. Sam squinted in the low light, staring straight ahead as the SUV passed through the tunnel of oaks and maples. There was sunlight in the distance, an oval of illumination, so far out of reach. Sam felt goose bumps prickling his flesh. The trees blocked out any trace of the blue sky, their bushy limbs clasped over the road like the hands of a strangler.

Sam could hear the slosh of gasoline in the trunk. That had been their last order of business before hitting the highway out of town: a quick stop at a gas station to buy and fill two ten-gallon gas cans. That was the kill switch. If they found no answers in the third-floor bedroom, or if the house came violently alive and they were unable to even reach the wall, they would burn the whole damn place to the ground. Sam wasn't certain if that would stop the entity for good, but he hoped it would weaken it. It might buy them enough time to come up with a Plan B.

Their bodies swayed as the SUV rumbled down the winding lane. Sebastian's head was lowered, his eyes staring at the floor. Sam wondered what he was thinking. Since they'd discovered him at Adudel's brownstone, Sebastian had been remarkably clear, his mind alert. There hadn't been one single moment where he seemed lost to some insatiable disease. Something had changed him since their trip to the house last year. And the closer they came to returning, the more frightened Sebastian appeared.

He doesn't want to go back, Sam thought. *He doesn't want to end this.*

"Sebastian?" Sam said softly.

Sebastian turned. "Yes, Sam?"

"Are you sure you want to do this?"

The old man smiled, but there was sadness in his eyes, as if he knew he were about to lose something irreplaceable. "Whatever the house is doing, it can't go on," he said.

The SUV broke through the darkened passageway and sped into the sudden, brilliant light.

The house was before them, crouching low in the overgrown yard. The tallgrass appeared healthier than ever. Thick and vibrant.

But their eyes were drawn to the beech tree, the hanging tree, whose twisted branches had been devoid of life last autumn. In the months since, it had experienced a disturbing resurgence. Vibrant strings of green leaves draped its body like living jewelry. Thick vines snaked up its gnarled trunk, wrapping tightly to its splitting bark, holding it together, keeping it whole. A few leaves fluttered free in the light breeze, but the rest stuck tight, the long strands of greenery swaying back and forth like pendulums counting down the seconds to their arrival.

TWENTY-EIGHT

12:45 p.m.

SAM SLAMMED THE back door of the SUV shut. He carried the dark canvas bag slung over his shoulder by a tan nylon strap. The chisel and hammers clanked faintly within. Moore insisted on carrying the twenty-pound sledge, relishing its weight in her hands.

The five of them walked up the gravel drive. To each side, the tallgrass rippled, independent of the breeze.

As they reached the front porch, Daniel paused. He stared up at the third-floor window.

Sebastian followed his gaze. "What do you see, Daniel?"

Daniel whispered something, too low to make out.

"I'm sorry, what was that?" Sebastian asked.

Keep them moving, Sam told himself. *If they wait too long, they'll start to question the plan. They'll turn back.*

"Come on, let's go," Sam called back as he started up the front steps. His boots knocked softly on the wood as he crossed to the front door. Unlike last autumn, there were no vines curled around the doorknob. It was free for him to turn.

Sam paused and glanced around the front porch. The vines that had once covered the planks had also withdrawn. They must have retreated into the tallgrass. It made no sense, but then again, few things did.

Behind him, Wainwright bounced lightly and found that the wood had no give under his feet.

"It's sturdier," he said. "The porch. It seems almost brand new."

Sam turned back to the front door.

Here we go.

He twisted the knob.

The door opened easily.

Did we lock it when we left last year? Sam tried to remember. *Maybe someone entered after us and forgot to lock it.*

Or maybe the house wants you to enter, his mind suggested. Sam pushed this away. Such thoughts would only lead to fear.

Sam steeled himself and stepped inside.

At first glance, it appeared the rooms were as they had left them. But soon they realized the interior was also in better condition. The house was impossibly clean. Not a speck of dust told of the passage of time. The wood of the walls and floor seemed richer than before. Even the furniture, still in place as instructed by Rachel Finch's will, looked freshly cleaned.

Healthy. The house seems healthy, thought Sam.

They tested the light switches as they hesitantly crept through the rooms. No power. This was not a surprise; the electricity had vanished with the removal of their generator on the first of November. In the kitchen, Wainwright twisted the knobs on the sink. No brown gunk. No freshwater. Nothing.

They moved down the narrow hallway, toward the main room. A wave of panic seemed to wash over Wainwright. "What is it?" Sam asked.

Wainwright shook his head and forced himself to follow the others.

They moved through the next room and into the foyer. They found themselves once again standing at the bottom of the stairs.

"What do you think it has planned?" Sebastian asked.

"I don't know," Sam responded honestly. "It knows we're here. If it wants to do anything to us, it will."

The house creaked softly in the light wind, boards popping faintly in distant corners. No one spoke. They stood perfectly still, listening, straining to hear anything unusual—a footstep, a laugh, the echo of voices. They heard only the wind, whistling as it picked up briefly, pressing invisible hands against the windowpanes. Then the whistling faded. The wind died down. The weight of the intense stillness settled over them.

The summer heat receded the moment they stepped through the front doorway, an occurrence they should have welcomed but which instead unnerved them. There they stood, in the cold, quiet house, waiting for it to make the first move.

It's doing the same thing, Sam thought. *Watching us. Waiting.*

Moore adjusted her grip on the sledgehammer's handle, turned to Sam, and raised a thin, arched eyebrow.

"So?" she asked.

How did I become the leader? Sam wondered. He took a deep breath, letting the role he never asked for settle in.

"We break through," Sam said.

Moore nodded her approval. "We break through."

The stairs creaked beneath their feet as they crept upstairs. Moore weighed the wicked sledge loosely in her hands as she climbed toward the second floor.

Be ready, she warned herself. *This bitch can get to us in our own homes. No telling what it will do here.*

Wainwright stayed close behind Moore. Sebastian was third, his hand on the rail, making sure both feet were planted firmly on each step before moving farther. Sam followed, his hands ready to catch Sebastian if he were to tumble. As always, Daniel trailed them, wrapped in a troubling silence.

There were no ghosts waiting for them on the second floor. The stained-glass window at the far end of the hall offered a cheery alternative to the shadows that cloaked the top of the stairs. They passed the closed doors to their right and left, each taking furtive glances at their old bedrooms, memories of their first visit to Kill Creek rushing back to them.

When Moore turned the sharp corner into the alcove at the end of the hall, she stopped, her feet butting up against the first step of the next set of stairs. The others gathered around her, all taking a moment to peer through the gloom at the brick wall above them. Behind it, they had been told, was the third-floor bedroom, the place where the last gasp of air had left Rebecca Finch's lungs, the room Rachel Finch had sealed shut after her sister's death.

"Fuck it," Moore said, and she trudged up the stairs, reared back the sledge, and let out a fierce cry. The hammer's head collided with the red bricks, chipping a chunk away. It skittered down to the bottom of the stairs.

Sam stared at the chunk of brick, afraid. It was as if they had just sucker punched a bully, the red shard of brick like a drop of blood against the wood floor.

If the house wasn't awake before, it is now.

Above, the pounding continued, the clanking of the hammer growing louder as Moore put more muscle into it. But unlike the first swing, the subsequent ones had little effect on the wall. No matter how hard she attacked the bricks, their edges remained intact, the mortar secure. Before long, despite the coolness of the house, beads of sweat were rolling down her face.

"Anyone who thought this wall was gonna come tumbling down can kiss my ass," she called to the others.

Sam set the canvas bag down, and Wainwright quickly unzipped it. He rifled through the various items in the bag, pushing aside the Bible that Moore had purchased and snatching up a chisel and the smaller framing hammer. He took the stairs two at a time, all the way to the top, and set the edge of the chisel into the mortar between the bricks. Soon there was the clank of two hammers working, their heads pounding in a steady rhythm. Gray dust floated through the air as tiny bits of mortar sprang free, but still the wall held fast.

With a slight groan, Sebastian pressed his hands against either side of the narrow stairwell and lowered himself down onto the first step.

"You all right?" Sam asked.

Sebastian smiled wearily. "Yes, yes of course."

He's lying, Sam thought.

Sam watched Moore and Wainwright at work, arms whipping around in half circles, Moore's sledge brutally attacking the wall, Wainwright's hammer connecting with the butt of the chisel. A dense cloud of mortar dust was building around them.

Wainwright pulled the neck of his shirt up over his nose and mouth, shielding his lungs from the abrasive air.

"I'm sorry you had to come back here," Sebastian said suddenly. He had turned his attention to Daniel, who was standing a few feet behind them. "It must be especially hard for you, considering . . ."

Sam watched Daniel, unable to predict his reaction. Daniel's slack cheeks reddened, a rim of tears rising to his eyes. He clenched his jaw, fighting the sorrow, swallowing it, pushing it down, down, down into the pit of his stomach, where he had held it for nearly six months. Anger flashed across his face, wild and untamable, and then it was gone, his moist eyes drying, his face returning to the disturbingly blank expression he had worn since they'd found him in Chicago.

Ignoring Sebastian, Daniel swiveled around to Sam. "The elevator. Can't we take that up?"

Before Sam could respond, Wainwright called down from the top of the stairs, "There's a wall on that side too. Brick, just like this one. Besides, there's no electricity. The elevator wouldn't work anyway."

Muttering something under his breath, Daniel lowered his head and stepped farther back into the hallway.

"Daniel?" Sam asked, not bothering to mask the concern in his voice.

"I'm okay. I'm okay."

"You sure?"

Daniel nodded, a bit too enthusiastically. The tears were back, threatening to spill over. "Yeah. Yeah, I'm just going to go downstairs for a second. Maybe step outside, get some air."

"I'll go with you," Sam said.

Daniel threw a hand up in the air. "No!" he barked. Then, with more restraint: "I just need a minute." He hurried off down the hallway.

"Should we go after him?" Sebastian asked once Daniel had disappeared down the far stairs.

"No, he'll be fine," Sam replied. There was doubt in his voice.

TWENTY-NINE

1:50 p.m.

DANIEL COULD STILL hear the hammering echoing through the upper half of the house, a mean, destructive clatter that seemed to chip away at his very skull, an invisible spike attempting to break through to his brain.

When he reached the first floor, Daniel paused, one hand on the knob at the end of the stair rail. He closed his eyes, trying to push an image from his mind.

Claire. Her twisted and bloody body wrapped in metal. The engine puffing steam around her. One eye closed. One eye open, the pupil dilated, burst blood vessels mixing with the beautiful blue iris, staining it purple. That glazed eye, staring out through the wreckage at nothing, seeing nothing, sensing nothing. Gone. Gone, forever.

Daniel choked back a sob, instantly furious with himself. Every time he cried it was as if the last bit of Claire he held inside him were draining out, spilling to the ground, lost. He wanted to hold the tears in—to hold *her* in—close to his heart. Instead, they slipped free, his daughter with them, the vacuum of space within him growing larger, consuming him, his heart, his soul. What had once been a paradise was now a black abyss, the vastness of space without a single star to light the way.

I want her back, he pleaded with the darkness. *I want my daughter back. I know you have her. I'll do anything. Anything. Just give her back. Give her back to me.*

It was pointless, he knew. She was dead. There was no coming back.

But the house had, hadn't it? This goddamn abomination of a house had become alive out of sheer will. It had twisted itself into their lives from miles away, like an invisible vine creeping across the country, into their houses, into their families, into their minds.

It has Claire. It told *me it has her. If it is holding her, it can release her.*

Daniel closed his eyes.

"Please give her back," he whispered.

The void surrounded him. Silent. Infinite.

Without warning, a jolt rocked his body, electricity coursing through him from head to toe. His thick fingers clutched the railing, nails digging into the wood as the sensation overtook him. His first thought—his only thought—was that this was the heart attack his doctor had always warned him about. Then came a flash of images—Claire as a baby, held in Sabrina's arms; Claire's baptism; riding her first bicycle; cheering with the junior high varsity squad; with her date for Winter Formal. They were snapshots he knew well, filed away in a photo album somewhere, back at his house in Chicago. But these were more real than those flat, lifeless photographs. These were three-dimensional, a strange sense of motion given to the images. Claire's eyes blinked. Her smile widened. He could almost hear her laugh.

At the back of his skull, his brain hot like an electrical socket, a voice crackled through curtains of ancient whispers: *You could have saved her.*

And then it was over. His body released from whatever had taken hold, the electric shock dissipating from the very ends of his hair, the tips of his stubby fingers. A low sigh escaped him, from the deepest corners of his lungs.

Around him, the house's wooden joints began to creak, as if the building were being gently rocked on its foundation by the almost undetectable sway of a minor earthquake. It lasted only a few seconds, then the movement ceased, order restored.

He stood at the bottom of the stairs, the house quiet around him. The wind picked up outside, whistling through a crack in a wall.

Daniel took a few short breaths, testing his body, making sure everything was working normally. He felt no pain, no shortness of breath, no tightening in his chest. Whatever that was, whatever had passed through him, was gone.

From high above came a thud, and the entire house seemed to shudder. Daniel cocked his head, attempting to locate the sound. It was within the walls, hidden. A second thud followed the first. Then a faint, steady squeak. He recognized it now. Gears turning. Machinery at work.

Watching the area just to the left of the staircase, Daniel imagined a system of gears and belts turning, sending something down to him. When the squeaking reached the first floor, a third thud echoed through the foyer as the machine came to a stop.

It hit him in an instant, embarrassing in its obviousness.

The elevator.

He moved farther into the foyer, and the iron accordion door of the elevator came into view. Through the grate, Daniel could make out the rich wood walls of the elevator car. It must have been at the top floor when they arrived. Something triggered it just now, an electrical surge perhaps, and it descended.

Except there is no electricity, Daniel realized. *We tried the switches ourselves. The juice is off.*

Daniel tried to view the entire car. It seemed empty, but the patchwork of iron partially obstructed his view. There could be something in there. A shadow. An occupant.

Daniel touched hesitant fingers to the accordion door. Took a breath. Cautiously collapsed it open. The elevator was empty. Just to be sure, he searched the entire car from floor to ceiling, finding nothing except . . .

Daniel cocked his head, confused. The light at the center of the ceiling was on, its opaque glass cover glowing from within, silhouetting the corpses of dead bugs piled at the bottom.

So there was power. They must have been mistaken. Maybe the breakers for the lights were off but the elevator had never been shut down. It was a long shot, but it was the only explanation that made sense.

He was faintly aware of his feet moving, carrying him forward into the car. His hand reached out and grasped the accordion door, pulling it closed. There were buttons before him, three in all, stacked atop each other like the shimmering spine of a distant constellation. He pressed the top button: *3*.

He waited for those familiar sounds to return—the squeaking of gears, the thud as a chain was pulled taut—but there was only silence. And then the elevator was moving, the foyer vanishing from sight as Daniel passed between floors. The second-story hallway appeared, Sebastian's scuffed black shoes visible at the far end, Sam's back jutting out from around the corner. The elevator continued to rise without a sound. No heads poked out from the alcove, no startled eyes watched as Daniel ascended past them.

Up, up, up he went, higher into the house. The last sliver of light from the second-story hall slipped across the floor of the elevator. Then it was extinguished, darkness enveloping Daniel, the crisscross pattern of the accordion door barely visible before him.

He should have been frightened by this journey. Yet there was no fear, only the sense that he was being drawn toward something good, to a very special place the house had reserved only for him. A goofy grin spread across Daniel's face, his cheeks still wet with the tears he had shed at the foot of the stairs.

The stop came suddenly. Daniel placed a hand against the wall of the car to steady himself. On the control panel, the lit third button blinked off, announcing his arrival.

"No," Daniel whispered. He pushed the accordion door open.

Just as Wainwright had said, there was a brick wall here too. Daniel felt his stomach drop. With a trembling hand, he reached up and touched the bricks.

Instantly, they crumbled. The top row went first, then the next, and the next, the bricks falling away from him like a breaking wave. Just like the elevator, they made no sound as they crashed to the floor.

The doorway was open.

Daniel squinted in warm sunlight. His grin widened, the carefree smile of a drunken man.

With an almost irrepressible sense of excitement, he stepped out of the elevator and into the third-floor bedroom.

THIRTY

2:07 p.m.

AT THE TOP of the stairs, Wainwright and Moore continued pounding the brick wall. They had been at it for almost an hour, coming down only to dig through the canvas bag in hopes of finding a utensil that would finally do the job.

It's not working, Sam thought. He tried to swallow and found that his throat had constricted.

The chisel and sledge had knocked a few chunks of mortar loose, but the bricks held tight. It was a miraculous thing, the barrier, hastily built over two decades ago, impervious to harm.

Sebastian was just outside the alcove, pacing nervously in a small circle.

"Maybe we should just go," he suggested.

Sam shook his head. "You know we can't do that."

"I know," Sebastian admitted. There was a heavy sense of resignation in his voice.

Moore trudged down the stairs, the sledgehammer held out in both hands.

"The bitch isn't budging." Her face was caked with gray dust, streaks of sweat cutting dark rivers down her cheeks. "Your turn."

The offer pleased Sam. Standing around watching was making him feel more and more helpless. He took the hammer as Moore

slipped down onto the bottom step. At the top of the stairs, he settled
in next to Wainwright, who pounded the edge of the chisel with fading strength. Sam reared the sledgehammer back and slammed it into
the bricks with all his might. The enthusiastic show of muscle seemed
to encourage Wainwright, who began backing each blow with more
power.

Soon, their attack was perfectly timed, their individual strikes
syncing into one sound, like the ticking of a monstrous clock.

He could hear them, through the wall—*clank, clank, clank!*—like
trapped miners desperately fighting for daylight.

The irony was almost palpable as Daniel stepped freely from the
elevator and into the room. He felt like an astronaut on some distant
planet, the first man to walk on its alien terrain.

Like the rest of the house, the third-floor bedroom was immac-
ulately clean. He traced a finger over the surface of a heavy maple
dresser. No dust.

There was a single window to his left, the pane no more than two
feet by three feet. Yet the sunlight streaming in was blinding, a warm
yellow beam of otherworldly luminance.

Hadn't he seen boards over that window last year? Surely he had
imagined it. There weren't even nail holes in the perfectly smooth walls
on either side of the frame.

Beneath the window was a queen-size bed covered in a
hand-stitched quilt. Beside the bed, a wheelchair was parked, abandoned, its occupant long gone.

Daniel sucked in a mouthful of air. It was impossibly pure. Almost
alpine. The crisp, cool air one would find at higher elevations, far above
the timberline. The clarity of it excited him, tickling his lungs with the
hint of frost.

Along the wall to his right was a wooden shelf lined with picture
frames. Each frame was turned away from the room. Carefully, Daniel
flipped the first frame around. It housed a black-and-white photograph of two young girls, around eight or nine years old, with identical
flower-print dresses and black hair pulled into ponytails. They were
mirror images of each other, right down to their dour expressions.

Daniel turned the next frame. This photograph was beginning to yellow and fade. It was of the girls again, now women in their thirties, flanking an ancient man with a face like cracked, weathered leather. The man had the same gray eyes that they did. This must be their father.

The third photograph was more familiar—the sisters posing in front of the house on Kill Creek. One of them was now in a wheelchair, her mysterious accident happening sometime between the second and third photo. So these were the Finches. Rachel and Rebecca.

Daniel moved farther into the room. The sunbeam that drifted in through the bedroom window fell warmly on a silver jewelry box. Daniel lifted the lid, and instantly the tinny strains of music flooded out. He recognized it as Bach, although he could not place the concerto. As the tune played, Daniel explored the interior of the jewelry box. It was lined with red velvet, several necklaces hanging from the top portion, a series of small compartments in the lower section housing rings. It was not flashy jewelry—no diamonds or precious stones. Almost all of it was silver, although not a single piece was tarnished. They were as bright and smooth as if they had been polished only moments before.

At the edge of the box, where the lid was hinged to the back, something white peeked out. Daniel gave it a light tug. It was paper, yet thick and glossy. His pulse quickened; the excitement, so unexpected, seemed to course through his veins. Each new discovery in this room was his and his alone. While the rest of them pounded stupidly on the other side of the wall, Daniel was inside. Entry to this secret place had been granted only to him.

Grasping the sides of the jewelry box with his fingers, he lifted out the inside tray. There, beneath it, was a stack of pictures, devoid of color, their grainy quality harkening back to the early days of photography. They were candid shots of a white-haired woman, her eyes clouded by cataracts, her mouth open slightly as if about to speak. She sat at a round table, hands clasped in those of a man and woman on either side of her. They looked on expectantly, waiting.

A medium, Daniel realized. *This is a séance.*

There were only four pictures, all from the same angle, each capturing the same moment with very little time elapsing between them. In each progressing photograph, a smoky, serpentine line emerged farther and farther from the old woman's mouth, stretching out over the table like a ghostly arm.

Daniel flipped the last picture over. Penciled at the bottom in small, deliberate print was the word "grandmamma."

What a strange lineage the Finches had come from. Finding this house, a place of so much potential power, must have been terribly exciting. Living under this roof, walking these halls each day and night—surely it did not take them long to realize what they owned. Harnessing its energy would have been their first priority, awakening the slumbering entity that rumor and gossip had invited in.

Daniel set the photos back into their secret hiding spot and replaced the inner tray of the jewelry box. He closed the lid, the classical tune that emanated from within instantly snuffed out.

Something squeaked behind him. The wheelchair, being nudged forward just a bit. He heard the light scrape of shoes on the floor as feet shuffled in place. Suddenly Daniel had the overpowering sensation of someone standing behind him, watching him, waiting for him to turn. He felt eyes on him. He listened closely and believed he could hear the whisper of breath being drawn.

Balling his hands into fists, preparing for a confrontation, Daniel spun around. His fists instantly unclenched. His heart skittered abruptly, like a needle scratching across a bumped record.

At first, the person before him was simply a shadow, silhouetted against the brilliant light of the window. But even before she stepped forward, even before the reflected sunshine fell upon her face, he knew who it was. He could tell by the way the hair fell across her shoulders, by the hint of curves on her budding body, by the trace of perfume—a mix of spice and flowers—that permeated the air.

The challenge was not guessing the young woman's identity but believing that it could be true. His mind tried desperately to reject it. There was no way it could be real. It was a trick of the light. A hallucination projected by his grief-stricken mind.

His tears convinced him otherwise. They sprang from his eyes like deep, long-hidden water from a cracked stone, washing freely and uncontrollably down. His entire lower jaw began to tremble as if from some abrupt, intense chill. A bubble of saliva popped between his lips as he fought to form the single word that would make it all come true.

"Claire."

A warm smile lit up her face. And now the sunlight began to shift, freeing itself from the sun outside to rotate around her, brightening her, bringing her away from the shadows and into perfect view. It was as if the sun orbited her. She was the center of everything.

It was her, his daughter, his Claire, alive. She held out a hand, and on her pinkie Daniel saw the ring he had given her two Christmases before, a silver band with a cutout of a cross in the middle. A rosy hue rose to her cheeks, the color of life.

Daniel slipped his hand into hers. The warmth confirmed what he already knew, that his beautiful daughter was no longer dead, that she had come back to him, snatched from the cold darkness of the grave by this glorious house.

"Claire," he said again, the name now leaping freely from his tongue. Still the tears came, his wet cheeks shimmering in the sunshine. She wiped them dry with her thumb. Her lower lip stuck out in a slight pout, poking innocent fun at her emotional father.

When she spoke, her voice was not the frog-like croak of the undead but the sweet, tender song he never thought he would hear again. She said, "Daddy," and the word was pure Claire, love tinged with a hint of teenage sarcasm. Daniel pulled her close to him, hugging her, feeling her arms wrap around his waist. The last of many walls constructed since her death collapsed to rubble, and Daniel sobbed into her shoulder, dampening the lacy white dress—

Her funeral dress. We buried her in that dress!

—that hung lightly on her petite body.

"I love you," Daniel cried. "I love you so much. So much, baby. Oh my God, I've missed you. It hurt so bad." He was rambling, he knew. But there was so much to tell her. So much he had held inside, thoughts he could not share with his own wife, emotions reserved only for the daughter he thought he would never see again. "I've missed you. I've missed you. I've missed you."

"I know," Claire cooed into his ear. "But I'm back. Everything could be just the way it was. I could come home to you and Mom. It'll be like nothing ever happened, like I never went away."

Daniel tightened his grip on her. Her use of "could" scared him. It sounded speculative rather than certain. "I want you to come home, sweetie. I'd do anything to have you back. Anything. Anything."

He felt her lips against the side of her face. "That's good, Daddy. That's perfect."

Daniel frowned. The movement of her lips did not exactly match the sound of her voice. The words were lagging behind by a half second or so. And that wasn't the only strange thing. Her voice seemed to be coming from *behind* her, as if someone were crouching down and speaking in her voice.

"Daddy? Are you listening to me?" she asked.

Daniel scolded himself for thinking this moment could be anything but miraculous. *It's Claire. It's your daughter!*

"I can come home. But I need you to do something first." Her parted lips did not even seem to move as she spoke.

"Anything," Daniel repeated. And he meant it. In his soul, awakened from its comatose state after nearly a year, he meant it.

"I can leave this house, Daddy, but you have to do exactly as I say. If you don't, you'll never see me again."

The sharp stab of terror tore through Daniel's body. Every molecule threatened to spin free. The thought of losing her again was too much. He couldn't bear it. Not again.

Claire pressed her mouth up to his ear, as if fearing the secret words would be sucked away into the vacuum of the bedroom. At first, his mind rejected what she said. It was too strange, too unexpected. He could not do that. Anything but that. Then she raised a hand to his face, her fingers tracing the edge of his hairline, running through his sandy hair, and that fear sprang back like a striking snake—*You're going to lose her again! And this time it will be forever!*

She repeated the instructions over and over; each time, the sting of shock subsided a bit more until they were just words. Ordinary words. He closed his eyes. The only sound he could hear was her voice, Claire's voice, and it was like music, a heartbreaking song recalled from another life.

The instructions began again, and now she was slipping something into his hand. A handle. Heavy on one end. Like the hammers they had used to attack the brick wall at the top of the staircase. The weight of it forced his hand down suddenly and, as if from far, far away, he heard a sound—*chink!*—like metal biting into wood.

Once more, she told her father what he must do. And then she pulled away, kissing him lightly on the forehead. Her lips were soft and wet. She was so real. So real.

Daniel looked into his daughter's eyes, and she gave him an encouraging smile.

"Do it, Daddy," she said, her head cocked, her eyes wide. She smiled, and the words filled his ears, even as her grinning lips remained motionless. "Do it for me."

THIRTY-ONE

3:18 p.m.

THE LIGHT WAS gone in an instant. One moment, the warm after-noon sunshine threw a mosaic of colors on the lower half of the stair-case; then it vanished, a gloom overtaking the steps.

Sam glanced at Wainwright, who had stopped chipping at the mortar around one particular brick. He set his hammer and chisel down on the top step, wiping his forehead with the sleeve of his shirt.

"I can barely see anything up here," he said.

It was true. Without the sunlight from the alcove window, they were practically working in the dark.

"What's going on out there?" Sam called down to the others.

Moore was standing at the window, peering through the stained glass, out to the west of the house. "Looks like rain," she announced. "Big, fat black cloud just passed in front of the sun. Where the hell did that come from?"

There was a sound. Fingers tapping. All over the house.

"What is that?" Sam shouted.

They all listened. Not fingers. Rain. The soft pitter-patter on the roof. Raindrops began to spit at the windowpane, obscuring the glass.

"This is pointless," Wainwright said, motioning to the wall. His voice was little more than a whisper. "These bricks must be held in place by something more than cement." He sighed. "We're not going to get through with these tools."

"Yes, we will," Sam said.

"I don't know, Sam. . . ."

"We will!" The sudden anger surprised even Sam. He glanced away, embarrassed.

Wainwright cleared his throat and waved at the dust swirling about them. "I need to step outside for a second."

"We don't have time."

"I can't breathe up here," Wainwright said pointedly.

Clenching his teeth, Sam tightened his grip on the cast-iron skillet—

Hammer, his mind corrected him.

But it wasn't. It was the skillet from his mother's stove. He held it by the handle. Its blackened body glistened. Blood. His mother's blood.

Sam looked up, startled. Wainwright was hurrying down the stairs. Moore called after him as he passed, "Check on Daniel, will ya? He's been gone awhile."

Sam looked down at the object in his hand. It was a hammer. It had always been a hammer. Its head was dented from bashing the hard brick.

At the bottom of the stairs, Moore was talking to Sebastian, somewhere in the hall, out of sight. With both hands, she wiped the dust from the sides of her shaved head and stepped out of the alcove.

Sam was alone.

That was when he heard it, a voice through the wall. He turned and stared at the bricks.

It was a woman's voice, muffled by the barrier between them.

"Sammy?"

There was a rush of air, and he was back in that kitchen, in his childhood home, the storm raging overhead, his brother and mother fighting, his awful, drunk mother yelling abominations, the ugliest words in the English language. Little Sammy was there by the stove, frozen in place, watching helplessly as his mother suddenly slapped Jack, slapped him so hard, he fell to the ground. She was on her son in an instant, straddling him, hands around his throat. She was saying what she had said so many times when she was drunk, that she wished she had never had them, that they had ruined her life, that they were a curse. They took her happiness. They deserved nothing but misery. But her words had never felt more potent, more real. Jack's eyes bulged in disbelief. His lips lapped the air stupidly. There was no breath. His mother had made sure of that. Just as she had given the boy breath, she planned to stop it. She was going to kill him.

And there was Sam, ten years old, watching his mother strangle his brother. His beloved Jack, who had taught him to throw a baseball and smoke a cigarette. His brother, who called him names and gave him noogies and wet-willies, his brother, who stood up for him when older boys called Sam a pussy and a fag.

Jack's bulging eyes stared desperately at Sam. Burst blood vessels shattered the whites of his eyes into pieces of red-stained glass.

End her misery, they pleaded. *End her awful life that she hates so much. End it. Kill her.*

Kill our mother.

Jack's face was turning purple.

Sam reached for the nearest object and his fingers found the handle of her cast-iron skillet.

He swung it. He knew the second his arm came down that it was too hard. The dull thud of metal on skull was the most horrible sound he would ever hear. The back of his mother's head caved in. Blood splattered little Sammy McGarver's face.

Sam stared in horror at the gore-soaked cast-iron skillet in his hand. The impact still reverberated up his arm and into his shoulder.

But it wasn't a skillet.

It was a hammer.

And he hadn't bashed in his mother's head.

He had swung the hammer hard against the wall, and a single brick had jostled loose. He pushed the brick with his index finger, and it moved slightly in place.

"Moore!" he yelled down the stairs.

Moore hurried into the alcove. "What's the matter?"

"One of the bricks." Sam stared down at her, his eyes wild. "It moved."

Bounding up the stairs, Moore grabbed the chisel and planted its sharp head against the mortar. With her other hand, she whipped the smaller hammer around in a powerful arc and brought it down hard on the butt of the chisel.

The sound of the impact was like the chain of a millennia-old beast snapping in half.

The brick inched out from the wall.

Moore froze. She wasn't sure she could believe what she had just seen. She pounded the back of the chisel again, and again the brick jumped.

"Holy shit," she whispered. "We're getting through. This bastard is coming down!"

A thin layer of cold sweat swept across Sam's body. Suddenly he didn't want the wall down. He wanted to pack up the tools and drive far, far away from this house.

Because you know what's on the other side. You know she's there, waiting for you.

Moore was digging excitedly at the mortar bordering the brick. Grasping it by its edges, she gave it a little tug. It wiggled in place like a loose tooth.

A rare smile rose to Moore's face. "Don't just stand there. Help me," she said.

Leave the wall, Sam's mind warned. *Leave this house.*

But Sam knew that he could not do that.

Whatever was on the other side, it would end here.

At first the lighter did not strike. Wainwright tried again, flicking the little metal wheel. This time the lighter came alive, a flame flickering in the light breeze. He held it to the end of a cigarette. Heard the faint sizzle as it lit. Sucked in sharply to get the tip nice and red. He exhaled the first puff of smoke, watching it waft out into the cool drizzle.

Wainwright leaned against the frame of the back doorway and smoked. The sleeves of his slim-cut linen shirt were rolled up to the elbow, and his arms were covered in a gray dust. He ran his fingers through his shaggy hair, and more dust drifted into the air.

Although he was sheltered here, nice and dry, he could sense the coolness of the afternoon rain, driving the oppressive heat down into the soil. He cocked an ear, trying to make out the sound of Sam's hammering. It appeared the attack on the wall had stopped for the moment. All he heard was the soothing rhythm of raindrops as they spattered the trees and bushes surrounding the house.

He had a perfect view of the woods to the south and the hint of a trail snaking through them. The opening to the path had been obvious last October; now the foliage was overgrown, making the trailhead difficult to pick out.

He took another drag and savored the hint of sweetness in the smoke, rolling it slowly over his tongue before expelling it. His nerves were fried, like the exposed wires of an old garage sale lamp. The cigarette helped, but not much.

He was beginning to doubt if coming to Kill Creek would result in the answers they sought. The house had offered nothing since their arrival, not even a supernatural display to confirm their fears. No orbs of light. No ghostly apparitions. Nothing. Only a wall that refused to come down. Nothing unexplainable about that. They had rushed back to the middle of nowhere expecting a confrontation with ultimate evil and had found good masonry instead.

Wainwright sucked the last drag from the cigarette, then stubbed it out on the doorjamb and flicked it into the yard. It landed halfway between him and the trailhead, a sliver of white in the deep green carpet, like the protruding tip of a fractured bone.

He was turning back toward the kitchen, his hand reaching to pull the back door shut behind him, when he caught a glimpse of the girl. It was only that—a glimpse—but in his mind he could still see it, the deep brown skin, the dark hair, obscured by the thick curtain of leaves. He paused. Glanced back. She was gone.

You saw nothing, he told himself. *No one was there.* He wanted to believe this because his first instinct had been something different. His first thought had been, *There's Kate.*

He started to back into the house as he watched the wall of trees for any sign of the girl. The rain pelted the leaves, giving the woods a strange sense of movement, the branches nodding, as if encouraging him to explore.

There she was again, farther down the trail this time, barely visible through the cover of green. In an instant, she was gone again, lost to the dense forest.

Wainwright moved out from under the roof's overhang and into the sprinkling rain. His wild hair was instantly wet, clinging like curling fingers of ivy to his forehead. He blinked as the raindrops collected on his eyelashes, wiping at them to keep his vision clear.

It wasn't her, his mind insisted. But it had looked like her. Even in the fleeting glimpses, he had noticed that this woman carried herself like Kate. Except there was an odd stutter to her movements, like a film with random frames removed.

Pulling the overgrown branches away from the trailhead, Wainwright stepped through the rip in the forest and onto the path. The branches snapped back into position behind him, blocking his way. The message was unintentional but nonetheless clear: there was no turning back.

At first he did nothing. He simply stood at the edge of the trail and continued to scan the area for the girl. The tops of the trees provided momentary relief from the growing storm, their bushy branches deflecting the rain.

"Kate?" he called out, feeling instantly foolish.

It isn't Kate. It can't be. It's the bloody house. Or it's nothing. It's your imagination.

But what if . . .

A sound worked its way to him, beaten down by the steady patter of the rain. He cocked his head, trying to force his ears to separate the noises like audio tracks on a computer, the falling rain on one track, the bristle of blowing leaves on another. And on a third track, a sound he may have imagined, a woman's voice from farther down the trail.

"O . . . here." He heard it this time, he was sure of it. *Over here,* she had said. Even the voice sounded like Kate's, playful yet commanding, each word warmed by that Southern twang.

He began to walk, hesitantly at first, then driven forward, his feet moving faster as he rounded the first curve in the path.

"Over here!" the voice said. "Hurry it up!" It was closer, just around the next bend.

Raising an arm to shield his face from the overgrowth, Wainwright burst into a clearing. He expected to find her waiting for him, smiling warmly. But the clearing was empty save for the creeping vines that seemed to be overtaking the countryside.

"Kate?" There was no hesitation now; he called the name with confidence, sure she must be nearby.

Only the rain responded, growing in intensity, pounding the cover of trees in an effort to break through.

Wainwright walked the edge of the clearing, a complete circle no more than forty feet in circumference. On one end, opposite where he had entered, was the next leg of the trail, its entrance barely discernable. She must have slipped through just before he arrived, pushing deeper into the woods.

He decided to follow the path until he found her. But as he took his first step, something creaked underfoot. He bounced lightly in place, finding that the ground had an unusual give. The creaking became a crack, the sound of weak wood splintering.

The well, he thought, remembering his own warning from their first visit. *If I'm not careful, these boards will snap and I'll fall—*

It came at him in a flash of light, what little sunlight remained in the day glinting off of metal. The image was too confusing to process. A flashlight? A star? A coin? The possibilities rushed by, unfiltered by reason. Then instinct kicked in, his face flinching, his hand swinging up to block the incoming object.

He heard the impact before he felt it—a sickeningly dull thud, like the smashing of a pumpkin. The force of the blow caused him to stumble back a few steps, the rotten boards protesting loudly beneath him. His tongue licked wildly at something that was wedged between his teeth, *through* his teeth, a metallic object, cold and sharp at its edge. His mouth was wet, too wet, filling with a gushing liquid.

Blood.

His mind raced, panic shorting out his senses, keeping him from making sense of what was happening. Through this, through the throb that was quickly enveloping his face, through the confusion as his tongue lapped stupidly at the metal edge in his mouth, another sound came to his attention. A whimpering from off to his side.

"I'm sorry," the new voice was saying. It was a man's voice, pathetic and grief-stricken. "I'm sorry," he said over and over. "I'm sorry, I'm sorry."

Without warning, Wainwright was pulled forward, his feet stumbling as the metal object was yanked from his face. His mouth was overflowing with blood; he could feel it coursing down his chin, soaking his shirt.

"I'm sorry," the voice insisted at a near-hysterical pitch. "I have to! I'm sorry!

For an instant, the whimpering ceased, replaced by a grunt, as if the man were putting all of his energy behind one action. Wainwright's wild eyes caught a glimpse of the glint again. This time it came at an angle, allowing him to make it out, to see the awful thing that was about to strike him. A blade, flat and tapered, like a sharpened stone. An ax. No, smaller.

A hatchet.

There was only time for this single thought, and then the impact jerked his head back, his neck bending at an unnatural angle. Something sloughed off the top of his head and it hit the ground with a terrible, soggy splat. Blood was drenching the back of his shirt. And then the darkness consumed him. It was not as he had imagined it. He had expected death to occur in the snap of a finger. But this was the sensation of his mind powering down, like a computer hard drive spinning to a stop. There was only blackness, and then . . . there was nothing.

Daniel stared down at the mess he had made, his chest heaving with each breath.

The second strike had taken Wainwright's scalp clean off. The clump of hair and flesh lay on the forest floor, wetted by the occasional raindrop. Where the hair had once been, the top of his skull was caved in, the pinkish-gray tone of brain visible through jagged bone.

Letting the hatchet slip from his hand, Daniel dropped to his knees, his body quivering as he began to weep. "I'm sorry," he whispered to the lifeless body. "I'm sorry. I'm sorry."

Wainwright's face was split straight down the middle, the nasty work of the hatchet's first blow. The blade had bitten deeply into his head, creating a canyon from just below his hairline down to the middle of his mouth. His two front teeth had been knocked in; one was folded up like the landing gear of an incoming plane while the other hung loosely by a thread of nerves.

The blood was more than Daniel could have ever expected. It soaked the earth around Wainwright's head, turning the already mushy ground into a reddish-black swamp.

Sitting on his legs, his knees digging into the dirt, Daniel stared at Wainwright's mutilated face, the glazed eyes parted by that terrible slash in the skin. Daniel couldn't look away. He had done this. He had murdered this man, with no warning, with no obvious motive.

The light touch of fingers grazed Daniel's shoulder. He peered back at the girl standing behind him.

Claire. Even as the storm above grew in strength, she was a beacon of light, a shining star in the gloom.

She bent her neck, her head turned down at an odd angle, and her voice seemed to rise up and over her, cascading down her shoulders like mist over a mountain ridge.

"Thank you, Daddy."

The sensation of her hand on his shoulder gave him strength, strength to get back on his feet, to pull the wood planks from the top of the well, to drag Wainwright by the feet and slide him, headfirst, into that man-made hole in the earth.

The body, Daniel thought. *That's all it is now. A body. No life. Nothing to mourn.* It was simply a means to an end.

She was smiling down at him, and the sight warmed his soul. His body stopped shivering. The tears dried up.

He was strong again. He could do this. He could finish the job. For her.

Daniel shoved over the boards covering the well to expose about three feet of the mouth. It was just enough to fit the body through. Wainwright was heavier than he looked, but with some effort, Daniel managed to drag the limp corpse closer so that its feet dangled over the edge. He gripped the young man—

Body, he corrected himself. *It's nothing more than that.*

—by the shoulders and, lifting with his legs as he had always been taught, he tipped the body up until it slid easily over the lip of the well. It plunged into the darkness. As he had with his cell phone six months earlier, Daniel listened for the object to splash into the water below.

There was no sound. Wainwright was swallowed by the earth.

Nearby, Claire giggled.

Daniel turned to her.

Her head was bobbing with laughter, her lips pulled into a tight grin, but once again he had the feeling that the sound was not coming from her but from something behind her.

Like a puppet.

No! his mind roared. *That is your Claire!*

Yes, it was his Claire, and her laughter was like breath in his lungs.

Daniel bent over and grabbed the carpenter's hatchet by its blood-streaked handle. He wiped the gory blade on his pant leg and started toward the trail that would lead him back.

To the house.

To them.

THIRTY-TWO

3:50 p.m.

HE WAS BACK in his bedroom.

Not the cozy, rustic room in his house in upstate New York, but the place he had called home for one night last Halloween.

Sebastian sat down on the bed, just as he had six months before. Through the door, he could hear the muffled voices of Sam and Moore on the stairs, followed by the pounding of hammers. He should be out there, helping them.

What help could you possibly be, old man? You don't even want to be here.

"None of us want to be here," he said aloud, but the sound of his own words embarrassed him.

You're a coward.

It was true, although he had no real reason to fear the house. Like the others, Sebastian had returned home only to be struck by inspiration. Like the others, he had spent the past few months pounding away on a keyboard, his fingers barely able to keep up with the story racing through his mind.

But it was different for you.

"Yes," Sebastian said to the empty room.

He was not driven by terror as Sam, Moore, and Daniel had been. As he wrote, he became aware of a presence in the house, a figure that lurked at the corner of his vision. But he was not afraid. The further he got into the new book, the closer the figure approached, until one day it put a hand on his shoulder and said in that warm, rough voice, "It's good, Sebastian. It's really good."

Richard.

He knew it couldn't be true. Yet every day when he returned to his computer, Richard was there, standing behind him as if waiting for pages to read, just as he had done when he was alive.

Listen to yourself, his mind ordered. *The thing in the house with you was not Richard. Richard is dead. There's no coming back from that.*

I thought it was my imagination, he insisted.

You were lying to yourself.

"I know," he said.

He'd gotten more than just Richard back, though. His mind had returned to him, the lapses into dementia growing rarer until they ceased entirely. Sebastian felt more alert than he had in years. He was operating at peak performance, all cylinders firing, as he passionately wrote what could be the best novel of his career.

He got up from the bed, his hand on the footboard to steady himself. Slowly, he crossed to the bathroom and stepped inside. He flicked the light switch, remembering only when the bulb above did not react that there was no electricity. The bathroom was a cocoon of shadow, the only light falling in through the open doorway.

Gripping the pedestal sink with both hands, he stared at his reflection in the mirror. He was a silhouette against the backlight of the bedroom, a featureless black curtain.

"Why are you here?" he asked the shapeless form before him.

He already knew the answer, no matter how badly he wanted to avoid it.

Because I know it wasn't right. Because I know it wasn't really Richard.

It was the house.

That was the reason why, once he had written the last page of his book, he had driven four hours into Brooklyn to visit Dr. Adudel. He had to find out what was truly happening to him. Perhaps whatever lurked in the house empathized with Sebastian. After all, they were both old. They were both being forgotten. Maybe what the house was doing wasn't bad. Maybe it was trying to help him. He made the trip to Adudel's three times before the day the others arrived. Only then did Sebastian finally get his answer.

I'm the storyteller.

"I never asked to be," he said to his faceless self.

"You didn't have to ask," a voice said from the darkness behind him. "You were chosen."

A second form was reflected in the mirror, a shadow among shadows. It was moving closer.

Sebastian closed his eyes tight. "Leave me alone," he said.

He felt fingers brush his neck.

"I gave you everything you wanted," Richard said. "But I can take it back. Unless you leave. Leave this place. Now."

It isn't Richard.

"Go home, Sebastian. Go home, my love."

It's isn't him!

Sebastian opened his eyes again.

It wasn't a mirror before him but a window, and through it he saw warped wooden planks set into the forest floor, beside which lay the crumpled form of Wainwright. He saw the basement, flooded knee-deep, and in the black water floated the body of T.C. Moore. He saw the hallway, just outside this bedroom, and sprawled across the ground was Sam McGarver, his face and torso mutilated, a dark lake of blood pooling around him. He saw the front yard and the flashing lights of police cars as bullets ripped through Daniel Slaughter.

He saw himself, in his garden at home, Richard by his side.

"Leave this place," Richard said.

Sebastian gasped and pushed away from the sink, away from the mirror.

The mirror. It's only a mirror.

So it was. A simple mirror over the pedestal sink, reflecting his dimly lit face.

He looked so old. The color that had warmed his cheeks was gone. Liver spots peeked through thin receding hair.

Sebastian felt something tug at his mind, like fingers pulling a loose thread, threatening to unravel his memories.

Sam stood over Moore as her sweaty hands tugged at the brick, inching it slowly away from the wall.

"Just pull the thing out!" he barked.

"I'm trying!"

"Let me do it!"

"I've got it, McGarver! I've got it!"

Moore adjusted what little grip she had, her fingertips slipping as she wiggled the brick back and forth, trying desperately to work it free. It was right smack at the center of the wall.

If we can get this one out, Sam thought, *we could get a crowbar through. We could pry more bricks loose. Bring this whole damn wall down.*

His hands quivered slightly as he watched, his fingers twitching as Moore tried to draw the brick out.

"Just get your goddamn fingers around it and pull!" he said, his impatience getting the better of him.

"Sam, what do you think I'm trying to do? I've got a quarter of an inch to work with. Just back off, okay?"

Sam did as she said. He glanced around, realizing for the first time that they were completely alone. "Where are the others? Where's Sebastian?"

"Fantastic," Moore snapped. "We're about to open Tut's tomb, and they're all off playing grab ass."

There was the loud, abrasive scrape of brick on cement. Sam peered over Moore's shoulder as the chipped red block came out a full inch. It was enough for her to wrap her fingers around each side. Planting a foot against the base of the wall, she leaned back. She sensed Sam there, ready to break her fall should the brick slide easily out. Taking a deep breath, she shoved off from the wall, the brick held tightly in her hands.

There was no fear of falling; the wall gave up another two inches but refused to let the brick go just yet.

"Shit!" Moore barked.

She released her grip just long enough to wipe her damp fingers on her pants. As she did, the brick began to wiggle by itself, drawn back into the wall by some phantom force. Her hands were around the brick at once, pulling desperately at it, trying not to lose ground. Each tug was equally matched from the other side as something attempted to keep the wall from coming down.

"Grab my shoulders," she called back.

Sam did, his hands grabbing Moore roughly.

She called out the instructions, her voice rising to a near yell. "On three, you pull as hard as you can. I'll do the same. One." She planted her heel into the top stair, the tip of her shoe pressed hard against the wall. "Two." The veins in her hands bulged, her fingertips bone white. She clamped her fingers around the brick like a vise. "Three!"

It happened in one fluid motion, Sam heaving Moore back just as she pushed off from the wall. And then they were falling, tumbling down the stairs, the edges of steps scraping their shoulders and backs. They landed at the base of the stairs in a heap, Moore a jumble of arms and legs beneath Sam, all eyes on the object in Moore's hand, so ordinary in any other situation, so extraordinary here.

The brick.

"You did it," Sam said with disbelief. Then, louder, the excitement palpable: "You did it!"

And then a wave of dread blew over Sam like a cold wind. *You did it. You're going to open that wall, and whatever was tugging on the other side of that brick will be there, nothing between you.*

He stared at the brick, still clutched in Moore's hand. Each of their stories had led them to this point, to the secret room beyond the wall, four different paths converging at a crossroads, a hidden place not on any known map. They were in uncharted territory. Stepping beyond the staircase into the third-floor bedroom meant giving in to the power of the house, acknowledging its invisible pull on each of them. It had lured them back for a reason. They were about to discover what that reason was.

The missing brick left a gaping hole at the center of the wall, black like a necrotic wound. From this, there came a sudden sucking sound as air was drawn sharply through the gap and into the secret room. A whistling rose to their ears, the air rushing faster and faster. They could feel it passing by them, pulled down the hallway and up the staircase to disappear through that small brick-sized space.

"We have to get the rest of that wall down," Moore said finally.

Sam gave a small nod. "Okay."

They were halfway up the steps when they heard the voices. Sam slowed, fearful that it was his mother again, or something pretending to be his mother, something that wanted to mock him from the darkness. But as they regained their position on the top step, the noise began to transform, splitting from one sound into several discernable sounds, each with a different rhythm, the uneven tempo of words. It reminded Sam of standing in a hushed crowd, a ripple of disobedient whispers rising and falling around him.

"What is that?" he asked.

Moore shook her head. "Hell if I know."

Sam lowered his ear to the hole. The suction was intense, pulling his head toward the wall. He fought it, listening as the voices collapsed upon each other like waves. He could not make out what they were saying, but their pace was urgent, as if what they had to share could wait no longer.

"I've heard this before." It was Sebastian, once more at the base of the stairs. Neither of them had heard him approaching.

"Sebastian?" Sam asked, confused. "Where were you?"

The old man ignored the question. "I heard it in my room, the last time we were here. I heard it in my sink. Down the drain."

In any other circumstance, Sam was sure Moore would have scoffed at this. But not here. They both nodded as if Sebastian's admission were the most natural thing in the world.

Without warning, the voices changed position, the whispering behind the wall cutting out like a radio being clicked off. They picked up a beat later, down in the second-floor hall, muffled slightly by the closed doors.

Sam cocked his head toward the new location. "Now it's coming from the bedrooms."

The noises leapt from room to room, first confined to the bedroom at the end of the hall, then relocating instantly to the door nearest the main staircase. The voices alternated at random, hitting each room like the off-key bars of a broken xylophone.

Soon the spaces between the shifts began to grow briefer, the noises coalescing into one voice, the words spoken in unison, a chant, still too low to make out yet spoken with that same unnerving urgency. They whirled around Sam, Moore, and Sebastian like an aural cyclone.

Sebastian tugged on the sleeve of Sam's shirt. "We need the others. They should be here."

He's right. Best to band together, to enter the third floor as a group.

Moore was already on her feet and squeezing past Sebastian in the narrow stairwell. "I'll find them. You two get the rest of that wall down."

Sam retrieved the smaller hammer. Crouching down so that he was level with the hole, he peered into the darkness, trying to make out anything, a single detail, a hint of what may await them once the wall was down. The dim light outside tried to slip between the cracks of boards covering what Sam assumed was the front third-story window, that all-seeing eye perched atop the house. From what he could tell, the room was bare except for a single piece of furniture. Some sort of chair. Two circular posts flanked it. Wheels.

Rebecca Finch's wheelchair.

Other than that, the room was empty.

THIRTY-THREE

4:08 p.m.

THE CHORUS OF whispers rolled across the first floor like fog, billowing up in the corners of the foyer before folding back in the opposite direction. Moore could hear them more clearly down there, away from the others, the words seemingly directed toward her. They were voices, she was sure of it. Hundreds of them. Male and female. Old and young. At one point, she even thought she heard the terrified wail of a baby.

Wainwright and Daniel were nowhere to be found. She moved from room to room, calling out their names. There was no response.

In the kitchen, she found the back door locked tight. She parted the heavy velvet curtain that hung over a nearby window, peering out through the pouring rain at the woods behind the house. There was no sign of movement, only the heavy branches swaying as the fat raindrops pelted them. The storm had given the world outside a sickly greenish-yellow hue, the flora deepened by several shades, leaves cloaked in shadow. It was not the kind of thing one saw in Los Angeles, where a single crack of thunder was enough to send motorists skidding off the road. No, this was a warning of worse things to come. The rain would not let up, the wind would grow more intense, hail would pelt the roof's weathered shingles.

The purr of a woman's voice snaked around Moore's feet, murmuring something unintelligible. Glancing down, she instantly zeroed in on the source—an electrical outlet just off to her left. The sound emanated from the outlet's tiny slits, the soft buzz of electricity carried beneath it. Her jaw and her fists clenched simultaneously. The damned voices made her mad. The house was taunting her, thumbing its nose at her, daring her to fight back.

Fight back against what? she wondered.

She kicked the outlet, hard, hoping the voice would falter, retreat farther back into the wall. It did not. The words poured out, whispered so quickly that they became one long series of jumbled consonants and vowels. With some concentration, she was able to pick out a recognizable word here and there. "That," the woman said. And "House." And "Bad." After a few minutes, Moore began to recognize the same words again and again, consistently repeated in the precise order. At one time, an entire sentence became clear—"You kids, stay away." She waited another full minute, watching the second hand on her watch as it spun past the quarter mark. There it was again, right on time. Whoever this woman was—a past inhabitant, a frightened neighbor—her warning appeared to be on a loop, repeated over and over by the house, infinitely.

But there was an end, abrupt and unexpected. The woman cut off mid-sentence as two new voices, those of young boys, took over. "Dare you to knock on the door," the first one said. "I'm not scared," replied the second. It played like an audio snapshot, a moment in time captured by the house. It had overheard this, a dare between two friends.

Overheard? Seriously? How the hell can a house hear?

"Dare you to knock on the door."

"I'm not scared."

Then, suddenly, the whispering from the outlet ceased and Moore became aware of a new voice, calling out from another room. She turned toward it, attempting to discern its location. Moving across the kitchen, her footsteps soft and silent, she followed the sound to the basement door. Resting one hand on the knob, she pressed her ear up against the door, surprised to find that her pulse had quickened, that fear was bubbling just beneath her anger.

"Help!" It was a young man's voice. He was clearly in distress. "Anybody up there? Please, I need help!"

Wainwright, Moore realized. Throwing open the door, she rushed down the rickety stairs into the absolute blackness of the basement. She recalled the last time she had done this, hesitantly creeping down with a camera and flashlight to illuminate her path. Now she raced into the void. She yelled his name out loud, "Wainwright! Where are you? I'm coming!"

The ambient light from the kitchen did little to brighten her descent, but it was just enough to reveal the arch of a person's back, rising from the darkness at the foot of the stairs like the hump of a white whale. Her first thought was that Wainwright was injured; perhaps he had slipped on a step and tumbled to the basement floor. But something wasn't right. The body before her was too pale, too cold, a lifeless color, like flesh completely drained of blood.

She slowed her pace. "Wainwright?" With an unsteady hand, she reached for the crumpled form resting oddly on the cool cement.

It seemed to anticipate her touch. It shifted, pushing itself away from her. At the same time, its face twisted toward her, into the light.

Above her, the door began to swing closed, the light on the stairs quickly reduced to a mere sliver.

Moore recoiled, whipping her hand away from the thing at the foot of the stairs.

The face staring back at her was not Wainwright's; it was barely recognizable as human. It grinned with cracked, dirt-crusted lips pressed tightly against rotting black teeth. Its flesh was gaunt, cheekbones poking sharply beneath skin bruised purple by pools of trapped, coagulated blood. A few thin strands of ratty black hair hung over its eyes; the rest had fallen out long ago, its scalp dotted with red fleshy craters, like the volcanic surface of some distant moon. A low, raspy chuckle seethed through its clenched teeth, its body quivering as it laughed at her.

"Theresa," it hissed.

Moore's stomach clenched into a fist. She thought she was going to vomit.

"Oh God . . ."

The faint outline of a tattoo covered the rotten flesh of the thing's back. She knew it well. It was the snarling face of a tiger. Bobby had been so proud of that piece of shit backpiece, just another pathetic attempt to feel like a man.

I've made a mistake, Moore thought.

And then the door slammed shut, the light extinguished, the darkness engulfing her. She could hear that thing, that abomination, pulling itself up the stairs toward her, its splintered fingernails digging into the wood.

Its voice bubbled up through the wall of mucus in its throat:

"Why do you make me hurt you?"

Instinctively, Moore began to retreat, taking a step back. Then another. And another.

The door. She could make it. But she had to run.

Now. Run!

She was turning to make her escape when something darted out from between the steps and slammed into her left ankle, biting deeply into her flesh. She heard the crack of breaking bone, but it was too late to stop her forward motion. The weight of her body came down on her left foot and there was a sickening snap as her ankle split clean in two. She roared with pain, hands grasping blindly in the darkness as she lost balance, teetering backward, her broken ankle folding at an unnatural angle.

She was falling. Back down the stairs. Back toward the dead, rotten thing waiting on the basement floor. She could hear that awful, gleeful chuckle rising, and with it the wet crackle of phlegm-filled lungs.

Her right shoulder hit the ground first, ramming into the merciless concrete, the ball of her humerus popping clean out of its socket. Muscle tore as her body came down on her dislocated arm. The pain was excruciating, momentarily distracting her from the white-hot throb of her ankle. She gave a frightened whimper, disgusted by the weakness she heard in it but unable to stop herself.

T.C. Moore had written of absolute terror. Her characters often found themselves being tortured by godlike beings from other worlds, their flesh peeled back with pliers, their fingernails snapped off, their orifices defiled in unspeakable ways. She had relished in the suffering of her hapless heroes, convincing herself that there was a crossroads where pain met pleasure. She insisted that this was what it meant to be truly alive, the sensation of agony transformed into ecstasy. What Moore's fans did not know was that she had never experienced such a moment of transcendence. She had suffered horrible beatings at the fists of her ex-boyfriend, one bad enough to split the pupil in her eye. But it had never broken through into pleasure. Pain was pain. There was nothing wonderful about it.

The anguish she was encountering on the basement floor was beyond anything she had ever imagined. It was mentally blinding, her mind filled with an intense white flash even as the blackness of the surroundings smothered her. Her arm flopped uselessly at her side, her foot bent against the broken bones so that it jutted away from her body at a ninety-degree angle. Her entire body seemed to throb, the pulse of her speeding heart captured in her swollen arm and leg like a hive of angry bees ramming her flesh to escape. She could feel a wetness on her ankle, the open wound where something had sliced into her.

With her left hand, Moore pushed herself up, propping her back against the wall. The dead thing was nearby; its giddy laugh had ceased, but she could still hear it breathing. She swiped at the open space around her, wanting to make contact and not make contact at the same time. Touching it would be awful, perhaps too awful for her frazzled mind to handle, but not knowing its location was somehow worse. She could picture it—rotten flesh stained by the damp earth, those terrible teeth exposed in a lipless grin, cloudy eyes staring hungrily through the abyss.

She swung her arm around to her side, and her hand collided with something almost rubbery in texture. With her fingers, she traced the object, attempting to determine its dimensions. Her fingertips slid across something slick. The dampness of breath heated her palm. The thing leaned closer, and Moore realized what was happening.

She was touching a face. Her fingers were on its teeth. And it was *smiling*. She could almost see it through the darkness, a pale orb hovering inches away from her.

"I found you, Theresa," it chuckled as sickening black bile poured down over its lapping tongue.

With her dislocated arm and broken ankle screaming in protest, Moore scrambled madly away. The edge of the first step smacked into the base of her back, and she pushed herself up onto it, trying to scoot up the stairs like a child who had yet to learn to walk.

The thing did not follow. It shrank back into the shadows.

Moore sat on the step, her chest heaving as she drew in fast, frightened breaths. As if from another world, a sound filtered down to her—the muffled clank of a hammer on brick.

Rearing her head back, she yelled up the stairs, "Sam!" She tried again, drawing out the word until her voice cracked: "Saaaaaaaaaam!"

"He can't help you," someone spoke in the darkness.

Moore turned toward the voice, trying to force her eyes to see in the pitch-black room. "Who is that? Who's there?"

Feet shuffled, the grit of the concrete floor scraping beneath shoes. "It doesn't have to be bad. I can make it quick. I promise."

"Daniel?" Moore's mind tried to make sense of it, but she found that she couldn't. It was beyond sense.

What doesn't have to be so bad? Make what quick?

"I have to," Daniel said. "You understand, don't you? You know that I have to do it?"

"Do what, Daniel?"

There was that scrape again; he was moving closer. "I have to. I'm sorry."

"Daniel, I'm hurt. I need your help. Help me up the stairs."

"You saw her, didn't you?" From the sound of his voice, he was now only a few feet away.

Moore winced as she pushed herself up another step, trying to put distance between them. "Saw who? Daniel, what are you talking about?" She managed another step, groaning as her mangled foot knocked against the post of the handrail.

"I saw you touch her face," Daniel said.

"Her?" Another step, her arm trembling weakly under her weight. "Who do you think that was?"

There was a long pause. Moore had the ridiculous notion that Daniel had exited the room, her mind temporarily forgetting that the staircase on which she was sprawled served as the only way out. Leaning on her elbow for support, Moore craned her neck to look up the stairs. She was halfway to the door. She could just make out the sliver of light beneath it. She grasped the back edge of another step. Her muscles bulged beneath the sleeve of her shirt as she pulled her aching body farther up the staircase.

She was close, so close. The light beneath the door was brighter now, almost within reach.

The bottom step squeaked loudly, and Moore knew that Daniel was coming after her.

"It was Claire." The voice seemed to hover over Moore in the darkness like a spider dangling from its web. "It was my Claire."

All of the traps Moore had ever set in her mind, those glorious mental contraptions designed to position others right where she wanted them, they were nothing compared to the trap this house had set for her.

The hatchet struck Moore in the stomach, a powerful blow that drove her back against the stairs. There was a cracking noise. The world began to tremble. Something snapped beneath her.

She was falling through the shattered stairs. She landed back on the hard floor of the basement.

Daniel was coming back down the stairs, down to finish what he had started.

Blood seeped between her fingers as Moore clutched her stomach. There was nowhere to hide.

Then, from within those impenetrable shadows, came a voice. Not the gravelly voice of the thing pretending to be Bobby.

It was a woman, prim and proper, an iciness to her words.

"You come into our house, you have to play by our rules," the voice said.

Moore peered into the darkness, trying desperately to make out the person speaking.

"But our game is fair. Oh yes, you have a choice." The voice sounded like it was right in front of Moore, but all she saw was darkness. "You can stay where you are, and he will find you. Or you can come to me and I will take all of your pain away."

That first step squeaked again as Daniel reached the bottom of the stairs.

The voice said, "Do you want that? Do you want me to take away the pain?"

I do, Moore admitted to herself. She wanted the pain to end. She had lived with it for almost her entire life and all she had ever wanted, more than fame and money and sex and power, all she wanted was for the pain to *end*.

"Come to me."

Daniel was a large, heaving shadow at the foot of the stairs. The hatchet was gripped in his hand. Blood fell in thick drops from its blade.

My blood, Moore thought. *That's my blood!*

"Come to me, and you'll never feel the pain again."

There was an eye in the darkness, a single pale orb floating like a frozen, distant planet. A woman's eye. Cold and powerful.

"Come."

Daniel's head snapped to the right and he glared at Moore through the shadows. Without a word, he stormed toward her, raising the hatchet into the air.

Pain is pain, Moore thought. She scrambled quickly toward the darkness and into the arms of the thing waiting there.

THIRTY-FOUR

4:35 p.m.

THE RAINDROPS HIT the dry, thirsty earth but it refused them, their liquid bodies, like tears from the sky, rolling aimlessly across the brittle surface of the creek bed. It was not long before the individual droplets found each other and merged, first creating snakelike rivulets of rain that coursed from bank to bank, then joining into a single sheet of water, its level rising with every inch that fell.

The furry green vines that draped the countryside like exposed muscle began to awaken at the soothing touch of the cool rain. Their movement was subtle, the constrictions slow like the stirrings of an animal roused from hibernation. As the creek bed filled with rainwater, the vines wriggled beneath the surface, leafy worms digging in the dirt.

Still the ground did not drink. Kill Creek, with the exception of a few stagnant puddles, began to flow once more.

There was a moment of all-consuming strangeness, and then there was a click and Sebastian's mind was clear again. It reminded him of the television he had bought with the paycheck from his first published novel, a heavy wooden monster with a protruding black-and-white eye, antennae sprouting haphazardly from its head. Back in those days, there were only a handful of channels to receive, which meant that you had to wade through several patches of static as you turned the dial in search of a healthy signal.

For six months, Sebastian had been free of these spells. He felt reborn, relishing every moment of this new age of lucidity. But now things had changed. He was tempted to leave the group and return home. Panic had invaded him and it was growing stronger the longer he stayed in the house. He did not want to lose his mind. He did not want to be plunged forever into the nothingness.

The house giveth, and the house taketh away.

It wasn't quite the same sensation as before, though. Instead, it was as if the dial had become stuck between channels, two separate images dog-piling each other.

One minute he was on the stairs, watching Sam pound away at that profoundly stubborn brick wall. And then the sides of the house began to ripple.

The digestion of memories, he thought, not sure exactly what it meant.

He could still see the house as it was, the hallway stretching out before him, empty and barren, ending in the top of the far staircase that led down to the first floor. But superimposed upon this was a duplicate image, similar but not exact, a glimpse out of time. Sometimes this was all that occurred before the dial would finish its turn to the next channel, the present returning to him, clear and genuine. Other times, transparent forms would pass before him, people he did not know, their clothing reminiscent of times only vaguely familiar, a woman and a man, black and white, like that old television he had owned so long ago.

From the top step, Sebastian could hear the clank of Sam's hammer chipping at the brick. The sound reverberated through him, from the center of his chest out, like a stone tossed into a mirror-still pond.

But every time he became accustomed to these ghostly images . . . *click!* The hallway would once again be empty, the washed-out colors regaining their full vibrancy, the apparitions gone in the blink of an eye, and all memory of the occurrence gone with it.

Once more, they were alone.

When Sam was in the third grade, he and his father decided to plant a row of rosebushes as a surprise for his mother. She was gone for the day, visiting her father at a rest home called Holiday Resort (the "holiday" consisting of Grandpa King sucking on an oxygen tank and battling a mean case of emphysema, the result of many happy years of smoking).

Sam's mom wouldn't be back until late evening, and his father was confident that they could get the plants in the ground in time. Even at three months shy of nine years old, Sam knew his mother would not truly appreciate the gesture. She would force a smile and say how beautiful they looked, and then she would go into the house to pour herself a vodka and tonic with a twist of lime. What she truly thought of Sam and his father's hard work would come out later—

You think a few puny roses can make up for this rathole of a house?

—but there in the warm afternoon sunshine, both Sam and his dad, a thin, meek fellow with a weak chin and even weaker backbone, convinced themselves this gift would actually make her happy.

The rosebushes were lined up in a row along the back side of the house, eight in all, their thorny branches waiting patiently to prick soft flesh. The thorns reminded Sam of a shark's teeth, jutting off in all directions, like the rotating blades of a garbage disposal, made to tear, to shred, to destroy.

His father returned from the garage with two shovels, handing the shorter one to Sam. The plan was to plant the bushes in the long stretch of soil between the back patio and the house. His father insisted that once they got into the groove, the job should only take them a couple hours, three at the most.

Then, while digging the first hole, they hit something hard. Cement. The edge of the shovel scraped angrily against the buried slab. No problem, his father insisted, just move a little to the right and dig again. Sam did as he was told, but his new hole was only a few inches deep before his shovel let out another painful screech. Concrete, same as the last.

After the fourth hole led to the same results, Sam's father began to realize the frustrating situation they were facing. The house's foundation had been sloppily poured, and the excess concrete had been allowed to run off and dry, leaving a layer, hard as stone, surrounding their home.

Not one to easily lose his cool, Sam's father disappeared back into the garage and returned, moments later, with a pickax in one hand and a sledgehammer in the other. First he used the pickax, its pointed edge chipping at the cement like the horn of some strange metal beast. Shards of concrete flew, pecking at their faces, but the slab refused to split. The sledgehammer also had little effect, denting the rock-hard surface but otherwise leaving it intact.

After an hour, Sam's father was covered in a mixture of sweat and powdered stone and filled with something close to rage. He threw the sledgehammer to the ground, muttered a few choice curse words under his breath, then surveyed the yard and pointed out a patch of soil along the picket fence at the far end. The rosebushes were set easily into this new location. Sam's mother came home to a pleasant surprise and a forced smile, and for a few fleeting moments, all was right with the world. But with Sam and his dad, there lingered a sense of defeat, the knowledge that they had gone to battle with the concrete slab and lost.

That same sensation now came to Sam, rising from the back of his throat like the bitter taste of bile. He had managed to free four more bricks from the wall, but the others were holding tight with otherworldly conviction. With the absence of five bricks, the hole was almost large enough for Sam to poke his head and shoulder through. He could have reached a hand in had he wished, but the fear of something grabbing hold kept him from doing so. Instead, he peered into the gloomy third-floor bedroom, searching for anything. A clue. A tiny detail that would make all of the other unbelievable occurrences fall into place, making sense of this inexplicable adventure they were on.

Except for that ancient, abandoned wheelchair, there was nothing.

The whispering voices emanating from the house had stopped a few minutes before, leaving Sam and Sebastian in a stillness that was, for some reason, even more disconcerting.

Sebastian was at the foot of the steps, facing the small window that looked out into the backyard. The rain pelted the windowpane, tapping it like a child asking to come in. "Quiet," he said.

"I know," Sam said. "Whatever the house was saying, it's stopped."

Sebastian shook his head. "That's not it. I mean it's quiet. No sounds at all. Not even from the others."

Sam cocked an ear, listening. There was only the rain—on the window, on the roof—accompanied by the occasional rumble of thunder. Otherwise, the house was completely silent. No footsteps. No muffled voices. No doors clicking shut. "You're right. It's like they're gone."

With the hammer still clutched in his hand, Sam moved down the narrow staircase and peeked around the corner. He called out each of their names: "Wainwright! Daniel! Moore!" Each one bounced its way down the hall, retreating into the depths of the house until even the echo was consumed. There was no answer.

"Maybe they stepped out for a smoke," Sam offered.

Sebastian shook his head but continued staring out at the back lot. The reflection of raindrops cast shadows rippling down his cheeks. "They're not exactly old chums. They would rather be here helping you than palling around on the front porch." He took in a deep breath and glanced at his wristwatch. "Besides, they've been gone for far too long."

He was right. It had been half an hour since Moore had left to look for the others and over two hours since they had last seen Daniel. Could it have been that long? The afternoon had escaped them, the task of breaking through the brick wall consuming their day.

"What do you say I go have a look?" Sebastian suggested.

"No," Sam said, a bit shocked by the sternness in his own voice.

That was our mistake, he thought. *The house split us up without us even realizing it.*

Sebastian started down the hall. Sam opened his mouth to call out, but the sound of heavy footsteps stopped him. Sebastian came to a halt, just past the first set of bedroom doors.

"There they are now," Sebastian said.

A hulking black form appeared at the top of the stairs. The dark, faintly human figure stood motionless for a beat, like the shadow of a mountain, shoulders heaving with each deep breath. And then he moved slowly into the light.

Upon seeing Daniel, Sam's first thought was that he'd cut himself. But there was too much blood. Splattered beads of it dotted his face, already drying to a brownish red. His polo was soaked through, its wetness shimmering in what little light there was. His hair was slicked back, with what Sam first assumed must be water or sweat, but now realized was thick globs of blood. This was not the Daniel they had come to know, the man who had tugged self-consciously at the edge of his shirt in an attempt to pull it over his bulging belly.

This Daniel seemed to have no idea that he was caked in gore, that his arms were streaked with it, that it dripped from his fingers like scarlet tears. Sam's eyes followed the jagged lines of red down his arms to his right hand and the carpenter's hatchet clutched there. On one end was the flat head of a hammer; the other narrowed into a hatchet. Its blade was shiny-slick with a thick coat of crimson and dotted with pale flecks that Sam assumed must be flesh.

Sebastian took a step toward Daniel and held out his hands. He made a sweeping motion from head to toe, as if bringing everyone's attention to the bloody mess of Daniel Slaughter.

"What's happened, Daniel?" he asked, his voice beginning to shake. "Are you hurt?"

Daniel's fingers tightened on the hatchet's handle, and an icy sliver of terror ripped through Sam's body. "Sebastian, stay back!"

"But, Sam, look at him. Something's wrong." Then, to Daniel, "Where are Moore and Wainwright? Have they been injured? Was it the house?" Sebastian moved one step closer to Daniel, and then, just as Sam had done, his gaze moved down to the bloodstained hatchet. "What is that?" he asked, the truth dawning on him. "Daniel, what have you done?"

"Sebastian, get away from him!" Sam cried out.

As he took in a deep breath, Daniel's eyes began to glisten with tears. He clenched his jaw, shaking his head slowly. He began to mutter something under his breath, a blubbering mess of words that were at first unrecognizable.

Sam watched Daniel's lips as he recited the words over and over like a prayer. *What is he saying?*

Daniel's voice began to rise, the words floating like a swarm of black gnats down the hall. "I'm sorry," he said. "I'm sorry. I'm sorry." His eyes darted between the frail form of Sebastian and the dust-streaked face of Sam. "I have to."

A horrible realization dawned on Sam. *He's going to kill us! He's killed the others, and now he's come for us.*

Sebastian must have come to the same conclusion. He took a step backward.

Daniel's entire body flinched. He tightened his grip on the hatchet.

"I hid the book," Sebastian called back over his shoulder. "Before I went to see Adudel. I hid it so no one could find it. You don't have to worry. No one will ever read it."

Sam watched as Sebastian's posture stiffened. He stood up straight, tall, and proud. His hands clenched into fists.

In that awful moment, he realized what the old man planned to do.

"I won't be its storyteller, Sam," he said. "Is the hole big enough yet? Can you get through the wall?"

"Don't, Sebastian."

"Is the hole big enough? Look, goddammit!"

Sam glanced over at the wall. He had hoped to make the hole bigger before crawling into the room, but maybe he could squeeze through.

Maybe.

"Is it?" Sebastian yelled.

"Yeah. I think."

"Then go."

"No, Sebastian!"

"Go, Sam!"

A roar filled the hallway, a sound of such pristine ferocity that for a brief moment Sam thought an animal was preparing to charge them.

It was—an animal that had once been Daniel Slaughter, a blood-soaked beast with murder in its eyes. The roar twisted back into Daniel's open maw like a cyclone spinning into the sky. It became a terrible, high-pitched moan, shrill and helpless: "You understand! I have to! I have to do it!"

"GO!" Sebastian cried. "NOW!"

The heavy footfalls came quickly, rattling the floor with each step. Daniel bounded down the hallway toward Sebastian, one hand stretched out to grab the old man, the other slicing the air with that death-caked hatchet. Even beneath the smudges of blood, his face burned bright red. He huffed and puffed like a locomotive as he charged, his loose clothes rippling around his body. Tears streamed down his flushed cheeks, that high-pitched moan like a boiling teakettle.

"Sebastian!" Sam screamed.

The old man glanced back over his shoulder. And he smiled.

Daniel's bloody fingers grasped at his prey. His hand came down on Sebastian's shoulder with such force that Sam was positive the old man would shatter beneath it, disintegrating into a cloud of dust and bone.

The hatchet followed, swung at an angle. Its blade sank deeply into Sebastian's side. Ribs split like twigs. The old man groaned in agony as he threw all of his weight forward, pushing Daniel and toppling them both to the ground.

"I'm sorry!" Daniel shrieked, swinging the hatchet wildly as he shoved Sebastian's frail body off of him. Daniel scrambled to his feet. He raised the hatchet to bring it down on the old man's skull.

Sam did the only thing he could. He clapped his hands loudly and cried, "Hey! Over here!" It was ridiculous, he knew. It was the way one might get the attention of a disobedient dog. But it worked. Daniel's head whipped toward Sam, his face wrinkled into a hideous sneer. For the first time since this standoff had begun—

How long had it been? Seconds? Minutes? Hours?

—Sam got a good look at Daniel's eyes. Something had gotten inside him, *infected* him, forcing him to complete his unthinkable deeds.

Infected, Sam thought. The word was right. Daniel looked as if he were at the mercy of some unimaginably high fever, the rising temperature of his overworked body boiling away all coherent thought.

He was mad.

"I have to," he said, his voice now low and guttural, like a death rattle.

"That's right," Sam said. "So do it. I'm right here. Come and get me."

There was no time to be afraid. Daniel's feet pounded into the wooden floor as he resumed his charge, and Sam spun quickly around, arms reaching for the sides of the narrow passage, the very tips of his toes grazing each step as he flew up the stairs.

He could hear Daniel coming after him; each stair he mounted groaned in agony. He could hear the excited pant of Daniel's breath as he scrambled up the staircase, so close that Sam could almost sense the heat on his back. But all the while, Sam kept his eyes on one thing—the hole in the brick wall, just wide enough for him to slip through, just small enough to keep Daniel out.

The thick edge of Daniel's middle finger slid down Sam's back, and Sam dove, the voice of his father suddenly shouting in his ear, a command from his years playing Little League baseball back in Kansas: *Slide! Slide!*

Sam slid, the sharp corners of the bricks cutting into his stomach as he passed through the black mouth he had cut into the wall.

He was swallowed by the darkness.

Sebastian listened as Daniel's thundering footsteps moved quickly down the hall, away from him. His side was on fire. Even the slightest movement sent needles shooting through his entire body. But he had to move. He had to move quickly before Daniel returned.

Gritting his teeth to hold in a scream, Sebastian dragged himself across the floor, toward the door of the closest bedroom. *His* bedroom.

He reached for the doorknob, but his fingers only grazed it. His fingertips left streaks of blood on the brass knob. His entire hand was covered in the red stuff.

He shivered as shock threatened to overtake him. He had to stay present, he had to be in this moment or it would surely be his last.

Clenching his teeth, he forced his body to rise up. Something snapped in his chest. Another rib, fractured by the blow. Something pushed through his skin—the jagged edge of a bone—and he felt a gush of fresh blood course down his side.

Daniel's muffled voice snapped him to attention, echoing down from another world.

"Get back here! Let me do this! I have to do this!"

He was still after Sam, although the frustration in his voice made Sebastian think that perhaps Sam was temporarily out of reach. He hoped so.

Sebastian's fingers took hold of the doorknob. He fought against the slickness of the blood as he turned it.

The door gave a merciful click, and Sebastian pushed it open. Digging an elbow into the wood floor, he dragged himself inside the bedroom. He scooted up against the wall and quietly pushed the door shut.

The latch clicked back into place.

For the moment, he was safe. For the moment, he was alive.

But I shouldn't be, he thought.
I shouldn't live through this.

THIRTY-FIVE

5:02 p.m.

EVEN AS SAM hit the floor, he never stopped moving. He scooted with his feet, pushing himself farther into the room, his body cleaning a path through the thick layer of dust as Daniel swiped the hatchet through the hole in the wall.

The first thing Sam noticed was the cold. The third-floor bedroom had to be at least forty degrees cooler than the rest of the house. When he exhaled, his breath misted into an icy cloud.

The room was nothing more than a large, empty square. Thick dust covered the wooden floor. On the far side was a pile of toppled brick, and beyond this, the elevator car, its accordion door open.

Once he was halfway across the bedroom, Sam allowed himself to stop. Daniel was still much too large to climb through the hole in the wall, but that didn't stop him from trying. He pressed his body up against the bricks as if expecting his form to mold to the shape of the opening, like a child trying to force the wrong puzzle piece into place.

"Get back here!" he yelled. "Just let me do it! Let me finish this!"

Sam propped himself up with his arms, his chest heaving as he attempted to catch his breath. "Daniel, stop. Please. Think about what you're doing."

Daniel let out a furious howl, a sound that made Sam think of an animal caught in a steel trap.

"It's not too late to stop," Sam told him. "We can walk away from here. We can fix things."

"Shut up!" Daniel yelled. His voice bounced around the room like an echo chamber, ping-ponging from wall to wall. "You don't understand!"

"I want to understand, Daniel."

"You can't!" Only half of his face was visible through the hole, but Sam could see fresh tears on his beet-red cheeks.

He watched as Daniel glanced to the right, focusing on something just over Sam's shoulder. There was nothing there, of course, only the empty wheelchair, the broken spokes of its bent wheels draped in an elaborate spiderweb.

"I don't know if I can," Daniel said. Saliva bubbles popped between his lips as he cried.

"Daniel? Who are you talking to?" Sam asked.

Daniel stared at the wheelchair. He saw something sitting there. Something that offered him much-needed words of support. His face darkened. The tears stopped flowing. He began to nod, understanding. Then his insane glare was on Sam again, the tiny glimpse of old, reasonable Daniel gone in an instant, pulled under by the current of dark waters.

"Okay," he whispered. "Okay. I can do it. For you."

Sam gave a startled yelp as Daniel began to ram the wall. *Thud! Thud!* The force with which Daniel slammed his shoulder into the bricks made Sam cringe. The barrier would hold, he was sure of it. He was safe for the time being, unless there was another way in. . . .

The elevator, Sam thought suddenly, a jolt of panic ripping through his body. He hopped up and raced across the room, leaping over the pile of bricks and into the elevator car. He jammed a finger into the button for the first floor. Nothing happened. The elevator did not move. Sam gave a frustrated cry. He hopped up and down in the car, but it stayed put.

I'm going to die in here.

No sooner had Sam thought these words than he became aware of the faint sound of something scattering on the wooden floor. Daniel was still smashing into the wall like a wrecking ball, his teeth bared, a long string of spit dripping from the corner of his mouth. Yet where before the wall showed no signs giving, it now buckled inward a bit, the mortar between each brick crumbling to the ground. Daniel must have sensed it, for his attack increased in both frequency and power. He began to hum excitedly under his breath.

It was difficult to accept. Sam had hammered away at that wall for hours and only managed to loosen a handful of bricks. And it was about to cave against Daniel's immense weight.

There was only one other way out: the small window that graced the north wall.

Unfortunately it had been boarded up years ago. Several thick planks were secured to the wall on either side of the frame. An obscene number of nails held them in place. Many of the heads were bent at odd angles, as if whoever had hammered them in had done so in a rush.

It's a prison, he realized. *Those boards were there to keep someone in. To keep Rebecca in.*

Sam's hand gripped something. A handle. He looked down.

He was still holding the small hammer. He had forgotten it was even in his hand.

Sam rushed to the window and began bashing at the boards. They did not budge. Like the brick wall, they refused to give, even though they were already covered in countless dents from a previous attack.

She tried to get out of this room. The thought sent a chill through his body.

"Come on!" he cried. He hammered at the flat ends of the boards. The head of the hammer savaged them, splitting off slivers of wood, but the boards held tight.

Behind him came the thunk of a brick dropping to the floor. Seconds later, it was followed by another.

He's coming! Sam's mind screamed. *He's going to get you! He's going to kill you! Just like Moore! Just like Wainwright! Just like—*

Sebastian. Poor Sebastian.

He saw the old man smiling back at him as Daniel raised the hatchet high into the air.

With a mighty cry, Sam swung the hammer into the end of the middle board.

It moved.

One of the rusty nails gave an angry howl as it was wrenched from the wall.

It was enough for him to slip his fingers in between the board and the wall. He gripped the end, put one foot on the wall and pulled back with all of his strength.

Like the first brick in the wall, the board seemed to pull back, to fight against him, but Sam would not yield. Veins bulged in his arms, raising the damaged flesh beneath his tattoos as he forced the board free. The nails shrieked, and then Sam was falling backward, the board in his hand. He threw it aside.

Dim light passed through the sliver of grimy window.

Sam was immediately back to work, bashing the next board free. One by one, they fell until the tiny window was completely exposed. He clawed desperately at its latch with sweat-drenched hands.

The mad humming from Daniel was rising in volume as he pounded faster and faster at the wall. It was disturbingly sexual, as if the excitement of bursting through the obstruction was bringing him to climax.

Sam's fingers slipped from the latch. He swung the hammer down on it, but the latch would not move.

"Come on! Come on! Open, you son of a bitch!"

The head of the hammer slipped and his hand grazed the latch, tearing the tender flesh of his palm. Streaks of fresh blood glistened on the tarnished metal. It was no use. The latch stuck tight.

He let out a whimper, a noise that both infuriated and frightened him in its helplessness.

A third brick fell, and Sam knew there was no time left. In only a few seconds, the wall would topple and Daniel would rush him, hatchet slicing the air.

Sam swung the hammer again, but this time he aimed for the windowpane. It broke through with an ease that thrilled him. Shards of glass showered the floor like hail. He ran the head of the hammer around the edge of the frame, chipping away the remaining shards.

From across the room he heard the thunderous rumble of the wall coming down. A brick, propelled by Daniel's powerful attack, came skidding across the floor, stopping a few inches from Sam's foot.

Sam dashed back across the room. The intricate network of spiderwebs ripped like silk tendons as he grabbed the wheelchair by the armrests and lifted it from the floor. He paused, noticing the savagely bent wheels. The chair had once been used as a weapon . . . or a tool.

He remembered the dents in the wood planks hiding the window. He looked quickly around and saw similar dents in each wall. Even the ceiling looked as if someone had tried to claw their way through it.

She was locked in here. Rebecca Finch was locked in this room.

To die.

He considered the wheelchair clutched in his hands, and a sudden thought occurred to him:

Scratches on the ceiling. Smashing the chair into the window.

Rebecca could not have done this.

Who was locked in here?

Daniel bounded into the room.

Sam had no time to plan the action; in one fluid motion, he hoisted the heavy metal chair in an arc over his head, his eyes never leaving the intended target.

It was a direct hit. The edge of one wheel collided with Daniel's chest and sent the large man falling back through the now-open doorway. He thudded onto the steep staircase behind him.

Racing to the window, Sam mashed his hands down onto the exposed frame. He could feel the shards he had missed biting into his flesh like glass teeth, but he ignored the pain, propping himself up through the hole where the window once was. Rain pelted his face as he maneuvered his body through the tight space, only vaguely aware that he was now dangling over three stories of open air. The roof of the front porch was directly below him, and the hideously twisted beech tree just past this.

"I can't let you go!" Daniel's voice boomed as if his mouth were inches from Sam's ear. "I have to do this, you understand? For her!"

Move it, asshole! Sam's mind ordered. *Faster! Faster!*

Sam did as he was told, swiveling around onto his butt and taking hold of the edge of the rooftop. He kicked wildly with his feet as he pulled himself up and out of the window. Once, his shoes made contact with what felt like Daniel's shoulder, and a wave of terror shook Sam's entire body. But he did not stop. The muscles in his forearms burned white-hot as he lifted himself away from the windowless frame and up toward the roof. The heavy rain made getting a grip difficult, but somehow he managed. He had no choice. It was either keep hold or fall to his death.

He flopped onto the roof's sandpaper-rough shingles like a landed fish. His arms were trembling as he strained to drag himself farther onto the roof.

Something grazed his leg and a gush of warmth ran down his ankle.

He's cut me! He's cut me with that fucking hatchet!

A fresh hit of adrenaline screamed through him and, growling through clenched teeth, Sam dug his fingernails into the shingles, dragging himself those last few feet onto the roof. He was instantly on his back, pushing himself farther and farther up the steep incline.

He blinked in the rain, the water coursing down his neck and under his shirt like hundreds of clear, wet snakes. He lay there, letting the storm drench him, trying in vain to steady his breath. He glanced down. A bloody gash peeked out through the cut in his pant leg. He parted the material to inspect the wound. He could see the inside of his flesh, like a cross section of sedimentary rock.

Sam closed his eyes and a few hot tears slipped free. They streaked down his trembling cheeks and were instantly washed away by the unrelenting storm.

From the bedroom below, Daniel swiped the hatchet out into the air. Even with the weight he had lost in the past six months, he was still too large to fit through the window. He let out a furious roar. The entire house seemed to shudder beneath Sam. And then it answered its new caretaker, those hundreds of phantom voices whispering, the sound emanating from every board, every nail, every stone.

Sam began to scale the sharp incline of the roof, his back hunched, his fingers gripping the abrasive surface of the shingles. When he neared the peak, he leaned on the brick chimney for support. Had the house been smaller and the roof steeper, the unrelenting rain may have sent him sliding right over the edge, a fall that would have left him with a broken back at best. But the immense size of the structure meant that the roof rose at no more than a forty-five-degree angle. He had to concentrate on keeping a foothold, but at last he made it to the top.

Sam straddled the peak of the roof. He was higher than the treetops, with a clear view for half a mile in each direction. The bulk of the trees seemed to trace the winding creek, cloaking it in a dense green garment. He followed it around the side of the house to the front yard. Around the bridge they had crossed when they arrived, the trees shrank back, exposing the creek bed. Except it was no longer a bed. The afternoon storm had managed to dump enough water onto the dry earth to get a stream flowing. It seemed unlikely that the creek could be rejuvenated in just a few hours, but there it was, a growing deluge rippling through the countryside like blood down a wound whose scab had been peeled free. At this rate, the waters could spill over the banks in less than a day.

The land was brilliantly green. As Sam glanced over the yard from high on his perch, he thought he could make out an uneven pattern woven into the grass, like the leafy tentacles of some long-buried sea creature.

He rested, soaked to the skin, the rain pouring over him, and Sam became aware of the house vibrating beneath him. It pulsated in an odd arrhythmic way like a murmuring heart.

It's speaking to him, Sam realized, *speaking with its collected voices.*

The house had heard every muttered warning, every campfire tale whispered throughout the years, growing more powerful as its infamous reputation spread. Adudel had been right; this place could not risk being forgotten. Whatever entity now resided within its walls, it found life through a legacy of tragedy and fear. It had been weak when they visited the previous year, banished to the shadows that cloaked each dusty room. At that time, it was little more than a local legend.

But then the writers arrived, and their visit went viral, viewed millions of times. The renewed interest must have been like a shot of adrenaline, jolting the house awake after years of hibernation. Rachel Finch had done the very same thing in the eighties by luring Adudel to the house. That she had encouraged him to embellish his story only confirmed Sam's hypothesis—that the house went through periods of dormancy, like a regressed cancer, waiting for its name to reenter the collective consciousness so its power could spread beyond its property line.

Which is exactly what it had done, following each of them into their homes, into their very minds, forcing them to propagate its disease the only way they knew how—by writing.

But their novels—which made connections to the house through surprisingly similar details—were not the endgame. The books that had devoured months of their lives were a way of breaking them down and, ultimately, bringing them back together. No, the punch line to the house's cruel joke was for them to return by their own free will.

It had lured them back to kill them. Their brutal deaths would be the ultimate ghost story.

No, Sam realized, *we're nothing more than a publicity stunt for a story already written.*

Sebastian's book.

Sebastian could be its storyteller. He could make the house famous once more. Except Sebastian's spirit could not be fully broken. He was willing to refuse this Faustian bargain. For his friends. For what he knew was right.

The house hasn't won. Not yet.

There was still Sam, hiding out on the rooftop, and Sebastian . . .

Sam sat up straight, the action nearly knocking him over one side of the roof. Daniel had left Sebastian behind in the hallway to die. But maybe . . . just maybe . . .

The third-floor window Sam had climbed through faced the front yard, which meant that the bedroom closest to where Sebastian had been attacked was on the back half of the house. Looking down the other side of the roof, Sam tried to imagine the bedrooms beneath him. He pointed a finger at the southwest corner, then moved it slowly to the left, past what would have been the tight alcove. Next came the bedroom at the very end of the hallway. And finally the second bedroom from the end, the one he had slept in on Halloween.

Carefully, Sam climbed over the roof's peak and began to move down the south side. Several times his feet slipped on the wet shingles, but eventually he made it to the edge. Now came the hard part. A metal rain gutter ran the length of the house, and by peering over the roof, he could see a short ledge just outside the bedroom window. But there was no telling how much weight the gutter could hold, and the ledge offered little room on which to stand; he was lucky if it was six inches wide.

"Screw it," Sam told himself.

Stretching out along the end of the roof, he grasped the gutter so tightly, the color was pressed from his fingertips. He took a deep breath and let one foot slip over the edge, then the other, his body falling into open air.

THIRTY-SIX

5:2I p.m.

SEBASTIAN KNEW HE was dying.

His hands were beginning to shake. A cold sweat had broken out over his entire body. He needed to get to a hospital immediately. But he couldn't risk dragging himself back out into the hall. Daniel could be there, and Sebastian would have no hope of escaping. No, all he could do now was wait until someone else found him or Daniel came to his senses.

At the very least, Moore and Wainwright were also injured. At worst, they were dead.

The ghost of a memory appeared in his mind, an image through a window—bodies in this house, the bodies of his friends—and then it was gone, dissipating like morning mist.

Sebastian thought of Daniel. There was no easy way out of this for him. But showing some mercy on Sebastian and Sam might count for something in the eyes of the law.

If Sam is still alive.

He had heard the shouts coming from the staircase leading to the third-story bedroom. This had been followed by a heavy clatter that could only be the brick wall toppling to the floor. He had no idea what this meant, but he hoped with all his heart that Sam had escaped. Then the voices had begun again, floating up through the floor like smoke from a fire below. The conspiratorial din of gossip.

Sitting on the floor, his back propped against the wall, Sebastian stared at his pale, bony hands and whispered to them to stop shaking. The movement made him uneasy. He could get through this. The bleeding from his side had stopped for the moment. He certainly had internal injuries, but he could make it out alive. All he had to do was stay calm.

The sight of his trembling hands was becoming too much to bear. Sebastian clutched them together and held them to his chest. He closed his eyes, searching his mind for some form of reassurance, an image perhaps, a reminder of happier times. Yet all of his memories were fading like old photographs. He thought of Richard, back before the symptoms of his cancer made themselves known. He thought of having tea in the garden just behind their house, purple clusters of hydrangeas blooming in the shade of a young redbud tree. He clutched to this image like a drowning man to a passing log, attempting to lose himself in the safety it offered.

Out in the hallway, a floorboard creaked. But Sebastian did not hear it. He was drifting off toward the garden and Richard and the smile that promised everything would be all right.

When he opened his eyes again, he was there. The clarity was startling. He blinked in the dappled sunshine. Breathed in the moist summer air. Smelled the fragrant aroma of lemon peel tea.

"Richard?" he called out.

There was no reply.

The old wooden rocker, Richard's preferred seat in the garden, showed the slightest hint of disturbance, as if someone had just abandoned it.

"Richard? Where are you?"

An arbor overgrown with crimson trumpet vines signaled the end of the garden and the beginning of what Sebastian called "the back lot," where his meticulously pruned and weeded flower bed gave way to the natural wild of the forest. Someone was moving among the trees.

"Richard! It's me! It's Sebastian!"

The person appeared to hear his voice, pausing before the thick stump of a rotted oak. It was not Richard, but a woman, her skin a few shades darker than the bark of the tree that sheltered her. She stared at him as if confused by his voice.

"Hello," he said, moving a few feet in her direction. "Who are you?"

She said nothing, but as he neared, she began to shake her head slowly. For every step he took toward her, she took one in the opposite direction. Still her head shook.

"My dear, what on earth is the matter?" Sebastian asked.

She backed farther and farther into the shadowed woods, her face obscured by the diminishing light. Now her hands were raised, her palms held out toward him as if asking him to stay back.

But Sebastian did not listen. He followed her deeper into the forest and the darkness that welcomed them both like a lover's arms.

Daniel stared dumbly at the smear of blood on the floor. The sight of it did not worry him. It was not his blood.

Sebastian was still alive. And from the path of blood, it was clear he had crawled into this bedroom.

He pressed his ear up against the door but heard nothing. His fingers tightened on the hatchet. Its handle was slippery with blood and sweat.

In the beginning, these quiet moments led to the desire to call off his assault. He would find himself thinking about these people as friends, remembering bits and pieces of a time before Claire's death when everything had had worth. But that time had passed. There was no going back. He had to see this through to the end.

He glanced over his shoulder and there was Claire, her strawberry blond hair dancing in the light, a warm, loving smile for her daddy.

So there were still two more. But only two more, and then she would be with him. Their sacrifice would mean the re-formation of his family. What man wouldn't do everything he could to save his family?

In the stillness, Daniel listened as the thud of his overstressed heart forced out sharp, shallow breaths. Soon he became aware of another sound—the soft click of a latch withdrawing.

Slowly, the bedroom door swung open on squeaky hinges.

Cautiously, Daniel peeked inside the room.

And there was Sebastian, back to the wall, staring off into space. The lower half of his shirt and his pants were wet with blood. The old man had not been the one to open the door.

It was the house. The house had let Daniel in.

"For her," Daniel whispered as he moved into the room, the door swinging slowly shut behind him.

The tips of Sam's shoes touched the window ledge. His right foot slipped on the wet concrete, the weight of his body shifting unexpectedly, and for a moment he was sure he was going to fall. He tightened his grip on the metal gutter, his fingernails scraping painfully against it. The panic lasted only a few seconds, and then his foot found the ledge once more.

Beneath the overhang of the roof, he was sheltered for the moment, although the rain pelted his hands and sent long streams of water running down his arms. Thunder crackled overhead, a strange electrical quality to it, like the fizzle of an exposed wire.

He had gotten lucky; this window looked into the bedroom in which Sebastian had taken refuge. Sam stared at his reflection in the glass, squinting to see past this, into the murky room. He thought he could make out some movement within, just to the right of the bed.

Making sure his grip on the gutter was solid, Sam carefully tapped the base of the window with the toe of his shoe.

"Sebastian," he said, just loud enough to penetrate the window.

Something glinted in the darkness, catching what little light there was, like the sliver of a moon in a black sky. Then it was gone, reclaimed by the shadows.

Sam knocked the window again, a bit louder this time. "Sebastian. Can you hear me?"

A face slammed into the glass and Sam jerked back, one hand losing its hold on the gutter above. He fumbled to keep his feet on the ledge, knowing there was nowhere to which he could retreat. The face was twisted into an awful grimace like the gnarled bark of an ancient tree—eyes wide, mouth gaping in a crooked moan. Blood smeared the windowpane, leaving a swath of deep red.

"Sebastian . . ." Sam could barely find the breath to mutter the name.

The elderly writer stared out at him as if to ask why, why this was happening to him, why he deserved such a fate. He was Sebastian Cole, legendary author, godfather of modern horror. Without him, there would be no Sam McGarver. And now he was being murdered.

Digging his fingers into the side of the gutter, Sam reared back his foot and gave the window a hard, swift kick. The pane was thin; the force of the kick should have easily shattered the glass. Instead, a spiderweb of cracks shot out from its center, but the pane held.

Sam attacked the window, over and over. "Sebastian! Hold on! Just hold on!"

Sebastian mouthed something, a silent plea, and then sadness flooded his face, the realization of defeat. From behind him, another face rose up, specked with blood.

Daniel bared his teeth, a cross between a grin and a growl, and in that moment, as time seemed to screech to an unbearable halt, Sam found himself face-to-face with a monster. He had written of madness in several of his books, but no words ever committed to paper captured the purity of this insanity. There was nothing left of Daniel Slaughter. There was only this thing, this blood-drenched creature, a puppet of Kill Creek.

Sam was not aware of speaking, but he heard his voice echo in his ears, yelling, "Daniel, no!"

He was too late. The hatchet rose into the air, so stained with flesh and blood that it resembled a prehistoric tool, a sharpened stone used to massacre enemies. Sebastian's eyes rolled back as he caught sight of the weapon. He watched helplessly, awaiting his end.

It was swift. One moment, the hatchet hung above Sebastian like the blade of a guillotine; the next, it was gone, buried deep into the pale flesh of the old man's neck. A geyser of blood sprayed the window, the crimson fountain obscuring Sam's view.

With no thought of falling, Sam kicked off from the ledge, hoisting himself out into the air and swinging back toward the house, his feet held flat in front of him. This time, the window gave in, the pane exploding in a shower of glass. A sliver still held by the wooden frame sliced Sam's leg, but he felt no pain. He had to get inside. He had to stop Daniel.

His feet hit the large man in the chest, knocking him back a few steps as he fought to keep his balance. Then Sam was swinging out again, away from the gaping hole left by the demolished window and into the pouring rain.

Get back to the ledge, Sam's mind ordered. *Get your footing, climb through the window, and put this bastard down!*

Sam kept his eyes on the window ledge, his hands pulling up on the rain gutter to bring his body back toward this target. In only one second, he would be inside the house. From there, he had no plan except to get the hatchet away from Daniel.

The rubber soles of his shoes squeaked as they made contact with the concrete ledge. At the same time, a cold gust of wind blew down from the purple clouds, causing the curtains that hung inside the shattered window to billow out like the sails of a ship. And from between the drapes burst Daniel, hatchet swiping the air. The blade slid across Sam's belly, a damp scarlet patch immediately seeping through his shirt.

"Just let me do this! Let me finish it!" Daniel shrieked, the last of his words obscured by the crash of furious thunder overhead.

Sam pushed off with his feet, once more leaving the ledge and swinging into open air. Daniel thrust his arm out and whipped the hatchet back and forth in a desperate attempt to make contact. The action was wild, unplanned, and Sam's rain-slicked fingers could no longer keep their grip. He felt them slip free from the gutter. Watched as Daniel grew farther and farther away. It was not until he was almost to the ground that Sam realized he was falling.

THIRTY-SEVEN

5:50 p.m.

SAMMY? THE VOICE called from the watery depths of the past. *Why are you doing this? Why are you hurting me?*

Sam opened his eyes. He had no sense of time. Had it been a minute? An hour? He blinked in the falling rain, raising a hand to shield his eyes from the downpour. Pain screamed up his leg as he shifted his body. His entire foot throbbed with the steady beat of his heart.

Sam shook the fog from his head and tried to push himself up into a sitting position. This slight movement sent a lightning bolt of pain all the way from his ankle to the base of his brain. He heard himself cry out even as he tried desperately to remain quiet. He knew Daniel would be coming. If he had been out for long, Daniel could be upon him in seconds.

As a moan squeezed through his clenched teeth, Sam forced himself to stand up. His right ankle was broken, the flesh already swelling up like a fat purple sausage. He tried to put some weight on it and almost toppled over, the pain excruciating.

You're lucky to be alive, he thought, and then that final image of Sebastian flashed across his mind—eyes rolled back, mouth agape, hatchet biting deeply into his neck, the fountain of blood splashing against the bedroom window, hot and thick. Sam knew he wouldn't be alive for long. Not if Daniel found him like this, out in the open, unprotected with a broken ankle.

The sound of the front door slamming got him moving. He hobbled along on his left foot, trying to put as little pressure on his right as he moved. He bit his lip to suppress a cry, his eyes tearing more with each step.

He could hear Daniel clomping down the the front steps, could just make out his grunts as he marched angrily around the house. Normally, Sam could outrun Daniel, but not with a broken ankle. If Sam didn't find a hiding place quickly, there was a good chance Daniel would catch him. And then . . .

Sam knew what happened then. He would get the hatchet, just like the others.

It was all the motivation he needed. He pushed the pain to the back of his mind, forcing it down into a small, dark place.

He quickly scanned the area around him with wild eyes.

The woods. Too far. Too little protection.

The back door. No good. He would have to backtrack, and Daniel was coming.

At the base of the house, near the southeast corner, Sam spotted an indentation in the ground. It was overgrown with weeds, but it was clearly a depression, dipping down a couple feet. Through the wild grass he could barely make out the reddish hues of a rusty grate and beyond this, the blackness of a tunnel.

The crawl space.

"Sam!" Daniel roared from around the other side of the house.

Sam had to move.

Forgetting his injured foot, he took a quick step forward and his ankle buckled, bending at an unnatural angle. He only had time to let out an anguished yelp before he fell flat. The palms of his hands mashed down into the thick mud.

Sam glanced quickly to his left, just as Daniel rounded the corner. A demented smile rose to Daniel's face as he saw Sam lying helplessly on his stomach. He tightened his grip on the hatchet. The rain washed over him, turning a light pink as it mixed with the blood that covered his face, his chest, his hands.

"Sam," he whispered hungrily.

Something in Sam's mind clicked and his body responded, moving without thought, pulling him across the yard toward the weed-shrouded crawl space. Sam could almost feel the *thump-thump-thump* of Daniel's footsteps as he bounded over the rain-slicked grass. But Sam did not look back. His eyes were fixed on that rusty square and the blackness it covered, the blackness that meant escape. Soon his fingers were touching the cold concrete that bordered the hole, one hand reaching out for the weathered metal grate.

A flash of panic lit up inside him like ignited gunpowder: *What if the grate is like the brick wall and the boarded-up window? What if it won't budge? What if I can't remove it in time?*

But it did budge. It easily ripped free with one yank. The rusted screws snapped just below their heads.

Sam flung the grate aside and wriggled into the dark tunnel. The musty odor of damp earth enveloped him. He could hear himself whimpering pitifully at the thought of safety, and the sound terrified him.

He was halfway in when Daniel caught him. A hand grabbed Sam by his bad foot and wrenched it back, pulling him like a snake from a hole. The pain was unfathomable. Black spots exploded before his eyes, the dark threat of unconsciousness. "No!" he screamed. Tears began streaming down his cheeks, as if his body were trying to physically expunge the pain.

"Where do you think you're going?" Daniel's voice was low and raspy, barely recognizable as human.

Sam began to kick wildly. He knew how horribly futile the action was. So even he was surprised when his foot connected with Daniel's chin, whipping the man's head back sharply. Sam felt Daniel's grip loosen, then release completely. Immediately he was on the move, doing what he and his brother had called "the army crawl," dragging his body forward with his elbows. Six inches. A foot. Two feet. Three.

Daniel lunged at the crawl space, his large hand swiping at the open air, his fingers straining.

"Goddammit!" Daniel cried suddenly. He yanked his hand back as if realizing he had just plunged it into scalding hot water. "Come out of there, you fuck! Come *out!*"

Sam listened to Daniel's labored breaths. He could now only see Daniel from the neck down, his body crouching as the storm pounded down on him. Farther and farther Sam scooted into the crawl space, the opening becoming smaller, the outside world narrowing as he tried to put distance between himself and this nightmare.

It was the memory of the spiders that made Daniel jerk back from the crawl space. Those slick black bodies began to scurry about his brain, the splash of red on their bellies warning him to stay away. He could almost feel them beneath his skull, scampering over each other in a mad, hedonistic frenzy, their spindly legs tapping the spongy gray matter in an odd staccato rhythm.

That childhood terror scratched at his brain stem like a mangy, rabid dog at a back door, begging to be let in. But he wouldn't let it in. Because it wanted to destroy him.

A hand slipped into his, and the army of arachnids that filled his head was gone in an instant. Claire, his wonderful daughter, was beside him. Yet her hand was so much colder now, the warmth of life fading, it seemed, with every ticking second.

He turned to her and a gasp slipped from his trembling lips. She was smiling a smile that belonged only to him, but her teeth, which braces had straightened to perfection when she was twelve, were now as crooked as a rotted picket fence, their once-white brilliance stained black. They hung loosely in her puffy gray gums.

"Daddy," she whispered, and a line of blood slipped from her hairline, coursing down the side of her face. Its color was devastatingly bright against the pallor of her flesh. "Daddy, you have to hurry. Don't let him get away, Daddy. I don't have long."

Fresh tears rose to Daniel's eyes. He was so close. He wouldn't fail. He couldn't. Not now, after all he had done.

"Daddy," Claire said once more. She pressed her head against his shoulder. "Daddy . . ."

Daniel tucked his daughter under his arm and glared furiously at the dark mouth of the crawl space.

Don't worry, baby, he thought. *He hasn't gotten away. There's still time.*

THIRTY-EIGHT

6:11 p.m.

DAMP AND COOL as the grave.

Sam tried desperately to push the words from his mind, but it was no use. The crawl space was just that—damp and cool as the grave—and the thought of his life ending here, in the belly of the beast, was horrifying.

Yet he pressed on, crawling like the beloved G.I. Joe action figures he'd had as a kid, elbows digging into the moist earth.

Move it, soldier! he commanded in his best drill sergeant bellow. *Move it or lose it, you maggot!*

"I'm moving," he replied. "I'm moving."

Sam did move, but slowly. The light was almost nonexistent. Every time he inched forward, he reached out to feel if the path was clear. He must have crawled twenty feet. Maybe more. Even in the dark, he could sense other sections of the crawl space shooting off from the main tunnel.

He saw something scramble past.

He stopped. Listened.

Only the sound of the rain pounding the ground outside.

He began to crawl again.

His hand grazed something smooth and spongy. Some kind of root. He traced it in the blackness, trying to determine its dimensions.

It seemed to have five rounded points protruding from a thicker, flatter chunk that rose from the muddy soil. And on the back of each point was a slick, hard shell, like a fingernail.

Because it was a fingernail. He was touching a hand.

Sam had no time to process this thought. The hand grasped his, squeezing tightly until he imagined he could hear his bones cracking.

He screamed, a sound that lacked any pretense, any self-consciousness. It was the sound of pure terror, expelled from his lungs like an unclean spirit.

A jolt rocked Sam's mind, an electrical surge that cleared all thought but one: *Get away.*

Tugging madly at his arm, Sam tried to pry himself from the hand's clutches. The confines of the crawl space made it difficult; the back of his head cracked painfully against the top, his elbows scraped raw against the walls. None of this mattered. He had to escape. The hand held tight, refusing to let him go.

And then something unexpected happened: the hand released him. Sam tumbled backward, farther into the crawl space. He lay on his back, drawing in sharp, desperate breaths.

The whispering voice of the house sank down around him, a thousand fragments of a thousand words:

I've heard about that house . . .

Dare you to go inside . . .

. . . guy died in there . . .

. . . saw something in the window once . . .

My sister tells me her best friend went in . . .

. . . couple witches live in it . . .

They're witches . . .

Witches . . .

. . . want you to stay away from there . . .

Because . . .

Witches.

. . . because it's haunted . . .

Haunted . . .

. . . it's haunted . . .

That place is haunted, don't you know?

Sam knew. All too well.

A black shape scrambled up to his feet. His first thought was that it was an animal. A raccoon, perhaps, or a skunk.

But it was not an animal. It reared back, its shoulders against the ceiling of the crawl space, its charred skin peeling away from its skull, eyes nothing but gooey clumps in the sockets where heat had caused them to burst.

"Hello, Sammy."

It was his mother.

She grinned, and a cloud of dark gray smoke floated out of her toothless maw.

Sam screamed.

A chuckle rose from deep in his mother's chest. She tipped her head, and thick, congealed blood poured from the hole that little ten-year-old Sammy McGarver had bashed in her skull.

She grasped his broken ankle and squeezed.

The pain forced an even greater scream out of Sam.

His mother's chuckle grew louder.

"I hope it hurts, Sammy," she said, laughing. "I hope it hurts like hell!"

Sam rolled frantically around, fighting to free his ankle, kicking with his good foot. He reached out his hands and grasped desperately into the dark.

His mother's laughter died down to a raspy purr. "Sammy. Why did you do this to me? Why did you hurt me?"

He dug his fingers into the dirt and tried to pull himself away.

"Because you're a killer," she said.

"No!" Sam cried.

"You're a killer, remember, Sammy? Remember."

"Stop it!"

"Remember what you did. What you are."

"STOP IT!"

Bone scraped bone as his mother wrenched his broken ankle. Sam shrieked, the world going momentarily white, and he was—

He was in the kitchen. Little Sammy McGarver, holding a bloody cast-iron skillet in his hand.

"Remember."

And there was his mother, dead.

No, not dead.

"Remember."

She was writhing on the kitchen floor, her cheek smearing an arc of blood across the linoleum.

She was still alive.

"Stop, Sammy." The voice was wet, spoken through a curtain of thick blood. He could see it bursting in red bubbles from her lips. "Please stop."

But Sammy didn't want to stop. He wanted her gone from their lives forever.

"Remember what you did."

He reared back the skillet and brought it down on his mother's head. The impact sent her face smashing down into the floor.

"Remember what you are."

"Stop!" Jack was screaming.

But Sammy didn't hear him. Sammy brought the skillet down again. And again. And again. Until he was sure. Until he knew she would not get up.

"STOP!"

Under the house, in the crawl space, Sam buried his face in the dirt and screamed.

"Now you remember," his dead mother said. Her breathing was like the clicking of beetles. "You're a killer. Say it."

Sam began to sob.

"Say it, Sammy."

He yelled it into the earth beneath the house on Kill Creek.

"I'm a killer!"

A low chuckle rose up from his mother's blackened chest. "That's right. That's right, my boy."

Get away from her, his mind commanded.

Sam stretched out his hands, reaching into the shadows, and he felt his fingertips connect with metal.

He craned his neck to see. There seemed to be some sort of metal grid at the end of the crawl space.

A grate.

Sam thrust his good foot out as hard as he could, landing a swift kick straight to his dead mother's face. She released her grip, only for a second, but it was long enough for Sam to scramble away. Turning in the tight confines of the crawl space, he kicked frantically at the grate. It clanked loudly, denting inward an inch or so. He kicked again and again and again, each time forcing the grate a little farther from its frame.

"Get back here, you little shit!" his mother screeched.

Fingers tore at his clothes, digging their nails sharply into his skin, leaving long, raw gashes as his mother struggled for a grip.

With a loud grunt, Sam delivered a mighty kick to the grate, and his heart leapt as he felt it give way, his foot passing beyond where the grate had been and into open space. He waited for the clatter of the grate hitting a hard floor but heard a faint splash instead.

Hooking his uninjured foot through the opening, Sam pulled himself toward the end of the crawl space. His broken ankle scraped against the rough concrete. White lightning shot through his body. Sam stifled a cry, forcing the pain out of his mind. The thing that looked like his mother must have sensed his escape, for its grasping intensified, taking whole fistfuls of his flesh in its eager hands—pulling, tugging, fighting to keep hold.

But Sam fought harder, managing to get halfway through the opening to grip the sides with both hands. He slid his body through, letting his own weight carry him, slipping out of the crawl space and into what he could only assume was the basement.

Water engulfed him, black and absolute. His tailbone bumped the concrete floor and Sam realized the water was about four feet deep, just enough to cushion his fall. He could still hear the howl of his mother, barely audible over the pounding of the rain, but she came no closer.

Letting his injured leg drift freely behind him, Sam half walked, half swam through the flooded basement. He was a wreck, his muscles groaning as he forced himself forward, his ankle a constant dull throb that seemed to have metastasized to his bones, making his entire body ache. His breathing was desperate, unsteady, a bit of stagnant water drawn in with each gasp. It was sour in his mouth, like spoiled milk. He hated to think what unspeakable things lurked just below its surface.

The door at the top of the stairs was slightly ajar, a shaft of pale light offering just enough illumination for him to make his way. All around him, water trickled from the walls, bleeding through the cracks.

He reached the bottom of the staircase and felt underwater for the first step, finding instead a handful of hair. A face hovered just above the surface.

It was Moore. Her black mane floated around her pale face like spilled oil. Her glassy eyes stared into the nothingness above them.

She's dead.

Sam stared at the corpse of his friend. The cold water around him drew the warmth and feeling from his flesh. He ran a hand down her side, stopping at her stomach. Deep red blood soaked the front of her shirt where Daniel's hatchet had bit into her. It pooled out into the water around her. Sam thought of the taste of the sour water and his throat constricted in revulsion.

He closed his eyes.

The sound of breathing. Shallow. Faint. But there was no doubting it.

His eyes flashed open as he pressed his hand flat against her chest, snaking his fingers under the straps of her cross-front shirt to feel her skin.

She was cold. Too cold. Yet there it was, the slightest rise and fall as her lungs sucked in tiny, desperate gasps.

He leaned down close to her mouth. A wisp of breath moved her lips.

She's alive. . . . She's alive!

"Moore," Sam whispered. He was afraid Daniel might hear him. He was even more afraid that the house would hear him.

Wrapping his arms around her body, he lifted her up onto the stairs, trying to get her out of the freezing water. He patted her cheeks.

"Moore!" Screw Daniel. Screw the house. He needed her to wake up. He needed her to live. "Moore! Please!"

Her eyes fluttered in their sockets, then slowly turned to him. She blinked. Once. Twice. Stared at him as her vision cleared. A single word escaped her lips, so faint that it was barely audible:

"Sam."

"Yes. Moore, it's me."

"Sam."

"You're alive. You're going to be okay."

She drew in a deeper, fuller breath. She swallowed. Her hands pushed weakly against the stairs beneath her. She wanted to move.

"I'm going to get you out," Sam assured her. "We're both getting out."

She nodded slowly.

"Fuck . . . yes . . ." she managed to say.

At the center of the staircase, several steps were missing where Moore had plunged through. It would be difficult to get her over that hole, but not impossible. He had to do it. They had to escape. And they were running out of time.

With his arm around her waist, his hand gripping the side of her shirt, Sam struggled to get Moore to her feet. Together they mounted the stairs, pulling their battered bodies toward the light above.

THIRTY-NINE

6:35 p.m.

THEY REACHED THE top of the stairs.

Sam feared Daniel would be there in the kitchen, waiting for them, hatchet raised above his head, psychotic grin playing at his quivering lips.

But the kitchen was empty. The back door was closed.

Sam clutched on to Moore tightly as he inched on his good foot across the kitchen, pausing to regain their balance at the island. They listened to the howl of the wind and the steady hum of the rain.

"Can you keep going?" Sam asked.

Moore winced, but nodded.

As they slowly moved toward the back door, Sam became aware of another sound just below the racket of the storm. Cocking his head to one side, he tried to separate it from the rain and thunder and wind, attempting to zero in on its source.

It was the voice of the house. Yet unlike the times before, its words were too faint to make out. It was as if the house were speaking to someone other than him, whispering a secret into someone else's ear.

Moore groaned weakly. Her hand was on that nasty gash in her stomach. Blood seeped through her fingers.

"Sam . . ."

"I know—we're going."

Somewhere above, a door slammed.

Footsteps ran quickly down the hallway above them. Sam tracked the movement from one end of the ceiling to the other, and then as quickly as they began, they fell silent.

"Is that Daniel?" Moore asked weakly.

Sam thought for a moment, then shook his head. "I don't think so."

"Then . . . who is it?"

Sam did not reply.

Trying desperately to keep his weight off his broken ankle, Sam hobbled them over to the back door. He twisted the handle and gave it a sharp tug. The door would not open. He flicked the lock and tried once more, but still the door wouldn't budge.

A floorboard creaked in the study.

Sam paused, listening, waiting.

The whispering of the house was still there, a constant, undulating wave of voices washing in and out.

One of the voices screamed, inches from Sam's ear.

"Shit!" He let go of the doorknob and stumbled backward. A lightning bolt of pain ripped up his leg. His ankle was killing him.

He glanced frantically around, but there was nothing beside him.

Moore began to slip farther through his arm. He tried to adjust his grip. "I need you to walk, Moore," he said.

She gave a frightened whimper. It was an awful sound coming from her. "I don't think I can."

"You have to. I can help you, but we're not going to make it out if we don't do this together. Okay?"

She didn't respond.

"Okay? Moore?"

"Okay." She planted her feet and forced her injured body to take as much weight as she could bear.

"The hallway," Sam whispered in her ear.

With his arm still around her waist, Sam guided Moore across the kitchen and into the hall. The passage was dim. The only break in the gloom was the arched doorway up ahead that opened to the foyer. He had to hope that the sounds he heard were just the house toying with them. If they passed the arched doorway and found Daniel staring back at them, he would kill them. There was no way they would be able to move quickly enough to escape.

Sam pressed a finger to his lips. Moore nodded, understanding. Sam slid up to the edge where the archway began until he could peer into the front entrance of the house.

Someone was there, on the stairs. A face was peering through the banister. It grinned, and the corners of its lips stretched unnaturally wide, its mouth spreading like a wound opening.

From the other end of the hall came the roar of an invisible wave. It thundered down the narrow hallway and crashed around Sam and Moore, the voices shrieking in their ears:

That house!

Go inside!

Witches! Witches!

Heard the stories!

Go inside!

The sounds swirled around them until they became the cackling of a cruel old woman, mocking their pain, savoring their fear.

Sam tucked his chin to his chest and waited for the onslaught to pass. And then—

It was gone.

In an instant, the house was silent.

He glanced through the archway, into the foyer. The thing on the stairs was no longer there.

He looked to the front door. There was nothing in their path. They could make it.

Moore was leaning against him, still clutching her bloody stomach. A thin layer of sweat covered her pallid skin. She took short, quick breaths.

"We're going to get out of here," Sam told her. "But we have to move. Fast."

There was doubt in her eyes, but she nodded.

Sam slipped his arm around her waist and stepped out into the foyer.

The door. Make it to the door. You can do this. Don't stop. Don't—

A loud thud from above rattled the entire house.

Sam was thrown off balance. He was falling, and Moore with him. His shoulder slammed into a wall. His legs buckled and he allowed himself to go down to the floor, Moore coming to rest beside him.

"Oh God, are you okay?" he asked.

She was staring up, trying to place the source of the sound. "What was that?"

There was another thud, and then the clicking of a chain being drawn over a pulley.

The elevator was moving.

Through the slats in the gate, they watched as the car slid slowly down. A final thud announced its arrival.

Sam peered into the shadows beyond the accordion door.

"It's empty," Moore whispered.

She's right, he thought. *It's just the empty elevator.*

But there *was* something. On the floor at the center of the car. A rectangular object.

A book.

Without warning, the accordion gate folded open, the metal screeching loudly as it collapsed. The book shot out of the elevator and slid across the hardwood floor. It came to a sharp stop a few feet away from them.

It was the Bible Moore had bought at the bookstore that morning.

From the shadows inside the elevator, something chuckled, low and guttural.

"I can see it," Moore said, her weak voice trembling. "It's watching us. It's smiling."

The very air in the house seemed to compress, to push in on Sam like a phantom fist clutching him, and a thousand voices screamed in his ears.

In the shadows of the elevator car, something stirred.

"Go!" he yelled, barely able to hear his own voice over the cacophony.

Ignoring his throbbing ankle, Sam crawled across the foyer, pulling himself forward with his left arm while dragging Moore along with his right.

He glanced back over his shoulder.

The movement in the elevator intensified, a black form wriggling higher and higher, as if it were being birthed from the shadows. A smaller black blob rose from the larger form, twisting out of the elevator to hover in midair. At its center, two eyes opened. Milky white orbs stared out.

"We have to get out of the house!" Sam dug his elbow into the floor and gritted his teeth as he pulled them faster. They were only a few yards from the front door.

Behind them, the thing was crawling out of the blackness of the elevator. It slipped past the gate, and the shadow swirled off into the air like smoke, revealing arms of pale dead flesh. Thick saliva crisscrossed its gaping maw like wet spiderweb.

Digging its grimy fingernails into the wood floor, it began to drag itself into the room. Its fingertips thumped against the floor as it took hold, nails biting into the weathered wood. The thing's twisted body slid farther into the foyer.

A ghostly wind snaked down the staircase, whipped around Sam and Moore, and blew off the last of the shadow from the creature before them.

"Oh my God," Sam heard himself say.

The thing crouching on the floor craned a neck like twisted rope, and they found themselves staring into the face of a witch. Decaying flesh hung in loose clumps from exposed bone. Where once there had been lips, strips of ragged skin stretched over teeth as gray and split as rotted wood. Her thin black hair, what hair hadn't been tugged free, was pulled into a tight bun. Tiny insects scurried across her scalp, the white heads of maggots poking out of a spongy, necrotic wound.

Her legs stretched out behind her, useless, like two dead, gray eels. Her jagged fingernails bit into the floor as she dragged herself closer.

The image of the ancient wheelchair in the third-floor bedroom flashed across Sam's mind. This was Rebecca Finch, former owner of the house on Kill Creek.

The Rebecca-thing opened its mouth wider and an awful sound spilled out, somewhere between a scream and a death rattle. Her dead, opaque eyes glanced around. She grinned, and a raspy chuckle worked its way from her collapsed lungs. She trained her sightless eyes on Sam.

"Sammy," she said mockingly.

"Open the door," Moore said.

Sam could not move. The front door was completely forgotten as he stared wide-eyed in horror.

The Rebecca-thing cackled louder. A slick black beetle scurried out of her mouth and along the white sliver of her cheekbone.

"Sam, you came all this way to see us?"

"Open the door, Sam," Moore pleaded.

"We knew you would bring the others," the Rebecca-thing croaked. "You're so weak, so afraid, so guilty, that you rounded them up, one by one, like a good little boy."

Moore groaned angrily and reached out for the doorknob, but it was too far. They had to get closer.

Rebecca Finch crawled toward them, her head bobbing loosely on her neck. Her cloudy eyes glanced from the terror-stricken face of Sam to Moore, arm outstretched, clothes still dripping with a mixture of water and blood.

"Your friend doesn't seem happy, Sam. But why would she be? You only bring misery. To your family. To Erin."

Sam moaned at hearing this abomination say her name.

"You destroy everyone around you. You bring nothing but pain."

Moore lunged for the doorknob, but she was still too far away. She collapsed to the floor, wincing as she clutched the bloody wound in her stomach.

The Rebecca-thing dragged itself closer to Sam. "Why don't you stay?" it asked, its tongue clicking with excitement. "Your other friends are here. They're upstairs, in our bedroom. They're staying *forever*."

Around them, the house began to undulate, boards splintering as a wave rippled through the floor and walls.

The Rebecca-thing shook with laughter, the sound growing louder and louder until it became a scream. Thick gray saliva dripped from its tongue as it shrieked with demented joy.

"Sam."

The voice was barely a whisper, yet somehow through the maelstrom, Sam heard her.

He looked down at Moore, her face pale, her skin slick with sweat.

You can save her, he told himself.

Suddenly the Rebecca-thing fell silent.

There was something at the top of the stairs. A tall, thin shadow. A woman. Black hair billowed around her pallid flesh.

Rachel, Sam realized.

She reached out to them with a gnarled, ancient hand.

"You're all a part of the story!" she called down to them. "They'll remember you forever, and the things that happened in this house! And they'll say your name in a whisper as they pass!"

Sam's hand found the doorknob.

It won't open. We're trapped. We can't escape.

He twisted the knob, and it turned.

The latch clicked, hinges squeaking angrily as the door swung inward.

The boards of the front porch groaned, and the Rebecca-thing shifted its dead eyes to the doorway behind them.

"Ah, there you are."

Sam spun around, but it was too late. With an angry howl, Daniel burst over the threshold and whipped the hatchet down. The blade split Sam's collarbone and wedged deeply into his shoulder. Sam cried out in agony.

"Kill him," Rebecca Finch cooed.

At the top of the stairs, Rachel joined in. The chanting voices of the Finch sisters echoed off the walls of the foyer. "Kill him! Kill him! Kill him!"

"Kill him, and your daughter will be free!" Rebecca roared.

With a sudden yank, Daniel pried the hatchet from Sam's shoulder, the blinding pain sending black streaks across Sam's vision.

Daniel mumbled something unintelligible. With one hand, he shoved Sam's head to the side, exposing his neck.

With his other hand, Daniel lifted the hatchet high into the air.

"Kill him!" the sisters sang. "KILL HIM!"

It won, Sam thought. *The house beat us.*

Images flashed through his mind: Erin in their house in Lawrence, the day they moved in; smiling, gorgeous, on their wedding day; staring sadly at him in the coffee shop last January; Moore smirking back at him in the VW bus on their way to Kill Creek; Sebastian in the hotel bar; playing one-on-one with Jack at the park in Blantonville, the court overgrown with weeds.

Memories.

He refused to lose them.

He had to hold on.

Daniel mashed his hand down harder against Sam's head, pressing his cheek to the ground. Sam could hear the house whispering through the floorboards.

Out of the corner of his eye, Sam saw Daniel's foot, stretched awkwardly behind him.

Sam kicked, and the bottom of his shoe collided with Daniel's lower leg. There was a sickening crunch as Sam's ankle split farther. His entire body was on fire, the pain unbearable.

Don't stop!

He kicked again, even harder. The force of the impact sent Daniel's leg flying out from under him, just as he swung the hatchet down. The giant man gave a startled cry, thrown off balance, arms flailing wildly as he tumbled forward. Sam managed to roll out of the way just as Daniel hit the ground with a thud.

The hatchet slipped from Daniel's hand and went skittering across the wood floor. Sam scrambled after it, ignoring the throbbing pain in his ankle, ignoring the searing agony of his savaged collarbone, thinking only of getting that hatchet into his hand.

Behind him, Daniel was pushing himself up. He swatted at Sam's leg, gripping his broken ankle and giving it an excruciating twist.

Sam's fingers grasped the handle.

You're a killer, his mind told him.

No. I'm not.

He flipped the hatchet around, the blade now to the back, the flat side forward, and he swung it, hard. The blunt steel bashed Daniel in the side of the head and he collapsed to the floor.

There was a moment of stunned silence. Even the house grew quiet.

Rolling onto his back, Sam watched as Daniel struggled to get to his feet. But his body would not cooperate; each time he tried to rise, he collapsed back down to his knees. Gripping the edge of the door-frame, he was finally able to stand. He lumbered out onto the porch like a drunk, each step an effort to retain his balance. When he reached the porch railing, he paused as if to admire the twisted form of the beech tree. And then he slowly turned, his back to the rail.

There was the sound of splitting wood as the railing gave way. The rusty nails holding the top plank in place snapped free, and the large man went sailing over the side, splashing down to the muddy earth.

In the foyer, the Rebecca-thing howled furiously. Her maw was open impossibly wide. Her white eyes bulged from her skull.

Movement at the top of the stairs caught Sam's eye.

Rachel Finch was on all fours, thrashing like a mad beast. Her thin lips were pulled back in a hideous snarl.

Sam winced as he scooped Moore up with his good arm, the hatchet still held in his hand.

"There's nowhere to run!" Rebecca shrieked after them. "SOON EVEN THIS HOUSE WILL NOT BE ABLE TO HOLD US!"

As they stumbled over the threshold, Sam glanced back.

The foyer was empty. The Finch sisters were gone.

FORTY

ALTHOUGH THE RAIN had not let up, the storm clouds that stained the sky a yellowish green at midday were showing hints of purple dusk as Sam struggled to help Moore down the porch steps and onto the front lawn. The wind whipped around them, tearing at their clothes with renewed ferocity. A few yards away lay Daniel, faceup, his chest rising and falling slightly with each shallow breath.

He's still alive, Sam thought. He hoped he hadn't made a mistake.

When they reached the SUV, Sam gently set Moore down on the ground, her back against the door. He gripped the side mirror for balance as he set the hatchet on the roof of the car.

"What are you doing?" she asked, frowning.

Sam nodded toward the house. "We can't leave it like this."

"Like what?"

"Intact." In all of Sam's life, in the hundreds of thousands of sentences he had written, never had a single word held so much power. "This house is over a hundred and fifty years old. If we can get a fire going, it should go up like dry brush, even in the rain. It won't take long."

"No," Moore said. A bit of color had returned to her face. The hand on her stomach was still caked with blood, but even that was beginning to dry. For now, the bleeding was under control. "Just forget it. Let's just go."

Rainwater dripped from Sam's face as he bent down beside her. "Moore, there's something in that house, something that made Daniel go mad, something that doesn't want to be forgotten."

"But we're out now. We made it."

He took her hand in his. "You know that doesn't mean we're safe. If we leave the house intact, once word gets out about what happened here, whatever is in there will be stronger than it's ever been. And there's no telling what it will do. To us."

The fear was trying to take hold of her again. But she seemed to push it back, at least for now.

With one hand on the side of the SUV, Sam hobbled around to the back and opened the hatch. The two gas cans were still there, right next to the splitting maul Wainwright had insisted on buying and never even removed from the car. Sam grimaced, fighting through the pain as he carefully lowered each plastic can to the ground.

Suddenly a wave of panic washed over him; he had nothing with which to start the fire—no match, no lighter, nothing.

He called over to Moore. "You have a lighter?"

Moore shook her head apologetically. "Don't know where mine is."

"Shit," Sam growled. He closed his eyes, trying to picture their arrival. Wainwright had been driving. He remembered the kid smoking. He usually had his lighter on him, but maybe if he had a spare . . .

Once again using the SUV for support, Sam moved to the driver's-side door. He opened it and ran a hand over the seat, his fingers digging into the cracks. He found nothing. He leaned across the seat and twisted the knob on the glove compartment. The door popped open. Inside was their rental agreement, a map of Kansas City, and the SUV owner's manual. He ruffled through the contents, unaware of the little prayer he whispered under his breath. The glint of metal caught his eye. He shoved the map aside, revealing a pack of smokes and a silver Zippo lighter. He let out a sharp breath, took the Zippo in his hand, and flicked the flint. A healthy orange flame sprang forth.

"Wainwright, you wonderful asshole."

The wind was blowing even harder, the rain falling in diagonal sheets. Each drop was like a beesting as Sam dragged the first gas can across the yard and up the front steps. Above him, dark clouds swirled angrily, as if the storm itself disapproved of his intentions.

By now his ankle was almost completely numb. He stepped on it as lightly as he could, but the pain was nowhere as intense as before. Either the nerves in his foot were fried, or the part of his brain that warned him of his injury had decided to close shop for the day. His shoulder, on the other hand, was a live wire, but he did his best to minimize the movements of his arm as he hobbled across the front porch.

The foyer was just as they had left it—streaks of Daniel's blood across the wood floor, but no trace of the things that had been Rebecca and Rachel Finch.

Sam stepped cautiously into the house. Except for his labored footfalls echoing lightly around him, all was still.

He crossed to the staircase and placed the gas can on the fourth step, removing the cap. Reaching between the balusters, he carefully tipped the can over. Gasoline gurgled from the opening and cascaded down the stairs, pouring out across the floor below.

Careful not to lose his balance, he took a few steps back toward the open doorway. With his breath held, Sam flicked the lighter. The flame danced before his eyes.

"Sam?" a weak voice called down from above. "Sam, help me."

Sam glanced up. From within the curtain of darkness at the top of the stairs, the voice spoke again, soft and pathetic: "Help me, please."

Sebastian!

But he knew it wasn't. Sam had seen the geyser of blood that had erupted from the Sebastian's neck. The old man must have bled out in seconds.

But what if . . .

It wasn't Sebastian. It was the house. It had always been the house.

"Sammy, what are you doing?" the darkness asked. It was his mother, her voice commanding. "You stop that. Stop it right now."

Pushing the voice out of his mind, Sam bent down and held the flame to the shiny pool of liquid still spreading over the foyer floor.

"What the hell do you think you're doing?" The thing in the shadows was furious now, no longer the sweet voice of Sebastian or the hateful voice of Sam's mother, but a thousand overlapping voices shouting from another world.

"STOP!"

The gasoline ignited in a flash. Sam snapped the lighter shut, extinguishing the flame, and stumbled backward onto the porch. His eyes remained on the floor inside, on the blue-tipped flames that coursed hungrily across it.

The fire. Jack had started the fire. Their mother was dead inside. They knew she was gone. Their father would be home soon. Sam had saved Jack. But Jack knew the price his little brother had paid. No one else needed to know. Jack would make it look like an accident.

Jack. Beautiful Jack, who had taught Sammy to throw a baseball and smoke a cigarette.

Inside the house, the flame reached the east wall and attempted to crawl up it. Sam's face began to glow orange in its light.

Panic. His mother was in there. The woman who cursed her children's names, who blamed them for every one of life's miseries. But his mother, all the same. He ran. Into the burning structure. Tried to pull her body out. Jack was grabbing Sammy by the back of his shirt. Sammy was screaming, "Mommy! I'm sorry! Mommy! Wake up, Mommy! I'm sorry! I'm sorry!"

The entire kitchen was in flames. A beam was falling. Onto his mother. Onto the bloody mass that had been her head. Part of the door-frame collapsed, and Sam was pulled to the ground. He recoiled at the smell of his own burning flesh as the flames devoured his left arm.

And Jack was once again dragging him by his shirt. The sound of ripping cotton. The roar of the fire as the flames raced through the old house.

The foyer was engulfed now. The flames were beginning to creep up the stairs to the second floor.

The flickering orange light.

Jack had taken off his own shirt to wrap Sammy's burned arm. They stood side by side, watching their home burn. Somewhere in the distance, sirens wailed.

The flame hit the mouth of the plastic gas can. There was still a good amount of gasoline inside, ready to be devoured.

The thousand voices of Kill Creek cursed him, transforming into something guttural, bestial, like a record slowing on a turntable until the words became inhuman.

Sam stumbled down the front steps as, inside, the flames shot into the plastic tub. First there was a flash, and then the gas can exploded in a ball of fire. Plastic shards slapped wetly against the walls, the molten fragments sending tendrils of flame across the wallpaper like fiery snakes.

Sam limped over to where Moore sat with her back against the side of the SUV.

"Do you think the rain will put it out?"

Sam shook his head. "By the time it does, it'll be too late."

The ground seemed to shift beneath them, Sam's foot catching momentarily on the grass.

"I need to get Daniel," he said.

"No," Moore was saying. "Leave him."

Another clump of grass hooked Sam's shoe, nearly tugging it off. He glanced down in time to catch a glimpse of a furry green vine slipping through the weeds.

"What is that?" he asked.

Moore opened her mouth to respond, but whatever words she intended slipped silently into the air. They watched the tallgrass ripple, not blown by the stiff wind but drawing back and forth like ocean waves. From the house to the edge of the creek, the yard was alive, an undulating green animal.

"Get in the car!" Sam ordered, yanking the back door open so Moore could climb inside.

He had just started to turn toward the driver's-side door when an incredible force rammed him from behind. Sam was knocked off his feet. He skidded to a stop on the rain-slicked grass. He gasped, the breath knocked from his lungs. He struggled to push himself up, blinking as the rain spattered his face, staring up through watery eyes at the blurry image of Daniel, blood oozing down the side of his head. He glared at Sam with milky white eyes.

"No," Sam managed to say.

"Yes," he whispered, his grimace widening to an impossibly large smile. His voice was the thousand voices, traveling through eons of time and space to purr in Sam's ear: "Yes."

Sam felt the spiky pelt of a vine twisting its way up his leg. It reached his knee and constricted, the tiny sharp hairs on its hide poking through his pant leg to bite his skin.

There was a jerk, and the vine began to retract with amazing speed, pulling Sam swiftly over the yard, away from Daniel. Sharp stalks of tallgrass tugged eagerly at Sam's clothes as he passed.

He came to rest beneath the beech tree. Its crooked trunk seemed to curl up to touch the low-flying clouds. From the top of the tree, another vine came winding down, so quickly that Sam's eyes could barely follow it. He had no time to fight it off, only to feel its needlelike husk wrap ruthlessly around his neck, pulling up, up, into the air, lifting him off his back. He began to kick helplessly, his feet swishing the open air. He clawed at the vine, leaving mean red scratches down his neck as he tried desperately to wedge his fingers beneath it. The harder he fought, the more the vine tightened, until his throat closed to a thin slit, the slightest of gasps drawn through it.

The hanging tree, he thought, and his eyes flashed to the window of the third-floor bedroom. There, framed by the jagged edges of shattered glass, lit by the wild light of the flames below, were the awful faces of Rebecca and Rachel Finch. They were hideous mirror images of each other, white eyes staring out from even whiter flesh, faces of the dead, pleased at Sam's fate even as their beloved house burned around them.

The vine wrapped tighter around Sam's throat, and the black cloak of unconsciousness began to creep into the corners of his vision. Through this dark tunnel, Sam stared up at the phantasmal shapes of the Finch sisters, who in life were seduced by the power of the house and in death remained devoted, for unfathomable reasons, to feeding its legacy. With the ghost stories of believers. With the bodies of Sam and his friends.

From what seemed like a world far away, Sam heard the vine snap. He saw a thin strand, like a piece of green twine, fall free. His body was beginning to tingle, but he could still feel something pressing against the top of his foot.

A branch, he realized with a rush of excitement. His shoe was caught beneath it, holding him in place.

The vine slid roughly up his neck to his chin, leaving pink burns in its wake as it attempted to lift him higher.

Sam fumbled blindly with his fingers, finding the trunk of the tree, too thick to grasp. His face was hot with blood. He could almost picture himself turning bright purple, eyes bugging from his skull.

With his foot wedged securely below, he traced the edge of the tree trunk until his hand wrapped around the slender arm of another branch. Desperately, he grabbed hold and pulled downward, the force so great that, for a split second, he feared he was going to break his neck in the process.

There was a crack just above his head as the vine snapped in half, and suddenly Sam was falling, his arms slapping the rough bark of branches as he plummeted to the earth.

He landed in a heap, staring up through the branches at the dangling end of the severed vine. Already it was whipping down toward him, readying another attack.

Sam sprang up, hobbling away from the tree as quickly as his injured foot would allow. The tallgrass swelled around him in an attempt to hold him in place, but he broke through, ripping it out by the roots in greedy handfuls.

Twenty yards away, Daniel stood over Moore, his hands clenched into fists.

She was saying something to him.

Begging for her life, Sam guessed, and the thought of Moore begging anyone for anything made him sick.

Something on the roof of the SUV caught Sam's attention.

Adrenaline coursed through his veins, supplying a temporary reprieve from the pain of his wounds, propelling him to the SUV. He snatched the carpenter's hatchet from the roof, and then he was behind Daniel, the blade rearing back.

No! a voice screamed in his mind, from the dark place where the fires had once burned. *No, Sam, don't!*

It was his brother's voice.

I have to, Sam thought.

One minute, T.C. Moore was staring up at the towering form of Daniel Slaughter, and the next, the sharp blade of the hatchet was slamming into the side of Daniel's head. The edge of the blade cut all the way to his orbital bone, its sharp corner slicing his eye. A gooey substance, like undercooked egg white, slipped down over his bottom eyelid. And then a crimson stream began to pour out from the wound. It soaked the shoulder of Daniel's shirt and coursed down his chest. He swiped at the hatchet, confused by the object now lodged in his skull.

Sam caught a glimpse of a name crudely carved into the wooden handle: *Goodman.*

Daniel turned to stare at Sam with his one good eye, his expression like a confused child, asking, *Why? Why did you do this?*

The giant hulk of a man slumped to his knees, his face going slack, his remaining cloudy eye rolling back into his head. His fleshy lips cupped the air like a landed fish, straining to put that last bit of breath into a final plea.

"S . . . sss . . . sorry." The words puffed from Daniel's mouth like smoke rings. "I-I'm . . . ss-sorry." A scarlet bubble rose between his lips and popped. And Daniel Slaughter was gone.

There was now only one directive—to escape.

Sam slid behind the wheel of the SUV and slammed the door shut. Moore was sprawled across the backseat. Her breathing was steady, her color encouraging. As soon as Sam was in the car, he clicked a button, and the auto locks engaged. They could hear the tallgrass whipping frantically at the steel frame of the car, the force rocking it back and forth. Without a word, Sam pressed the ignition button, and they both breathed a sigh of relief as the engine instantly fired.

He jammed the gearshift into reverse and slammed down on the gas with his good foot. The wheels of the SUV spat gravel. He spun around quickly, the car slipping a bit off of the driveway; then he hit the brakes, threw the car into drive, and peeled off down the path.

In his rearview mirror, Sam caught sight of the house, engulfed in flames, just as the second-story windows exploded in multiple fireballs. The inferno had spread quickly to every floor. By the time it was finally extinguished, there would be little left of the house. "Look," Sam said, pointing ahead through the windshield.

Moore pushed herself up in the backseat and saw what lay ahead—the surging waters of Kill Creek washing over the wooden bridge. In one afternoon, the storm had turned this barren creek bed into a raging river. The force of the waves surging against the bridge's support beams was causing it to sway. A few pikes had already split in nasty spear-like shards.

"It might not hold us," Moore called out from behind him.

"It has to."

"But—"

"It has to," Sam said again, leaving no room for argument. He pressed the accelerator flat against the floorboard, the SUV rocketing forward as the tires found traction.

The first half of the bridge began to collapse the second the car made contact. The crisscrossed beams beneath it split clean through, carried off by the whitecapped rapids. The rest followed instantly, the bridge dropping down into the creek as if chasing the SUV's bumper.

The back wheels bit into solid ground just as the last of the bridge fell free, the SUV leaving behind it a gaping chasm where the bridge had once stood.

Sam did not slow as they raced beneath the canopy of trees and toward the on-ramp to K-10. But he did glance over his shoulder to see the sky painted an angry orange as the house on Kill Creek burned.

PART FIVE

UNDER THE RUG

December 15

It is easy to understand why books of this nature become bestsellers. People are just so desperate to believe in something bigger than themselves. But in the end, Adudel's account rings false, the imaginative ramblings of a man who has devoted his life to a field that is based on speculation and garners few accolades beyond those of his equally eccentric peers.

—excerpted from the New York Times *book review of* Phantoms of the Prairie *by Dr. Malcolm Adudel*

FORTY-ONE

TELL ME.

There was the house, the way it was before the fire, back when fear controlled Sam's life. In his hand he held a hatchet that did not belong to him. Its weight was foreign to him. It felt like the weight of a life.

On the porch sat Daniel, his chin in his hands as if he were completely bored with the situation. At the side of his head, a deep red chasm opened. He looked to Sam with innocent eyes. He was the man Sam had met over a year ago, caring and humble and comforted by faith.

Tell me who you are, the voice said again.

Sam glanced down at the hatchet in his hand. It was no longer a hatchet. It was a muddy gray hand, attached to the end of an arm that sprouted like a root from the bloodstained earth.

The silence woke him.

Sam opened his eyes to watch his breath spill from his mouth in an icy mist. He was warm beneath the blankets, but the world outside was cold and unforgiving. Sunlight spilled in through a window still kissed by frost.

His hand slid beneath the covers to the other side of the bed, reaching instinctively for Erin, for his wife.

She was there, her body hot beneath flannel pajamas. She rolled over on one side and scrunched her pillow up around her sleepy face. "I don't want to get up yet," she said.

Sam smiled. "We don't have to."

Leaning over, Sam slipped an arm around her, nuzzling his lips into the space just below her earlobe. He kissed her lightly, feeling a shiver of goose bumps prickle his skin, not because of the winter air but because she was here, back with him, and his heart beat right once more.

Erin came out of the door with two steaming mugs of fresh coffee. She had pulled a heavy wool sweater on over her flannel pj's, her feet nice and snug in fur-lined boots. Sam had changed into jeans, a thick hoodie, and a corduroy jacket. A wool cap was tucked down over his ears. He sat on a metal porch chair, his hand to his head, lost in thought.

"You okay?" she asked.

He smiled warmly and took one of the mugs, the steam curling into the golden morning sunlight. "Yeah," he said. "I'm good."

A heavy snow had fallen during the night, obscuring the brittle brown grass and hanging in fat clumps from the barren tree branches. The day was finally beginning to warm, although the thermometer on the front porch showed the temperature to be just above freezing.

For a few minutes, the two of them sat in silence, sipping their hot coffee and looking out at the wintry paradise of their street.

The fallout from Sam's experience at Kill Creek had been pretty much as expected. He knew that when lying, it was best to stick as closely to the truth as possible. So when officers from the sheriff's department came to visit him at Olathe Medical Center, just outside of Kansas City, Sam told them the story he knew they wanted to hear.

Sam, Sebastian, Moore, Daniel, and Wainwright were eager to see one another after nearly six months, so they decided to have a reunion at the site of their first meeting. The plan had been to drive down to Kill Creek and take one last look at the house, for old time's sake. He admitted they had planned a bit of what he guessed the officers would call "vandalism." After pondering on it for six months, they just had to know what was behind that brick wall at the top of the second-floor stairs. So they loaded up their rental SUV with tools and drove out to

Kill Creek Road. Daniel wasn't quite himself, but the rest of the group rightly assumed he was still emotionally fragile after the death of his daughter.

None of them could have guessed that returning to the house would make the poor guy snap, but snap he did, violently attacking and killing much of the group with a hatchet he must have found somewhere in the house. Sam managed to take cover in the crawl space, at which time Daniel used the spare gas from the SUV to set the house on fire, probably in an effort to force Sam out. It worked. Sam was able to get Moore, who had also been attacked, out of the house, only to find Daniel waiting for them in the yard. A struggle ensued and, were it not for Sam gaining control of the hatchet, he doubted they would have survived.

It was the same exact story that Moore told, right down to the smallest detail, and once all of the bodies were retrieved, the evidence appeared to corroborate their statements. Daniel's wife and his pastor could attest to the fact that, since Claire's death, an unrelenting darkness had enveloped the man.

Sam felt guilty for pinning everything on Daniel, but for the most part, it was the truth. More importantly, it was the truth that had to be told. The press, of course, had a field day with the fact that Daniel's last name was Slaughter. Each headline was more salacious than the last, until even the journalistic reports verged on fiction.

A few months later, after Sam had gone from front-page news to little more than a footnote in the *Lawrence Journal-World*, life began to take on the faintest hints of normalcy. His ankle and collarbone healed as well as could be expected. He still had a bit of a limp, and on rainy days his foot ached like a son of a bitch, but often the injury was noticeable only to him.

Moore spent two full weeks in the hospital. The hatchet made a nice little mess of her abdomen, but somehow the blade slid right between the overlapping coils of small intestine, miraculously avoiding any life-threatening internal damage. A few stitches here, a few staples there, and Moore was on the road to recovery. Physically, at least. She had become strangely quiet. No foul remarks. No sarcastic quips. It appeared the experience had changed her most of all.

Sebastian was memorialized in countless magazines and newspapers as the influential writer he truly was, but within two weeks, an

A-list actor died when his twin-engine Cessna crashed in Northern California, and so the world's fair-weather grievers quickly turned their tearstained faces to the fresh tragedy. There were rumors of a missing manuscript—a final novel by Sebastian Cole—but so far, no such novel had been found.

Wainwright was remembered in countless online posts and in an official statement from his father, which proved to be less about the pain of losing a son and more about promoting Donald Wainwright's tabloid empire. WrightWire struggled to carry on but, without the leadership and financial backing of its founder, the site quickly became just another home for hardcore genre fans.

Sam was only in the hospital for a few days, after which he returned to his house in Lawrence with a cast on his ankle and a sling on his arm. He was pleasantly surprised to find Erin waiting for him. She insisted she was only there to make sure he got back on his feet (or foot, as it were), but after a week, she began staying overnight. By the end of August, they were once again sleeping in the same bed, and by Labor Day, the intimacy that Sam had thought forever lost was back.

One night in late October, as the anniversary of his first trip to Kill Creek rolled round, Sam broke down crying. He needed to tell her everything, even if it meant losing her forever. So through tears that seemed to know no end, he told her about Kill Creek, and then he told her about his mother. Whether or not she chose to believe him, it was the truth, down to the darkest detail. Erin silently absorbed his tale for what seemed like an eternity. And then she held him in her arms. Sam knew this wasn't the end of his redemption but only the beginning. It would take months, even years, before the past could become just that—the past.

Sam stared into the swirling brown coffee in his cup. A few snowflakes fell into the hot liquid and were immediately gone.

"What's the matter, Sam?" Erin asked.

Sam furrowed his brow. "Just something on my mind." He did not continue.

Erin brushed the snow off the bench along the porch railing and sat down. She put a hand on his knee. "What is it?"

Tell her.

"It's just . . . there's something that hasn't sat right with me, since that day."

Erin took a sip from her coffee, steam billowing up around her flushed face, but she said nothing.

"When I was in that third-story bedroom," Sam said, "there were scratches on the walls. On the ceiling. The wheelchair was bent all to hell, like somebody had used it to try to bash their way out."

Another snowflake fell into his coffee. Its flawless geometry melted away in the blink of an eye.

"That was Rebecca's room, but she was in that wheelchair. She couldn't have done all that."

"What are you saying?" Erin asked.

Sam sighed. He knew he should let it go. For his sake and for hers, he should leave it in the past. But he just couldn't. Not yet.

"Adudel had a photo from when he went to the house. Rebecca was dead at that point. But the woman in the photo with him, the one who claimed to be Rachel, her hair was pulled into a bun, just like Rebecca used to wear. I don't think . . ."

He took a swig of coffee and gathered his thoughts.

"I don't think that was Rachel. I think the house gave Rebecca her legs back. It gave her what she most desired—just like it tried to give Daniel his daughter. I think the house gave Rebecca her legs, and in return she walled up her sister in that third-floor bedroom. I think Rachel died in the room, trying to tear her way out."

There was no response from Erin. For the moment, she had forgotten the coffee cup in her hand.

"Why would she do that?" she asked finally.

Sam shrugged. "Maybe Rachel had second thoughts. Maybe she wouldn't go along with the plan to bring someone in to document the experiences in the house. Maybe she didn't want the house to grow stronger. So the house tempted Rebecca, and she accepted."

Out in the yard, a cluster of sparrows had landed in the fresh snow, pecking around for anything of value beneath the powder.

"I still dream about that house," Sam told her.

The suddenness of the statement caught Erin off guard. She rolled the warm coffee over her tongue and swallowed, thinking. "What do you think it means?" she asked.

"Nothing," Sam said. It was the truth. There was no reason to think otherwise.

Sam sat alone for a while longer, watching the icicles drip from beneath the overhang of the roof.

When he went back into the house, he found Erin curled up under a blanket on the leather couch, a black-and-white movie playing on the television.

"*The Thin Man*," she informed him. "Wanna watch? It just started."

Sam stared at the TV, at Nick and Nora Charles trading witty barbs, then shook his head. "No, thanks. Not right now. I'm gonna try to get some work done."

"Okay." Erin watched him as he moved quietly up the stairs. "I'll come get you for dinner."

Upstairs, in his study, Sam sat down at his desk and wiggled the mouse, listening as the computer's hard drive spun to life. The screen blinked on, revealing a blank white page.

For a moment, he sat with his hands in his lap, letting everything else melt away until there was only the memory of his childhood.

He was halfway through the first paragraph before he realized he was typing. He did not bother to reread what he had so far. He pushed on, knowing that the words may not be perfect, but that they were right.

When Erin came upstairs to announce dinner, she heard the clacking of keys and went away without a sound.

Sam McGarver sat at his computer and felt the story pour through his fingertips. He did not write for his fans. He did not write for his publisher or his agent or even for Erin. He did not write for his past or for Kill Creek.

He wrote for himself.

EPILOGUE

"YOU GOOD? NEED anything? Water? Coffee?"

Sam shook his head. "I'm good, thank you."

The production assistant gave him a pleasant smile and then hurried back through a glass door, disappearing into the control room.

The man across the table from Sam, a kind-faced bald gentleman with a neatly manicured gray beard, motioned to a pair of large headphones on a nearby stand.

"Try those on. It helps to hear your own voice."

Sam did as he was told, pulling the headphones down over his ears. Immediately, all sound from the room was cut off. He felt as if he were drifting through endless space.

The sound of the void.

"Can you hear me?" The man was now directly in Sam's ears.

"Yeah," Sam said into a microphone mounted on a metal arm before him. He felt his mouth move, felt the breath pushing the words past his lips, and then they were instantly piped into the vacuum of the headphones. Too crisp. Too perfect. As if his very thoughts were being transmitted. There was something uncanny about the sensation.

The man adjusted his own microphone and checked his watch.

"Well, I guess if she doesn't show, it'll just be you and me."

"She'll be here," Sam said. He had no information to support this, but he knew it was true.

He rubbed the scarred flesh of his left arm. He wanted to get this over with. He knew there would be questions about what had happened last spring, but that wasn't why he was there. The book resting on the table between them was the one and only reason Sam had agreed to this interview.

Across the spine, in a font that probably took a room full of executives way too long to agree upon, was the title *A Thinly Cast Shadow*, followed by, in smaller print, *40th Anniversary Edition*.

They were there to talk about Sebastian Cole. To honor him. To remember him.

"Have you seen her?"

The too-present voice in his ears startled him. He looked across the table at his interviewer, now cleaning his glasses with a handkerchief.

"Excuse me?"

"Moore. Have you seen her since . . ." He let his words trail off.

"No," Sam said. "Haven't even spoken to her since we were in the hospital."

"Hm," the man said as if already bored by his own question.

There was a sharp pop, and a third voice, that of the unseen sound engineer, informed them: "One minute until we're live."

The man cleared his throat and took a sip of water from a tall, thin glass. "Okay, well, I guess we'll get started—"

A heavy soundproofed door opened, and suddenly she was there in the booth with them. She was dressed in a tight dark gray sweater, leather skirt and leggings, and a sleek black trench coat that stopped just below her hip. Her long dark hair had been cut short into choppy daggers.

Without thinking, Sam hopped up from his chair, his head jerked sharply to the side as the headphone cord went taut. He stripped the headphones from his head, angry with himself for feeling like a high school kid on a first date.

"Hi," he said.

She smiled warmly. *Warm.* That was a word Sam never thought he would use when describing T.C. Moore.

"Hi, Sam. It's so good to see you."

Her hands slipped around him and she pulled him close, hugging him.

"How are you?" he asked.

"Good," she said. "Really, really good."

Sam heard the tinny voice of the engineer calling out from his headphones: "Fifteen seconds."

The man across the table motioned to a third seat. "Ms. Moore, if you don't mind, we're about to begin."

Moore took her seat. Sam did the same, securing the headphones over his ears.

The man clasped his hands on the table as if he were about to say grace. He leaned in close to his own microphone, emblazoned with the red, black, and blue logo of NPR. When he spoke, his voice was velvet.

"Welcome to the latest edition of Book End. I'm Rupert Taylor, and with me today are Sam McGarver and T.C. Moore, two of the most famous names in horror literature, here to discuss the master of the macabre, the late Sebastian Cole, and the fortieth anniversary edition of his masterpiece of supernatural terror, *A Thinly Cast Shadow*."

He paused, attempting to find the best way to broach the next subject.

"Before we discuss the book and its legacy, I want to acknowledge the story that I know our listeners are expecting to hear, and that is the events at Kill Creek."

Here we go, Sam thought. This wasn't a surprise. He knew there would be questions about it. He had prepared a polite bit of discouragement for this very moment.

"I'm sorry," Sam began. "I understand the curiosity, but that subject is still very difficult to talk about. Ms. Moore and I went through a very scary, very traumatic experience, one that resulted in the death of Mr. Cole. I don't have anything else to add that your listeners don't already know."

"It's okay, Sam. They're just curious," Moore said.

Sam stared at her, confused. What was she doing? Nothing good could come from talking about that place.

The man licked his lips and leaned in closer to his mic. "Well, um, we all know the official story, but there are many who believe something . . . *stranger* happened."

Don't do it, Sam thought. *Don't tell them. No one needs to know.*

Moore leaned back in her seat and crossed her legs. Her hands were resting on her knee. There was something odd about them. They were not the hands of a middle-aged woman. They had an ancient quality, as if they were made of brittle paper that, when punctured, would allow the air to turn the bone within to dust.

"There are things that happened that can't be easily explained," Moore said finally.

"Such as?"

"Well, I hate to be a tease, but I'm actually writing a book about it."

Sam sat up straight. *No.*

"It's a book I started shortly after our first trip to Kill Creek."

No, this can't be.

"It's a work of fiction, but it is very much based on fact—"

"Moore," Sam interrupted.

"Because you see, Sam and I, we share a bit of a secret."

"Moore, what are you doing?" Through the headphones, he could hear the fear in his voice.

She turned to him, and for the first time since she arrived, Sam looked directly at her face. Something was off.

"I'm sharing our story, Sam," she said.

What was it? Something was not right about her, but what?

"They deserve to know the truth."

Despite the dim, intimate lighting in the booth, Moore's eyes seemed to shimmer, her pupils like two perfect—

Her eyes. That's it. Her eyes!

The pupil of her right eye was no longer ruptured. Where before it resembled a drop of ink running into the iris, it was now a flawless black circle.

A memory came rushing back. Moore floating in the dark water of the basement. Her corpse-like face staring up. Eyes wide.

Both pupils identical.

Even then, she had been changed. She was dead. He was sure she was dead when he found her. And then she was alive.

This wasn't Moore. This was something else.

He could still hear the shriek of that twisted obscenity that had once been Rebecca Finch: *Soon even this house will not be able to hold us!*

"I guess I just feel very lucky," T.C. Moore was saying from a million miles away.

"With your help, Sam, I made it out."

ACKNOWLEDGMENTS

I wrote the first draft of this book more than ten years ago, but with a career mainly in reality and children's television, I couldn't seem to get anyone interested in a horror novel by a first-time author. So the fact that it is finally in your hands is a testament to many amazing people who deserve my profound thanks:

Adam Gomolin at Inkshares, who saw the potential in my original manuscript and was there with me in the trenches for every single rewrite. He encouraged me to push myself outside my comfort zone, challenging me to beat even the moments I thought were working perfectly well. Turns out those moments could be better.

My editors, Matt Harry and Pamela McElroy, for their many, many reads through the book to hone it both creatively and grammatically.

Avalon Radys and the entire Inkshares team for keeping the train moving, and for holding the door so I could hop on at the last second.

Jamie Dorn, J.F. Dubeau, Alex Rosen, and Phil Sciranka for taking the time to read my ghost story and giving their invaluable input.

Jorge Gonzalez and Chris Contreras at the Tracking Board. Without the Launch Pad Manuscript Competition, this book would still be sitting on my hard drive.

Rock Shaink, who has been not only a huge champion of this novel but also of me as a horror writer.

Jed Elinoff for his friendship and for helping hold down our many forts while listening to me talk about how little sleep I was getting as I rewrote . . . and rewrote . . . and rewrote.

Charles Kephart, who read the very first draft of *Kill Creek*. He has encouraged me through friendship and kind words for years.

The friends, family, and complete strangers who supported me by preordering the book on Inkshares.

The Kansas towns of Coffeyville and Lawrence and the University of Kansas for shaping who I am and inspiring me to write a Midwestern ghost story.

The countless horror authors and filmmakers who inspired me growing up and continue to feed my love of horror. Every sentence of this book is in some way because of them.

My parents, Warren and Sherry, who never questioned why their son had so many pages from *Fangoria* taped to his bedroom wall.

My brilliant, hilarious, creative, beautiful daughters, Aubrey and Cleo, who cheered me on through every rewrite and never failed to ask, "How many pages do you have left?" *A lot, girls. A lot of pages.*

And, most of all, my wife, Kim, who lived through the insanity with grace and patience, who lifted me up in moments of doubt and took on way too many burdens so her husband could stare at a computer screen for months. If this book is the darkest parts of my soul, you are the brightest.

GRAND PATRONS

INKSHARES

INKSHARES is a reader-driven publisher and producer based in Oakland, California. Our books are selected not by a group of editors, but by readers worldwide.

While we've published books by established writers like *Big Fish* author Daniel Wallace and *Star Wars: Rogue One* scribe Gary Whitta, our aim remains surfacing and developing the new author voices of tomorrow.

Previously unknown Inkshares authors have received starred reviews and been featured in the *New York Times*. Their books are on the front tables of Barnes & Noble and hundreds of independents nationwide, and many have been licensed by publishers in other major markets. They are also being adapted by Oscar-winning screenwriters at the biggest studios and networks.

Interested in making your own story a reality? Visit Inkshares.com to start your own project or find other great books.